DAMAGED

THE VIGILANTES, BOOK ONE

STONI ALEXANDER

SILVERSTONE PUBLISHING

This book is a work of fiction. All names, characters, locations, brands, media and incidents are either products of the author's imagination, or have been used fictitiously. Any resemblance to actual persons living or dead, locales, or events is entirely coincidental. The author acknowledges the trademarked status and trademark owners of various products referenced in this work of fiction, which have been used without permission. The publication/use of these trademarks is not authorized, associated with, or sponsored by the trademark owners.

Copyright © 2021 by Stoni Alexander

Developmental Edits by Johnny Alexander
Copy Edits by Proof Before You Publish
Cover Design by Better Together
Cover Photo by Period Images

All rights reserved.

In accordance with the U.S. Copyright Act of 1976, the scanning, uploading, and electronic sharing of any part of this book without the permission of the publisher is unlawful piracy and theft of the author's intellectual property. Without limiting the rights under copyright reserved above, no part of this publication may be reproduced, stored in or reproduced into a retrieval system, or transmitted, in any form, or by any means (electronic, mechanical, photocopying, recording or otherwise) without the prior written permission of the above copyright owner of this book.

Criminal copyright infringement, including infringement without monetary gain, is investigated by the FBI and is punishable by up to five years in federal prison and a fine of $250,000.

Published in the U.S. by SilverStone Publishing, 2021
ISBN 978-1-946534-16-3 (Print Paperback)
ISBN 978-1-946534-17-0 (Kindle eBook)

Respect the author's work. Don't steal it.

To S.H.
For being one of the good guys

ABOUT DAMAGED

Stryker Truman

I'm *not* one of the good guys...not even close. I'm a heartless savage hunting down the thug who murdered my mother. Watching her die in my arms has turned me into a killing machine. Revenge runs bone-deep for me. It's burned into my soul, baby.

When I become the one with a damn target on my back, my life turns into a raging dumpster fire. But not because my company gets breached or because some SOBs are trying to off me.

There's this woman...the *one* woman I can't freakin' stand. An impulsive cop who arrested me for a crime I didn't commit. She gets too close to me, she's gonna learn about all the ones I *did* pull off.

The problem is, I'm crazy attracted to her. Insane, over the top, can't-get-her-outta-my-head kind of attraction. She pushes all my buttons and makes me madder than hell. If anyone can bring me to my knees, it's her.

Turns out, I took a vow of celibacy. And I don't break so easily.

Except the hot cop is now a detective...and I gotta help her with a serial-killer case 'cause I got wicked-good hacking skills. But that's all I'm gonna help her with...

1

THE BODY

Stryker Truman skimmed the lengthy rap sheet on his laptop. "These guys are hella dangerous. Four have been on The Most Wanted List for over a decade. We're gonna end their killing spree tonight."

Pausing, he regarded the three men sitting around the poker table in the Travesty room of The Dungeon, Stryker's member-only nightclub. No one spoke. Two of his guys were struggling to make eye contact and one was tapping his fingers on the table.

"The suspense is killing me," Stryker said. "Someone's gotta say *something*."

After a sigh, Quincy said, "I'm out."

"Do you think we need one more guy?" Stryker slid his gaze from Quincy to Brooks to Rhys. "You do, don't you?"

"I just got engaged," Quincy said, rising to his feet. "Keeping this a secret from my woman is eating me up. I'm out."

Muscles running down Stryker's back grew tight. *Dammit*. This mission needed to happen, tonight. He pushed out of the rickety wooden chair, extended his hand. "You're a good man, Quince."

As Quincy shook it, he chuckled. "Me? A good man? No, I'm a

cold-blooded killer. I love you guys, but I'm done with these missions. We're sending out a 'Save the Date' soon. I have no idea how this wedding stuff works, but I found the right woman and I'm done leading a double life." He tossed a nod to Brooks and Rhys before shutting the door behind him.

Stryker eased back down. "We can do this job with three. Brooks, run through the specs again."

"No, we can't," Brooks replied. "These guys are over-the-top violent. We can't do it with three."

"Brooks is right," Rhys added. "We've gotta stand down."

"Fuck," Stryker said, slapping his laptop shut.

Knock-knock-knock. "Stryker, it's Mavis."

Stryker glanced at the monitor on the wall. His general manager stood outside the door. Turning to his team, he said, "I'm stupid enough to think I can do this on my own."

After standing, Brooks gripped Stryker's shoulder. "We're close friends, right?"

"More like brothers." Stryker hitched his hands on his hips. "You gonna lecture me?"

KNOCK-KNOCK-KNOCK. "Stryker, it's important," Mavis said.

"I'll see you at work, tomorrow," Brooks said. "Don't do this one alone. It's a suicide mission if you do."

Brooks opened the door. "C'mon in, Mavis. Our game ended early tonight. Have a good one." Brooks took off.

Mavis and her cloud of cigarette smoke entered the private, sound-proof room. In reality, poker games never happened there. It was used for mission strategy only. Something that *wasn't* going down tonight.

"I'm taking off," Rhys said. "Sorry you didn't win, Stryker. You had a good hand, though." He shot Mavis a smile and was gone.

"What's the word?" Stryker plucked the lit cigarette from Mavis's hand and stomped it out. "Stop with the smoking. It's against code."

She barked out a laugh. "This is my reward for tending bar the past hour. It's a madhouse down there. If you're so worried about code, thin out the crowd."

It was after eleven. "Why are you tending bar?"

"April's a no-show, again." Mavis picked up the flattened cigarette and stared at it like it held the answers to the universe. "I'm filling in for her, but I can't tend bar and manage the club. It's busier than usual for a Thursday." She glanced around, her gaze settling on the back door across the room.

He didn't like that Mavis was in Travesty. If she used her master key to check out *that* room, she'd learn *her* key didn't work. That would lead to a shit-ton of questions, none of which he would answer. He needed to get her the hell out of there, so he tucked the laptop under his arm and left. As soon as she joined him in the dimly-lit hallway, he shut the door, making sure it was locked before they walked down the hall together.

Stryker was pissed. His mission had been aborted and one of his guys had bailed. "Do I need to do rounds?"

"I need you to stop by April's and check on her." Mavis entered her office and dropped the cigarette butt into the stump-filled ashtray before easing down behind her desk. "It's the second night she no-showed. I'm concerned."

"Did you call her emergency contact?" he asked.

Mavis swiveled the computer monitor toward him. "She put *me* down."

He chuffed out a grunt. "Not helping." He texted himself April's phone number and address. Before heading out, he turned back to Mavis. "She better have a damn good reason why she's not here."

He took the stairs to Level One. Pounding music and loud conversations interrupted his thoughts. L1 was packed. *This is crazy.*

Once outside, he checked with Tank, his line manager. "Are we at max?"

"We're close," Tank replied.

"Nobody else goes in until twenty leave." Stryker slid into his black Mercedes-AMG GT 63S and entered the address. On the way, he called April, got no answer and hung up.

"Siri, call Dakota Luck," Stryker said.

Seconds later, his friend answered.

"Hey," Dakota said. "You guys all set for tonight?"

"We had to abort."

"What happened?"

"Quincy dropped out."

"Tonight, or altogether?"

"For good," Stryker replied as he turned west on Arlington Boulevard. "Brooks and Rhys didn't think we could handle it with three. Pussies."

"We'll regroup."

"I was gonna do it alone, but—"

"Not smart, Stryker."

"Do you think these guys coulda killed her?"

"The gang leader is old enough, but my gut says no. Don't go off half-cocked without a team," Dakota said. "They're ruthless."

"So am I, but I got a work thing I gotta handle." Stryker pulled up to April's three-story apartment building in an older Arlington neighborhood. "I'm out."

"Don't do anything stupid."

"I live for stupid." Stryker disconnected.

The front door of the brick building was locked, so he buzzed April's apartment. No response, so he pressed another button on her floor.

"What's up?" asked a woman through the box.

"I'm here to see April."

"Buzz April, then."

"She's not answering. Can you let me in?"

She hung up. *So helpful.*

He buzzed another resident, but got no reply. *How the hell am I supposed to get in?* He called April again. Her cell phone rolled to voicemail.

A woman in her thirties, wearing a T-shirt and shorts, padded down the hallway. After giving him the once-over, she spoke through the locked glass door. "Lemme see your ID."

Stryker showed her his driver's license.

She smiled up at him. "You her boyfriend?"

"Her boss."

"Where does she work?" asked the neighbor.

"The Dungeon. She's my head mixologist."

The tenant sized him up again. "I don't remember April mentioning her hot boss."

Stryker pulled out a business card from The Dungeon and flipped it over. Printed on the back was *Guest Pass for Two. Two Complimentary Drinks.*

She pushed open the glass door and stepped aside.

"Thanks for letting me in." He handed her the free drink card.

"Should I ask for you at your club?"

"I'm not there much." Stryker pointed down the quiet hallway. "This way?"

The neighbor led him to the third floor and stopped in front of a closed apartment door. "This is my place. April lives at the end of the hall on the left. Stop by for a drink. I'll be waiting." She winked before heading inside.

Stryker wasn't interested in a drink, a late-night booty call, or anything else from April's neighbor. After knocking on April's door, he said, "April, it's Stryker."

No response.

He tried the door. To his surprise, it was unlocked, and he stuck his head inside. "April, you here?"

The unexpected stench stung his nose. *No fucking way.* He moved inside, leaving the door open. The living room was dark, but the kitchen light was on. The place looked neat and orderly. Not sure what he was walking into, he pulled his Glock from the back of his pants.

April wasn't in the kitchen, so he continued down the short

hallway toward the dimly-lit bedroom. As he stood in the doorway, his brain stuttered to a stop. She was lying on her bed, propped against pillows, wearing a modest white wedding gown, the train draped over her legs. Her hands were folded in an X over her chest and her long dark hair lay neatly over both her shoulders. Her skin was ashen and her lifeless eyes stared straight ahead.

God, no.

He strode over, pressed his fingers against her carotid artery. Nothing. April was stone-cold dead. He wanted to pound on her chest and breathe life back into her. He wanted to scream at the universe to bring her back. But that wouldn't change a damn thing. He was too late. Moving quickly, he unearthed his phone.

"What's your emergency?"

"This is Stryker Truman. My employee didn't show for work, so I stopped by to check on her. She's dead. I need the police."

"Did you say she's dead?"

Dammit to fucking hell. "Yes. Based on the position of her body, she was murdered. Coulda been a suicide."

"Did you try CPR?"

"Her body is cold. Her neck appears bruised. She's been dead for a few days."

"I'll send a team right out."

He rattled off the address and hung up. Then, he stared into April's dead eyes while rage swirled around him. His thoughts flashed to his mom, the haunting image seared into his brain.

Pushing out those painful memories, he refocused on his employee. April's neck had purpled, a sure sign she'd been strangled. The rage swirled faster and faster, consuming him in a vortex of helplessness.

He'd dropped his Glock on the bed, so he shoved it back into his pants. Though he was licensed to carry, he untucked his shirt to hide it. The police would have questions, no need to point the spotlight on himself. He was guilty of plenty, but killing his employee wasn't one of them.

"Hello," called a man. "Arlington County Police."

"Back bedroom," Stryker replied.

Two officers entered the room, their guns drawn. "Did you call for us?" asked one of them.

Stryker had been staring at April, but he couldn't shake seeing his mom's face. To his surprise, he was trembling. "Yeah, I did."

"Sir, please step away from the bed."

After he stood, he shoved his hands into his pockets.

"Please leave your hands where we can see them," instructed the second officer.

Stryker dropped them by his sides. "Name's Stryker Truman."

"Can you tell us what happened?" The officers holstered their weapons.

"I own a nightclub in Arlington and April Peters is my head bartender." The second officer stepped away to make a call. "According to my general manager, she was a no-show last night and tonight. When she didn't return my GM's calls, I checked on her."

Two EMTs entered the room, pushing a gurney.

"Were you in a relationship with Ms. Peters?" asked the primary.

Here we go. "No, she was my employee."

"Was she deceased when you arrived?" he asked while an EMT felt April's carotid.

"Yes."

"Did you move her?"

"No."

The second officer returned. "Homicide has been called."

After speaking quietly to the officer, the EMTs left, without April.

"I'm gonna kill the SOB who did this to her," Stryker muttered.

"Mr. Truman, please don't make statements like that."

Stryker pulled two cards from his wallet. "I run Truman CyberSecurity in Reston and I own The Dungeon in Arlington. Have the detective call me. I gotta get some air."

"We can't let you leave, sir," said the officer. "The homicide detective will want to question you."

"I'll be in the living room." Without waiting for permission, Stryker left the bedroom, but the vivid memory of his mother's lifeless eyes stayed with him.

He hadn't been able to save her, either.

2

DETECTIVE EASTON

Homicide Detective Emerson Easton heard "wedding gown" and high-tailed it to the crime scene. A fresh-faced officer she didn't recognize met her in front of the low-rent apartment building. Patrol cars with their lights flashing had some neighbors milling around on the grass. Didn't matter that it was after midnight. Curiosity never slept.

"What's the word?" she asked, not slowing to chat.

"The vic is on the third floor."

She yanked the lobby door and almost pulled her arm out of its socket when the damn thing didn't budge.

"Sorry." The cop radioed and another officer opened the locked door from inside.

"Are the crime techs here?" Emerson asked.

"Not yet," replied the senior officer.

She eyed the rookie. "Can you wait here to let them in?"

"No problem," he replied.

She offered a tight smile before hurrying inside with the second officer. Rather than take the waiting elevator, they climbed the three flights. The late-night activity had concerned neighbors lining the hallway or peering out their front doors. She acknowledged them with a nod. The officer stopped outside a closed door.

"Please keep the neighbors out," she said.

"I was going to start questioning them."

Her phone binged with a text. After reading it, she said, "The tech team is five minutes out. I don't want any evidence compromised by curious neighbors."

He nodded. "Sure thing."

"What is the vic's name?"

"April Peters. She hadn't shown up for work and her boss came looking for her. He's waiting in the living room."

Emerson pulled on shoe coverings and disposable gloves before entering the apartment. Her stomach churned. The stench of death always did that to her. On her short list of hates, death topped them all. And she hated that, for some, it came way too soon.

When the lone man in the living room turned, the intensity in his wicked eyes stilled her breath. *Oh, no. Not him.* It had been a year and a half since she'd last seen him. His dark brown hair had grown past his shoulders, his scruffy beard and moustache drawing her back to those turbulent, ocean-blue eyes. That towering body of hard-muscled steel stood well over six feet tall, and her brain stuttered as she soaked in that surly Adonis of a man.

"Here to arrest me, again, Easton?" Stryker shoved his phone in his pocket.

Death might top her list, but the stormy sea of a man glaring down at her was a close second. The only thing that topped her dislike of him, was his total hatred of her.

She glared at him. "If the evidence points in your direction, I will."

"You don't use evidence," he bit out. "You go on a hunch. Is that keen gut of yours already hard at work jumping to *inaccurate* conclusions?"

You're a total tool. Rather than continue flinging mud, she shifted her gaze past him. "I understand you found the victim."

He nodded once. This time, she caught a flash of pain in his eyes. Nowadays, she was better at reading people. If she'd had that skill when she'd first met him, she might not have been so quick to arrest him.

"Stay here." She brushed past him.

When she entered the bedroom, the horrifying sight was a déjà vu of a crime scene from the previous month. Female, Caucasian, early thirties. Like the first victim, she was brunette, five six to five nine and wearing a full-length wedding gown. She was leaning against propped pillows with her hands crossed over her chest. Possible cause of death: strangulation. The victim's dead-eyed stare sent chills through her. *So tragic.*

Then, the sorrow vanished, replaced with determination and a sense of loyalty toward the deceased. She would do everything possible to find the monster who did this. For the sake of the victims, and to prevent anyone else from losing their life in this monstrous way.

The crime techs arrived. After speaking briefly with one of them, she left to find Stryker, but he was waiting inside the bedroom doorway. His hard-muscled body dwarfed the space, but it was the empathy pouring from his eyes that caught her attention.

"Thanks for sticking around," she said.

He arched a thick, black eyebrow. "Like I had a choice."

"Can you ID the victim for me?"

"April Peters."

"Is this how you found her?"

"Yeah. Felt her carotid. Might've sat on the edge of the bed." He paused. "Yeah, I did sit. Seeing her like this was shocking. This is fucked up."

"I know."

"Forensics will find my prints on the front door handle. It was unlocked. As soon as I entered, I smelled—that's when I knew something was wrong."

"Got it. Did you move her?"

"No, I wanted to perform CPR, but it wouldn't have brought her back."

"Thanks for the details."

Emerson never liked when a civilian found a body, especially when the victim had been posed for shock value, so she wanted to get Stryker away from the crime scene. After placing a comforting hand on his arm, she said, "Let's head back into the living room."

He held her gaze for an extra beat before saying, "You're the boss."

Once there, Emerson pulled out a small notepad and pen from her back pocket. "How'd you get into the building?"

"I buzzed, got no response, so I found a neighbor on this floor. I didn't get her name."

"The officer said Ms. Peters worked for you."

"Head mixologist at The Dungeon."

"How long did she work there?"

"A while. My GM manages the staff."

"When did you last see her?"

"Last week. Tuesday." He paused. "No, Wednesday. I stopped by around ten."

"Stopped by here or the club?"

His icy stare cut right through her. "The club, Detective. I've never been here before tonight."

Ignoring the bite in his tone, she continued. "What do you know about Ms. Peters?"

"Nothing. I didn't know she'd been a no-show at work until Mavis, my GM, told me. What can I tell my staff?"

"Only that she was deceased when you found her."

"Got it."

Emerson studied him for an extra second. "I'm sorry you had to see her like this. Do you need me to help you find a grief counselor?"

"I'm good."

"It might help you process this."

"I've seen worse."

Hmm, okay. She wanted to ask, but she needed to stay on point.

"We done?" he asked, interrupting her thoughts.

"For now."

Stryker studied her, his intense gaze raking over her face. "Still got my number?"

Emerson hadn't deleted it from her phone, but he didn't need to know that. Before she could reply, he took her pen and pad and scribbled out a number. "For when you want to interrogate me again."

"I'm gonna need to review the surveillance at your club and talk to some of your employees."

He stepped into her personal space. Rather than step back, she tilted her face upward and stared into his fury-filled eyes. "This time, I'm playing hardball, Easton. No warrant, no access."

Glaring at him, she said, "Your refusal to cooperate makes me think you've got something to hide."

"I wasn't the enemy then, and I'm not now," he ground out.

"I'll let you know when I get the warrant."

"I can't wait." His low growl filled the air before he took his angry self and stormed out. Of all the men she wanted to interact with, Stryker Truman was at the bottom of her list.

Though Stryker needed to burn off his anger, he'd use it. It kept him from slowing down, forced him to stay vigilant. Being mad, all the damn time, had turned him into a cold-blooded predator.

He jumped in his car and drove onto the main road, opened the sunroof and dropped the pedal. The throaty roar of his Mercedes' exhaust reminding him that this baby could fly.

April's posed body in the wedding gown popped into his thoughts. *Who the hell would do that to her?* He tightened his fingers around the steering wheel. Sorrow he couldn't process, but anger… no fucking problem.

The universe must really wanna stick it to me. I gotta deal with Easton again. Detective Emerson Easton brought the mother-loving heat every single time. He was off-the-charts attracted to her. But he flat-out could not stand the woman. Sure, she was cool under fire. Easton was beautiful, sexy, and the biggest pain in his ass he'd ever met. Eighteen short months ago, she'd wreaked havoc with his life, then cost him millions when several high-profile clients severed ties. It took months to repair those damaged relationships and earn back their trust.

It was almost one in the morning when he pulled back into The Dungeon's parking lot. Some idiot had parked in his spot, despite the curbside warning.

Owner's Spot
You park here, you get towed.
$500 big ones. NO Exceptions.

After muttering a string of obscenities, Stryker called for a tow and blocked in the car with his own. The early May breeze blew through the sunroof and he rolled down the window.

While waiting, he pulled up the surveillance footage from his club. He had no idea how far back he'd need to go, and he had no clue what he was looking for. Hell, he didn't even know if April had a boyfriend, or several. She could have been a club member and played here on her nights off.

Three men staggered out of the club, their drunken laughter catching Stryker's attention. None of them wore masquerade masks. *They're L1 members.*

Members on L2 and L3 always wore them, even if it was a simple, black masquerade mask. His private club catered to wealthy and well-known Washingtonians. Many liked the anonymity that The Dungeon provided.

"Fuck," one of them blurted. "Some asshole blocked us in."

"Damn, that's a nice car," said the second.

"We should break the windshield," said the third, and they started laughing again.

Stryker stepped out of his vehicle. "You break my glass. I break your necks."

"Oh, shit," one of them uttered.

"You idiots park in my spot?" Stryker glared down at them. Late twenties, average builds. He dwarfed them by a good six inches. *I got this.*

"Fuck, yeah," said the third. "Who the hell are you?"

"The owner. You got names?"

The first two rattled theirs off. The third crossed his arms. "I'm not stupid enough to tell you."

"Hey, man, this is the owner," said the first guy. "Take it down a few."

"This is a great club," added the second. "Don't blow this for us."

Stryker snapped a pic of them, then tapped his IDware app. "Whose car is this?"

"Mine," said the third, who pulled a switchblade from his pocket.

"An Uber or the cops," Stryker said. "You decide."

The one with the knife stepped forward. Stryker stood his ground.

"Dude, don't do it." His friend held him back, but he broke free.

"Put the blade away or I'll use it on you." Stryker's phone binged with the search results, but he stayed locked on the idiot.

Raising the knife, the man lunged toward Stryker. Stryker grabbed his wrist, twisted it hard, and squeezed.

"AAEEEE!" As soon as he dropped the weapon, Stryker shoved him to the ground, then grabbed the knife.

"Wrong choice." Stryker dialed 911.

"What's your emergency?"

"A drunk at my club attacked me with a knife." Stryker gave his location and hung up. Then, he called his line manager. "Tank, parking lot. Now."

As the man rose, Stryker tossed a nod to the other two guys. "Stand over there."

Both guys moved away.

Tank came jogging into the parking lot. A former marine, Tank was built like one. "Hey, boss man." Then, Tank eyed the guy. "You couldn't stop, could you? I threw you out and you pissed off the owner. Stupid move."

"Police are on their way," Stryker said to Tank. "Hold him."

While Tank kept the troublemaker from bolting, Stryker canceled his membership, then tagged the others. "You two are on my shit list. Pull this crap again and you're out." He called them an Uber.

"Thank you," said the first guy.

"Sorry, man," said the second.

"You don't even know who I am," muttered the third guy.

Stryker showed him his phone. "That's you, that's your online membership, and this is me deleting your account and banning you from my club." Stryker tapped two keys, and the guy was marked as NFW—No Fucking Way.

"I can use a different name, douche," said the asshole.

"You gotta stop," said his friend. "Just stop talking."

"I'm not afraid of the owner."

"You should be," said Tank.

"I've got facial ID software," Stryker explained. "Unless you have major reconstructive surgery, you can't get back in my club."

"What the hell?" he mumbled. "Who are you?"

"He's one of the best hackers in the world, *douche*," Tank said. "He can eff up your life with a few clicks on the keyboard. You picked the wrong man to piss off, dude."

A car pulled in and slowed. "Someone call for an Uber?"

The two guys thanked Stryker and hurried into the waiting vehicle. As the car pulled out, a police cruiser drove in. After

Stryker spoke to the officer, the guy was arrested, cuffed, and taken away.

Stryker's head was pounding by the time the tow truck arrived. "Hey, Stryker, how you doin'?"

"Never better," Stryker bit out. "Get this car outta here."

"Unless you need me, I'm going back inside," Tank said. "It's pretty crazy in there tonight."

"It's crazy every fuckin' night," Stryker grumbled.

With a laugh, Tank headed toward the entrance.

Within minutes, the vehicle was towed away, and Stryker parked in his spot. The thirty-minute time suck hadn't helped his mood.

When he walked into his club, the blaring music only magnified his already pounding head. Pushing into the crowd, he made his way through the wall-to-wall bodies to the rectangular bar on L1.

"Where's Mavis?" he called out to Parker, who was slinging drinks.

"Either filling in for April on L2 or in her office," Parker replied. "She said you went looking for April. Did you find her?"

After stepping inside the bar, Stryker pulled a cold one from the fridge, popped the top, and chugged half the brew. He'd tell his staff about April after the club closed.

"We'll catch up later." Not waiting for more questions, Stryker hoofed it toward the stairs.

Mavis wasn't tending bar on the second floor, so he continued up to L3. Passing the private kink rooms, he stopped in front of Mavis's office.

Knock-knock. "It's Stryker."

"Yup." Mavis's throaty rasp cut through the silence.

He shut the door behind him. His GM was sucking down a lungful of nicotine. She exhaled the smoke and crushed the cigarette into an already cluttered ashtray. "You were gone a while. What's the word on April?"

Stryker eased into the black leather guest chair. "I found her."

"Good," Mavis replied. "Is she helping out downstairs?"

Stryker wasn't going to sugar coat the truth. "She's dead."

Mavis reached for another cigarette. "Oh, God, no. That can't be right."

"Leave those." Stryker tossed the pack in the trash.

Mavis nibbled a fingernail. "What happened?"

"No idea."

"And?"

"I called the police."

"That's terrible. I'm so sad."

For Stryker, sad had morphed into fury decades ago.

"Was she killed?" Mavis asked. "Suicide? Did she have a medical condition? You gotta tell me something."

The eerie image of April in the wedding gown crashed into his thoughts. "That's all I got."

"Are you letting the staff know?"

"After we close." He pushed out of the chair. "I'll be in my office." After shutting the door behind him, he took the back stairs down to his private office in the basement. His dungeon in The Dungeon.

The retina scanner cleared him to enter his inner sanctum. He stepped inside the large room and the motion detector triggered the low-lit recessed lights. Dropping onto his worn chair, he sat in silence and stared at the six dark screens hanging on his wall. *What the fuck happened to April?*

Hair on the back of his neck prickled as the depravity of the situation took hold. He dug out his phone and dialed.

"You better have a damn good reason for waking me," his attorney said, his voice groggy.

"I'm being questioned by a homicide detective about a murder."

"Dammit, Stryker, what did you do now?"

He gave him the short version, ending with, "It's the cop who arrested me—"

"Emerson Easton?"

"Yeah. She wants to review the club's surveillance and talk to my employees. I told her to get a warrant."

"Not cooperating makes you look guilty."

"Not news," Stryker replied. "Last time I cooperated, she arrested me."

"That nightmare I remember. So, I gotta ask...did you kill—?"

"For fuck's sake, of course not," Stryker replied.

I've got blood on my hands, but it's not hers.

3

BOOMSLANG AND JUSTICE

As soon as Stryker left, Emerson called three judges for a search warrant. She got through to one who told her he'd help. Next, Emerson checked April's front door and windows. No sign of forced entry. Her gut told her that April knew her assailant. There were no dirty dishes in the sink, no glasses of half-drunk booze, no crumbs on the counter. *Had the killer stayed to clean up?*

If so, this criminal was brazen, which made him that much more dangerous.

Emerson spoke with neighbors. No one heard a thing. No loud music, no raised voices. Not even a scream from April's apartment. Nothing.

A shudder ran through her. The possibility that a serial killer could be stalking his next victim fueled Emerson to work harder and smarter. She didn't stand a chance in hell of catching him if she didn't work day and night to find him.

She drove home in silence, her thoughts laser focused on the crime scene, the images of April and the first victim etched into her brain. She'd need to discuss strategy with her captain first thing in the morning. The public needed to be warned, but knowing Captain Perry, she wouldn't want to unnecessarily terrorize women in the

DMV. People needed to be vigilant, not prisoners in their own homes.

Emerson pressed the garage door opener, drove inside, and shut the door. While she wasn't scared a criminal would target her, she always watched her six. Opening the door to her townhome triggered the security system, so after bolting the lock, she punched in the code. Once the alarm went quiet, she reactivated the system.

Meow, meow, meeeeoooooow.

Like every night, there he was, waiting for her. "Hello, Pima, how's my little guy doing?" She knelt to scratch the cat's head while he rubbed against her knee, his rhythmic purr a comfort. "Let's go upstairs."

Pima knew the routine well and scampered up the steps ahead of her, then took his position near his water bowl in the kitchen. Her return home meant the black cat with the bright yellow eyes got a treat. She shook the can of kibble and he rose on his hind legs, pawing at the air. "Maybe I should quit my job and we should join a circus."

She dropped a few treats in his bowl before trudging upstairs to her bedroom. After stripping naked, she walked into her bathroom and turned on the shower.

The stench of death would stay with her for days, but the shower helped. She stood under the warm spray and tried to detach from her latest case, but each one clung like a disease...until she solved them. Her mind replayed the evening. The gray pallor on the young woman's face. The simple, white wedding gown, the positioning of the victim's body on the bed. April Peters was thirty-five, just three years older than Emerson. Unless terminally ill, most women in their thirties didn't even think about death. They were too busy living.

But death was a regular part of Emerson's life. It was her chosen career, week in and week out. Death was inevitable, but the objective of life was to cheat the grim reaper for as long as possible. Her victims were robbed of that chance.

So was Doug. Doug was robbed of that, too.

Thinking about her brother filled her with anger and bitterness. *I failed him.* Pain slashed her heart. *But I'm never giving up.*

As she dried off, she thought of Stryker. How could she not? Built like a steel tower, his ripped muscles had stolen her attention the first time she'd met him. But it was the intensity in his eyes that drove her wild. He always looked pissed off, like that fiery gaze was intended just for her. Because it was.

She imagined him having a beautiful smile, but she'd never seen it. Not even once. That's how much he despised her.

Pima moseyed in with a toy in his mouth. He dropped it and started batting it around. She picked it up and threw it into her bedroom. Off he raced after it.

She half-dried her hair, then pulled it into a loose ponytail. Her favorite sweats were in the hamper, so she settled for a T-shirt and yoga pants.

In the kitchen, she flipped open her laptop and logged in to work. If she didn't start filling out the police report now, it would eat up too much investigative time during the work day. She was too wired to sleep, anyway. The cat came flying into the room, hopped on a chair, then onto the table. As he made his way toward her, she stopped typing. And then Pima did what he always did, he decided her laptop would be the best place to sit.

"Not happening, Pima." She blocked him with her arm. He sat on the table, curled his tail around himself, and stared at her. "Stare away. I've got work—"

Her phone binged with an incoming message. It was three in the morning and she knew exactly who was texting her.

She clicked on the app labeled, "Survivors" and read the private message.

"Hey, Boomslang, is my insomnia buddy awake?" Justice asked.

"Of course," Emerson replied. "What's your excuse?"

"Work," Justice replied. "Yours?"

"Same."

Ever since joining the online chat group for survivors who'd lost loved ones in the DMV—District, Maryland, and Virginia—Emerson had developed an online friendship with Justice.

"Someone wants to say 'hey.'" Emerson snapped a pic of Pima and uploaded it to their chat.

"What's he doing?" Justice texted.

"His favorite thing. Staring at me."

"What for?"

"A treat, a head rub, to lay on my laptop the second I stop guarding it."

"LOL."

"How you doing, for real?" she asked.

Justice kept things chill, never said much or got too emotional. She liked that.

No reply. She waited a few more seconds, then clicked back to her police report.

Bing.

"I've had better days," Justice replied. "You?"

"Wanna talk about it?" she asked.

"No. Good to know you're out there. How 'bout you?"

She wanted to tell him what she did for a living. That she spent her days, and a lot of her evenings, searching for killers. Instead, she typed, "Missing my bro."

"I'm sorry," he typed. "How can I help?"

"Talking now makes a diff. Knowing I'm not alone in my grief, you know?"

"We can't bring them back. Gotta go on without 'em. Never gets easier."

"Talk soon. Try to sleep." She clicked back over to her police report.

Five months ago, when her brother had died, Emerson struggled to process his unexpected death, so her captain suggested grief counseling. She, along with her mom and dad, worked with a great therapist. After several family sessions, Emerson told the psychologist she was dropping out.

"I'm happy to recommend a different counselor," Heather Sharpe had said.

"I love working with you, but I'd like to try a group," Emerson had told her. "Something online would be perfect."

That's when Heather Sharpe suggested Emerson join her online support group for survivors. Members could participate from the privacy of their homes, using their real names or anonymous ones. The climate suited Emerson, so she popped in weekly for sessions. Late one evening, a few months back, someone calling himself Justice had been online, so she pinged him to see if he was okay. That was the beginning of their online friendship. Nothing heavy. Two survivors checking in with each other on occasion. Having him there made her feel less alone, especially late at night.

His online profile listed him as a male who'd lost his mom years earlier in a murder.

Since Heather knew the true identities of everyone in the group, Emerson felt safe opening up about her feelings, something she normally kept close to the vest. Since joining the group, Emerson had become curious about Justice.

Curious, that's all.

At half past seven in the morning, Stryker punched in the security code at The Dungeon and flipped on the lights. "Too damn early," he grumbled.

While standing behind the bar making coffee, his phone rang. NO CALLER ID flashed on the screen. He answered, "Running late?"

"It's a fine fucking morning, isn't it, Truman?"

Carlo Spinetti's gruff voice turned his stomach. "What the hell do you want, Spinetti?"

"What happened to your manners? I'll go first. How you doin'?"

Stryker said nothing.

"Have you ruined anyone else's life lately?" Spinetti continued.

"Don't put that on me. You fucked up your own life."

"You're gonna regret helping the FBI," Spinetti said. "You enjoy that beautiful May sunshine while you still got a nose to sniff those pretty fuckin' flowers."

"Go to hell." Stryker hung up.

Spinetti's threat hung over him like a virus. Carlo Spinetti had been convicted of Internet fraud and was serving his sentence in a white-collar camp at a Maryland state prison. And it was Stryker's hacking skills that helped put him there.

"Dirt bag," Stryker said while pouring himself a cup of joe.

The front door opened and Captain Tiana Perry walked inside. Shaking off the annoying call, Stryker poured a second cup, then greeted his longtime friend. Tiana offered a warm hug.

As Arlington County's first Black and female police captain, she was opening doors for all women in the DC region.

With mugs in hand, the two got seated at a nearby table.

"I read my detective's report," Tiana said, after sipping the hot drink. "April Peters worked for you. You doing okay?"

One of the things he liked about Tiana was that she got right to the point. No bullshit, no small talk.

"I appreciate the concern," Stryker replied, "but you're not here to check up on my mental state."

"I need you to play nice with my detective."

"Not happening."

"Why do you hold grudges, Stryker? You gotta let all that go."

"Tiana, you weren't the captain when it all went down. Easton derailed my cybersecurity company, cost me millions, and damaged my reputation."

She glanced around. "You own a kink club. I think you damaged your own reputation."

Stryker chuffed out a laugh. "But I wasn't running a damn brothel out of it."

"Last year, you offered me off-the-books hacking help to get a violent criminal off the streets," Tiana continued. "I've got a possible serial killer on my hands. Put aside your personal feelings and do it again."

Serial killer? "Assign it to a different detective and you've got yourself a deal," Stryker said before setting down his mug.

"Cooperate with the investigation."

"I am," he replied.

"That means, don't force my detective to get a warrant just to review your club surveillance. Emerson is good," she continued, "but she needs someone who can scour the dark web, use that fancy facial recognition software you have—I can keep going. The list is endless."

"The PD has a data forensics team," Stryker pushed back.

"And they're stretched to the max." She set down her mug. "I'm asking you to make yourself available to her. Become a primary, *confidential* resource. She's got two dead women and the cleanest crime scenes we've ever seen. Do the right thing."

Silence.

Tiana was waiting this one out. Not the first time he'd seen that determination in her eyes.

More silence.

Dammit. He wasn't gonna win. For April's sake, he'd play nice with Easton, despite their rocky history. "I'll do it to stop a killer."

Tiana smiled. "That's all I'm asking. Use those crazy-good hacking skills and help me—help Emerson—before this lunatic takes someone else's life."

Instead of squeezing into the crowded elevator, Emerson trotted up the stairs and into Homicide. Despite getting a whopping three hours of sleep, she was ready to work. She shoved her handbag in her desk drawer and made her way to the break room. Between thinking about the killer and knowing she'd have to deal with Stryker, she'd had a restless night. Chasing down a psychopath would be the easier task. No doubt, Stryker would put her through hell just so she could view the surveillance at The Dungeon. Steeling her spine, she filled her mug and returned to her desk to check email.

Even though the judge had agreed to send over the search warrant, it hadn't come in yet.

Bing!

She read the incoming email. *Ah, crap, I forgot about this.* Huffing out a sigh, she pushed out of her chair as a coworker did the same.

"Why does this always happen to us?" asked fellow detective, Nikki Cardoso.

Emerson glanced around the department. None of the other detectives seemed fazed by the email. "Let's beg out."

The women beelined for the captain's office but Tiana Perry wasn't at her desk.

"Looking for me?" Captain Perry asked as she approached her office.

"Good morning, ma'am," Emerson and Nikki said as they moved out of the doorway.

After entering, the captain asked, "Do we have a problem?"

"We got an email," Nikki began. "Something about being interviewed for *DMV* Magazine."

Captain Perry sat behind her desk and logged in to her computer. "That was arranged weeks ago."

"We don't have time," Emerson said. "Can you assign someone else?"

"Detectives, you were chosen by Media Relations, along with a dozen others from different departments." She tucked her short, dark hair behind one ear. "This is a great opportunity for the public to see that we bring value with our Abuse Prevention program, our LGBTQIA+ Liaison Team, even our lost bicycle hotline number."

"The public can read all that on our website," Emerson protested.

"Everyone isn't on our website, but everyone reads *DMV*." She lifted her copy off her desk as her phone rang. "Captain Perry," she answered. "Be there shortly."

"The police chief is holding a press conference this afternoon," the captain said to her detectives. "The public needs to know we've got a possible serial killer in the area."

"The hotline's gonna go berserk," Nikki replied. "Mostly with people freaking out."

"We're not disclosing anything that would compromise the investigation, like the wedding gown or alleged cause of death," Captain Perry explained. "Not yet."

"Who's my secondary?" Emerson asked.

Captain tossed a nod in Nikki's direction. "Cardoso."

One bright spot in all of this. The two detectives worked well together.

"Captain, please assign different detectives for the magazine interviews," Emerson said.

"Complete them," the captain said. "The journalist signed an NDA, so he won't disclose any details about your cases."

Emerson fought the urge to roll her eyes. *What a time suck.*

"Dismissed."

As Emerson and Nikki made their way back to their desks, Emerson wanted to hit the restart button on her day.

"I'll be in court this morning," Nikki said. "Email me a list of follow-ups and I'll get started this afternoon. Try to have some fun with the magazine interview."

"Fun?" Emerson deadpanned. "What's that?"

"Something you should be having on a regular basis." Nikki threw her computer bag over her shoulder. "Whatever happened to the guy my husband and I fixed you up with?"

"We had coffee, but he wasn't for me."

Nikki glanced over Emerson's shoulder as the captain's assistant escorted a young man into the bullpen. "You're up."

As Emerson eyed the journalist, she told herself she'd get rid of him in fifteen minutes, twenty, tops.

The captain's assistant stopped near both women's desks. "Detective Easton, Detective Cardoso, this is Lyle Barnham, an investigative reporter with *DMV* Magazine."

Looking to be in his mid-twenties, Lyle kept his dark hair military short. His black-rimmed glasses were too large for his oval face and slender build.

Offering an obligatory smile, she shook his hand. "Call me Emerson."

"Sure thing, Detective," Lyle said.

The assistant chuckled as she made her way back to her desk.

"I've gotta leave," Nikki said.

"Can I interview you another time, Detective?" Lyle asked.

"Sure thing," Nikki said before taking off toward the elevator.

"Have a seat, Lyle," Emerson said.

Lyle sat in the guest chair beside her desk. "Thank you for talking to me."

Let's get this over with.

"*DMV* Magazine is doing a six-piece article on your department," he began. "I'm interested in learning what happens behind the scenes. You know, learn how detectives gather evidence, solve crimes, catch the bad guys, but also how law enforcement makes a positive impact in the community." He paused to smile. "You know, get to the heart of the Arlington City Police Department."

"Arlington *County*," she corrected.

Lyle's cheeks pinked. "Right. I knew that."

"I've got about fifteen minutes, so ask away."

"I was given permission to shadow a criminal investigator. Rather than ask a bunch of stagnant questions, I was hoping to follow you around this morning."

Earth, swallow me now.

"Have you toured the precinct?"

"Nope."

"You can ask me some questions while I take you around."

Lyle asked a lot of questions. How is evidence collected? Where is the evidence held? How long does it take for a coroner's report? What's a typical day in the life of a homicide detective? She kept her answers high-level and short, while Lyle shoved his phone in her face to record her answers.

As Emerson brought Lyle around, she now had a valid reason for popping downstairs to forensics. The team wouldn't have any information on April Peters, but it didn't hurt to be seen there. She believed the squeaky wheel got fixed faster.

Once there, she introduced Lyle, then made her way to the crime scene photographer.

"I took bets you'd be by this morning." The tech glanced at his watch. "You're late. I pegged you for getting here thirty minutes ago."

"I've been working with the reporter."

"I won twenty big ones," the crime tech said. "And to show my gratitude, I've got these for you." He opened a drawer and handed Emerson a folder. "Crime scene pics, from last night."

"I owe you a beer." She flipped open the folder and a slash of pain cut through her. The photos of April Peters were downright creepy.

Lyle peered over her shoulder. "That doesn't look good."

On a grunt, she closed the folder. "Thanks for these," she said to the crime tech.

In the hallway, she asked Lyle who he wanted to question next.

"Can I hang with you a little longer? I signed an NDA and won't write about anything I see. I'm interested in how an investigator approaches their cases, especially from the beginning."

"Each case is different," Emerson explained as she ushered him toward the stairs.

Lyle stopped in front of the elevator.

"I'm walking the three flights," Emerson said. "You can meet me upstairs."

"I'll stay with you."

They returned to Homicide and she retrieved a folder from her desk before heading into a conference room. She tacked up the photos from the first murder on a bulletin board, then did the same for the second. Emerson noted the similarities and differences in her victims. At some point, she realized Lyle was standing inches away from the bulletin board, staring at a close-up photo of Gloria Stanton, the first victim.

"What caught your attention?" Emerson asked.

"What's that discoloration around her neck?" Lyle asked.

"She's been strangled. Autopsy report is due back any day, so my answer is unofficial."

"How do you stay detached from all of this?"

"Who said I did? These people's lives have been cut short. They have families, friends. It's tragic." She jotted down a few notes for follow-up.

"How do you find the killer?" Lyle asked.

"One clue at a time."

"Do they ever get away with it?"

"Unfortunately, yes. We've got over twenty cold cases dating back fifty years. Some never get solved."

"Bummer," he replied.

Lyle hung around for another thirty, then told her he had to get to class.

"What are you studying?"

"I'm getting a Master's in journalism. Would it be okay if I followed up to see how you're progressing with your cases?"

"I'm sorry," Emerson replied. "I've got a full plate. I hope my answers helped with your story."

"No problem. Thanks for your time and good luck." Lyle headed out and Emerson turned back to the crime scene photos.

The first victim, Gloria Stanton, had worked at an Arlington dive bar for six months. She'd waited tables and served drinks behind the bar. Emerson had talked to management and questioned some of the regulars. Everyone knew Gloria, but no one knew much about her. Like April, Gloria lived alone. Emerson couldn't find any of Gloria's family. Neighbors in the apartment building said Gloria kept to herself.

The unsub—unknown subject—must have known that about both women and used that information to befriend them and gain easy entry into their apartment. *Did he dress them post-mortem or convince them to put on a wedding gown? Maybe he forced them to at gunpoint. What kind of sick game is this killer playing?*

After jotting down several notes, she returned to her desk and pulled up email. *Yes! I got it.* She texted Stryker. "Mr. Truman, it's Detective Easton. I've got that warrant. When can I speak to your GM?"

Stryker's executive team sat around the conference table finishing up their Friday meeting at Truman CyberSecurity, the premiere cybersecurity company in the region. Their goal? Stop hackers from breaking into their clients' software systems and holding those companies ransom, or stealing their secrets and selling them to foreign governments or enemies of the state.

Stryker had once been a black hat hacker, but turned to white hat hacking after getting caught by the FBI. As part of his plea deal, he agreed to make his services available when the Bureau needed to catch a major cybercriminal. In the past decade, he'd helped out a handful of times. The majority of his time was spent protecting government and civilian organizations from the very hacker he used to be.

"Brooks, you're up," Stryker said to his VP of Sales and Client Retention.

He and Brooks Johnson had been close friends since college. On a bet, they'd grown their hair long. These days, Brooks' black dreads trailed down his back. Years later, their playful rivalry was still going strong, though Stryker had declared Brooks the winner a long time ago.

Not only had Brooks helped Stryker grow the company into the powerhouse that it was, he also managed recon in Stryker's vigilante team.

"This week, my team closed eight new accounts and renewed annual contracts with sixty-four clients," Brooks said.

"Nice work," Stryker replied. "How many did we lose?"

"None," Brooks replied.

"Even better."

Next, Stryker addressed Danielle Fox, his Manager of Data Breach, Government. "Whatcha got, Danielle?"

In addition to being one of the best hackers he'd ever met, she'd been with him since she'd graduated college—first, as a hacker, then climbing through the ranks to earn a seat in his inner circle.

"My teams found eighteen ways to breach the FBI, eleven for NSA, and sixteen for State," Danielle replied. "We passed that info along to the agencies, so they can make the fixes."

"Good job." His phone buzzed with an incoming text, but he ignored it. One by one, he asked each exec if they had anything more to discuss.

"Only TGIF, baby," Danielle added, and everyone laughed.

"Before I forget—" Stryker pulled out his phone and glanced at the text from Emerson before pulling up a QR code. "I've got the charity event tix."

Everyone, but Danielle, scanned the code.

"Can't make it?" Stryker asked her.

"I've got a thing that evening."

"Tix for you and a guest," Stryker explained to the group. "Includes parking and grub. You buy your own booze and if you show up, you better donate."

"When is it?" someone asked.

"Thursday night," Stryker answered.

"I'm out," Brooks replied.

"This coming Thursday?" asked another exec.

"How did you get hired, here, exactly?" ribbed Danielle.

Stryker laughed. "Play nice, Fox."

Stryker's assistant popped her head into the conference room. "You about done?"

"Yup," Stryker replied, as his three-year-old nephew pressed his face against the glass of the conference room. When he saw Stryker, he grinned, then toddled toward the conference room door, squeezed past the assistant, and tumbled onto the floor.

After pushing to his feet, he said, "Hi, Uncle Syker Tooman."

Everyone laughed as Stryker picked up Aaron. "How's my big guy?"

The assistant held open the door so Stryker's sister could enter. She was pushing a stroller, the seat piled high with bags.

Trudy said hello to his staff, then set one of the bags on the table. "Open it."

"Is this what I think it is?" Brooks lifted out a large, plastic plate of homemade chocolate chip cookies covered in clear plastic wrap. "You are an angel. These are the best cookies I've ever eaten."

Danielle lifted out a second plate from a bag, pulled off the cellophane, and bit into one. "Mmm, this is better than—"

Stryker's sister laughed. "They're not *that* good." She placed all the bags, save one, on the table. Word spread fast. Within seconds, the room was filled with hungry employees snatching up the homemade treats. Trudy pushed the stroller out the door, then turned back to Stryker. "Got a second?"

Brother and sister walked down the hall toward his corner office, the tyke still in Stryker's arms. When they entered his office, he set the child down. Trudy pulled out a plate of cookies, removed the outer wrap, and handed one to her son, along with a sippy cup. Then, she set the plate on Stryker's small conference table.

"We need to talk," Trudy said.

"So, you didn't stop by to deliver cookies and spread springtime cheer?"

"No."

Stryker and his older sister were close. Her husband was a high school math teacher and Trudy stayed home to care for their three young children. Money was tight, but Stryker made sure they were never without.

"I got you something." Stryker pulled out a credit card and handed it to her. She just stared at it. "Take it."

"For what?"

"I added you as a second user on this account. For groceries."

Her eyes widened. "I can't do that."

"Look around. I built this. Mom and Dad aren't here to share it with us, so that means more for us. Take the card." He smiled. "Buy food. You and the hubs get a sitter and go out to dinner without the kids."

Tears filled her eyes. "You are so good to me."

"That's because I like you. You wouldn't be saying that if I didn't."

She laughed.

"Uncle Syker Tooman."

Stryker knelt. "Whatcha got there, buddy?"

The child had pulled a LEGO DUPLO car from his mom's diaper backpack. "I made this with Gam-pa."

After rolling the car around on the floor with his nephew, Stryker gestured for his sister to sit. "What's going on?"

Once she sat, she started fidgeting with her ring. His phone buzzed with a text. Detective Easton, again. "Warrant burning a hole in my hand. When can I talk to your GM?"

While he didn't want to deal with the hot detective and her saucy attitude, he'd agreed to play nice. "Gimme a quick second," Stryker said to his sis. "I gotta handle this."

Stryker typed out a text. "The Dungeon, 7pm." He added the Arlington address and hit send. Then, he added her to his personal VIP list at the club before turning back to Trudy. "What's going on?"

"Dad contacted me."

Gritting his teeth to keep from screaming obscenities in front of his nephew, Stryker said nothing.

"Can I have more cookie, Mommy?" Aaron offered her a huge grin. "Peeeeeaaaase."

Trudy handed her son a small one, then turned back to Stryker. "Say something."

"You're not done talking," Stryker bit out.

"About a month ago, Dad called me. He got my number from Aunt Heather."

Up went Stryker's eyebrows. "Why didn't Heather let you know?"

"She did. She told me he'd been in touch and wanted to see me. See us. Anyway, Heather asked if she could pass along my number. I told her yes. A few days later, Dad called me."

Stryker had a sudden urge to punch his fist through a damn wall. Nothing pissed him off more than thinking about his father. "And?"

"We met for coffee, just the two of us. He looked older, a little heavier. It was weird to see him." She fiddled with her ring.

"Go on, drop the bomb on me."

"He was very remorseful about leaving and asked if I'd consider giving him a second chance."

"Based on the car Aaron is playing with, I'm guessing you did."

She nodded, but said nothing.

Aaron appeared beside Stryker. "Gam-pa was nice." His cheeks were smeared with chocolate and Trudy cleaned him with a wipe.

"I forget that children have giant ears and a sponge for a brain," Stryker said while playfully poking his nephew in the belly.

Aaron giggled. "Tickle monster."

"He asked for your phone number," Trudy whispered.

Heat blasted Stryker's chest. "No."

"And I gave it to him."

Not takin' his call. Problem solved. Deadbeat Dad would move on and Stryker would hit the delete button on the SOB...again.

Trudy stood. "I hope you'll reconsider. He's old and lonely."

"Sixty-something ain't old. Where's he been for the past twenty?"

"Florida."

Stryker shook his head as he lifted the child, razzed his cheek, then set him in the stroller. "Thanks for coming by, buddy."

"Bye, Uncle Syker Tooman."

Trudi hugged her brother. "Just give him a chance. You sure you still want me to have this credit card?"

"I'm not interested in talking to him, but I'm not gonna punish you for being a—"

"Softie," she interrupted.

"Bonehead," Stryker replied.

"What's a bonehead, Mommy?" Aaron asked as Trudy wheeled him toward the door.

"I love you." She waved the credit card. "Best brother ever."

4

FORCED TOGETHER

Emerson had been summoned to Captain Perry's office. "Did you read my police report?" Emerson asked.

"Yes," Captain Perry replied. "You didn't have to finish it at three this morning."

"I couldn't sleep, plus, I want to get started with the case today."

"You're dealing with a deviant mind. You'll have to use all your best resources if you want to catch him or her. To help, I've secured you a confidential resource."

"A CI?"

"More like a confidential partner. He can help you gather information…er…faster." Captain Perry offered a warm smile. "Go through the normal procedures to secure whatever you need, but this person can get you most everything much, much quicker."

"Sounds great."

"Not too long ago, he helped me with a high-profile case. We wouldn't have caught the unsub without his phenomenal hacking skills."

"Can I get his name and number so I can contact him?" Emerson asked, phone at the ready.

"It's Stryker Truman."

Emerson stared at the captain in disbelief. "My off-the-books resource is Stryker Truman?"

"Correct."

Emerson could not believe how an already bad situation could get any worse. "That's not gonna work."

"He's already proven to be a great asset to the department."

Emerson flashed the warrant. "So, I won't be needing this."

The captain smiled. "Show it to him anyway. It'll break the ice."

A single piece of paper would not melt that glacier of a man.

"He can't work here at the precinct and you can't be seen at his cybersecurity firm," Captain Perry continued, "so you'll work at his club."

"He sent me a text to meet him there tonight."

"Excellent." The captain rose. "He's eager to help out."

Her contentious relationship with Stryker sent a shudder through her. She did not want to work with him.

"Questions?" asked the captain.

"Any chance you can find me a different informant?"

"No. And this resource stays between us."

"Understood."

The drive home was filled with a numbing silence. Since her brother had died while working an undercover case, Emerson had grown more and more frustrated at work. Though she loved being a detective, she couldn't get past the disappointment. No matter whom she'd spoken with, no one would investigate his death. The ME had ruled it an accidental overdose, the department had expressed their condolences, and everyone had moved on. Everyone, except Emerson.

Doug didn't do drugs.

Now, she was forced to work with Stryker. Solving a double homicide was stressful enough, but partnering with him would make an already challenging situation impossible. In this case, however, she did have it coming to her. Stryker couldn't stand her and she didn't blame him. The previous times she'd interacted with him had ended in a total disaster. *Epic fucking fail.* Back then, Emerson had been the bad guy.

She let herself into her townhouse and was greeted by her talkative feline. She cracked a smile at his two-legged dance before heading upstairs to change. After staring at her clothes for what felt like forever, she texted her best friend. "What do I wear to a kink club?"

Dots appeared, then, "I'm guessing as little as possible," Danielle replied. "But the *real* question is why are you going to a kink club????"

She texted back, "Work."

"Should I check with my sister?" Danielle replied.

"NM, I got this. When's our GNO?"

"Wednesday. My sister wants to come. Okay?"

"Of course," Emerson typed. "I love Claire-Marie. Gotta run. Wish me luck."

"You don't need luck. You pack heat. Aim low." Danielle added a laugh emoji and several heart emojis.

Emerson settled on black jeans, a white shirt, and a long sweater. She threw on a little blush and tinted lip balm, slipped into work heels, and stared at herself in the mirror. "I look like a prude."

With her Glock secured in its holster, she patted Pima and left.

After parking in the lot, she eyed the members waiting in the long Friday-night line that wove its way around the building. In addition to wearing clothes that showed off their best assets, some wore simple black masks that framed their eyes. And there were several whose ornate masks covered most of their faces. A chill crept through her. Sex with a stranger was a fantasy only. *I couldn't do it if I couldn't see his face.*

Exiting her car, she made her way over. The distressed brick, three-story building looked like it was one hot second from being demolished. The windows had been blackened and she had to search for a club sign. *This has gotta be the place.* She spotted a sign beneath the lone light bulb that hung over the front door.

The Dungeon

Emerson's skin prickled. She felt like she was about to enter a medieval torture chamber. Five minutes after standing in a line that didn't budge, she texted Stryker. "Should I flash my badge so I get jumped to the front?"

No dots appeared.

Seconds later, a humongous man with arms bigger than her legs walked over. "Detective Easton?"

"Did my clothing give it away?" She bit back a smile.

He chuffed out a hearty laugh. "I'm Stryker's line manager, Tank." He showed her his phone. Stryker had sent him a picture of her standing in line.

The bouncer brought her inside. The high-tech music reverberated in her chest and the low-lit lighting created an intimate setting. Clubbers stood in small groups or twosomes talking. Some were masked, but the majority weren't. As Tank led her around the dance floor, she eyed the couples pressed together, swaying and grinding to the beat. She hadn't been with a man in a long time and a touch of envy ran through her. Sometimes, she wanted to escape reality doing something other than watching a movie with her cat. She wanted a man's hard body on her while his large hands caressed her skin. Her insides tightened at the sexy thought.

An oversized rectangular bar stood toward the back of the room with a large area nearby for members to mingle. On the other side were a mix of tables and horseshoe-shaped booths that afforded some privacy.

As Tank approached the elevator, Emerson's heart picked up speed. "I'll take the stairs."

He led her to a fire door and stilled in front of the wall scanner. The light turned green and he opened the door. "Stryker'll meet you on the third floor."

On the way upstairs, she wondered how bad it would've been if she'd stepped into the elevator. By the time she reached the top floor, she had convinced herself that she needed *more* exercise, not less. She yanked open the heavy door and headed down the quiet hallway. Black walls, candelabra lights set on low. *Definitely sexy.*

A couple exited a room and walked by, arm in arm, both masked and both wearing leather. A door at the far end of the hallway opened and Stryker appeared. A surging wave of adrenaline rolled through her. His massive body dwarfed the space and her cheeks warmed.

One step at a time, she made her way toward him, the matador sizing up the bull. The only thing missing was the smoke billowing from his nostrils. Despite their contempt for each other, he was a smokin' hot man. She couldn't deny that he was part man, part beast, and all testosterone. He'd pulled some of his long hair into a half-up top knot. Her whisper-soft moan floated in the air. His sexy man bun was her hot button. She imagined freeing his hair as he planked over her, his soft waves brushing against her bare skin.

Stop, Em. Just stop.

Stryker did not greet her with a smile, but, then again, she wasn't offering one of her own, either. The man wore his anger well. She hated having to work with him, but she loved that she could see him again. He was super easy on the eyes. *Staring is not a crime.*

"Detective Easton, let's see that warrant."

She fished it from her handbag. After skimming it, he handed it back to her. "This'll work." He waited for her to enter the office, shut the door behind him. The woman standing beside the glass desk was leaning on a hand-carved cane.

"Hello, ma'am. I'm Detective Easton."

"Call me Mavis."

As Emerson eased onto the guest chair, Mavis sat in her cushioned chair behind the desk.

"Thanks for talking to me about April Peters."

"What happened to her?" Mavis asked.

"The report from the coroner's office hasn't—"

"No.' Mavis cut her off. "Was she killed? Suicide? I feel absolutely sick over this. I had no idea anything was wrong. If she killed herself..." Mavis cleared her throat.

"It appears she was murdered. I'm hoping you can help me with the investigation."

Emerson glanced over her shoulder. Stryker's heated gaze drilled into her. He hadn't moved from his position as door guard.

"Mr. Truman, can you join us?"

Refusing to sit in the guest chair beside her, he got comfortable on the sofa across the room. And his hard stare sliced right through her.

Steeling her spine, she turned back to the GM. "Mavis, what can you tell me about April?"

Mavis clicked on her keyboard while she read from the computer. "I hired her almost three years ago. In this industry, that's like a decade. April started in L1—"

"L1?" Emerson asked.

"Level 1," Stryker replied, the frustration in his voice not lost on her. "As in, the first floor. More members, more chaos. We put the employees in the pit, first. Sink or swim."

"She was a sweet young woman," Mavis said. "She showed up on time, did her job. No drama. Rarely called out sick. Better positions would open up, she'd express interest, and I'd give her a shot. She was head mixologist when she—" Mavis paused. "You find that son of a bitch and I'll kill him myself."

Ignoring that comment, Emerson pressed on. "Was she married? Boyfriend, girlfriend? Was she seeing anyone?"

"You'd have to ask a coworker. If I was tending bar, we were short staffed. No time to talk."

After several more questions, it was clear that Mavis knew nothing about her employee.

Emerson finished with, "Do staff list emergency contacts?"

"Mavis was hers," Stryker replied.

"I would have insisted she list someone else, if I'd caught that," Mavis said.

"Did she talk about family?" Emerson asked. "Mention a friend by name?"

"No, sorry." Mavis sighed. "I learned a lesson. Get to know my staff."

"Did she have any friends here I can talk to?" Emerson asked.

Stryker rose. "I got this."

"Thanks for your time," Emerson said to Mavis.

"I hope you catch him or her," Mavis replied.

With a nod, Emerson followed Stryker out. They walked down the hallway in silence. Most people made conversation, but not this one. His frustration rolled off him like angry waves crashing against the shoreline in a violent hurricane. But she wasn't deterred. Her new "partner" hadn't intimidated her a year and a half ago and he wasn't intimidating her now.

As they approached the elevator, she snuck a peek at him. His dark brows angled down while muscles in his jawline ticked.

Stopping in front of the elevator, he crossed his arms over his massive chest. "I don't want to work with you, but I want to catch April's killer."

"Ditto."

His eyebrow arched. "We agree on something." Then, he stepped so close his delicious scent—a combination of leather and soap—filled her soul. He smelled so good, so intoxicatingly sexy. *He smells like a man.*

"I need you to see something on the surveillance." His voice had dropped to a husky whisper, sending heat blasting her chest.

His gaze seemed to strip her bare while chaotic energy swirled around them. All she could do was breathe him in and relish everything Stryker. The attraction was powerful…and infuriating the hell out of her. She was stronger than this. He was just a man. A gorgeous, agitated man who hated her for doing her job.

Despite the silent battle raging between them, she liked feeling his fury and seeing the heat in his eyes.

"What do your employees know about April?" Emerson asked.

"After the club closed last night, I told them she died," Stryker replied. "That was all I said. The staff talk. If the killer works here, I don't want to tip them off. This stays between us."

"Nothing like a shit-ton of secrets from my confidential resource to get a girl's blood pumping."

Strangely, a smile tugged at his lips. "I need to bring you into my office."

"Okay...and?"

"No one comes into my dungeon."

"Because they never make it out alive?"

His lips twitched as he tapped the elevator button. "Because it's private."

The elevator doors swung open, but she didn't move. "I'm taking the stairs."

They walked down the three flights in an icy silence. Back on L1, Stryker led her through the noisy space where bodies were pressed together on the dance floor. *Are they searching for Mr. or Ms. Right or just looking for some late-night fun?*

Emerson's world was so different from theirs.

Stryker stopped in front of a door marked "Private". After the retina scanner flashed green, he pushed open the door. She entered another stairwell leading down.

"Your office is in the basement?" she asked.

"Right." He took a few steps, turned back.

A cold sweat blanketed her and she hugged herself from the sudden chill. He furrowed his brow. "Are you uncomfortable being alone with me?"

"No," she replied. "Are there windows?"

"No."

"One way in and out?"

He studied her for an extra beat, his gaze skimming her face, pausing on her mouth, then back into her eyes. "You claustrophobic?"

She hated admitting a weakness, but she couldn't go downstairs. "Is the basement my only option?"

"I got you," he said. "Can you find your way back to Mavis's office?"

"Yeah."

"I'll grab a laptop and meet you on L3, as in, the third floor."

Her thundering heart slowed down. "That's a better plan."

Stryker liked knowing the hard-assed detective was human...or leaning in that direction. From what he could tell, she was claustrophobic. He could work with that. What he could not deal with was how strikingly beautiful she was. The more he stared at her, the more agitated he got. She had this amazing way of riling him up simply by existing.

Didn't help that he'd sworn off women ever since the "incident". Four months ago, after connecting with a member, she'd followed him home, knocked on his front door, and expected he'd invite her in. He did not. She dogged him at the club and kept showing up at his house. The stalking ended after he got a restraining order and blocked her from his club. But he'd learned his lesson and had gone cold turkey ever since.

Stryker Truman was on a sexual strike. More pissed off he could not have been.

He grabbed a laptop from his private office in the basement and returned to L3. Emerson wasn't waiting in Mavis's office.

"Seen the detective?" he asked his GM.

"Not in the last five minutes," Mavis replied. "Scare her away already?"

"She must have wandered into a room."

After eyeing his laptop, Mavis pushed out of her chair. "I take it you want to use my office."

"For ten minutes, then I'm gonna need you to relieve Parker on L2."

Mavis snatched her pack of crumpled cigarettes. "I love win-win situations." With the help of her cane, she was gone in seconds.

Stryker went off in search of the sultry detective. Most of the doors on L3 were closed because they were in use. On occasion, when members were finished playing, they'd leave the door to the suite open. As he suspected, he found her in the Guilty Pleasures room, staring at the kink toys hanging on the wall.

He stood in the doorway admiring the spectacular view.

His libido could only take so much of the sultry detective. Those intense eyes that drilled into his, the way she moistened her lower lip with a slow roll of her tongue. And he'd lose his ever-loving mind if he caught another whiff of her. He'd never met anyone who smelled so fucking good. If he glanced at her rockin' hot body, he'd start to harden.

She was hitting all his buttons, but he wasn't gonna let his dick take the lead. Not this time. "See something you like?" he asked.

She eyed him so hard, his breath hitched. *Fuck, fuck me. Do not walk in.*

After pulling the nipple clamps off the wall, she said, "These have got to hurt."

He bit back a smile. "Wouldn't know. Never used 'em."

She rehung the sex toy, then ran her fingers down the feather wand.

He tracked her every movement. The way she slowly traced her fingers over the soft feathers, how she removed the whip and cracked it against her thigh. His cock twitched.

"If my career doesn't work out, maybe I'll become a dominatrix."

A deep groan rumbled through him. Never one to surrender his alpha tendencies, a vision of her standing over him in black latex had him fisting his hands. Despite his warning, he found himself walking toward her. With every step, blood rushed to his groin. "Smack it on your hand."

Whap! The smack of leather against bare skin filled the silence. "That's a good sting." Her voice had dropped.

His cock started pulsing. "Awakens the nerves."

"Put out your hand," she commanded.

Stryker rarely took orders from anyone, but he found himself lured by her bossiness and held his out, palm up.

She cracked the whipped against his skin, the sharp sting sending streams of pleasure through him.

"I should be punishing you for what you did to me, not the other way around," he rasped out.

She faced him full on and stared straight into his eyes. "Maybe you should."

Their breathing had changed, the roar of it thundering in his ears. He needed to tamp down on the mounting arousal, but his feet were cemented in place.

Tap-tap-tap. "Stryker, can I sanitize the room?" asked an employee.

Emerson hung the whip on the hook and marched out, leaving him with a burning desire to take her up on her sexy offer.

They entered the office and he shut the door.

"Where's Mavis?" she asked.

"Smoke break." Stryker sunk into a guest chair and opened the laptop.

When she dropped into the seat beside him, he became hyperaware of her essence. She smelled like a field of wild flowers. He didn't remember her smelling like that when she'd arrested him. Back then, she stunk of rotten eggs.

"You've got multiple businesses to run," she began, "and you're doing this out of—"

"Obligation." Stryker leaned back in the chair. Her wavy golden hair tumbled down her back, those big brown eyes with a soulful gaze, and her hot, tight body commanded his complete attention.

"So helpful." Pausing, she glared at him. "Captain Perry said you can speed up the process, but I haven't made any progress with the first murder, which happened last month. We had a wiped-down crime scene. No cell phone, no laptop. I couldn't find any social media accounts or next of kin. The victim, Gloria Stanton, worked as a bartender at Good Times Bar-n-Grill in—"

"Arlington," he replied.

"Right. Bar staff and patrons knew nothing about her. Most only knew her first name. Said she was a listener, not a talker. She lived alone in an older apartment complex with no surveillance. Her neighbors said she was quiet, kept to herself. I need to know if she was a member here."

"Got it. What about her car?"

"There's no record of her having one. Her landlord said she'd lived there a few months. She listed an emergency contact that went nowhere. This poor woman was totally alone."

"The killer probably knew that about her."

"Since both women were found strangled and wearing a wedding gown, I'm focusing on April Peters's case."

"Understood," Stryker said. "I'll analyze her cell phone data, search the dark web for postings by the killer. Sometimes these psychopaths upload pics from their crime scene. I can also check the Internet for police reports on similar murders."

"That'll be great."

"Not all tonight. This takes time."

The tight lines around her eyes softened. "Of course."

"Let me show you what I found." Stryker started the video. "Volume is pointless with the crowd."

In unison, both he and Emerson leaned close, their shoulders brushing against each other. She moved away, the space leaving him cold.

"This is from a coupla weeks ago," Stryker explained. "That's Parker Sandler, one of the bartenders. He came in early to restock the liquor. His shift ended at eleven."

Instead of leaving the club, Parker pulled up a stool at the bar and ordered a beer from April. Whenever she had a lull, she'd talk to him.

"Lots of eye contact," Emerson said. "Look, she touched his arm."

"You got a Ph.D. in psychology, now?" Stryker fast-forwarded. Parker stayed until the club closed, then helped April clean up. She grabbed her backpack and they left out the front door. Stryker flipped to a different camera. Parker walked her to her car. She hugged him, then got in. He walked to the other side of the parking lot and jumped in his car, then followed her out of the lot.

"Looks like they're friends," she said. "Maybe more. Have you talked to him?"

"No." He opened a different browser and logged in to The Dungeon's employee website. "He called out sick the first night she didn't show for work."

"What about last night?" Emerson asked.

"He was here, but he kept checking his phone." Stryker ran the video showing Parker checking his phone every ten minutes.

"Most people are phone obsessed," she said. "I'm going to need to review the surveillance going back a few weeks, maybe longer. Can I get a copy?"

"You can review it here."

"Making this difficult for me, aren't you?"

"If I were playing hardball, you'd know it. Parker is on L2. You okay with strippers?"

"Come again?"

He paused while the atmosphere turned electric. Those were some loaded words. She hitched a brow and waited.

"Some people aren't comfortable around topless women. I can bring him up here so you can talk to him."

She exhaled a grunt. "I need to find a killer, Mr. Truman. Naked women cozying up to a pole won't faze me."

They continued staring into each other's eyes while her sensuality lured him in. He wanted to kiss her so damn badly.

"Let's do it up here," she said, breaking the silence. "It's private."

The longer he stared, the more he wanted her. Wanted her beneath him, on top of him. He wanted to taste her and have her, again and again. *Fuck, she's killin' me.*

She cleared her throat, booting him from his fantasy. He texted Mavis to send Parker up. Emerson snagged his attention again. This time, by raking her fingers through her hair while her breasts pushed against her tight, white shirt.

She's making me crazy. "I'm gonna stay with you."

"I don't need a bodyguard." She removed her long sweater, but he did not drop his gaze.

"My club, my rules." He slapped his laptop shut, the frustrating grinding through him.

"I'm going to sit here," Emerson said. "If you won't leave, move to the sofa or sit at Mavis's desk and work...or in your case, *pretend* to work. I don't want him to feel like we're ganging up on him. I'm soft-pedaling my approach."

"A new strategy," he grumbled. "I can't wait to see this."

She grunted out her frustration, which had him biting back a smile. He liked annoying the detective. She had it coming to her for all the aggravation she'd caused him.

He tugged out his hair tie, dragged his fingers through his hair. He caught her staring at him—more like, full-on gawking. He could not get a read on this woman. Good thing he didn't give a fuck.

Tap-tap.

Stryker opened the door. No denying Parker looked uncomfortable. His hands were shoved into his jeans' pockets, his cheeks were flush with color. "Mavis said you wanna talk to me."

Emerson stood. Her easy-going smile sent a blast of heat through him.

"Hi, Parker, I'm Detective Easton. I've got some questions about April Peters." She gestured to the chair. "Can we talk for a few?"

"I'm not in trouble or anything, am I?" Parked asked as everyone sat down.

"No trouble," Emerson said. "I could use your help."

Her voice had taken on a laid-back tone. The tightness around her eyes was gone, too. Easing back in Mavis's padded desk chair, Stryker was more interested in watching Emerson than in staring at the computer screen.

"Were you and April friends?" Emerson asked.

Parker cleared his throat. "I guess. We'd started talking, you know." He wiped his palm on his jeans. "I liked her. She was cool."

"How long have you worked here?"

"A few months." He glanced at Stryker.

"Things going well?" she asked.

"Sure, it's steady work. Members are good tippers."

"You called out Wednesday this week. Can you tell me about that?"

"Sure, yeah." Again, he glanced at Stryker. "I'm not gonna get fired, am I?"

"It's all good, Parker," Stryker said.

"Wednesday?" Emerson pushed.

"Okay, right. I got a migraine. Took some meds and passed out. Best way to shake 'em is to sleep it off." Parker swallowed.

"Did anyone see you that evening?"

"Um…no. I live alone," Parker replied. "I got a roommate, but he pretty much lives with his girlfriend."

As Emerson continued questioning him, Stryker's opinion of the hard-ass detective shifted…a little. Her approach had changed in the last year and a half. Now, as a rookie detective, she exhibited more control and her relaxed style of questioning seemed to be working on the anxious bartender.

"I was thinking about asking her out," Parker confessed. "But I wasn't sure how she felt about me."

"Was she seeing anyone else?"

"I dunno."

"So, you said your migraine went away and you came to work on Thursday. Everything go okay that evening?" she prodded.

"Um, yeah. I had something I—all good. Yup, all good."

"You sure?"

Parker nodded.

Emerson scribbled something in her small notepad. "Were you and April friends on social media?"

"I don't have any accounts."

"Do you know if she did?"

"No idea."

"Thanks for your help." Emerson handed him a business card. "If you think of anything that might help, call or text me."

"Sure thing. I've gotta get back downstairs and relieve Mavis." Parker shut the door behind him.

Emerson pressed her finger against her mouth. "Shh." Those soft, plump lips were a magnet Stryker was fighting to resist. Was she torturing him on purpose? All he wanted to do was kiss her, sink his tongue inside her mouth and—

She opened the door, leaned into the hallway. And he glanced at her tight, sexy ass.

Fuck me.

Then, back into her eyes as she retreated inside and shut the door.

"He's gone," she said. "He's got an alibi, but no witnesses. I'll get his address and see if there are street cameras near his house."

"I can help with that," he said.

"Thank you." This time, she flicked her tongue over her lip while she wrote in her notebook. He didn't remember her being so damn tempting the first time around.

"I've gotta start reviewing the club's surveillance." She pulled a thumb drive from her worn leather handbag.

"Detective, I've got over fifty cameras in my club. If you use a thumb drive, it'll take you months to review everything. You don't have months."

"Well, what do you propose I do?"

"View the videos in my office."

"At your cybersecurity firm?" She looked like she was holding her breath.

"No, Easton, in my basement office, here."

With pursed lips, she stared at him for several seconds before sucking down a deep breath. "I can't—"

"You can."

"No, I can't." She slung her bag over her shoulder and walked to the door. "I'm sorry, I can't." She marched out, taking her fear, her frustration and a whirlwind of hotness with her.

I'm in hella trouble.

5

THE KILL

Emerson was dying to kiss Stryker. Press her lips to his and let go. She wanted to rip off his clothes and screw him on the sofa, the bed, and up against the damn wall. Her insides were screaming for a release. She was trying to ignore the urgency between her legs, but she couldn't. Their combative connection was filled with animosity and savage energy.

She stalked over to him and snaked her arms around him, pulling him flush against her. Rising up on her toes, she leaned in, didn't wait for permission, and kissed him.

His gruff, gritty groan sent electricity flying through her. He lifted her in the air and she wrapped her legs around him. He fell backwards onto the bed, rolled them over, and thrust inside her.

She cried out, the euphoria cascading through her sex-starved body, the pleasure sending her higher and higher. Their collective moans, coupled with his hands —those amazing man- hands—raked her body. Arching into him, her strangled cry was stopped by his mouth on hers, biting and nipping at her lips.

When he took her nipple into his mouth, the orgasm ripped through her, explosive pleasure sending her flying high. But it was his release that rocked her world. As he stared into her eyes, told her she was the sexiest, smuttiest woman he had ever known. "I could fuck you every day," he whispered.

A sudden pounding on her legs squelched the euphoria, while her feet stung from a series of sharp jabs. She started kicking Stryker away, but the onslaught of discomfort wouldn't stop.

Emerson jerked awake and bolted upright in bed. Pima pounced on her feet, tucked beneath the comforter. Then, the damn cat crashed down on her again, this time biting her big toe.

"Ouch!"

The cat's sharp claws dug through the linens and into her foot. She jerked away from him. "Pima, you interrupted my sex dream. Dummy. How could you do that?"

She laid back down and the feline sat on her stomach staring down at her, his wild purring almost as loud as her heavy breathing. She was covered in a thin line of perspiration, her insides throbbing with unrelenting need.

"Wow, that was some dream. My God, that man has seeped into my subconscious." As she turned on her night table lamp, the cat hopped off. It was three thirty in the morning. After pushing out of bed, she padded into the bathroom for water.

Hours earlier, she'd left the club in a huff. Not acting like a professional wasn't helping her solve these murders, but she was *not* ready to face her fear. Just the thought of going into a windowless basement made her stomach clench and her heart pound. No way could she force down her insecurities while trying to act like a badass cop.

I've gotta get over myself and do it.

After sliding back under the covers, she reached for her phone. She tapped on the Survivors app and checked for messages. None.

She needed sound advice from an impartial person on how to handle the situation. As she scrolled through the online members in the private chat group, she felt comfortable reaching out to two of them for help. The first was her therapist, Heather Sharpe.

"Dr. Sharpe, my work requires me to face my claustrophobia. I'd

DAMAGED

like to set up a virtual appointment with you. My sched is pretty crazy right now, but I'm hoping we can find something sooner than later. Please let me know your avail. Thanks."

She sent it, then scrolled to Justice and typed out a message. "Hey, insomnia bud. I have a prob. Could use your advice." She hit send.

Like most nights, dots appeared. "Whatcha need?" he replied.

"I have to face a fear with someone I don't get along with. It's a work thing, so no choice. I don't want this person to see me weak. How to proceed?"

Nothing for a minute, then his response. "Deep breath. Small steps. Confidence you'll be okay. Do it for you. BTW, how could anyone not like you?"

She smiled. Justice was right. So what if she has a panic attack in front of Stryker? Her gut told her that if she did, he might be the best person to help her through it. And if he was a total tool, she'd manage through it for the victims. She'd do it for April Peters and Gloria Stanton.

"Great advice," she texted him. "Thanks for your help. What's keeping you up so late?"

"Nothing special," he replied.

"You okay?"

"Who the hell knows," he replied.

"Wanna talk about it?"

"Maybe another time."

"Get some sleep." She closed the app and set down her phone. Lying there in the dark, her thoughts floated back to her sexy dream. The way Stryker had held her in his arms and kissed her naked body. How she'd loved giving herself to him and how easily he'd been able to pleasure her.

Not happening, so stop dreaming about him.

Stryker reread the text exchange with Boomslang before setting his phone and wallet in the cubby. As he finished pulling on his tactical gear, he thought about asking her for coffee. Or a drink. Dinner was too much and a lunch date wasn't his style. Dating, in general, wasn't his thing, but some chick who'd named herself after a venomous snake intrigued him.

He stepped into his combat boots, fitted his Glock with a silencer, and searched his pockets for a hair tie.

Brooks was getting ready next to him and Stryker held out his hand. After scrounging in his cubby, Brooks handed him a hair tie. Stryker pulled his hair into a man-bun before turning his thoughts to the mission.

A surprise attack on a ruthless gang in the DMV. In the dead of night, the leader and his four highest-ranking members would be exterminated. These five criminals were wanted for sex trafficking, child pornography, multiple murders, and sexual assaults. All five were repeat offenders, but they'd always managed to find their way back into society.

Today was the day they'd meet their maker, Stryker Truman style.

He checked his secondary weapon before dropping it into the holster. With ski mask in hand, he turned to his team. "We ready?"

Rhys pulled on his ski mask. "All set."

Brooks nodded before pulling up the hoodie and grabbing the key to the SUV.

To replace Quincy, Stryker had called in his close friend, Sinclair Develin. Known in DC as The Fixer, Sin's expertise was getting his high-profile, high-paying clients out of scandals. When needed, he would join Stryker on a kill.

Sin slid a blade into a sheath strapped to his ankle, then stood and holstered his Glock. "I covered the SUV's plates with deflectors when I got here."

"Good," Stryker said. "Let's get this job done."

The four men slid comm devices into their ears and left out the secret back door inside Travesty, down the fire escape, and into the waiting vehicle. Brooks always drove, stayed in the vehicle, and was tasked with ensuring each man got out, dead or alive.

The men had spent the last two hours in The Dungeon's Travesty room reviewing every detail surrounding the attack. Before they could get to the leader, they'd have to take out his guards and closest allies.

Riding shotgun, Stryker pulled up the surveillance cams pointed at the target home in a Maryland suburb, north of the beltway. Months back, Rhys had donned a utility jacket and made a few house calls in the neighborhood. He managed to leave behind six small cameras so Stryker could track the gang's activity.

"The house is owned by an uncle of one of the members," Stryker said. "Word is that he got sick and the nephew moved in to help. They took over the house and the uncle was never seen again."

"So, we might find a decomposing body," Rhys said. "You know I hate that."

"That's why you're getting a head's up," Stryker replied.

Additionally, several women lived in the home. Because they never left, Stryker didn't know if they were prisoners. No problem. Once Stryker and his team were out, ALPHA operatives would swoop in and handle the rest.

ALPHA, a top-secret government organization buried deep within the Department of Justice, was focused on catching or eliminating the country's most dangerous criminals.

The men rode in silence. Now wasn't the time for idle conversation. As Stryker mentally prepared, he flipped from one surveillance camera to the next. Their destination street was quiet. Adrenaline coursed through him, his heart pumping out eighty-three beats a minute. Twenty beats faster than normal, but the rush from the mission kept him sharp.

Brooks pulled into a neighboring street, cut the lights, and killed the engine.

"Where are the ALPHA ops?" Stryker asked Sin.

"Twenty-three minutes out," Sin replied. "If this goes right, we'll be gone by then."

Brooks set his Glock on his thigh as the other three strapped on their night goggles. Stryker pulled out his phone and tapped the IDware app. A miniature screen inside their night goggles displayed a green light next to his IDware icon.

"Software on," Stryker said to his team.

"Got it," Sin said.

"Ditto," Brooks replied.

"Nope," Rhys said. "Nothing for me."

Dammit. Stryker opened the back of the SUV and fished out a pair of goggles. "Try these, but keep your head down."

Rhys replaced the goggles. "This works."

Stryker closed the back hatch and slipped on his leather gloves. Down the street, a dog started barking. The balmy evening air meant perfect sleeping weather, and the neighbor with the dog had left windows open. The damn dog had heard them.

"Move the vehicle," Stryker said to Brooks.

"Good luck," Brooks said as the men took off down the street.

With weapons in hand, they crossed the street, heading toward the house at the end of the court.

As soon as it was in sight, Rhys murmured, "Moving into position." He split off, jogging between two homes, heading for the back of the property.

"It's you and me, brother," Stryker said.

"Always is," Sin replied.

"I've got eyes on one of the guards," Rhys said. "He's sitting on the steps leading to the back door." After a brief silence, Rhys said, "He's down."

Stryker and Sin approached the dark two-story home. A first-floor window was open. They peered inside. Two men were watching TV in the living room. "That's him," Stryker murmured. "That's Rowdy."

"The other is his personal bodyguard," Sin murmured. "We've

gotta get past them, take out the others, kill Rowdy's guard, then deal with him."

"Rhys," Stryker said. "We need to enter through the basement."

"Copy that," Rhys replied.

Stryker and Sin made their way into the backyard. Within seconds, Sin had picked the lock on the basement door and all three men slipped inside. A man slept on the sofa. IDware confirmed him as one of the five gang members.

Rhys and Sin split up to clear the lower level.

Stryker stood over the sleeping man. His eyes fluttered open. He bolted upright, reached for his sidearm—

Pop! Pop!

Two bullets to his head. He slumped forward. Stryker pushed him backwards and shot him in the heart.

"Two back here," Sin whispered into his comm.

"Confirmed gang members?" Stryker replied.

Pop! Pop! Pop! Pop!

"Confirmed," Sin replied. "Both down."

"We can take out the guard on the first floor," Stryker said. "Rhys, you can stay with Rowdy while we cover the top floor."

The basement door flew open. Two men came running down the dark stairs and started firing. *BANG! BANG! BANG! BANG! BANG! BANG!*

Pop! Pop! Pop! Pop! Pop! Pop! Pop! Pop!

Both of Rowdy's men dropped. Rhys was writhing on the floor. "Brooks, Rhys is down," Stryker said.

"On my way," Brooks replied.

Rhys winced. "It's my leg."

"Get him outta here," Stryker said to Sin.

Sin helped Rhys stand, then wrapped his arm around Rhys's waist and hurried him out of the house. Outright fury sent Stryker bolting up the stairs three at a time. The first floor was clear. He continued to the top floor. Cleared the first bedroom, then the bathroom.

Anxious whispers were coming from the back bedroom. With his handgun at the ready, Stryker entered the dark room. Two women were huddled in the corner, but Rowdy and his guard weren't there. He hurried out and strode toward the only room he hadn't checked.

Just as he approached the entryway, Rowdy's guard appeared, raised his weapon—

Pop! Pop! Pop!

Stryker hit him once in the head, twice in the chest. The guard dropped. The room was empty, but Stryker heard someone breathing in the closet. *It's gotta be Rowdy.*

"Rhys is secure," Sin said into Stryker's comm. "I'm coming up."

"At least two women in the back bedroom," Stryker whispered, covering his mouth with his hand. "Assume they're armed."

Stryker opened the closet door. Rowdy aimed his gun at Stryker's head.

Pop!

Stryker shot the pistol out of his hand and kicked the weapon out of reach. Then, he raised his goggles and stared into the eyes of one of the most wanted men in America.

"You're never gonna make it out alive," Rowdy growled.

"Neither are you," Stryker bit out. He pulled out his phone and showed Rowdy the screen. "This is the prosecutor who put you away twenty years ago. Amanda Truman. Remember her?"

"Look, chump, I've been tried so many times, it's like Alphabet Soup."

"Look at the damn picture. Did you murder this woman on her front doorstep?"

"I'm not telling you, asshole. Who the fuck do you think you are coming into my house and killing my best guys?"

"ALPHA ops are four minutes out," Brooks said in Stryker's ear.

"Did you kill Amanda Truman?" Stryker growled.

"Who the fuck is Amanda Truman?" Rowdy yelled.

"Answer the question."

"If I did, the bitch had it coming to her."

Stryker shot him between the eyes, then unleashed two bullets into his chest. "Rot in hell." He shoved his phone in his pocket and bolted from the room.

"Sin, we gotta go," Stryker said.

Sin emerged from the back bedroom. "Brooks, let ALPHA know there are four women in the back bedroom," he said into the comm. "Two in the corner, two in the closet. None are armed."

"Will do," Brooks replied. "We've gotta get Rhys to a doc."

"We're on our way," Stryker replied as he and Sin bolted out of the house. They jumped in the waiting vehicle and Brooks sped off.

Stryker eyed Rhys in the back seat. "Where you hit?"

"Thigh, but I'm gonna be okay. I don't need to go to the—"

"I've got someone who'll patch you up," Sin said.

"ALPHA just arrived on the scene," Brooks said.

"Did Rowdy kill your mom?" Sin asked Stryker.

"My gut says no."

"You'll find him," Sin said.

"I made her a promise I'm gonna keep," Stryker replied. "Even if it fucking kills me."

6

THE SURPRISE VISITOR

Emerson slogged through rush-hour traffic on I-95 south, heading to the FBI Academy in Quantico. Almost a week had passed since April's body had been discovered, but Emerson had nothing to show for the hours she'd spent trying to gain solid footing on both murders.

After being ushered into a conference room, she was told that Agent Radcliffe would be in shortly.

A few moments later, Lynn Radcliffe entered, her computer bag slung over her shoulder. "Emerson, it's good to meet you."

"I appreciate you making time for me, Lynn."

"You've got two very challenging cases," Lynn said, as she got comfortable at the conference table. "Made any progress since we spoke?"

"Unfortunately, none."

"I had a chance to review both police reports you sent over," Lynn said. "Did you bring the crime scene photos?"

Emerson laid them on the table in two rows. Stanton first, then Peters. While Lynn studied the pictures, Emerson unearthed her laptop and logged in.

"There were no phones or laptops collected from either victim's home, correct?" Lynn asked.

"That's right. The second victim owned a cell phone, but the techs couldn't find it."

"Cause of death?"

"Strangulation for Stanton. The ME's report showed ketamine in her blood. I don't have the autopsy results for Peters yet."

"Ketamine is an easy way for the killer to gain power over their victim. They become paralyzed and helpless to fight back." Lynn studied one of the pictures. "You said Gloria Stanton was *not* sexually assaulted. Was April Peters?"

"Forensics came back with a negative on that."

"A small win in a dark situation," said Lynn. "So, with only two deaths, we don't classify this as the work of a serial killer."

"I contacted you because of the perp's bizarre MO and I want to get a jump on creating his profile. I'm concerned he's going to kill again."

"Got it. Based on what you told me, this does have all the markings of a spree serial killer."

"Right," said Emerson. "A thrill seeker."

"Let's start building our profile. I like to start with generalities, then we can create a profile based on what we've got to work with. The more evidence you collect, the more you can fill in the missing pieces."

"Sounds good."

"Because most serial killers are men, I tend to use the word 'they' or 'he.'"

"Understood," Emerson replied.

"Psychopaths lack remorse and empathy, which is why they kill so easily. They love killing and they don't fear repercussions—a very dangerous combination that spurs them to do it again and again. The killing satisfies a temporary need. Over time—and that timeline varies—the need overtakes him and he does it again. There's a glibness about them. They believe they won't get caught and, for some, it becomes a cat-and-mouse game with law enforcement. Most of them are charming. They can also lead a double life. Some have a loving spouse and happy children. Their families act as unknowing shields keeping their secrets well buried. No one would suspect that their friendly neighbor or helpful coworker is an evil monster."

When Lynn finished discussing general characteristics of serial killers, she asked about details surrounding Emerson's cases. "I know we spoke on the phone, but let's start from scratch. Assume I know nothing."

"Both victims are white females, late twenties to mid-thirties. Brunettes with long hair who lived alone. Both were wearing white wedding gowns, no veils, no shoes and no jewelry."

"Underwear?"

"Bras and panties for both vics."

As Emerson continued listing their commonalities, Lynn jotted notes on a white board. Once Emerson had finished, Lynn reviewed the crime scene pictures one more time.

"I've been doing this a long time," Lynn said. "I've been wrong, but fortunately, less than I've been right. I think your killer is a white male between thirty and thirty-five years old. He's either asking his victims to dress in a wedding gown—or he's forcing them into one—to relive an experience. Since he didn't sexually assault either woman, I'm presuming he's reliving something that didn't happen. Maybe his fiancée left him at the altar. Maybe the killer got married, but he and his bride couldn't consummate their marriage. Maybe she broke the engagement and he hates her for it. Rather than process it like a mentally healthy person, he's begun reenacting the ceremony with his preferred ending."

A shiver skirted through her. "Horrifying."

"Very." Lynn nodded.

"His victims let him in, so we presume they know him."

"Looks that way," Emerson replied. "No forced entry."

"On the phone, you mentioned having a person of interest," Lynn said.

"A bartender where Peters worked. He was nervous when I questioned him, so that doesn't fit the profile of someone being glib."

"You can't rule him out, either."

"I'm not. He called out sick the first night Peters went missing. The second night—the night her body was found—he was at work."

"No time of death yet?"

Emerson shook her head.

"Is he a POI for the first crime?" Lynn asked.

"I only discussed Peters's death with him. I'm going to press him harder when I talk to him next."

Lynn spun two photos toward Emerson. "Let's talk about these poses."

Their conversation continued into the early afternoon. When they finished, Lynn walked Emerson to the lobby. "I hope this was helpful."

"Extremely." Emerson shook her hand. "Thanks for your time and expertise."

"Let me know if you have questions or run up against any challenges. This killer is good, but he'll slip up. Most of them do."

Emerson spent part of the drive back to Arlington trying to get the ME's office to give her a time frame for April Peters's tox and autopsy reports. The department was short-staffed and behind on delivery. It would be another week or two before she got the results.

Her partner, Nikki, was chasing down the phone records, but those were taking longer than she'd like. Emerson needed to know if Gloria Stanton was a member of The Dungeon, and there was only one person who could tell her that. But, she'd been terrified to face her fear and venture into the basement of the club.

Once back in Arlington, she was en route to a sandwich shop when an excited young couple stopped her.

"Excuse me," said the man. "We're getting married today."

"Congratulations," Emerson said with a smile.

"We're all turned around," said the woman. "Our wedding celebrant is waiting for us where we pick up our marriage license, but—"

"You're almost there," Emerson said.

After she directed them toward the building, the man turned to his fiancée. "Ready to get hitched?"

"I can't wait!" Grinning, they clasped hands and hurried off.

The cold reality of her cases smacked the smile off Emerson's face. *Gloria Stanton and April Peters will never marry. They don't get to have a family or grow old with someone. Some psychopath took that away from them.* Determination had her digging her phone from her bag. Time to face her fear.

With sweaty palms, she called Stryker.

"Truman," he answered.

"It's Detective Easton."

"Ready to work?"

"I am. When can we meet?"

"Lemme check." Silence. "How's four?"

"When?"

"Today."

"That would be great. Thank you."

"Yup." He hung up.

He was a man of few words, but he was being cooperative. A small win. After grabbing takeout, she walked inside the PD and up to Homicide. Just as she finished eating, her desk phone rang with a call from her captain.

"Detective, can I see you in my office?"

"Yes, ma'am."

In addition to Captain Perry, an officer from Media Relations was waiting for her. She closed the door behind her.

"Easton," began Captain Perry. "The journalist—"

"Lyle Barnham," added the Media Relations officer.

"Mr. Barnham filed a complaint about you," said the captain.

DAMAGED

Seriously? "Why?" Emerson asked.

"For refusing to work with him again," said the MR officer.

Emerson swallowed down the sigh. "Captain, I took him on a tour and answered all of his questions."

"Let him tag along with you," Perry said. "He might prove to be an asset in this case."

"I don't—" Emerson protested.

"He told me his publisher wants to—and I quote—'be a friend to the department'," said the officer.

"Great," Emerson said, biting back the mounting frustration. "Why doesn't he work with someone else while I solve these crimes?"

The captain shook her head. "Work with him, Detective."

I am not getting a break. "Of course."

The Media Relations officer stood. "He'll be contacting you directly."

Emerson waited until the MR officer left. "Captain, I want to talk with you about my brother's death."

"I'm sorry but the case is closed and out of my hands."

"I know I've brought this up several times since Doug died, but I'm convinced he didn't die of a self-inflicted overdose."

"And I believe you, but the tox report is all the evidence the department has."

"I want to go undercover and infiltrate the gang."

Captain Perry's jutting eyebrows creased her forehead. "This isn't a bunch of kids hanging on the street corner selling a little weed. This is an extremely dangerous group of individuals. It took Doug eighteen months to earn their trust. I'm sorry, Emerson, but I can't recommend you for that assignment."

"Then, can we honor Doug at the fund raiser?"

"He'll be mentioned."

Emerson's blood pressure soared. She wanted to scream, but throwing a tantrum wouldn't bring back her brother. Being "honored" and being "mentioned" were two completely different things. Her brother was a good cop who got killed because he was close to making an arrest. He wasn't a user hooked on heroine.

With nothing left to say, Emerson returned to her desk. She had zero interest in working with Lyle Barnham. And her interest in working for the police department was fizzling fast. Her faith in the organization had hit an all-time low. How could no one see what she saw? Why wouldn't anyone back her on this?

Truth was, Stryker had a packed schedule, but he needed to see Emerson. Though he told himself it was to help her catch a killer, he hadn't stopped thinking about her. Over the past week, she'd unpacked herself in his brain and he could not evict her from his thoughts.

Stryker's assistant buzzed him. "Cooper Grant is here."

His office door opened and his childhood friend sailed in. Cooper was Assistant Special Agent in Charge of the FBI's DC office.

"No bottle of scotch, so you're here on business," Stryker said. "Never a good thing."

"Ah, you love me, scotch or not," Cooper said, before closing the door.

"Debatable."

Cooper's smile fell away. "I've got good and bad news."

"Hit me," Stryker said.

"There's chatter Spinetti has a contract out on you," Cooper said.

"Is that the good news?"

"No, idiot, that's the bad news. You need to hire protection."

This time, Stryker chuffed out a laugh. "I'll be fine. No one's gonna kill me."

"You run a cybersecurity firm. What do you know about defending yourself?"

While Stryker loved Cooper like a brother, he kept his dark side hidden from his law enforcement friend. The only thing worse than someone putting out a contract for him, was Stryker going to prison for his vigilantism.

"Spinetti called me last week," Stryker said.

Up went Cooper's eyebrows. "How the hell did that happen?"

"He got himself a burner and then he dialed. Not too difficult."

"And he threatened you?"

"He didn't call to thank me."

"Dammit, Stryker, hire a damn security detail."

Not happening. Stryker did not need men trailing his every move. "I can take care of myself. What's the good news?" Stryker asked, redirecting the conversation.

"I'm up for promotion."

"Congrats, my brother." He studied his friend. "You don't want this new job, do you?"

Cooper sat on the edge of the sofa and raked his hand over his beard. "I'm burned out. I'm tired of the criminal getting off on a technicality. I'm tired of our evidence getting fucked up and becoming inadmissible in court. The bad guys are winning."

Stryker pulled out two shot glasses and a bottle of scotch from his credenza. "Remind me, what are you interviewing for?"

"Special Agent in Charge."

Stryker poured their drinks, handed one to his friend.

"Why the hell are we drinking in the middle of the afternoon?" Cooper asked.

"To a promotion you don't want."

They tapped their glasses together and downed the booze.

"What's the problem?" Stryker asked before storing the bottle.

"The position's in Vegas. I don't want to transfer again."

Stryker smiled. "Looks like the contract on my life *is* the good news."

Cooper's phone rang and he silenced it. "Gotta run. Watch your back."

"I'm a better shot than you are."

"When was the last time you fired your weapon or even went to target practice?" Cooper headed for the door.

"Call me when you head to the firing range. We'll see who's the better shot."

"You're on. Let me know if Spinetti contacts you again," Cooper called out over his shoulder.

Stryker needed to head out himself. He was meeting Emerson in forty minutes. As he shut down his computers, his assistant popped in.

"You have another visitor."

"Not now." Pushing out of his chair, he rounded his desk.

But she stood there, stone faced.

"What's wrong?"

"He says he's your father."

His brain froze. *"What?"*

"The atrium receptionist called me after she'd sent him up here. I told him you were in a meeting, but he waited. I didn't want to interrupt your meeting with Mr. Grant, so I stuck him in the executive conference room."

"It's okay." Stryker had never given his assistant instructions on how to handle his non-existent father.

"I'm sorry," she replied. "I can tell him he needs to make an appointment."

Stryker could see how anxious she was. In all the years she'd worked for him, he'd never brought up his dad. His smile elicited a sigh from her. "I'll handle it."

She returned to her office and Stryker slid his laptop into his computer bag, threw the strap over his shoulder, and strode out. As he passed the glass-enclosed conference room, his dad looked over. Tyler Truman could not hide his surprise. The last time he'd seen his son, Stryker had been a fifteen-year-old kid, wrecked over his mom's death.

Over the past twenty years, Stryker had learned how to control and channel his rage. Seeing his father unearthed a world of hatred toward the man who had abandoned his children during the lowest point in their lives. The closer he got, the harder his fists tightened. He wanted to deck the man, then tell him what he really thought of him.

Tyler Truman rose. "Stryker, it's been a while. You look good, son."

Pain slashed through him. His father had lost the right to call him "son" when he walked out the door and never came back. When Stryker refused to shake his dad's outstretched hand, his dad's face turned bright red. His embarrassment was nothing compared to how Stryker felt.

"Now's not a good time," Stryker said.

"Is there somewhere we can talk?" His dad glanced out the glass windows. "I just need a minute."

One damn minute wouldn't make up for the lost decades. "Your minute started twenty seconds ago. What do you want?"

"To apologize. I'm sorry I left. I made a mistake."

Stryker stared at him for several beats. "Twenty years later, you're apologizing for leaving. But you never contacted us. Not once. What's your angle? You need money?"

"Trudy said you're all about giving second chances," Tyler said.

Stryker stared at the stranger with the thinning hair and heavy bags under his eyes. He was wearing a suit and tie, the turquoise tie clip an outdated eyesore. He didn't pity him. How could he? He didn't even know the man he'd once called dad.

"I'm so proud of what you've accomplished," Tyler continued. "This is impressive. Can you give your old dad a tour? How about I come back when you've got a few minutes?"

Stryker did not want to see him again. "Wait here."

He found his assistant working at her desk. "Can you give Tyler Truman a brief tour?"

"Sure."

"Brief," Stryker repeated. "Don't take him into the government pods. Don't answer any personal questions about me."

"Of course not." She offered an assuring smile.

Stryker headed toward the elevator, stopping in the conference room. "My assistant will take you on a tour. Don't pop in again." Before Tyler Truman could reply, Stryker left.

As he entered the waiting elevator, his frustration had turned his shoulders to lead. Since he wasn't alone, he pushed his feelings aside and asked Garrett how his new baby girl was doing. He checked in with Shayna about her new hacker pod. Each employee got a few seconds of his attention. He valued them and made damn sure they knew it. Something he didn't feel when his dad had left.

He paused at reception where four employees manned the phones and welcomed visitors. "If Tyler Truman returns, do not send him upstairs."

As Stryker pushed out the front door of his half-billion-dollar company, he slid on his shades and grumbled, "Not *everyone* deserves a second chance."

He slipped into his Mercedes and drove out. Despite the warm sun and clear blue sky, his bad mood followed him all the way into Arlington. As soon as he pulled into the club's parking lot, he spotted her in her car. Seeing Easton had this dizzying effect on him. On one hand, he liked working with her. On the other, he didn't like being infuriated every damn time he was around her. She'd put him through hell and he was still fuming.

As she exited her vehicle, he checked her out. Tight jeans that flared at the bottom, a shirt, and a jacket. This time she'd worn stilettos. He pushed out of his car, shouldered his computer bag, and paused to admire the spectacular view. With every step she took in his direction, his body temperature climbed. The straight-laced detective was bringing the heat and he burned for her in all the ways that made him a man.

A pissed-off man who hadn't gotten laid in months.

"Thanks for meeting me." Her smile—that brief, breathtaking upturn of her mouth—sent a surge of energy whipping through him. "Captain Perry gave me the bad news. We *have* to work together." She grunted out her displeasure.

Knowing their mutual dislike was still intact bolstered his spirits. "Sucks for me, too."

"We should try to get along."

"Ever heard of faking it?" he bit out.

She extended her hand. "Deal." Her soft skin and delicate fingers fit so perfectly in his large hand. Strange, he didn't want to let her go. One firm pump, and she released.

"Not gonna lie," she said, as he held open the door for her, "I'm not looking forward to working in your basement."

He locked the front door, turned off the security alarm, and headed toward his office. "Water?"

"What I need is liquid courage," she murmured.

"I can help with that."

"I'm a lightweight when it comes to booze. Gotta stay sober. I got the tox report back from the first murder and I feel like I'm already behind."

He grabbed two bottled waters then continued on to the basement door. He unlocked it and she breezed past him.

Wasn't expecting that.

She waited in the stairwell. He hotfooted it downstairs and unlocked his office door. Motion sensors triggered the lights. "Welcome to my inner sanctum." He turned around. No Emerson.

After setting his satchel on his desk chair, he found her sitting on the top step, hyperventilating, her eyes brimming with fear. He sat next to her, thinking she'd scoot over. She didn't budge. They were smooshed together, their thighs pressing against each other.

When she stared up at him, the fear in her eyes surprised him. "I can hold my own at a crime scene. I can manage through blood okay, too. But I cannot go down these stairs."

He had an idea. "Wait here." Never before had he taken pictures of his office, but he snapped a few photos and sat beside her again.

"My office." He flipped through the photos.

"Looks more like a command center."

"Once we get working, you won't even remember there are no windows."

"And only one exit."

"If you can't get past this, the captain will assign the case to someone else. You want that?"

"No, but you might."

"This isn't about me, not this time. What's got you so afraid?"

She gazed into his eyes and their too-close proximity had him glancing at her mouth. *So fucking enticing.* So. Damn. Infuriating.

"When I was a kid, my brother and I got trapped in our basement during a kitchen fire that spread fast. I was terrified. There were no windows and the smoke was coming in through the closed door. The firemen had to break it down to get us out."

"That's rough. Anyone hurt?"

"Nothing beyond smoke inhalation. We were lucky. That was the beginning of my claustrophobia. After the house was repaired, we moved back in. My mom and dad had the basement redesigned with a door leading outside and two windows. But I never played down there again."

"Did you talk to someone about it?"

"I've gotten good at avoiding the problem altogether." Breaking eye contact, she stared into her lap. "Someone close to me passed away suddenly and I was having a hard time…you know…coping with… well, everything."

"I'm sorry."

She nodded, but wouldn't look at him. Her hair had fallen over her cheek, hiding her face. He wanted to brush it away and tuck it behind her ear, kiss her sultry lips and take away her pain. But he kept his hands, and his mouth, to himself.

"My therapist has been great. Even though the claustrophobia is unrelated, I'd mentioned it to her. She's been helping me—or trying, anyway. I'm sorry I'm making this difficult for you."

"I needed that apology a year and a half ago," he murmured.

She stilled, their gazes locked on each other.

The overwhelming urge to kiss her had him biting back a growl. He needed air...or to get as far away from her as possible. This woman was bringing him to his knees and all she'd done was show a little vulnerability.

"I...um...I. This isn't gonna—" She stopped.

An idea took root. "Look, *Detective*, we don't like each other and don't want to work together. Go ahead and take off. I'll spend as much time as I can over the next several months—five minutes here and there—" She gasped. "I'll let you know if I find anything. Lemme walk you out."

She bolted to her feet. "No! I can do this," she said, and flew down the stairs. As she entered his office, she let out a half scream, half cry.

On his way down, he clamped down on a smile. He would keep her so busy, she'd forget all about being in a secure, windowless room.

Pushing her away was not what he wanted to do. He wanted her in his arms while he kissed the hell out of her. He wanted her in his damn bed, moving beneath him. But his gamble had paid off. Pissing her off had lit a fire inside her. Her iron-willed nature was the bait he needed to get her ass into his private workspace.

He guided her to a chair and she dropped into it. He eased down beside her and fired up the console. She was shaking so hard her teeth were chattering and her forehead glistened with perspiration.

"Doing okay?" he asked.

After typing in the series of passwords, all six monitors on the wall burst to life. He clicked to the surveillance three days prior to April's last day.

Emerson put her hand over her heart. "I can't catch my breath."

She was a greenish white. He scooped her up, grabbed a bottle of water, carried her to the far corner of the spacious room and laid her on the bed. Rather than leave her, he sat on the edge and held her hand. "Do you know Tantric breathing?"

"No."

"Put your hand on your diaphragm," he instructed. When she did, he said, "Breathe in and feel your diaphragm fill with air." Stryker inhaled this way. After a breath, she mimicked him.

As they breathed in sync, he stroked her hand with his thumb. Soft, gentle caresses to help her calm down. They seemed, however, to be having the opposite effect on him.

"We're in a safe space," he said. "You can leave whenever you want."

She gazed up at him. "I want."

I want, too. So. Damn. Badly. She had the power to send all his demons away. Every fucking problem would fade to black. Her face, that body. Their bodies gliding as one.

"To leave," she added, and a smirk brightened her eyes.

"Smart ass." He smiled.

To his surprise, she smiled back. His chest warmed and he held her gaze while they breathed in unison. He could get damn used to staring at her. "You're doing great." He opened the bottle and handed it to her.

"Thank you for helping me."

She looked too sexy lying on his bed. There was only so much torture he could take. "Ready to work?"

Emerson drank down some water. "Gloria Stanton was murdered a month ago. Also posed on her bed in a white wedding dress. Can you tell me if she's a member here?"

This was a good sign. She was moving past her fear. "Yup." He squeezed her hand before pushing off the bed. "I'll put her name in the database. If you've got a pic, I can use my facial recognition software."

She rose up on her elbows. "I didn't know you have that."

"Mine's proprietary. I call it IDware." He sat in his well-worn chair and typed the victim's name into his club's database.

"Not only that, it's available, which is half the battle," she said.

"The crime lab was hit with budget cuts. Requests take forever to get completed."

He scanned for a Gloria Stanton, but her name didn't appear. When he turned back, Emerson stood beside him. He admired her determination. "Problem is, a lot of members use fake names. The only real form of ID is their name on a credit card. That's not something I can easily find."

"I understand."

"But together, we can try."

Her hands shook as she pulled up a chair and rolled beside him. She sat on the edge, her back ramrod straight. Before he could check himself, he caressed her back. "You're doing great, Easton."

She put her hand on her chest. "My heart rate must be a hundred and fifty."

"You can do this."

She offered a tight smile. "You got me this far, let's keep going."

Emerson was struggling to keep it together. Before he'd laid her on the bed, she wasn't sure if she was going to vomit or pass out. Focusing on him and his steady breathing had helped. Staring at him was easy. He was sick handsome, but it was his inner strength that had saved her from really losing her shit.

Stryker's basement was a full-on command center. A black keyboard sat within his reach. Three laptops waited on the oversized console. Six monitors hung on the wall. The dungeon looked more like an FBI tactical center than the basement of a members-only kink club.

He dragged over a laptop and got busy. As his fingers flew across the keyboard, the monitors reflected the computer code he was keying in. "I'm scanning for her name, but the program needs us to manually request a new set of names."

After scanning for Gloria's name, he tapped the down arrow and the six monitors refreshed with a whole new list of names. You've got A through L. I got the rest. I've only owned the club for a few years, but this is the master list."

They worked side by side in silence, save for the sound of her heart still pounding away in her chest. But she had to give herself props. She was still sitting there. The real reason she hadn't fled the scene was the brick of a man beside her. She glanced over at him. He met her gaze.

"You okay?" he asked.

"I thought you didn't like me."

"Who says I do? The sooner we find the killer, the faster I can get you out of my life again."

She glared at him. "And here I thought you were a nice guy."

"Me? No, *not* a nice guy." Exasperation rolled off him. The air turned turbulent.

Staring into his eyes made her quiver for a completely different reason. Desire started deep in her belly. An aching, throbbing need she could not ignore. The push and pull were making her crazy. She wanted to kiss him so badly, press her mouth against his, and ride him for days.

He broke eye contact and continued scrolling.

"Are you trying to be a jerk or does it come naturally?" she asked.

His lips twitched, but he kept his attention on the screens. "Naturally."

And just like that, they were back to a frosty silence.

Being in the windowless space was starting to take a toll on her. She couldn't get her heart rate to slow and the muscles running down her back ached from anxiety. After finishing the water, she asked where the bathroom was.

"Corner."

There was no way she could walk toward the back of the room. "I'll hold it."

He pushed back in his chair. "I'll stand guard."

"You'll hear me peeing."

He laughed. "Your secret will stay with me." Then, he rose. "C'mon, Easton. Bio break."

She didn't budge.

"Do I have to carry you again?"

She shoved out of the chair and marched toward the back of the room. Panic took hold. She made an abrupt U-turn and beelined back to him. And despite their contempt for each other, she clung to him while her body shook.

And he held her in his arms like she was his. Like he cared for her more than he cared for himself. On the inside, she melted a little. But, she could not stand that he was seeing her at her absolute worst. "I'm going to ask Captain Perry to reassign the case."

"Like hell you are."

She tipped her face toward his and he kissed her. One long panty-searing kiss. She slid her tongue into his mouth and was rewarded with his. Her knees gave way and he held her flush against him. The kiss went on and on while she soared higher and higher. The desire in her belly exploded into full-blown passion. She raked her fingers down his back and grabbed his muscled ass.

Then, she pushed him away. Gasping for breath, she stared into his eyes. "Oh, God," she whispered. "That shouldn't have happened."

"You are the most dangerous woman I have ever met," he murmured.

Peering into his eyes, she asked. "Why do you say that? Because I pack heat?"

"You just are," he said and clasped her hand. As if walking on air, she went with him toward the back of the room. She loved how his grip was firm, but not tight. Holding his hand felt...right. She loved how good he was at distracting her from her phobia.

"You got this." He opened the door and closed it behind her.

"You're not leaving me, are you?"

"I'm right here."

The windowless room was clean and bright, so she focused on that...and on their sweltering kiss. When finished, she washed her hands. Her emotions were out of control, something that rarely happened. This man was definitely bringing out the worst in her. *Or maybe the best.*

When she opened the door, she said, "Thank you."

"Let's finish looking for Gloria Stanton. Can you do that?"

She nodded. On the way back to the console, she eyed the St. Andrew's cross and the row of kink toys hanging on the wall.

His personal playroom. A sudden rush of envy made her heart squeeze. *He's so out of my league, sexually.*

They returned to their seats and worked as if that kiss had never happened. But it had, and it wasn't something she'd soon forget.

The real thing was way better than her dream.

When they couldn't find Gloria Stanton's credit card in The Dungeon's database, Emerson concluded that she hadn't been a member.

He started shutting down his computers. "Ready to head out?"

She'd had more than enough of the below-ground room. Her stomach had been tied up in knots all afternoon. Once on the main level, she breathed. "Whew, that was crazy intense. Thank you for getting me through that."

"You did a good job."

"We still need to search your surveillance for anyone April talked to," she said.

"That's gonna be harder," he replied. "She was a bartender. She talked to everyone."

"When can we get together next?" she asked.

"I'll check my schedule and text you."

It was almost seven and employees were arriving for work. Parker entered the club and his attention flitted from Emerson to Stryker while the color drained from his face.

"Oh, hey, Detective. How's it goin', boss?"

This time, Emerson observed more and said very little. Was he a nervous person or did he have something to hide? She made a mental note to run his name through the system.

"I'll walk you out," Stryker said as Parker continued on.

The evening breeze helped her relax. Being outside lifted her spirits. She still couldn't believe she had spent three hours in a basement with no windows. She couldn't have done it without him.

She unlocked her car and opened the door. "It's none of my business, but do you live in the basement of your club?"

"It *is* none of your business."

"Are you always a jerk or just a jerk towards me?"

"Just you." He winked, then headed for his car.

He's got too much swagger for his own good. I could get into some serious trouble with that man.

7

GIRLS' NIGHT OUT

Emerson walked into the upscale restaurant and glanced around. Raphael's was the place to be and the eatery was crazy busy. Danielle Fox hurried over from her spot at the bar.

"I cannot believe we've never been here before," Danielle said. "You have got to check out the bathroom. It's uh-mazing."

Emerson laughed. Being with her best friend was the perfect way to walk herself off the ledge, which was what an afternoon with Stryker called for. That, and a strong drink.

"Our table's not ready yet," Danielle said. "Come to the bathroom with me." Looping her arm through Emerson's, she led her through the spacious dining room.

Once there, Emerson's mouth dropped open. "Wow, this is spectacular."

"I know, right?"

Small, ornate chandeliers dangled from the ceiling, the pristine marble floors sparkled like diamonds. No stalls here. Each toilet was a private oasis. When Emerson entered one, Danielle was right there with her.

"I can't have a moment alone?" Emerson asked.

Danielle just laughed. "We've been peeing together since we were six."

Even the hand dryer was a thing of beauty that purred when Danielle tapped it.

As Emerson washed her hands, Danielle eyed her friend. "You aren't okay. What's wrong?"

"It's nothing," Emerson whispered.

Danielle crossed her arms and blocked the door.

"You aren't budging, are you?" Emerson asked.

"Nope. Spill it, sister."

"I've got a case that's got me on edge. Plus, I ran into—" She stopped cold.

"Ran into who?"

"Never mind."

"Now, you're starting to piss me off."

"I ran into Stryker Truman."

"So?"

"He's your boss," Emerson whispered. "I can't talk to you about him."

"I never talk about personal stuff at work. Ever, Em. I promise. He doesn't even know we've been BFFs since the beginning of time. I've never even mentioned you."

Relief had Emerson smiling. "I've run into him a few times. One minute he's a great guy and the next, a full-on jerk."

Danielle ran her fingers through her long hair, then stared at Emerson in the mirror. She dug out a lipstick and handed it to her. "You need a little…I don't know…pink."

Both women were blondes with fair complexions, so whatever makeup Danielle used, worked for Emerson.

Emerson rolled on the lip color and handed the stick back. Next, Danielle held out a small makeup brush and her blush. Emerson refused. "I'm going to dinner with my best friend and her sister. Why am I putting on makeup?"

"You look like you could use it." Danielle dabbed the brush into the blush and then applied it to Emerson's cheekbones. "You know, people would die for your cheekbones. You could have been a model."

Emerson barked out a laugh. "Yeah, but I'd have to wear six-inch heels. I'm five-four."

"The only reason Stryker doesn't like you is because you arrested him," Danielle whispered. "He finally got the FBI account back at the beginning of the year. He lost a lot of business because of what happened."

Emerson's stomach roiled. "I feel badly about that, but at the time, I thought—"

"Don't worry about it," Danielle said. "Ancient history."

"Danielle, Emerson, are you in there?" Claire-Marie called out.

"I won't say a word," Danielle whispered while she crossed her heart.

"Thank you." Emerson opened the door.

Danielle's older sister, Claire-Marie, hugged them as the restaurant buzzer vibrated in Danielle's bag. "Our table is ready! Let's get this party started!"

After the women were seated in their booth, a server took their drink order. Now that Emerson's stomach had quieted down, she was famished. Tonight, Claire-Marie had pulled her dark hair into a ponytail that sat high on her head.

"You look like you're going to yoga," Danielle said, "but you're drinking."

"I'm playing later and like to give my partner something to hold on to." Claire-Marie waggled her eyebrows.

Claire-Marie was a CPA by day. At night, she liked her kink served strong.

"Where are you playing?" Emerson asked.

"The Dungeon," Claire-Marie replied. "It's big bucks for a membership, but worth it. I'm there at least once a week. I have guest passes if you guys want to check it out."

"I'm too much of a prude to get kinky with a stranger," Emerson said.

"You can just talk and get to know someone, first," Claire-Marie explained. "You can watch others play. You can play and not have sex or just have straight up sex. Lotta options."

The server returned, set the tequila shot in front of Claire-Marie, then opened the wine bottle and poured a small amount into Danielle's glass. She slid the glass to Emerson. "I'll drink anything. You try it."

After sipping it, Emerson nodded to the server who poured out three glasses.

"Cheers," Emerson said.

She and Danielle sipped the chardonnay while Claire-Marie tossed back the shot.

"I have fun news," Claire-Marie said. "I'm doing a photo shoot."

"That's cool," Danielle said. "How'd that happen?"

"I met this guy. Not a romantic thing. Anyway, he's a photographer who does a ton of local shoots."

"Did you check his references?" Emerson asked.

Both women stared at her. "Seriously?" Claire-Marie asked. "He asked me if I want to get together at a park—in public on a Saturday—and take some test shots. Not everyone is evil."

"Where'd you meet him?" Danielle asked.

Claire-Marie sipped the wine. "The Dungeon, and I ran into him at a coffee shop. He's cool."

"What does he do with the photos?" Emerson asked.

"He's a stock photographer, so he sells them to stock companies and people buy licenses to use them. I'm excited."

The conversation and laughter came easily as the three women continued chatting. Emerson talked to Danielle almost every day, but it was good catching up with Claire-Marie.

After their dinners were served, Emerson said, "Do you guys carry mace or pepper spray?"

"I have some." Danielle set hers on the table.

"No," Claire-Marie said. "My bag is a disaster. I'd never be able to find it. I'd just knee 'em in the balls."

Emerson carried one of each and slid the mace across the table. "Keep this."

"Why are you giving me your mace?" Claire-Marie asked. "What do you know that we don't?"

When she leaned forward, the sisters did the same. "I don't want you guys to freak out or anything, but there's a possible serial killer in the area."

"*What?*" Danielle shouted.

Several patrons glanced over.

"I want you guys safe, that's all," Emerson said.

"I never go home with anyone from the club," Claire-Marie said. "I play there and I leave. I don't even use my real name."

"Can you tell us anything else about the killer?" Danielle asked Emerson.

"Sis," Claire-Marie interrupted. "Chill out. Relax. You know what you need? A man…to help you take it down a few notches. When was the last time you got any?"

"Don't start with me." Danielle topped their wine glasses, emptying the bottle.

The server returned with a second bottle of white wine, which he uncorked.

"I think there's been a mix up," Emerson said. "We didn't order more wine."

"Looks too expensive for our wallets," Claire-Marie blurted.

"Compliments of the owner," said the server. "It's from his private collection." He set down three fresh wine glasses and poured the wine.

Danielle tried it. "Oh, wow. This is sooooooo good."

The server smiled. "I thought you'd like it."

Naturally suspicious, Emerson glanced around. "I don't know the owner. Who can we thank?"

"He said he'd pop over at some point and say hello." The server cleared away the dirty wine glasses before leaving.

Emerson glanced around the packed restaurant, but saw no one looking in their direction.

"Stop worrying," Danielle said. "It's all good."

"What's your story?" Claire-Marie asked Emerson. "Are you seeing anyone?"

"She works all the time," Danielle interrupted. "I can't believe you came out with us tonight."

"I had a stressful day and needed to unwind," Emerson said, then flicked her gaze toward someone approaching their booth.

Oh, my God, it's him. Her heart flipped and a zing of energy skittered through her. She could not escape him. Yet, she couldn't deny being elated to see him. Stryker had changed into a black dress shirt and black pants, his long hair pulled into a man-bun. She snuck a peek at his chest and spied a smattering of chest hair. *So yummy.*

He slid his gaze from woman to woman, but when his attention settled on Emerson, there was no denying the fire in his eyes. *He hates me so much.*

"Ladies."

"Hello, handsome." Claire-Marie patted the empty cushion beside her. "Join us."

Danielle groaned. "Hey, boss, what brings you by?"

"Easton had a stressful day and I wanted to help her relax," he replied.

Claire-Marie gaped. "You sent over the wine?"

"I did," he replied.

"Stop drinking it," Emerson mumbled. "It might be poisoned."

Danielle laughed.

"I'm not trying to kill you, Detective."

Emerson could not stop staring at his sexy mouth and those piercing eyes. *Too. Damn. Handsome.*

"So, you're the owner?" Emerson asked.

"One of five," he replied. "We own several restaurants in the area." He tossed a nod toward the back of the room and all three women craned to see. A long table was located in a private dining room enclosed by three glass walls and a glass door. Four men sat at one end of the table.

Claire-Marie had been smiling nonstop. "Food is great."

"So, how do you two know each other?" Stryker asked Emerson and Danielle.

"We don't," Emerson replied.

"Besties since first grade," Danielle said with a smile.

Stryker regarded both women for a long second. "Danielle, you never mentioned Easton." His gaze stayed locked on Emerson.

She couldn't look anywhere else. Her eyes were glued on him. His clothes, his hair, his face, that body. She could not stop checking him out, but it was the intensity radiating off him that was revving her engine.

"I don't talk about my personal life," Danielle replied. "What do you know about me?"

"You're one of the best hackers I've ever hired."

She beamed. "Exactly. And that's all you'll ever know. Ow." She glared at her sister. "Stop kicking me."

"Hi." Claire-Marie held out her hand and Stryker shook it. "I'm Danielle's sister, Claire-Marie. I love your club, by the way."

"Thanks." He directed his attention back to Emerson. "You doing okay?"

She raised her glass. "One more glass of the good stuff and I'll be feeling no pain."

"Stop by on your way out," Stryker said. "If you ladies can't drive, I'll call you a ride."

As he made his way toward the private room, Danielle went back to her food, but Emerson stayed locked on him. Turns out, she wasn't the only one tracking him. His swagger had caught the attention of Claire-Marie, who had twisted around to check him out.

"That man is a walking hurricane," Claire-Marie said to Emerson. "You're a lucky gal."

"*Me*? Oh, he hates me."

Claire-Marie barked out a laugh. "Honey, he's completely *gaga* over you." Claire-Marie got busy on her phone. When she finished, she showed them the wine Stryker had sent over. "This three-hundred-dollar bottle of vino is him telling you that he's interested. Definitely, definitely interested."

Emerson shook her head. "We do *not* get along."

Claire-Marie pushed her plate away. "Ever had a spite fuck?"

Emerson and Danielle exchanged glances, then burst out laughing.

"A what?" Emerson asked.

"I'd been dating this guy for a while," Claire-Marie explained. "I thought he was going to ask me to move in with him, but he broke up with me instead. It crushed me. I really liked him. Anyway, I got in great shape, dropped twenty pounds, and spite fucked him."

"Isn't that just backsliding?" Danielle asked.

"I had no intention of getting back with him. I just screwed him to show him what he was missing."

This time, all three women broke into laughter.

Emerson glanced at the owners' table. All five men were staring in their direction. Under the table, Danielle nudged her. Emerson glared at her best friend and Danielle waggled her eyebrows.

"Do you think he's handsome?" Claire-Marie asked her sister.

"Yes, but I'm not attracted to him," Danielle replied. "He's my boss. That's like being attracted to Dad."

"That's just gross...and weird," Claire-Marie said. "What about you, Emerson?"

She shrugged a shoulder. "He's okay." She really wanted to downplay this, but she wasn't convinced they believed her.

"The man's a god," Claire-Marie said. "A freakin' Adonis. He's got muscles on his muscles. That shirt could not contain him. And my God, his hair must be gorgeous when he lets it down."

"It is." Emerson had to admit that.

"When was the last time you did something for *you?*" Claire-Marie forked tuna into her mouth.

"Danielle and I got mani-pedis a few months back," Emerson said.

Claire-Marie shook her head. "You two are pathetic."

"I had a fun day," Emerson replied.

"Me, too," Danielle said, before taking a bite of her pasta.

"A spite fuck is exactly what you need—what you both need," Claire-Marie said.

"I've got my boyfriend, Billy," Danielle replied.

"Her vibrator," Emerson explained as she sliced off a piece of chicken.

Claire-Marie laughed. "Emerson, I dare you to spite fuck him. C'mon, sis, back me on this."

Danielle raised her wine glass. "Go for it, Em. Get wild with him."

Emerson flicked her gaze to Stryker. He'd been talking to one of the men at the table. As if sensing her, he slid his gaze to hers. Emerson warmed from his heated stare. Did she have the guts to do it? While sipping the wine, the liquid courage said "yes", but she doubted she could ever go through with it.

"A spite fuck will cure everything," Claire-Marie insisted. "You already picked your poison. Now, all you have to do is bone him."

The three started laughing again.

"Well?" Danielle asked. "Up for the dare?"

Emerson shifted her attention to Stryker. "I'll let you know what I decide."

They finished their meal, but when they asked the waiter for the bill, he told them it had been taken care of. They left him a huge tip.

Claire-Marie's friend had pulled up out front, so she hugged them both. "If you decide you want to be my guest at The Dungeon, text me. Off to kink myself out. Love you both." And with that, she bolted for the door.

"We have to stop by the table and thank him," Emerson said.

Danielle hiccupped. "No problem."

When Emerson rose, the alcohol went straight to hear head. "I shouldn't have had that third glass of wine."

Arm in arm, the women meandered toward the owners' private dining room. The second Stryker saw her, a shadow fell across his eyes. His expression turned primal. A low, moan escaped Emerson's throat.

"He is so gorgeous," she murmured.

"Spite fuck," Danielle whispered, then snort-laughed.

Stryker opened the door for them. "How was the grub?"

"Delicious," Emerson replied as they stepped into the fishbowl room. "Thanks for paying."

"Those bathrooms are"—Danielle hiccupped again—"excuse me…da bomb. I made a mental note to hang a chandelier in my bathroom." Another hiccup. She pointed. "Oooh, that table is so nice. Those are good chairs. I know good chairs and those are them."

Emerson pointed to the elaborate chandelier and Danielle gasped. "Soooo pretty."

"Feeling no pain, I see," Stryker said. "Looks like you got your liquid courage, Easton."

"I'm too busy babysitting to enjoy myself."

Stryker's smile sent a white-hot streak of desire surging through her. For that brief second, the anger he wore so well was replaced with the most beautiful person she'd ever seen in her life. A striking man who took her breath away.

"Stryker, you gonna introduce us or what?" asked one of the guys.

After Stryker introduced the men around the table, the guys started firing questions at them. "How do you ladies know Stryker?" asked the man closest to them.

"He's my boss," Danielle answered, then hiccupped again.

"At which company?"

"I'm a hacker," Danielle said.

"That's cool," said a different guy.

Danielle grinned at him. Emerson looped her arm through Danielle's. "We should go."

"What do you do?" one of them asked Emerson.

"I'm a homicide detective."

"Wait, is this *the* detective?" asked another. "Detective Easton?"

"That's me."

"The one who almost tanked your—" blurted one of the guys.

"How are you getting home?" Stryker asked, cutting off his friend.

Emerson and Danielle stared at each other. "I got an Uber over here," Danielle said. "I'm a worse lightweight than Emmy is."

"I drove," Emerson said, "but we'll take an Uber."

"I'll drive you home," Stryker said.

"Be careful with him," said the man with a crop of dark blond hair. "He's a wolf in sheep's clothing."

"Not funny," Stryker said. "There could be a serial killer out there."

The private dining room grew dead silent.

"Shit," Stryker mumbled.

"What are you talking about?" asked one of his guys.

"I'm investigating a couple of murders," Emerson said. "Stryker's just being cautious, that's all."

"I'm gonna take off," Stryker said.

His friends bro-hugged him while they slapped each other on the back. As Emerson and Danielle waited, Danielle whispered, "I think you should go for it."

Emerson laughed at her friend. "I think you should stop talking."

Danielle hiccupped. "Okey dokey."

"Stay out of trouble, idiots." On their way out, Stryker flashed his friends a smile and Emerson's whisper-soft moan caught his attention. "I heard that," he murmured.

"Drunk sounds," she replied.

C'mon. Have some damn self-control.

Stryker had spent his evening paying more attention to Emerson than to the dinner conversation around the table. The more he watched her, the more he needed her. By the time coffee had rolled around, he was back to being infuriated.

Because sex with Detective Easton was not gonna happen. *No fuckin' way.*

Screwing her did not count as helping her. Not that he wouldn't ensure the lady a good time, but she had trusted him at his club. The easiest way to burn that trust was to bed her. That kiss should never have happened. No way in hell would he tempt fate and do it again. Because if he kissed her, he sure as hell wasn't stopping there.

Shoving down his agitation, he held open the restaurant door. Arm in arm, the two friends breezed past him. Up until an hour ago, he had no idea Danielle knew Emerson, let alone was her best friend. And here he thought he knew his employees.

The valet pulled Stryker's car up. He opened the back door of his Mercedes and Danielle slid in. "Oooh, this is soooo nice. Me likey."

As he opened the door for Emerson, he murmured, "She's quite chatty after a few drinks."

"She's a very happy drunk."

"What about you?" he asked her.

"Three glasses of wine and I feel no pain. Dinner was excellent, by the way."

"Yuppers," Danielle said from the back seat. "I loved the chicken."

"You had pasta, Danny."

Danielle snickered. "Right, Emmy, you had the chicken. They were both eggselent."

"Danielle, what's your address?" Stryker asked.

Danielle rattled it off from the back seat. "Who was that man with you?"

"Which one?"

"The cute one." Danielle snort-laughed. "Dark blond hair."

"Cooper Grant," Stryker replied. "Wanna meet him?"

Danielle hiccupped. "Excuse me. Nope, no in...innerduction." She paused. "That's not a word."

As Stryker headed toward Danielle's, he glanced over at Emerson. She looked stunning. But she always did. He wanted to lay his hand on her thigh and wrap his fingers around her leg. He wanted to run his fingers through her long hair, then kiss her neck, her chin, working his way up to her beautiful mouth.

He hoped they solved the case soon. Working with her was an exercise in frustration. He pulled up to Danielle's, cut the engine, and walked the women to the door.

"I'll wait here," Stryker said.

"'S okay." Danielle hiccupped. "You can come in. Emmy used to live here with me. She lives in her brother's house, now." She hiccupped again.

Using her key, Emerson unlocked the front door, and they all traipsed inside. Stryker waited in the living room while Emerson took Danielle upstairs. He heard whispering and laughing, then Emerson came down alone. "Tomorrow, she's going to wish you hadn't seen her like this."

"I won't bring it up," he replied.

They left and Emerson bolted the front door. In silence, they walked to his car.

As Stryker pulled back onto the main road, he became aware that he was alone with her. He'd been alone with her this afternoon, too. All this one-on-one time was cranking the heat way, way up. He opened the sunroof, but the breeze didn't wick away the need coursing through him.

After giving him her address, she grew quiet. At a light, he glanced over. She returned his gaze. The pull was there, the magnetic tug to kiss her. The light changed. As he sped forward, he stifled the groan. Not kissing her was killing him.

He pulled up in front of her Alexandria townhouse. "Thanks for dinner and the ride. I know this is weird that we have to work together, and difficult for you because you can't stand me." She got out and took off toward the garage.

He cut the engine and hopped out. As the garage door opened, he said, "I want to make sure you get in okay."

"I'm fine."

"There's a killer out there and you're the one chasing him. Let me clear your place."

She pulled her Glock. "Together."

"You're not gonna shoot me, are you?"

Strangely, that made her laugh. "If anyone was going to get shot, it would be me...by you."

She keyed open the door. As soon as he stepped inside, he saw the wretched beast.

Meow. Meow. Meow. Meeeooow.

Stryker couldn't stand cats. They were insane.

The black monster ran up the stairs. He did appreciate the view of Emerson's glorious ass as he followed her to the main level.

"You want some water?" She pulled two glasses from a cupboard, filled one from the refreshment center of her refrigerator and offered it to him.

After filling and draining her own glass, she shook a can of treats and that damn animal started walking on its hind legs while pawing at the air.

"It's possessed."

She burst out laughing. "We're joining the circus. As soon as I catch this killer, Pima and I are traveling the country so everyone can marvel at his amazing tricks."

"Pima?"

"That's his name. P. I. M. A." She dropped the treats in his bowl and the crazy feline got busy eating them. More like attacking them in some kind of full-body heave.

"Even his purring sounds insane," Stryker grumbled.

That elicited another smile. Appreciating her beauty, he stayed locked on her. Then, he pulled out his Glock. "Ready?"

"Are you serious?"

"Unless you want me to stay here—"

Her lips parted, her tongue rolled over her lower lip and damn if his cock didn't move. The stare down continued. Someone had to make the first move.

"That kiss—" he said.

She shuddered in a deep breath. "Total mistake."

"I agree. Let's act like professionals."

"Ready to clear?" When she set her glass on the counter, she brushed against him.

That brief contact was enough to catapult them into each other. Her arms wrapped his neck, he snaked his hands around her waist. The explosive kiss was raw and intense. Mouths open, tongues searching. She could not stop moaning into him. He turned hard, his balls aching with a need that had him pulling her flush against him.

Ravenous for her, he pressed his palm against her ass and ground out a long groan. And then, he broke away, breathing hard, and out of his mind with a pent-up passion that made his head hurt.

"We can't do this." He sucked down a breath, but he couldn't stop the desire pounding through him. He was drowning in a tsunami of lust.

Disappointment flashed in her eyes. Her expression killed him.

She raked her hands through her hair and grabbed her weapon. "Let's clear the house. I've got to get some sleep."

Ah, fuck, I've offended her. With each room they cleared, the silence thickened. By the time they'd finished, a suffocating, blinding, deafening rage consumed him. They had to work together and he didn't need "complicated". A casual hookup wasn't gonna work, either.

They finished where they started. At the basement door leading to her garage.

"Thanks for tonight," she said, her tone chilly.

He was trying to do the right thing. How was not sleeping with her the wrong decision?

She walked him down the driveway. "I'm in court all morning, so if you text me about getting together—*to work*—and I don't respond, it's because—"

"You're in court."

"Right. Goodnight, Mr. Truman."

Ah, hell, we're back to that. "Detective Easton."

On a huff, she retreated into her garage. Once the garage door closed, he drove away. He had no idea how he was going to keep his hands off her. One thing was for certain. He was *not* having sex with her.

8

THE EVENT

As Emerson entered the posh DC hotel, her phone rang. "Hey, Mom."

Most times, when her mom called, her dad was by her side, the call on speaker.

"Hi, honey," said Tia Easton. "Dad and I wanted to let you know we're thinking of you tonight."

"Chin up," added Rick Easton.

"Thanks," Emerson said. "How are you guys doing?"

"We decided to spend the evening watching videos of when you and Doug were kids," said her mom.

Emerson's heart broke for her parents, but she pasted on a smile. "That sounds fun. I would much rather be spending my evening with you than going to this event."

"You're an Easton," said her dad. "Grit'll get you through it."

"We know the truth about Doug," added her mom.

"Yeah, we do." Emerson's phone buzzed with an incoming text.

"Are you in your dress uniform or an actual dress?" asked her mom.

Emerson took a selfie and texted it to her parents. "An actual dress, like a girl." She smiled. Her mom loved when she wore civilian clothes, but her dad was proud when she donned her uniform.

"You look beautiful," said her dad.

She'd worn a black halter dress that hugged her curves. The front landed above her knees, but the back of the dress trailed to the floor.

"Did Danielle do your hair?" asked her mom.

"Yeah, she's so good at updos. The best I could've done is a ponytail."

"Is she with you?" asked her mom.

"No, she couldn't make it," Emerson replied.

"You can call us after," said her dad.

"You know me," Emerson replied. "I'll just file the evening under bullshit and move on."

"Are you coming by this weekend?" asked her mom.

"Of course."

"Dr. Sharpe mentioned she was going to be there tonight," her mom said.

"Why?" Emerson asked.

"Her nephew is being honored," her dad replied.

Emerson didn't know their therapist had lost someone in the line of duty.

"We love you, honey," her dad said. "And we're proud of you for going."

"Love you guys." Emerson hung up and read the text from Captain Perry.

"Please find me when you arrive."

Forcing down a plethora of emotions, Emerson followed the signs toward King Ballroom. Tonight's event honored officers who had been slain in the line of duty the previous year. The gala paid tribute while also helping to raise money for their families. Her brother should have been one of the honorees, but the department had refused her repeated requests.

Despite Doug Easton's twelve years of service, including the last four where he served as an undercover officer, Doug was not being remembered as a hero. He wasn't being remembered at all. Never mind that he'd put his life on the line to infiltrate a dangerous Northern Virginia drug gang and that he was close to making an arrest before his death.

It was as if her brother had never existed at all.

The coroner's report listed his death as a drug overdose, a lethal combination of heroin and fentanyl. The Eastons had refused to believe he was using, so Emerson had pushed for more answers.

A detective had been assigned to investigate Doug's death, but he'd gotten nowhere, so the case was labeled an accidental overdose. The world went on, but for Emerson and her parents, they lived in a hazy, gray limbo.

The past several months had been rough. Emerson wasn't just mourning the loss of a beloved brother, she was angry at the world. Justice had not been served. On more than one occasion, Emerson had considered taking matters into her own hands, but she was smart enough to know that trying to make inroads into a drug gang was dangerous, especially on her own.

Immediately following Doug's passing, her mom had wanted Emerson to change careers, fearing something would happen to her, too. With the help of a family therapist, the Eastons were treading water, at least on the outside, but for Emerson, she was submerged in sadness and anger. For as long as she lived, she would never believe her brother had died from a self-administered drug overdose.

As she rounded the corner en route to King Ballroom, she spotted Captain Perry and her husband in front of the closed ballroom doors talking with her therapist, Dr. Heather Sharpe, and a man Emerson assumed was Heather's husband. Then, her brain froze and her body warmed. It was Stryker. *No way. That man is everywhere.*

The captain looked over and smiled.

Stryker turned. He gave her the once-over slowly, and a shadow darkened his eyes. She loved that he was checking her out. He'd had every opportunity to take her to bed last night, but he didn't. *Too late, buddy. Not happening now.*

He'd left his hair down, the long strands framing his handsome face. Then, she stole a glance at his duds. The man was rocking a dark suit, starched white dress shirt, and a bright red power tie. His bulging muscles stretched against the fabric. *My God, he's hot.*

The captain broke away from the group. "Hello, Emerson. Doing okay tonight?"

Of course not. "Yes, Captain."

"Call me Tiana in social settings." She offered a warm smile. "I'm hoping you can help me with something."

I don't even want to be here and now I have to work the event?

"I'd like you to host our guest of honor."

Hoping it would take her mind off her frustration, Emerson nodded. "Okay."

An officer from the department interrupted their conversation. Tiana excused herself and hurried off with him into the ballroom.

So, who's the guest of honor?

Several officers were handing out programs and Emerson snagged one, then skimmed until she found what she was looking for. *This can't be happening.*

The Civilian of Honor was Stryker Truman.

"Detective." Stryker's ravenous gaze set her body on fire while her heart rate jumped into the triple digits.

Their connection was immediate and intense. As she soaked up his rugged beauty, she felt an overwhelming urge to touch him. She resisted the desire to trail her fingers down his arm and stroke those hard muscles beneath his suit. Every cell in her body wanted him. Every fiber in her being needed him.

For a woman who remained calm under fire, her body responded like the building was ablaze and she couldn't do a damn thing to stop the inferno from consuming her.

But her fiery thoughts were trumped by the myriad of emotions swirling through her. The event was something she hadn't wanted to face and, now, she had to put aside her grief in order to ensure Stryker had a lovely evening. *The irony of life.*

"Congratulations on your award." She extended her hand and Stryker slipped his into hers. But this time, after shaking it, she did not let go. "I've been tasked with babysitting you...er...I mean, hosting you."

"That's what I hear. Ready to play nice?"

"Like you, I'm still faking it."

"Yup," he replied.

Heather Sharpe joined them. After hugging Emerson, she introduced her husband, Gordon.

"My mom mentioned you'd be honoring someone tonight," Emerson began. "I'm sorry for your loss. I didn't realize—"

"We're here to support Stryker." Heather beamed. "We're so proud of him."

Emerson shifted her gaze from one family member to another.

"Heather and Gordon are my aunt and uncle," Stryker explained.

"Stryker's been with us since he was a teen," Gordon said. "He's like a son to us."

"How do you two know each other?" Stryker asked Emerson.

"Your aunt is my therapist," Emerson replied. "She's been helping my family through a tragedy."

"I'm sorry for your loss," Stryker replied.

After hotel staff propped open the doors, attendees began moving into the ballroom. Emerson suggested they find their seats.

"After you guys," Stryker said to his aunt and uncle.

As they made their way into the ballroom, Stryker's fingers grazed Emerson's, sending adrenaline zipping through her. His skin on hers made her fingers tingle and her insides warm. He glanced over at her. When she met his gaze, the air became electrified.

"Where are you sitting?" he asked.

"Right beside you," she deadpanned.

"Table three."

Heather and Gordon were also assigned to table three. Emerson offered the chair beside Heather to Stryker.

"You can sit there," he said, sandwiching her between him and his aunt. Four seats remained empty at their table.

As Emerson glanced around the ballroom, Claire-Marie's challenge floated into her thoughts. *I dare you to spite fuck him.* She snagged a quick glance at Stryker. *No way. I can't do that.*

But Emerson did want to do that with him…so badly.

As he read through the evening's program, she checked him out again. He stopped reading and peered into her eyes. An untamed intensity that she found addictive rolled off him like a thunderous avalanche.

"Everything okay?" he asked.

He's my reward for making it through this evening. "I'm here…with you. What could be better than that?"

Stryker bit back a smile as Gordon pushed out of his chair. "I'm grabbing cocktails."

"I'll join you." Stryker stood. "What's your poison, Detective?"

You, you're my poison. She rose. "I told the captain I'd host you."

"I'm going right over there." He pointed to a bar twenty feet away. "And I'll be back before you can miss me."

"Miss you? That's *so* not happening."

He arched a brow. "What can I get you?"

"Sparkling water, please."

"Not repeating last night?"

"God, no. Plus, I don't drink at work events."

"Good call."

She glared at him. He leaned close, wrapped his hand around her arm, and whispered, "You look stunning, Emerson."

Her breath hitched. *He called me by my first name.*

His killer smile was the key that ignited her engine. And all she could do was smile back, like an idiot.

When he got in the drink line, a handful of women flocked over like vultures descending on their next meal. They flirted and giggled. Each one touched his shoulder or caressed his arm. One was so bold as to tug on his hair. She understood why they were flirting with him, but she didn't much like watching it. Still, she couldn't stop herself from eyeing the spectacle.

Stryker Truman was a gorgeous man with a number of successful businesses. He was also thirty-five years old and unattached. Who wouldn't want to snag a guy like that? *Me. I wouldn't. But I wouldn't mind letting loose on him for a few hours.*

He pointed to Emerson, and the woman who would not stop touching him, glowered at her. Emerson pinned on a subtle smile, meant only for Stryker. The woman moved on, but Stryker kept his attention laser-focused on Emerson. Instead of shrinking under his intense stare, it fueled her. She loved how his gaze never left hers, how he didn't check out the beautiful women parading by for his attention.

Her attention was diverted when the captain and her husband, along with another couple, sat down at their table. After more introductions, Heather pivoted toward Emerson. "I texted you a few times for a virtual appointment, but didn't hear back," she whispered. "Are you doing okay?"

"I was in a work situation where I had to face my claustrophobia," Emerson murmured.

"How'd you do?"

"I was a wreck, but my partner helped me through it."

"That's wonderful. A good partner, in anything, can make all the difference."

"Unfortunately, I have to do it again," Emerson said.

"You know you can do it, since you've already succeeded once."

Emerson nodded. "Doesn't stop the stomach ache and heart palps."

"Try counting the number of seconds separating you from the exit. That might help ground you. Deep breaths help, too."

"Thank you." Emerson paused. "I've struck up a friendship with someone in your survivor chat group."

"Wonderful. Who is it?"

"Justice."

"I see," Heather replied.

"I'm thinking I might want to meet him sometime. Nothing big. Coffee, maybe."

Stryker set down their sparkling waters. "Are you two talking about me?"

Emerson steeled her spine. "Why does everything have to revolve around you?"

On a chuckle, Heather leaned back in her chair.

"Excuse me." Captain Perry rose. "Time to kick off the evening."

"You'll do great, honey," said her husband.

They shared a smile before Tiana headed toward the front of the room, stepped behind the podium, and addressed the audience.

"Good evening. I'm Captain Tiana Perry, Arlington County Police Department. On behalf of Chief Watson and everyone in the ACPD, we'd like to welcome you to the twelfth annual Fallen Heroes Fundraiser." She paused for applause. "Losing one of our own in the line of duty is devastating for family, friends, and fellow officers. By supporting the families of the fallen, we honor their lives and ensure their legacies live on. Your generous support helps them get back on their feet by providing them with the funds needed to stay afloat. It also allows children of fallen officers to attend college. If you're sitting at a table with someone who's lost a beloved friend or family member, we hope you'll share a kind word. Thank you for being here with us this evening."

As Captain Perry made her way back to the table, Emerson fought against the pain and the sorrow. She wanted to let the tears roll down her cheeks, but she'd never show emotion in public. Never appear weak or draw attention to herself. She missed her brother every single day and now, this. This wonderful event was being shoved down her throat and she was forced to sit there and face her own loss. Her brother would not be honored for his years of service. He would not be labeled a hero. He had been labeled a drug addict, and it was killing her.

Her chest tightened, tears threatening. "Excuse me."

With her gaze trained on the exit doors, she kept walking. As soon as she stepped into the quiet hallway, a small choked sob escaped into the air. Fortunately, no one was around to hear her.

Before pushing out of his chair, Stryker glanced over his shoulder. He had no idea what tragedy Emerson had suffered or how his aunt was helping the Eastons deal with their grief, but he was not going to leave Emerson alone with her pain.

He could tell something was wrong the moment he saw her. There was an anger in her eyes that mirrored how he felt most days. A gnawing frustration that plagued him. Every. Fucking. Day. The loss never left him. He'd replayed his mother's death hundreds of times, but always changing the outcome. The paramedics had saved her. He envisioned her one of the region's top prosecutors. Or, or maybe she'd retired early to spend time with her grandchildren.

Those fantasies only fueled his anger. His mother was dead and no fucking daydream could change that. The only ounce of justice he would garner would be hunting down and killing the motherfucker who took her life.

He strode out of the ballroom and into the quiet hallway. No Emerson. She wasn't at the nearby bar. He spotted the restroom sign and headed in that direction.

After opening the door, he called out, "Emerson, you in here?"

"Yes."

"Are you alone?"

"Yes."

He found her at the sink and glanced to make sure the stalls were empty. "You okay?"

"Just needed some air."

The brief flash of anguish in her eyes wasn't lost on him. "You wanna talk about it?"

"This is a tough night for me," she said.

"What can I do to help get you through it?"

"Nothing. There's nothing anyone can do. My brother should be one of the officers being honored. Instead, he'll be mentioned in passing." She broke eye contact. "Like his sacrifice didn't matter. Like his service didn't count."

"I'm sorry for your loss."

"I see the contempt in your eyes," she whispered. "I know you resent me. And I get it. And now, you have to help me solve these cases. Nothing like teaming with the enemy to really piss you off."

"Emerson, stop."

Silence.

"We can't change what happened between us," Stryker continued. "Sometimes life is fucking cruel. I haven't been making this easy on you. I hold grudges. It's part of my charm." He gave in to a quick smile. "C'mon. Let's get through this event."

She didn't budge. "I believed the sex worker who told me you were running the prostitution ring out of your club. I didn't question her again. I didn't push her for the truth. I jumped to a conclusion and I made a colossal mistake. I'm a better detective because of it, but I'm very sorry I made your life so difficult."

Stryker wasn't about forgiveness. He was about revenge, but he would make the effort for Emerson. "Forgiven."

Before he could check himself, he pressed his lips to hers and her whisper-soft moan sent bolts of energy careening through him.

She kissed him back, then again. Her kisses were soft and delicate. In that moment, he became addicted to her touch. To the way she could silence his demons and break down his walls with such little effort. He couldn't control his feelings, and he hadn't been able to stop thinking about her. Not having control infuriated the hell out of him, but he couldn't fight it anymore. He had to have her.

He kissed her again. He loved that she'd worn her hair up, and how the tendrils framed her pretty face.

"I'm so fucking angry," she whispered. "All the damn time."

That, he could relate to.

The door opened. "Oh, sorry," said a woman.

"Room's all yours," Stryker said as he led Emerson out of the restroom.

She released his hand. "We have *got* to stop kissing."

"Not gonna happen," he murmured.

The sadness in her eyes was replaced with a spark of joy.

Mission accomplished.

They re-entered the ballroom, which was filled to capacity. Having Emerson by his side affected him in a myriad of ways. She was close, but not close enough. He wanted to stroke her back or hold her hand. He spotted a few clients and acknowledged them with a smile or a nod, but he didn't stop to chat. Emerson was the only person he wanted to talk to. The one person he needed by his side.

After sitting down, she whispered, "Thank you."

Their entrées were delivered and conversations continued around the table, the chatter of the guests filling the room with a cacophony. But Emerson was doing less eating and more studying of the guests. She leaned close, brushed her sultry mouth against his ear, and whispered, "The Wedding Gown Killer could be anywhere, including here."

That simple caress of her lips against his skin, coupled with her intimate voice, had him fighting against the desire. But it had taken hold and he couldn't stop it if he tried.

When he regarded her, the look in her eyes told him that he had to have her. "Doubtful, but not impossible."

"I hate to impose, but I need to go back into your medieval torture chamber and view the club surveillance," she whispered. "I know you're busy—"

"I'll give you the club code and you can review it during the day. Just lock the front door when you're there alone."

Her eyes grew large. "Oh, I don't know if—"

He couldn't help but crack a smile. "I'm messing with you. You don't have to go down there by yourself." He checked his schedule on his phone. "I'm available tonight and tomorrow after work."

"Thank you."

A woman stopped by their table. "Hey, Stryker."

She bent down and her breasts bulged against her lowcut gown, leaving little to his imagination. He had no idea who she was. "How's it goin'?"

She stared at him. "We met at your club a while back."

That didn't help jog his memory, so he pressed on. "Are you here to honor a fallen officer?"

"Oh, sure. I'm here with someone who knows someone, or something. You're looking good."

"This is Detective Easton," Stryker said.

The woman glanced at Emerson, then glued her attention back on Stryker. "Hey, you heading to your club after?"

"I've got plans."

"Maybe another time." She smiled.

"My schedule's packed. Thanks for stopping by."

"You've got spinach in your teeth," Emerson said to the woman.

Pursing her lips, the gal hurried off.

"You could've hooked up with her, after you got me situated in the depths of hell," Emerson said.

"She would've had to floss, first."

As they shared a laugh, he caressed her bare back, her silky skin warming his fingers. His thoughts jumped to kissing her, stripping her out of her sexy dress, and losing himself in her all night long.

"I'm not interested in her." His voice was filled with need. *I want you.*

Desire flashed in her eyes while her tongue rolled over her lower lip. His cock twitched and he sucked down a slow, controlled breath.

His message had been sent...and received.

During coffee and dessert, a sergeant stood at the podium and shared the legacy of each fallen officer while a slide show flashed pictures on a giant screen. Once those had been read, the officer called out the names of other officers and staff who had passed away in the last twelve months. When he called out "Doug Easton", Emerson lowered her head. His aunt whispered something to her. As she lifted her face, she swiped a tear.

Day in and day out, revenge and loss fueled Stryker. Anger was his closest friend. He and Emerson had more in common than he'd expected. Grief is a club that no one wants to be in, but some become members sooner than others.

Captain Perry returned to the podium. "I want to end our evening on an uplifting note because I believe that hope and love carry us, especially when we are grieving. This year, our guest of honor is someone I've respected for years. He is generous, both financially and with his time—and he's one of the busiest people I know. He has donated so much money to so many local organizations I've lost track. He's kept our area shelters stocked with food and helped ensure our after-school programs are never without. He is a luminary, and someone I'm proud to call a friend. Please help me welcome our Civilian of Honor, Stryker Truman."

At the podium, he accepted Tiana's hug, but his heart felt heavy. He was not worthy of this honor. If they knew the *real* Stryker Truman, they would despise him, regardless of how much money he donated to help those in need. Detective Easton would have plenty of reasons to arrest him for crimes he *had* committed—and would continue committing—until he found his mother's killer.

Stryker gazed into the sea of faces while the applause continued. When the guests rose to their feet, he had to stop them.

"I don't deserve your kindness," Stryker said over the hoots and hollers. "This is a somber event and I don't want us to lose sight of that."

The attendees quieted down. Most of them sat, but some remained standing.

"Captain Perry is right," Stryker said after scanning the crowd. "I have never refused to help her out, because I'm not stupid. Who wants to get on the wrong side of the police captain?" He paused for laughter. "I'm not a man of many words, so let me get to the point. Thank you to the brave men and women in blue who protect us every day. Chasing justice is never easy and I applaud your bravery. Losing someone who died trying to make the world a better place is tough. But we have to carry on and honor their memory. Thank you for inviting me to share in their lives tonight." He stepped aside so Tiana could speak into the mic.

"Thank you, Stryker." She peered out at the crowd. "Ladies and gentlemen, thank you for spending your evening with us and for your generous donations. Safe travels home." She turned off the mic and stepped away from the podium.

After the applause ended, guests began moving about the ballroom. Some were chatting in small groups while others plodded toward the exits.

"Are you playing nice with my detective?" Tiana asked.

"I'm doing my best," he replied.

A handful of guests surrounded the captain, so Stryker set off toward his table. He spent a few minutes chatting with his execs from Truman Cybersecurity before continuing onward, scanning the crowd until he found his target.

Emerson.

She stood in a group, talking with several officers.

Their eyes met and his chest heated. His physical reaction to her was off the charts and annoying as hell. More so, he found himself mesmerized by her beauty.

"Nice speech," she said.

"Short and sweet," he replied. "I'm going to say goodbye to Heather and Gordon before we take off. Come with me."

As they meandered around attendees, Stryker placed his hand on the small of Emerson's back. Had she been his, he would have snaked his arm around her waist, pulled her close, and dropped a soft kiss on her lips.

Tiana's words rattled around his head. *Play nice with my detective.* The things he wanted to do to Emerson were anything but nice. They were hot and dirty, and so damn gratifying. Things that would quiet his tortured mind and temporarily silence his demons. Making Emerson scream his name in ecstasy would be the perfect way to play nice.

Back at their dinner table, Heather hugged him. "We're so proud of you. Are you coming over for Sunday Funday?"

"I'll swing by," Stryker replied.

"Emerson, you should come with him. Gordon and I call it our afternoon of insanity." Heather laughed. "It's a lot of fun. Kids, grandkids. The dog is the most behaved out of the whole group. We play games and have a cookout."

"Thanks, Heather," Emerson replied.

As soon as his aunt and uncle headed out, Stryker shifted his attention to Emerson. "Ready to hunt down a killer?"

She nodded. "So damn ready."

9

THE SPITE F*CK

While Stryker drove her to The Dungeon, Emerson snuck a peek at him. *So freakin' gorgeous.* But it was the perpetual frustration in his eyes that sent her pulse into the stratosphere. She wanted to comb her fingers through his hair, tug him close, and marry her lips to his. The constant pulsing between her legs would not stop, so she'd come up with a plan. If she managed through another anxiety-inducing evening in the dungeon, she'd reward herself with Stryker.

My spite fuck...if he even wants me.

Rather than take her through the front door, he guided her to the back of the club and over to a gray metal fire door. There were few cars back there and no foot traffic. The scanner cleared him to enter. After opening the door, he waited for her to enter.

The music was so loud, it thundered in her chest. She wanted to forget about the pressure of the case, tug him onto the dance floor and lose herself in the seductive beat. She wanted to remove his tailored suit jacket and let herself feel the hard striations of his cut muscles. She wanted to have fun, like everyone else in that room. But, she wasn't like everyone else in that room. She was there to catch a killer.

As they made their way across the room, her palms got sweaty. Like Pavlov's dog, she became hyperaware that she was heading below ground. Stryker waited for the scanner, then opened the door. Once they were in the stairwell, he closed it behind them.

She started shaking, but she followed, counting the steps, one at a time. When they got to the bottom, fear settled in her chest. After unlocking the door, he entered the cavernous room. The lights illuminated his way to the console. At the foot of the steps, she remained frozen in place.

After booting up his systems, he retreated to the restroom.

And that's when she panicked. She shifted toward the steps. Twelve and she was free. Little stars clouded her thoughts and she sucked down a breath to steady herself.

Then, she closed her eyes and focused on her breathing. In, slowly. Out, slowly. Again, and again. Stryker opened the bathroom door. Seconds later, he was by her side. She opened her eyes.

"You can do this," he murmured.

She walked on rubbery legs to the console, pulled out the chair, but couldn't bring herself to sit.

Stryker removed his jacket, and she soaked up his broad shoulders and chiseled chest pressing against his fitted dress shirt. Seeing him strip off a layer of clothing was the perfect distraction. This time, her insides came alive for all the right reasons. Next, he rolled up his sleeves.

When she sighed, he looked at her.

"You're doing great," he said.

"I'm sure my staring at you is creepy. You have a calming effect on me."

"Stare away, if it helps."

Together, they sat side-by-side. Like the previous time, they would divvy up the work. Stryker spent a few minutes keying in what they needed.

"I'll be surveilling L2, where April worked," Stryker explained.

"She filled in on L1, so you'll view those videos, going back two weeks before her death."

Dragging her eyes from him, she began studying the video. She worked until the claustrophobia crashed through her concentration and she became anxious all over again. After a few calming breaths, she refocused and continued working. It helped knowing Stryker was inches away, his confidence and inner strength a continual source of comfort.

There were so many people who rolled up to the bar, and half of them were masked. People started blending together. Had she seen that man before or was he new? Was he trying to chat April up or just making small talk while she mixed his cocktail?

While Emerson was searching for a man, she couldn't rule out a woman, either. After what felt like forever, she glanced at the time.

"Thirty minutes," she said. "If I've seen the same person more than once, I haven't caught it."

"I hear you," he said. "This is easier for me because I know some of the members, but I'm here so seldom these days. Plus, it's a revolving door."

After an hour, Stryker said, "Parker has shown up on his days off. Check this out."

She counted four different occasions where Parker spent part of his evening at the bar when April was working. He'd have a beer, sometimes two. He always paid. She seemed genuinely happy to see him. And he helped her clean up after the club closed.

"I requested a background check on him," Emerson said. "I hope to have it back next week."

Stryker hopped on a laptop, his fingers flying over the keyboard. "I'll run one now. It takes a coupla hours." He pulled out his phone.

"I'm having two waters delivered. You hungry?"

She shook her head. Stryker called someone upstairs. When he hung up, he headed for the stairs. "Where are you going?" Emerson asked, feeling the nerves resurfacing.

"To grab the drinks. I don't allow staff down here."

With a tremble in her hand, she forced herself to start the video again. When she heard Stryker climbing the stairs, she hurried over to the bottom of the steps.

"I'm right here," he said as he ascended.

She waited until he was heading back down, two waters in hand, before she sat back down. "I am beyond embarrassed."

He scooped her hands into his large one. "Your negative talk is hurting you. Applaud your wins and stop criticizing yourself. That's Dr. Sharpe speak."

"You sound exactly like Heather." She released his strong and soothing grip to drink down some of the water. "How did you come to live with your aunt and uncle?"

Sadness flashed in his eyes. "Long story. Let's get back to work."

Since he didn't want to talk about it, Emerson let it go. They turned back to the video and continued watching.

"This is crazy," she said, breaking the long silence. "We've been staring at the screen for way too long."

He dragged a laptop over and keyed in something. "Let me pull the members who were here the nights April worked over the two weeks prior to her death."

The longer they worked, the more frustrated Emerson became. It was almost three in the morning and she couldn't decipher a single pattern with the clientele.

"Parker's background check is ready." He clicked on the report and slid the laptop between them.

She rolled closer while they read the report. He'd been arrested for ignoring a restraining order on multiple occasions. According to the report, his longtime girlfriend had ended their relationship, but he wouldn't stop calling, emailing, or dropping by. She'd moved to a different apartment, but he was relentless. He was arrested, tried, and convicted. He'd served his time and was out. It listed The Dungeon as his place of employment.

"Looks like we found our guy," Stryker said.

"The me before I arrested you would have agreed, but just because he was arrested for stalking his ex doesn't make him a killer. Is he here?"

"I'll check." Stryker called upstairs to the bar.

"Most everyone's already gone for the night," Stryker told her. "Including Parker."

"What about Mavis?"

"She's off for a few days."

The longer she stared, the more she wanted to kiss him. *Go for it. Kiss him.* Despite how badly she wanted him, she needed to get out of the enclosed space. She'd pushed herself hard, bribing herself with an outlandish reward, but she was desperate for some fresh air. She stood and stretched.

"Where are you going?" he asked.

"Home. It's after three."

As he was shutting down, she said, "I'll grab an Uber."

"Like hell you will. I'll drive you home."

Stryker slid his laptop into his bag and they headed upstairs. The club was closed, the first floor was empty, and the staff had cleared out.

"Different place after it closes," she said.

"Peaceful."

"You don't like the mayhem?" she asked.

"In general or here?"

"Both?"

"Mayhem follows me, and I'm over the club scene." After he set the building alarm, they left out the front door. Several members were hanging out in the parking lot.

"Don't these people sleep?" she asked.

As they passed the group, Stryker slowed. "Everyone doing okay?"

They all responded that they were.

"Need me to call a ride for you?" he called over to them.

"We're good," said one of the women.

Once in his car, Stryker asked if Emerson had her weapon.

"No, it's in my safe at home," she replied. "You?"

"Always," he replied, and turned onto the main road.

"Why do you carry?" she asked.

"Because I can." Unless pressed, the short answer worked best for him.

"Can you stay for a drink?"

Their eyes met in the darkened car. "Yes."

His desire would not be extinguished until he was inside her. It was a raw, wicked need that he could no longer ignore. He'd put the brakes on things last night because she'd been drinking, but tonight, she was stone, cold sober.

He parked in her driveway, grabbed his satchel. With his weapon in his hand, they entered her home. After tapping the button to close her garage door, she turned off the security system.

The yellow-eyed monster waited on the steps. This time, Pima's meowing was laced with a heavy purring.

"Cats are fuckin' crazy," he grumbled.

Emerson laughed as they headed upstairs. In the kitchen, she shook the can of treats and the possessed feline did his bizarre two-legged dance.

She gave him treats, then sauntered close. With each step, his heart pounded faster, the blood surging south. "What can I get you? Beer, wine? I've got—" She barreled into him, the intoxicating rush of her—her flowery scent, her soft lips on his, her nails raking down his back—had him groaning into her.

The kiss deepened, the rush of passion turning him hard. He wanted to strip her bare and drive himself inside her until the ecstasy numbed him. He needed to lose himself in her until he was too spent to give a fuck about anything...except her.

Breathing hard, she slowed the kiss down while delicate fingers slipped in his hair. She tucked strands behind his ear with one hand, while the other held him flush against her. He was a prisoner in a cell from which he never wanted to escape.

"Come upstairs with me," she murmured. "I need you naked in my bed."

Should he put the brakes on this? Do the professional thing? But when she clasped his hand, the only *right* thing was taking her to bed.

Once in her bedroom, she said, "Stryker, I'm spite fucking you."

"Say what?"

"Sex with someone you don't like or who doesn't like you, just to show 'em what they could have on the regular, but aren't gonna get." Her adorable smile sent him light years away. "You hate me—"

"That's behind us."

Instead of rushing to get him naked, a playful expression danced in her eyes while she took her time unbuttoning his shirt. The serious detective, who hated confined spaces, had a fun side.

"Oops, there goes another button." This emboldened, light-hearted woman was so different from the terrified one in his basement. The tease was phenomenal, the desire to bury himself inside her building to a frenzy.

Next, came his undershirt. "Oh, God." She'd stepped back and ogled his pecs. "You've got a better chest then me."

"Not true."

She studied every inch of exposed skin—his chest, his abs and his arms—while she slicked her lips with her tongue. His balls had drawn up so hard, he wondered if he'd come seconds after sinking inside her. After unzipping and toeing off his dress boots, she undid his pants. As soon as they were out of the way, she gripped his cock like a joystick and stroked him through his boxer briefs.

Wetness covered the head of his cock while he groaned from the onslaught of welcomed pleasure. Slipping her hands into the waistband of his boxers, she pulled them down and knelt as he stepped out of them. Now, on her knees, she gazed up at him with hooded eyes.

Never before had he been stripped naked while his partner remained clothed. This woman was breaking all his rules. Ever-the-alpha, he was more than happy to let her take control—all night long.

And then, reality hit him. "Ah, fuck, I don't have a condom."

"I'm guilty of a premediated spite fuck. I bought extra-large condoms. Latex and non-latex. All new, all for you." She grasped his cock and spread his wetness with her thumb. And then, she said, "I want you in my mouth. Without giving me your entire medical history, what's your status?"

"I haven't had sex in months and I used condoms, even for oral."

Without a second's hesitation, she licked the wet head. "Should I cover you?"

"No. Taste me." His voice was strained, the lust rocketing through him.

She licked him again and again before taking him inside her mouth. "Mmm, mmm."

He was flying high, and flying high fast.

While cradling his balls, she kept her other hand on his shaft while she took him in farther and farther. When he touched the back of her throat, more juices seeped out. Her moans were turning ardent and restless, yet she didn't increase her speed.

The pleasure was unrelenting, the desire to release increasing with each suck. The sounds of her approval mixed with her guttural groans were too much.

He gripped her shoulders. "Too good. I can't hang on much longer."

She pulled back and lifted her face toward his, her luscious mouth wet from his juices. "Come in my mouth."

She resumed sucking him, but with more intention. Her ferocious growls, paired with her skilled hand and mouth, had him gritting his teeth and groaning out her name. He was being consumed by her, and the orgasm started deep inside. As he started to release, he warned her, so she could pull off.

But, damn. She did not. He shot into her mouth while pure pleasure exploded through him. As he regained his senses, he gazed down at her. She still hadn't pulled off.

Then, she let him go and rose. Her mouth wet, her heavy-lidded eyes dark with desire. She retreated into the bathroom, returning a few seconds later.

"Spite fucks do not include swallowing."

He smiled, feeling drunk out of his mind with euphoria. "Damn, you sucked me good."

After throwing back the linens, she extracted four boxes of condoms from the night table drawer and tossed them on the bed. With her gaze pinned on his, she sauntered back over and kissed him. He threaded his arms around her and kissed her back, hard. Tongues thrashing, bodies gyrating against each other, he was a man hell-bent on pleasuring her. Needing her to feel him deep inside her heat, making her moan and buck with pleasure.

Her husky sounds rumbled in his chest. He reached behind and unhooked her halter, then unzipped her dress while she peppered his face with slow, sensual kisses. Her breathing was ragged, her enlarged pupils blackened her eyes. He pulled the dress off and it dropped to the floor.

Their mutual moans filled the air while he caressed her bare back and ran his hands over her soft, curvy ass.

Meow, Meoooow. The black demon streaked by, batting a balled-up piece of tinfoil. Then, it started running around in circles before bolting down the hall.

"That beast is insane," Stryker bit out.

Her laugh came easily. He could get damn used to *this* Emerson.

He extracted himself and stepped back. "I've envisioned you naked for longer than I'll admit," he said, still staring into her eyes.

To his delight, she didn't cover herself or say anything disparaging about her body. She stood there—a strong, proud woman—and let him gaze upon her near-naked form. He loved that she was comfortable in her own skin. She was more beautiful than he'd imagined.

"You're a goddess," he murmured.

He had to touch her, but he needed confirmation they were moving in the right direction. "Emerson—"

"I'm clean," she replied.

"I want to touch you, everywhere. Are you good with that?"

She pressed her breasts against his chest. "Yes. Definitely." She ran her fingers down his arms, pausing to appreciate his triceps and biceps.

"I need to taste you, to feel your pussy juices dripping down my face."

"Yes, yes." She gripped him harder. "Please."

"What *don't* you want?"

"All this talking," she replied with an edge to her voice. "I will stop you or redirect you if I don't like what you're doing." And then, she stroked his ass, his pubic hair and his hardening penis. When her mouth found his, her kisses were ardent, vicious and desperate. She nipped at his lip and tugged him toward the bed. They fell sideways onto the mattress.

In a flash, he was on top of her, kissing her mouth, her cheek, moving down to her neck. Those tender kisses and nibbles elicited a series of low, wild whimpers.

"You feel so good," she whispered. "So, so good."

He fondled her breast and teased her erect pink nipple with his thumb. She began writhing under him, her breathing jagged, her urgent fingers kneading his shoulders and back.

He moved down to kiss her breast, then took her nipple in his mouth, turning him hard again. The harder he sucked, the huskier her whimpers grew. When he slipped his hand between her legs, she turned into a beast, thrusting her hips up and groaning wildly.

"Fuck me," she commanded.

"Not yet," he murmured as he kissed and sucked her other nipple, and ran his tongue down her abdomen until he dropped it into her belly button.

"I'm dying," she moaned. "This is *the* best torture. You're making me feel good, every- fucking-where."

He liked this dirty-mouthed detective. She didn't hold back, didn't lay there, either. She dragged a pillow under her head and watched with heavy eyelids as he slipped his fingers between her warm, wet folds. As soon as he slid two inside her, she cried out for more.

Desperate to taste her, he withdrew his fingers and moved into position. She smelled like delicious pussy and he breathed her in. When he placed his mouth on her, she released a long, low whimper. "I love that."

He lapped and circled her clit with his tongue, then licked the length of her. "Mmm, you taste so good."

The dirtier he got, the more she liked it. She began gyrating her hips up and down, so he licked her harder and faster.

"Yesssss, I'm—" She began shaking while she cried out. "Commmming."

A rush of wetness flowed down and he relished in her release while the aftershocks rocked her. Then, he gently stroked her while her tense muscles relaxed into the mattress. After she stilled, he rose up over her, cupped her pussy with his hand, and kissed her. She wrapped her arms around his back and smiled at him. "You've ruined me for spite fucks. That was incredible."

"That was the warm up. We haven't spite fucked yet."

"Oh, right. I can't think right now." Her lazy grin was a dangerous combination of beautiful and carefree. She was pushing all his buttons. This time, in the best of ways.

He eyed the assortment of condoms, picked one, and tore open the box. After covering himself, he planked over her. "Top or bottom, Detective?"

"I'll take my spite fuck on top, then you can have your revenge fuck."

He chuffed out a laugh. "What the hell is that?"

"You get to take out your revenge on me for arresting you and putting you through hell."

"Then, I'm gonna get a *lot* of revenge fucks for a long, long time," he replied.

Emerson was flying high for the first time in months. Tonight, she was giving herself permission to let go, just this once. Her job was stressful and she'd been struggling with her brother's death. The sexy, angry beast in her bed was the perfect distraction, even if just for a few hours.

Nudging Stryker back, she straddled him. While peering into his bedroom eyes, she stroked his erection, his cock sheathed beneath the condom.

"You are so damn beautiful." His sexy-as-hell smile sent streams of energy flowing through her. "With a rockin-hot body that I cannot keep my hands off."

"This is a spite fuck, Stryker." She lifted off him and positioned him at her opening. "We don't get along. You can't stand me. Stop with the compliments." With a glint in her eyes, she lowered herself onto him.

Moaning through the penetration, she shuddered in a deep breath. "So good."

When he was nestled deep inside her, she gazed into his eyes and began moving. The intense pleasure had her eyes closing, but she forced them to stay open so she could appreciate his face, the lust in his bedroom eyes. His sexy moans sent jolts of energy racing through her.

This man was the ultimate fuck. He was easy on the eyes, smart as hell, and talented in the sack. For one glorious night, he was hers. No promises, no expectations, no lies.

As the pleasure spread through her, she leaned down and kissed him. He wrapped her in his strong arms and stroked her back. So much intensity and tenderness in his touch. It was hard to process all that pleasure.

Their tongues tangled lazily, at first, then she pressed harder and he reciprocated. The faster she glided, the more ravenous their kisses became. Pushing up, she rode him hard, for her own gratification.

And then, she raised her arms in the air and fucked the hell out of him. He pawed at her tits, squeezing and tweaking her nipples. The quick stabs of pain rocketed her higher, the euphoria stealing her breath. She gasped for air as the torrent of arousal took her to the edge of ecstasy.

He massaged her clit and she lost control, the exhilaration overpowering and unrelenting.

"You're fucking me so good," he bit out. "You're gonna suck me dry, again."

The orgasm started deep inside and rolled through her. "I'm coming," she cried out between gasps. "Oh, yes, yes." The endorphins shattered her, her pussy tightening around him while he ground out his orgasm in a series of throaty groans.

"Fuck, Emerson, you're taking me."

Their kisses were wild and greedy. Their husky, satisfying moans filled the night while she floated on a silver cloud somewhere in the stratosphere. Stryker Truman did it for her. But their being together was circumstantial. Nothing more.

As she started to move off him, he asked, "Where are you going?"

"This is a spite fuck, not a snuggle fest."

He released a relaxed laugh. "Lay on me."

In truth, she didn't want to disconnect, but she was keeping it real. If he wanted to stay in fantasy fuckland for a little longer, she was cool with that.

She lay on him and he blanketed her back with his massive arms. Warmth flooded her. "That was fun."

"At the very least," he murmured. "You're trouble, Easton."

She lifted her face and stared into his eyes "This is a one-night thing. We both had a good time. Going forward, it's business as usual."

"Killjoy."

"You need a break or you ready to have your way with me?" she asked.

"You're insatiable."

"I'm making up for lost time."

Pima jumped on the bed, stopped short, and glared at Stryker.

"He's gonna attack me, isn't he?" Stryker asked.

Emerson laughed. "He's never seen anyone in bed with me before."

"How long have you had him?"

"Five months. He was my brother's cat." She didn't want to talk about Doug, but she didn't want to push Stryker away, either. Unsure which direction to take, she hesitated.

"We can change the subject," he offered. "Whatever you want."

She appreciated that he didn't push. "Doug didn't like cats, either."

"How'd he end up with one?"

Rolling off him, Emerson leaned up on one elbow. "The cat showed up out of nowhere. Doug figured he'd move on, but he didn't. He felt badly for it, so he fed it, and that was it. From that day on, Pima owned him."

"Sounds like a good man."

She smiled. "He *was* a good man and a great cop. I became a cop because of him." She swallowed down the sadness and cleared her throat. "When Doug died, my parents took Pima, but my mom's allergic. I couldn't let them take him to a shelter, so I kept him."

"Danielle said this was his place."

She nodded. "I loved living with Danielle, but I wasn't ready to let him go, so I moved in." Her throat tightened.

As if sensing her struggles, Stryker tucked her hair behind her ear and kissed her. "Where'd the name Pima come from?"

"It stands for Pain In My Ass."

He laughed. "I would have liked your brother."

Her eyes brightened a little. "You two would have gotten along great, but he was way too protective of me. Worse than my dad. I'm not sure you would have passed the Doug test."

"Woulda passed, no prob."

She ran her fingertip over his lips. "I don't want things to get weird between us because of this."

He peered into her eyes. "They won't."

"Plus, now that I got you out of my system, I'm moving on to my next conquest."

That elicited a chuckle from him. "Are you working today?"

"Yeah, you?"

"I've got an early meeting this morning," he said while checking his watch. "It's almost five. How 'bout a power nap?"

"Sleep together?" she asked. "This is a spite fuck, not sex and a snooze."

She could become addicted to making him smile. "How 'bout this?" he continued. "We sleep for an hour, then I get my revenge fuck before we head out."

"Deal."

After dropping a kiss on her lips, he pushed out of bed. As he retreated into the bathroom, she glimpsed a beautiful tat on his back. A large cross and sword etched in black ink lay between his muscular shoulder blades and trailed down his spine.

A moment later, he crawled in beside her. "Lay on me."

"You're not the boss of me," she said.

"I'll lay on you, then."

"I wouldn't have pegged you for a cuddler."

"I'm not."

She rested her head on his muscular pec and he folded her into a protective cocoon. He was asleep in minutes, but she lay there listening to him breathe. After what had just happened, how would she be able to keep her hands off him?

How was this a one-night thing?

10

THE BREACH

Stryker and Emerson were lying on a quiet beach, kissing. The afternoon sun warmed his back. Being with Emerson made him happy, a feeling he wasn't familiar with, but something he cherished.

A jackhammer interrupted Stryker's dream and he opened his eyes. The purring beast was sitting on his stomach glaring down at him. Emerson stirred, then reached out and rubbed Pima behind his ears and his purring took off like a jet engine.

Emerson was curled around him. As she extracted herself, she said, "My arm is asleep. I'm not sure we could get any closer."

"Me *in you* is closer."

Her sleepy smile and mussed updo were adorable. Stryker felt drunk. He didn't do adorable, but that's exactly who was staring at him. Adorable and sexy. So drawn to her, he leaned over and kissed her.

"I didn't hear the alarm," she said.

He glanced at his watch. "Dammit, I forgot to turn it on. It's seven thirty."

"Nice move." She pushed out of bed and he appreciated her backside. Stryker had a type and Emerson was it. Petite and blonde with dark eyes, and a body in proportion to her small frame. She was muscular and dainty at the same time. And smart. He needed a smart, feisty woman. Someone who would push his buttons and keep him up all night long.

Ignoring his boner, he followed.

She handed him a toothbrush wrapped in plastic. "Extra from the dentist. I use an electric." Then, she eyed his erection. "Good one."

"I gotta bolt," he said. "My revenge fuck will have to wait 'til later."

"Later?" She snickered. "I got mine. You got laid. We're done."

He cupped her chin, kissed her. "We're just getting started."

"You are one cocky man."

"I know what I like." He smacked her bare ass. "And I'm looking right at her. Don't you want to feel good? Don't you want to squirm with pleasure while I suck your tits and fuck you to the moon?"

Sucking down a breath, she gripped the sink vanity. "Wow, you are good with the dirty talk."

With a wink, he brushed his teeth.

He liked that things weren't awkward between then. What he didn't like was their *unfinished* business. After brushing, he raked his fingers through his hair and left the bathroom to get dressed.

Being late for his first meeting snowballed into a clusterfuck of late for the entire day. After pulling on his clothes, he returned to the bathroom. Emerson had pulled her hair out of the messy updo and had repositioned it into a ponytail that sat high on her head.

"I'm outta here. Can you turn off your security system?"

"You aren't taking a shower?"

"No time," he replied. "Plus, I'd much rather leave your scent on me all day long."

A too-brief smile touched her eyes.

He took off down the hall, making his way downstairs to grab his satchel.

"I can let you out through the front door." A very naked and incredibly sexy Emerson waved him over as she headed toward her front door. He wanted to stay, but he had to bolt.

As she punched in her code, he spied the tattoo on her upper back. The green snake was perfectly situated between her shoulder blades. It sat coiled and ready to attack.

"Nice tat. Is that a green snake, a pit viper, or a mamba?"

"It's a boomslang," she murmured.

His brain screeched to a halt. "What did you say?"

"The venomous snake is a boomslang. They've been called the cat of the snake world. Ever heard of them before?"

He held her gaze for an extra beat. "Yeah, I have."

"Can you meet me at the club tonight?" she asked.

Is she the same woman from the Survivors online group?

"Stryker, hello?" Emerson said.

Snapping out of his thoughts, he unearthed his phone and checked his schedule. "After seven."

She unalarmed and opened the door. He ducked down as if to kiss her goodbye, only, he didn't. "You owe me one." Then, he took off toward his car.

The early morning sun, paired with perfect May temps, beckoned. He couldn't remember the last time he'd taken a day off. He wanted to steal Emerson away, hop on his Fat Boy, and escape into the Virginia countryside.

As he drove out of her quiet neighborhood, he couldn't stop thinking about her tat. *Is she Boomslang?* His gut said yes. At the red light, he pulled up the photo Boomslang had sent of her cat. That was Emerson's kitchen table and that crazy animal was Pima. *Holy hell. It is her.*

His life couldn't get much more complicated.

He drove into the parking lot of Truman CyberSecurity. The office building that bore his company's initials—TCS—was nestled in an upscale business park filled with technology-oriented companies. While Stryker could have placed his name on the front of the building, he preferred keeping a low profile.

The majority of TCS hackers worked late and strolled in between ten and eleven. Admin arrived at nine, so Stryker got to the office at eight. On a normal day, that gave him an hour before the mayhem started.

His eight forty-five arrival left him little time before his nine o'clock staff meeting. He swiped his keycard and yanked on the front door, but it didn't budge. The indicator light was off, so he used his key to enter the two-story atrium. *If we had a power hit, why isn't the generator running?*

First to arrive, he glanced at the company sign—TCS—located behind the large, curved reception desk. Normally backlit, it was dark.

Sunshine streamed through the floor-to-ceiling windows, but the lights were out. He didn't expect the elevator to work, so he hotfooted it to the stairwell. Again, his keycard didn't work, so he keyed the lock and entered the darkened stairwell. After flicking on his phone's flashlight, he took the stairs two at a time.

The second-floor housed his commercial account teams. Large rooms with chairs and bench-style tables where pods of hackers worked. Account managers responsible for these accounts, along with leadership, worked in traditional-style offices. Using his key, he accessed the floor. The pods were void of staff and nothing had been disturbed, the offices were empty, too. The churning in his guts subsided as he made his way to the second floor.

Floor three was home to his military accounts. Its set-up mimicked the first floor with work spaces and private offices. He found no one there and nothing out of place.

His heart rate began to drop. He'd gotten worked up for nothing.

The fourth floor was home to his government agency accounts, which included the CIA, FBI, State Department, DHS, and NSA. His hackers were amongst the best in the business and the senior account managers for these agencies had earned the right to manage them.

As he bolted up the steps, dread made his stomach drop. The fire door was off its hinges. This floor had been breached. These accounts were amongst his most classified. The security alarm hadn't gone off, so he hadn't been alerted of the break-in.

He pulled out his Glock and headed toward the first workspace, hoping no one had been there when the break-in happened. Pod after pod lined both sides of the hallway. The glass door to the CIA pod was closed and he slowed to look through the wall of windows. Monitors were dark, laptops closed. Every managers' office door was closed and locked. The State Department pod hadn't been breached, nor had NSA.

As he approached the last pod, his chest tightened. The glass door to the FBI workspace had been removed. The room looked like a bulldozer had ripped through it. Computers and monitors smashed to pieces, laptops broken in two or damaged beyond repair. Mayhem everywhere.

Fuck, fuck me.

As he stepped inside, dread morphed into fury. A quick count identified at least nine laptops missing from the tables. Before heading to the top floor, he snapped pictures of the destruction.

With anger streaming through him, he climbed the stairs to the top floor, where he and his executive team worked, along with in-house attorneys, accountants, and other management. No one's office had been compromised, including his own. He felt no relief. Someone had deactivated his security system, killed the power, including the back-up system, and stolen laptops from a pod that supported a top-secret client.

After Stryker's arrest eighteen months ago, the FBI had terminated their contract with TCS. Even after the charges were dropped, it had taken him months to earn back their trust. This was going to wreak havoc with their already damaged relationship. The fury that hounded him day after day exploded in a torrent of rage. He pounded his fist into the wall, sending searing pain shooting up his arm. *Fuck. Fuuuuuck.*

Shaking his hand out, he stared at the hole in the drywall before heading back downstairs. His phone rang. It was Brooks. "We've been breached," Stryker said. "Where are you?"

"Atrium. You?"

"On my way down." Stryker strode into the lobby to find several employees standing by the reception bank. Brooks was on his phone.

"What's going on?" asked a staffer.

"We've been burglarized," Stryker replied.

Everyone started hurtling questions at him. He painted on a smile, trying to look relaxed. "Why don't you guys take off? We'll update everyone when we know more."

"Can we grab our laptops?" asked one of his hackers.

"No," Stryker replied. "Operational security. No one goes upstairs." His employees looked as concerned as he felt.

A few meandered toward the exit, but most didn't budge.

Brooks hurried over. "The police are on their way."

Stryker did not want the police involved. The media would find out and hound the hell out of him and his employees. He wanted to deal with this his way...off the radar. Find the motherfuckers and pump some bullets into them.

The sex high from a few hours ago had been replaced with something much more familiar.

Rage.

He showed Brooks the photos. "Nothing stolen but FBI laptops."

"That's got retaliation written all over it. Who'd you piss off now, Stryker?"

"Who haven't I pissed off?"

Stryker pulled out his laptop, logged in, and activated the search. Years ago, he'd installed a software package to track stolen or misplaced laptops, but the equipment had to be on for the geolocator to work. Even though computers should stay on site, an employee who ghosted on him might take their company laptop. The tracking software helped him retrieve his stolen assets.

DAMAGED

He got several hits for laptops located upstairs. No hits elsewhere, which meant the stolen laptops were off.

"No lucky break?" Brooks asked, peering at Stryker's screen.

"No. Maybe the assholes will turn them on."

An hour later, the building was swarming with police, TCS employees, and repair techs. He escorted two officers upstairs to show them the FBI pod.

"The crime techs are on their way," said one of the officers. "They'll dust for prints, so we've got to block off this area."

"Whatever it takes," Stryker replied.

Time to manage damage control.

After ushering them into the atrium, Stryker got an earful from the repair guys. The fiber optics lines had been cut going into the building, thereby preventing any communications. The back-up power lines from the generator to the building had also been cut. And the main power lines had been severed, killing the electricity.

Whoever had done this had fucked up his company...big time.

"This is a big job and we're gonna need a crew," said a technician.

"Not gonna lie," said another. "This is bad."

"No shit," Stryker bit out. "How long is it gonna take to get us back online?"

"Hard to know for sure. Maybe a few days. Gotta call my boss on this one."

That wasn't even the worst of it.

Stryker needed to tell his clients that the building had been compromised, that laptops used to hack into the FBI had been stolen, and that top-secret government information could be in jeopardy. Stryker's head pounded and he scrubbed his fingers through his hair.

One of the police officers walked over. "Mr. Truman, we found the point of entry." He pointed across the atrium. "The perps used glass cutters to remove a large piece of the side window and they stepped right in."

Too fucking easy. "I'll have that boarded up," Stryker said.

Stryker found Brooks on the phone with their insurance company. After hanging up, Brooks murmured, "Could this be gang retaliation from our hit last week?"

Stryker shook his head. "They would have come after us, not our company."

"That's comforting to know."

Brooks's sarcasm wasn't lost on him.

"We've got over twenty-five pods. Why target just one of them?" Stryker opened a window on his laptop and pulled up last night's security surveillance. "Check this out."

Stryker fast-forwarded until 3:12AM, when the video went dark. "That's when they cut the connection." He dragged the cursor back. "That's when it happened, but they're dressed in black with black ski masks." His chest heated, the anger surging through him. "No flashlight. They must've used night goggles."

"You sure this isn't some gang-related revenge?" Brooks whispered.

"My gut says no," Stryker replied.

"What next?" Brooks held out his hand.

Stryker fished a hair tie out of his satchel and handed it to Brooks. "IT needs to inventory the equipment. Can you call someone to board up the glass?"

"Sure thing." Brooks tied back his dreads. "I'll also send out a company-wide email telling everyone to stay home until they hear back from us."

"Remind them not to talk about this with anyone outside the company."

"You know, this is all they're gonna talk about."

Stryker nodded. "If the power isn't up by Monday, we'll send someone from each pod to the client site to work from there. I'll handle logistics for that."

Brooks slapped him on the back. "We'll get through this."

Stryker snapped his laptop shut. "I'll check in with the police before I head to the Bureau."

"Glad I'm not having that conversation. We're already on thin ice with them."

"Not gonna be pretty."

"The upside is that no one was here when they broke in. Things coulda been a lot worse."

"I'm sorry *I* wasn't here," Stryker said. "The outcome would have been very different."

Stryker found the officer in charge. After showing him the surveillance video, he forwarded it to him, then jumped up on the reception counter. "Hey, guys. C'mon over."

Once his employees had gathered around, Stryker addressed the group. "As you've heard by now, there was a break-in."

"Was anything taken?" asked a manager.

"We'll know more in the next coupla days. Do not talk to the media, not even 'off the record'. And do not post anything online. Understood?"

Lots of nods and thumbs up in response.

"Who do you think did this?" asked an employee.

"Not gonna speculate. You guys need to head out. The building is closed. Text your pod mates and tell them not to come in. Questions get routed to Brooks and me. Once we've got power, you can return to work."

No one moved.

Stryker painted on a smile. "You got paid vacation. Go have some fun." As the crowd headed out, he jumped off the counter and strode out of the building. *What a fucking disaster.*

As he sped down the toll road toward DC, he called Cooper.

"Hey, man," Cooper said. "You caught me between meetings. Wanna grab dinner tonight?"

"I need to talk to you."

"Shoot."

"In person."

"Bro, I'm in meetings all day."

"It's related to the FBI account at TCS."

"I don't like the sound of that," Cooper said. "Should I turn on the TV?"

"I need fifteen minutes."

"Where are you?"

"Toll road, heading east."

"I'll tell my assistant to interrupt my meeting when you get here. How bad is it?"

Bad. "Nothing we can't handle." Stryker let those words roll off his tongue like he wasn't in the middle of a total shit storm. In truth, he had no idea who'd stolen the equipment or what they were going to do, now that they had it.

The beautiful weather called for sunroof open, windows down, hair blowing in the breeze, music blaring. Stryker drove in silence and with the windows closed, his thoughts laser-focused on who the hell could have stolen his computers.

When he strolled into Cooper's office, he had more questions than answers. He couldn't sit, but he didn't want to alarm Cooper by pacing, so he leaned against the windowsill. Then, like ripping off a Band-Aid, Stryker blurted, "We had a breach."

"Jesus, no."

"They cut the lines outside, which shut down the security system."

"Not good."

"It was a targeted hit. Laptops were taken, but only from the FBI hacker pod."

The color had drained from Cooper's face. "How many?"

"At least nine."

"We have to treat this as a security threat. Those laptops could be on their way to Russia or China. Or it could be a domestic terror cell."

"I've got tracking software—"

Cooper sighed. "Why didn't you lead with that? That's great. Where are they? Should I call in a SWAT team?"

DAMAGED

"The tracking only works when the machines are on. The ones taken had been powered down."

"That's fucking irony." Cooper made a call. "Cancel my afternoon meetings." He hung up. "Since this could be terror or foreign-government-related, our espionage team has to investigate. You've got to shut down all ops during the investigation. Coulda been an inside job, so we've got to look into every employee."

"C'mon," Stryker protested. "An employee would only need to disrupt the surveillance. They wouldn't need to cut the power and the generator."

"You're probably right, but we gotta follow procedure on this."

"How long will this take?"

"Days, weeks," Cooper replied. "Months."

"I am so fucked."

"The thing that will save you is if someone opens up a laptop and turns it on," Cooper said.

"Let us know if you get any ransom demands."

"Yup." Stryker removed his suit jacket and rolled up his sleeves. "Got any aspirin?"

Cooper opened his desk drawer and tossed Stryker a bottle, then pushed out of his chair. "I'll get you some water."

Stryker downed two pills. "I'm good."

"Well, I need some water. Let's walk."

On the way to the break room, Cooper asked if anyone would want to harm Stryker's business.

"No idea."

"If you think of anyone, let me know."

The fifteen-minute meeting turned into a three-hour debriefing. Cooper called in several people who pelted him with questions. Their solution? TCS would stand down until a full investigation could be completed.

"Not happening," Stryker pushed back. "You can't shut me down indefinitely. I employ over four-hundred people."

"If your team is hacking into government systems to identify potential vulnerabilities, and the hackers are doing the same, we can't isolate the good guys from the bad," said Cooper.

"The second they turn those laptops on, we've got 'em," Stryker said.

"Not if they remove the hard drives and ship them halfway across the world," Cooper countered.

"What do you suggest, Mr. Truman?" asked one of the senior agents.

"Once IT gets me an inventory of what was stolen, we cease operations on those clients only. If the Bureau was the only account breached, we isolate that and deal with it."

"I don't know," said another.

Stryker was done going in circles. He was not letting the FBI shut him down. An investigation could drag on for months. No way in hell would he lose control of his organization. He pushed out of his seat. "Thanks for your time. Cooper has the surveillance. I'll get you the specs on the stolen laptops."

Cooper rose. "I'll walk you out."

On the way to the exit, Cooper said, "I know you, and you're gonna try to find these guys. *Don't.* You don't know who you're dealing with. This could be a terror cell."

"When I find them—and I will—I'll rip their fucking hearts out."

That made Cooper chuckle. "You're a hacker. What do you know about retribution?"

The men slowed at the exit and Stryker handed Cooper his visitor badge. "I'll call you tomorrow," Stryker said.

It was almost five. Stryker was hangry enough to chew his arm off, and in desperate need of taking out his frustration on a punching bag.

On his way home, he called Brooks. "Update me."

"IT inventoried the FBI pod. Eleven laptops are missing. We've got no power, so they're working until we lose sunlight. They're back in the morning. The technicians start tomorrow. Their plan is to get us back online by Monday. How'd your meeting go?"

"A clusterfuck. FBI wants to shut us down while they do a full investigation. They've got every right, but I pushed back."

"No surprise there," Brooks said.

"I told them we'd shut down any clients affected by the break-in."

"I take it your bossing them around didn't fly," Brooks replied.

"I left. We'll know more tomorrow."

"I called Maverick Hott at ThunderStrike," Brooks said. "He's sending a team to guard the building until power is reinstated," Brooks said.

"Smart thinking. Anything else?"

"A reporter called me. I told him 'No comment' and hung up." The call ended and Stryker finished his drive home in a fuming silence.

After changing into a T-shirt and shorts, he went for a hard run that ended at his gym. After beating the hell out of a punching bag, he lifted. Dripping in sweat, he returned home and showered.

He had fifty-four texts, eighteen missed calls, and a hundred and forty-seven unread emails. Scanning the texts, he found Emerson's.

"Still on for tonight?" she texted.

He texted her back. "Work ran over. How's 8? Dinner at club while we work."

She responded with a thumb's up emoji and a smiley.

The tightness in his chest lifted a little. Her simple reply was the best part of his day.

11

ROUND TWO

Emerson knew something was off the second she saw him. Stryker was waiting at the back door of The Dungeon, his hands curled into fists, his jaw muscles flexing in his cheeks. He was staring right at her, but not seeing her, the intensity in his gaze a powerful aphrodisiac. He looked sexier than hell in a black T-shirt and tight jeans, his muscles straining against the cotton fabric.

"Hey," he said.

"Hey, yourself. What's going on?"

"Different day, different shit."

"You want to talk about it?"

"Talk? No. But I can think of several other things I'd like to do. Starting with putting my fist through another fucking wall."

Another wall? "I'm a good listener."

He shook his head. "Let's get to work. I need a distraction."

As soon as they entered the club, the sensual beat of the music rumbled through her. If she hadn't been there to work, she'd have pulled him onto the dance floor, held him flush against her, and gotten lost in everything Stryker. She would have asked him to tie her up or role play a scene, just the two of them. She would relish in his beautiful body and angry mind, letting him release his inner wild on her. And she would take all of him until she had drained him of his frustration, leaving only happy, relaxed Stryker.

But Emerson didn't live in that world. Hers was reality-based, and they were working together to catch a killer.

Stryker flagged down a bartender on L1. "Two dinners, to-go."

"Hey, Stryker. What can I get you, ma'am?"

"A burger with everything but mayo. And a side salad." She peered up at Stryker. "Are you getting fries and do you share?"

That made him smile. His upbeat expression far too beautiful to be gone so fast.

"Two burgers, two fries."

"Is that the entire order or just your order, Stryker?" asked the bartender.

"My order. Detective Easton gave you her order. Text me when they're ready."

I'm back to being Detective Easton. Something's definitely wrong.

He turned and bumped into an unmasked woman.

"Hi, Stryker." She smiled at him. "How's it goin'?"

"Another glorious fuckin' day in paradise."

As he moved around her, she said, "I'm with Local 8 News. Who do you think broke into your company?"

Emerson stared at him. *What the hell? What did she just say?*

He glared at the journalist. "How did you get in here?"

"Through the front door." Her annoying laugh had Emerson biting back a grimace. "I'm a member."

"No comment," Stryker bit out.

The woman looked down her nose at Emerson. "I need to steal him. You don't mind, do you, honey?" Her lips split into a smile. "Stryker, let's me and you grab a booth. There are a million rumors flying around on social. Help me set the record straight."

Emerson squared her shoulders. "Honey does mind."

"Back off there, sweetie," said the reporter.

"No," Stryker growled. "Do *not* talk to her like that. If you want to keep that membership, don't hound me again." He clasped

Emerson's hand and pushed through the crowd toward the private stairs leading to his office. Instead of stopping, he continued to an elevator marked "Private".

Oh, no. Her heart rate quickened.

The scanner cleared him, he punched the down button and the doors slid open. After leading her inside, the doors closed and the elevator descended to the basement.

Emerson swallowed down the scream while her heart thundered in her chest. A muffled cry escaped her throat and she started shaking. The doors opened into the basement and Stryker stepped out, but she couldn't move. She hated being in the elevator, but she was too keyed up to go into the dungeon. Neither space was safe. She needed to get upstairs or she'd pass out.

He turned. In that brief second, a sea of emotions swept across his face.

"Oh, fuck, Emerson. I'm sorry." He rushed back into the confined space and held her in his arms.

She clung to him, trembling and humiliated. "I'm sorry," she whispered.

He pulled away and stared into her eyes. "I'm right here."

"I want to face my fear, but my body reacted before I had a chance to walk myself back."

"That's on me. I was being a total dick."

"It's not your responsibility to help me."

Sadness filled his eyes. "I can help you, but I failed you." He kissed her forehead. His soothing touch helped calm her, but she wanted him to kiss her on her mouth and distract her from the panic.

"Lemme grab a laptop. We can work upstairs in Mavis's office. She's on vacation."

Emerson would never be free of her phobia if she didn't confront it. And she would slow her progress on the case to a debilitating crawl. After the day she'd had, she needed to find something. Anything. She buried her face in his chest. "I want to overcome this. Give me a second."

He inhaled a slow, deliberate breath and she copied him. Slow inhale, slow exhale. They stood there for what felt like eternity, breathing as one. Her heart rate slowed and she stopped shaking. Gazing up, she offered a little smile.

"I can work down here." She released her vise grip. "I know this isn't professional, but you are the perfect person to help me. You're fearless and I admire that so much."

"Thank you," he murmured.

She took a step, then another and another until she was standing in his spacious dungeon. She stared at the console, his bed with the still-rumpled linens. Forcing herself to keep on going, she imagined windows. He pulled out a chair for her and she eased down.

"Nice job, Easton." He sat beside her and powered up the computers. The monitors sprang to life as she stayed focused on her breathing.

Sitting at his command center, Stryker was the epitome of power. His inner strength bolstered hers. And for a man who wore his anger like a second skin, he had shown her such tenderness.

His fingers flew over the keyboard while he accessed multiple software programs. "What are we looking for tonight?"

Their eyes met. "I haven't been able to find April's family. There are several April Peterses on social media, but the accounts are private."

"I can access those. What else is on the agenda?"

Sex. Sex is on the agenda. "You want to talk about the B&E at your company?"

A shadow darkened his eyes and he raked his hand through his hair. "No."

Not wanting to push, she let it go. "I'd like to start reviewing club surveillance for anyone who might have been stalking April."

"How far back you wanna go?"

"A month."

He turned back to the console, but she couldn't tear herself away. *Stop staring at him.* After several more seconds of soaking up all that rugged beauty, she dragged her attention back to the monitors on the wall.

Moments later, he said, "Surveillance is teed up going back a month. I'm in the three most trafficked social media platforms and I've pulled up all the women named April Peters. My IDware only works if they have a profile pic of themselves, so I'll manually check each account."

"Great plan."

They worked side by side, but she couldn't ignore the constant pull. She had this unrelenting urge to look at him, or stroke his arm. She inhaled a slow, calming breath and his baseline scent filled her lungs.

His phone buzzed with an incoming text. "Grub is ready. You good staying put?"

"Yeah." Rather than view this as being alone in a closed-off space, she would appreciate the much-needed break from her tempting partner.

"Back in two." He vanished up the steps and she fought against the fear that slithered up her spine. Though she wanted to bolt after him, she stayed rooted in the chair, reviewing the surveillance. Dozens of people sidled up to the bar in the course of a shift. April waited on everyone with a smile. Emerson had learned to distance herself from the victims, but her heart ached as she watched this lovely woman slinging back drinks.

Stryker returned and her body came alive and relaxed at the same time. He had such a powerful effect on her. He stroked her back, between her shoulder blades where her boomslang tat lay beneath her clothes. "Holding up okay?"

A tingle of excitement skittered through her. She could get damn used to his touch. "I'm still here. Are *you* okay?"

When he didn't respond, she glanced over. He was back to work, scouring social media accounts, while eating his burger. "You good with music?" he asked.

"Sure."

He pulled up a mix of seductive tunes.

Within ten minutes, Stryker broke the silence. "Got it." He threw a social media account onto a wall monitor. "April hasn't posted in over a year, but this is her account and that's her brother."

He went back to typing. The man's social media account appeared on all six screens, along with his name and a contact number.

"Wow, that was fast," she said. "You are good."

"I've been doing this a long time."

"How long?"

"Since I was fifteen."

"What made you want to get into hacking?"

"You ask a lot of questions, Easton."

"I thought we were beyond the formalities."

"It's your name, isn't it?"

He had her on that. It was her name. "You also have a great way of not answering my questions."

"Run me through what happens with April's body," he said.

"It's up to her next of kin."

"I'll pay for whatever he decides."

"What? Why would you do that?"

"If we find the killer stalked her here at my club, I'm responsible for what happened to her."

"No, you aren't, Stryker."

"If he wants her body sent back to Iowa, I'll pay for that. Or cremation."

"You sure?"

"If the words are coming out of my mouth, I'm sure."

Emerson dialed.

"Hello?"

"Hello, Mr. Peters?"

"You got him."

"My name is Detective Easton. I'm with the Arlington, Virginia police."

"I'm in Iowa. You sure you got the right guy?"

"Are you April Peters's brother?"

Silence for a few beats. "Is she in trouble?"

"Are you her brother?"

"Yeah." His tone had changed, the anxiety sending a quiver through his voice.

Emerson pushed out of the chair. "I'm very sorry to tell you this...your sister is dead."

Silence, then he whispered, "God, no. Please, no."

Emerson's heart broke. She wished she could be there with him while she told him the devastating news. She wished she could promise to find his sister's killer, but she couldn't do that, either. All she could do was try her best to console a man who had received shocking, devastating news.

"I'm very sorry for your loss," she said.

"Can you tell me what happened?" he asked.

"It appears to be a homicide. If you're up to it, I'd like to ask you a few questions."

"Yeah, okay."

"Did April mention any friends, anyone she was seeing?"

"We hadn't talked, you know, by phone in months. She would send me a text every now and then. I know she liked living in the DC area and she had a job she enjoyed. I don't think she had a roommate and she never mentioned a boyfriend. Sorry I can't be more helpful."

"It's okay. Do you think April would want to be buried in Iowa?"

"Right...um. I don't have money to pay for—"

"She has a friend who's stepping in to help with costs," Emerson said.

"If April's friend can take care of cremation, that would be appreciated. Can I give you my address so you can have her ashes sent home?"

Emerson took his address, expressed her condolences again, and hung up. Her heart was heavy and she needed a minute to collect herself.

Death was never fun. Never.

She made her way over to the console and sat back down. "Thank you for paying for April's arrangements. You're a good guy."

He shook his head. "Not a good guy."

As they stared into each other's eyes, his gaze turned molten. When his low, husky growl filled the air, desire pulsed through her. Fighting against the need to kiss him was like fighting against a rip tide.

Instead of moving toward her, he turned back to his computer, severing their connection. His abruptness left her feeling the chill of his rejection.

"I'm gonna find the motherfucker who killed April," he grumbled.

He wasn't just keeping his distance, he was pushing her away. But she had told him they'd had their fun and it was back to business. Dismissing her disappointment, she returned to scrolling through the never-ending footage of video surveillance.

It was after midnight when she spotted something. "Check this out."

She'd homed in on a masked member sitting at the bar on L1. He had an unruly mop of blond hair, a blond beard and moustache. He wore a blue button-down oxford with jeans and sat alone, nursing a glass of wine. She fast-forwarded. If a woman sat beside him, he would chat with her for a moment or two, then stop. He didn't seem to be hitting on anyone or even trying to engage in much conversation. Emerson fast-forwarded again. He finished the glass, spoke to the bartender, and retreated into the Men's room. A few moments later, he returned to his stool and ordered another glass of wine.

"Maybe he was waiting for someone who never showed, or he's shy," Stryker said.

Again, she fast-forwarded. When the lights flickered and the bartender announced last call, he ordered a shot, tossed it back, but stayed until the club closed. He walked out alone and continued on foot until he disappeared out of camera range.

"No car," Emerson said. "Or he parked somewhere else and walked over."

"There're condo buildings around the corner," Stryker said. "I'll use my IDware." Stryker placed his hand over hers, still clutching the mouse. She both craved and loved his touch.

A few clicks and they'd loaded Blondie's image.

While waiting for the software to find a match, he glanced in her direction. "You're doing a great job down here."

"I feel safe with you. And I'm over being embarrassed. You're right about the negative speak. I'm going to empower myself, even if I'm faking it."

"Nice." The longer they stared into each other's eyes, the more she liked what she saw.

Bing!

No matches found

"That can't be right," Stryker said.

"How does your program work?" she asked.

"It matches the image with the member's profile pic."

"He must not be a member."

"If he's a guest, where's the member he came with?" he asked.

"Maybe that person was playing in a suite, left with someone, or was on L2."

Stryker nodded. "Makes sense. My brain is fried. We gotta call it."

Pushing out of her chair, she stretched. "Thank you for putting in so much time to help me."

"You were the one bright spot in a very fucked-up day."

One minute he was calling her Easton, the next he was moving away from her. And now, this compliment.

"Why don't you tell me about the B&E?"

"Not giving up, are you?"

She hitched a brow and waited.

"They cut the fiber optic cables, cut the power lines, and disabled the back-up generator. They stole laptops from the FBI hacker pod. It was a targeted hit. The police and FBI are all over it."

"Are they shutting you down?"

"They're threatening to." His tone had turned gruff, his eyes cold. "The only thing that'll break this case open is if one of those motherfuckers turns on one of my laptops."

"You've got tracking devices on them."

"Damn straight."

"What can I do to help?"

"What the fuck can anyone do?" He shoved out of the chair. "If I find the SOB who did this, I'm gonna—"

She went right up to him. "I want that anger."

"No."

She hitched her hands on her hips. "Don't push me away. That's just your go-to—"

On a deep, sexy growl, he kissed her. She threw her arms around his neck while his hands kneaded her ass.

The explosion of their kiss, their fiery connection, and their lust had her raking her teeth over his tongue. Gasping for breath, she bit his lip. He ran his hands down her back, but when he clamped his hand over her breast, their kiss turned brutal. Their carnal sounds—a mixture of whimpers, groans, and grunts—had her desperate to take him inside her.

She furrowed her fingers through his hair, fisting handfuls. The kiss turned wild. Higher and higher she flew, the pulsating between her legs begging for a release. She wanted him, all of him. She wanted to feel his hardness filling her completely. She needed to finish what they'd started hours ago.

She broke the kiss, but she didn't push him away. Locked in his strong embrace, she stared into his eyes, brimming with desire, while his erection pressed against her. Her panties were wet, her body dizzy from the energy whizzing through her.

"I want your revenge fuck," she said, her voice gritty with lust.

"Hell, yeah."

Breaking free, she opened her handbag, pulled out a condom, and tossed it on the unmade bed. She tore off her jacket, set her Glock on the console, then flipped open the buttons on her shirt. When finished, she didn't slip it off her shoulders. She sauntered close and waited.

With the back of his finger, he caressed her skin. First, her chest, then the swell of each breast. His ravenous gaze making her crazy with need. He slipped his hands into the shirt, then lifted the material over her shoulders. It fell to the floor. Her attention was glued to his. His actions were slow, deliberate. He had this amazing ability to control the situation, his actions and her reactions.

Despite her accelerating heart rate, her breathing fell in line with his. She loved the level of control he exhibited. Moving slowly, she reached around and unhooked the strap. The bra fell away, leaving her breasts exposed. She pinched her already hard nipples. His husky groan turned her wetter still. "Suck my tits, Stryker. And fuck me for your own pleasure."

She shimmied out of her pants, then her thong. Now, naked, she waited...for him.

"You are so damn gorgeous. I need to be inside you."

Trembling from anticipation, she unbuttoned his shirt and helped him out of it. After he stripped out of his jeans and boxers, she stroked his cock, rubbing his wetness over the head. Her breathing had grown jagged, her body desperate to connect with his. One look into his feral eyes and she jumped into his arms and clung to him.

Beyond his beauty, there was a confidence that rocked her to her core. He was in total command, in complete control. Calm, yet intense. She'd never met anyone like him.

He laid her on the bed, then covered himself with the condom.

"I'm gonna fuck you good."

She spread her legs. The unrelenting pulsing had her groaning. He held himself up with one arm and she stroked his hard triceps. Then, he positioned himself at her opening, but he didn't press on. "Do you want me?" There was a playfulness in his voice that surprised her.

She couldn't regulate her breathing. She arched up toward his cock, nudging the head inside her. "Better," she rasped out.

He pushed on and she cried out. "So good. Deeper." He tunneled in more and stopped. She groaned through the excitement.

"Beg me, Emerson. Beg me to fuck you."

"I'm dying for you, Stryker. I need it hard and fast."

He was giving all of himself to her and she loved it. The faster and harder he pumped, the harder she gave it back to him. In and out, again and again. The fear, the loneliness, and the difficulty of her career faded away. All she saw were his beautiful eyes, locked on hers. The desire spilling from him into her, taking her higher and higher.

And then...his mouth found her nipple and she cried out. Pure, radiant pleasure had her groaning out his name as he pulled the powerful orgasm out of her.

"Oh, yes, yes. I...I." Her pussy tightened around him, and she cried out, her long impassioned groans sent him careening over the edge.

The orgasm pummeled him, the waves of pleasure quieting his troubled mind. "Fuck, Emerson. You feel so fucking good."

The sex had taken the edge off, but Emerson had been exactly what he needed. Once they'd caught their breath, she sighed.

"Revenge fucking is the way to go," she murmured.

Rooted inside her, Stryker could breathe. Something he hadn't been able to do all damn day. The anger, the fury, the revenge floated away. Being with her soothed his tormented soul.

He dropped a worshipful kiss on her mouth before letting his tongue tangle with hers some more. The kiss continued and he found himself getting worked up all over again. "You're a witch, aren't you?"

"I do own a black cat and I love Halloween."

"Look at you all relaxed."

"Crazy, huh? I forgot all about being in a windowless room below ground."

He laid beside her. "Sex, the cure for your phobia."

Stryker admired her tenacity. She might be terrified in the confined space, but she was determined to gain control over her fear. The day had been a straight-up dumpster fire, but being with Emerson had breathed life back into him.

"What did you do today?" he asked.

Instead of laying her head on his chest, she pushed up on her elbows. Normally, he wouldn't care that she didn't snuggle, but he wasn't ready to let her go yet. So, he tucked her hair behind her ear and caressed her shoulder, then her back.

"I spent most of it visiting bridal shops. Both victims were wearing a similar dress. No one carries the designer, but someone suggested I check consignment stores. Supposedly, it was a popular style a few years back."

Their moment of Zen, that brief escape, was fast behind them. *Back to fucking reality*. They cleaned up, dressed, and he shut down the computers.

Once outside, he walked her to her car. "I want to make sure you get home safely. I'll follow you."

"I'm a big girl, plus, I've got Pima to protect me."

He dipped down and kissed her. "Call me when you get home."

He rubbed the back of his neck, but the stress of the day wouldn't leave. "Today feels like a week. Is tomorrow Saturday?"

"Sure is."

"I've got to check in with my team in the morning. After that, I'm free. You wanna keep working?"

"I don't want to take up your weekend."

He shot her a smile. "Yes, you do."

"Wow, you are cocky."

"You might want to spite fuck me again."

She opened her car door and slipped inside. "You've got a point. Thanks for tonight."

"Which part?"

"The whole enchilada."

After she drove away, he hopped on his Fat Boy, pulled on his helmet, and took off in the opposite direction. As he rolled onto the main road, he regretted not following her home.

12

THE SLEEPOVER

With wine glass in hand, Emerson crawled into bed and sipped the smooth chardonnay. Pima hopped up beside her. As she petted him, her thoughts floated to Stryker. She hadn't had sex in months and she'd never been so attracted to anyone, both physically and mentally.

Being a logic-based person, she wouldn't read anything into the situation. They'd hooked up, twice. Period. As far as she was concerned, theirs was a convenience thing, for them both.

Emerson's phone buzzed with an incoming text from Justice. "Hey, Boomslang. Checking in. How was your week?"

"Long," she replied. "You?"

"Mixed bag," he texted back. "Whatcha doin'?"

"Just got home from working late. About to hit the hay. You?"

"I went to an event this week to honor fallen officers in the DMV. It was well done."

"No way! I was there. We could've said 'Hey' in person."

"Maybe we did. I met a bunch of people," he replied.

"Small world." *Should I ask him if he wants to get together for coffee?* Stryker popped into her head. *I forgot to call him.*

"Were you at the event with a guest or date?"

Was Stryker a date? No, he wasn't. "Neither. Why were you there?"

"Got invited," he replied.

She typed, "Maybe we can meet, sometime. Coffee?" *Should I send it?* She imagined Danielle encouraging her, so she hit send.

A text came in at the same time. "Coffee sometime?" he texted.

She smiled. "Sure," she texted back. "Looks like we're both thinking the same thing. I'll check my schedule and get back to you."

When no dots appeared, she called Stryker.

He answered, "Did you ditch your car and walk?"

"I'm so sorry. I forgot. I'm not used to calling anyone when I get home. I'm at home and I'm fine."

"Whatcha doing?" he asked.

"In bed, glass of wine," she replied.

"Mmm, sounds sexy."

She chuckled. "If you saw what I was wearing, you would not think I'm sexy."

"You're always sexy."

He made her smile. "Thank you."

"Emerson, you don't know me that well, but there's something I should tell you."

Here it comes. "You're in a relationship."

"No. I wouldn't have had sex with you if I was in a relationship."

"Hmm, good to know."

"I'm aware that you're self-sufficient and independent. You're a detective, so you don't need anyone to protect you. In fact, you're the one doing the protecting..."

Pause.

"I'm in your driveway."

She flew out of bed and peeked out the window. Sure enough, he was outside, straddling his motorcycle, his helmet on his lap, his phone in his hand. *That man is a whole lotta yummy.*

"Well, I'm good. Thanks for dropping by," she said, before hurrying downstairs.

She deactivated the alarm and went outside, closing the door so the cat wouldn't bolt. And she ran into his arms.

He pulled her close and kissed her so good, she melted into him.

"Did you miss me?" she asked.

"Hell, no, why would you think that?" His devilish smile lit her insides on fire.

"I just opened a bottle of wine. C'mon in."

They walked inside and she re-alarmed.

"I'm not staying," he said.

"Sure, you aren't." She led him into the kitchen and poured him a glass of wine. "If you flee the scene in the middle of the night, I'll know."

"So, I'm trapped?" He sipped the wine.

"Trapped."

"Where's demon kitty?"

"Probably waiting around the corner, planning a surprise attack. No worries. I'll protect you."

On the way upstairs, he said, "I was right."

"'Bout what?"

"How sexy you look."

They walked into her bedroom. "I'm in a tank top and pajama shorts. Hardly attractive."

"No, you're right." He kissed her. "You're stunning." He glanced around. "Can I grab a shower?"

"Towels in the closet."

He retreated into the bathroom and turned on the shower. She crawled back into bed and sipped the wine. Her phone binged with a text from Justice.

"Sorry about the delay," he texted. "Coffee sounds good."

"Great," she replied. "Looking forward to it."

A few moments later, Stryker turned off the shower. The bathroom door opened as her phone buzzed.

"Have a good weekend," Justice texted.

"You, too," she replied. "Thanks for checking in." Just as she closed the app, Stryker's phone binged.

She flicked her gaze to him and her breath caught. He was buck naked, water droplets sprinkled across his muscular shoulders and pecs. He'd used one of her hair ties to pull the sides of his hair into a bun, leaving the rest trailing down his back. Desire swept through her.

I won't be able to keep my hands off him.

"You're not working, are you?" He picked up the glass and drank down a mouthful. "It's after three in the morning."

She patted the mattress. "Just texting a friend."

He slid in beside her as Pima charged into the room, jumped onto the bed, and glared at him.

"Here we go," he grumbled.

She smiled. "He brought you a present."

The cat dropped a toy and continued staring at him.

"Throw it for him," Emerson said.

Stryker launched it out of the bedroom and it sailed into the hallway. Pima bolted after it. After leaning back on the propped pillows, he held out his glass. "To you, for being a kick-ass detective and for pushing through your fear to work in the dungeon."

She tapped her glass against his. "To you, for forgiving me, for being such a good spite fuck, and for making sure I'm safe."

After one more sip, he set his glass on the night table, and lay down.

She set down her glass, turned off the bedside light, and slid beneath the covers. Then, she pulled a condom from under her pillow. "Wow, how'd this get in my bed?"

He snaked his arms around her and pulled her onto him. Their kiss was filled with a passion that had her panting. She couldn't kiss him long enough or stroke his tongue hard enough.

"Inside me," she gasped, while stripping off her clothes.

As soon as he covered himself, she straddled him, and sunk

down. Their collective groans sent her flying higher. Emerson had one speed with Stryker.

Fast and furious.

Stryker needed to slow them down. If he didn't, it would be over too soon. He wanted to savor her, make their moment last.

Without breaking their connection, Stryker rolled them over so he was on top and in control. Because that's what he did. His kisses were soft and his thrusting was slow.

"Mmm, you feel good," she murmured.

He rose over her and worshipped her beautiful breasts. As soon as he took her nipple into his mouth, she turned into a groaning, writhing animal. He loved how responsive she was to his touch. To tease her and heighten her pleasure, he lightened the pressure.

She bucked her hips and pressed her hands against his ass, holding him hostage inside her. With a sly smile, she murmured, "You think you've got all the power, but you don't."

He stopped moving inside her. "I'm crazy attracted to you. If we keep up all this hard fucking, I won't last long."

She repositioned herself beneath him and he sunk in a little more. Then, she raised her arms over her head and said, "I like being trapped beneath you." Her voice was filled with a huskiness that made him harder still.

"That arouses you?" he murmured.

In the dimly lit room, her gaze darkened. "A lot. Makes for a good revenge fuck…I'm your prisoner and you get to have your way with me."

He wouldn't have pegged her for someone into CNC—consensual non-consent—role playing. "You'll tell me if I'm too rough?"

She hitched a brow. "Stryker, when have I been shy about speaking up?"

"Right."

"This is a fantasy I've had for a long time," she whispered. "It's dark. I've never told anyone about this, because I'm a LEO."

"What does your zodiac sign have to do with your fantasies?"

She smiled up at him. "L.E.O. Law enforcement officer." After wrapping her arms around him, she kissed him. One kiss led to several until he deepened their embrace. Wetness flooded her core as their kissing intensified.

"Let me go," she uttered. "You're keeping me here against my will." She started wiggling out from under him, as if trying to escape, then, she bit his earlobe.

He held her arms over her head and thrust harder. "You're mine," he murmured. "And I can do whatever the hell I want to you, whenever I want to."

When he increased his speed and intensity, her breathing turned jagged and her moans deep.

"Oh, God, Stryker." She climaxed hard beneath him, her insides squeezing him, and he surrendered to the pleasure.

Spasms of glorious ecstasy rocked him again and again. For the next moment or two, the monsters that plagued him would be silenced.

Nestled inside her, he snuggled close while being careful not to drop his full weight on her small frame. They breathed in sync until she broke the silence with an occasional sigh. She stroked his back while he trailed his fingers gently over her breast and around her tender nipple. Moments passed in a comforting silence.

"I wasn't expecting that kind of role play," he said, moving beside her.

"Too much?" Her brows pinched together with concern.

He ran his fingers through her soft hair, dropped a kiss on her mouth. "I love that you're full of surprises."

Relief softened her expression. "Do you have a fantasy you've never told anyone?"

"I do."

She rolled toward him. "Tell me."

"I'm always in control. For once, I'd like the woman to take charge. To dominate me."

"Hmm," she said while stroking his skin. "I wouldn't have expected that from you."

"Maybe we're talking too much." He retreated into the bathroom to remove the condom, and returned a moment later.

After he crawled back into bed, she said, "I'm guessing that in a scene, the people involved discuss it beforehand, so there're no surprises. Maybe we should do that next time."

"All I heard was there's gonna be a next time."

She smiled. "Busted." Her smile fell away. "I want you to know, I'm assuming you have a few sex partners at The Dungeon. That's your business, but I don't want to hear—"

"Only you. I've been celibate for over four months."

She shot him a little smile. "But you own a kink club. What's up with that?"

"A club member stalked me. I got a restraining order and blocked her from coming back, but that was it for me."

She stroked his penis. "Welcome back, my friend."

He smiled. "Are all your fantasies dark?"

"No."

"When did they start?"

"In college," she explained. "They don't make sense, especially since I'm a homicide detective. A lot of my victims are powerless over their assailants." She shrugged a shoulder. "But a sexual fantasy is very different from an act of violence. I choose mine. They don't."

"I like that you speak your mind."

"Thank you."

They fell silent for a moment.

"Earlier, in the elevator, you told me you admired me because I'm fearless," he murmured. "Truth is, I'm not. Two things scare the hell out of me."

She waited.

"Your demon cat."

She smiled. "And?"

"Never finding my mother's killer."

"Oh, wow. What happened to her?"

"Another time." He kissed her forehead. "Thanks for letting me crash here."

She fell asleep in minutes, but he lay awake thinking about the woman in his arms. A year and a half ago, she'd turned his life upside down. Was this something that could work, long term, or just a convenience thing?

He woke with the cat camped out between his feet while Emerson lay sprawled over his chest, her hair tickling his chin. He loved waking with her in his arms.

As soon as he moved, Pima started purring.

Emerson leaned up and kissed him. "Still here, huh?"

"I'm trapped, remember? House alarm?"

"Lucky me."

Pushing up, she combed her fingers through his hair and stroked his whiskered cheeks. "Your aunt is amazing. How is it that she and your uncle don't hate me?"

"Hate you? Why?"

"For what I put you through."

"The charge was dropped, the ACPD issued a formal apology, and the pimp was caught. Heather and Gordon thought it was a misunderstanding, plus, they were dealing with some crazy stuff themselves."

She pushed out of bed. "Roll onto your stomach."

"Why?"

She retrieved a bottle of body oil from the bathroom. "Because I told you to."

As he rolled over, she pulled off the linens and straddled his backside. And then, she started rubbing his shoulders.

"That feels phenomenal," he said.

When she found a knot, she dug her knuckles into it, then ran her fingers along the muscle until she kneaded it smooth. He lost track of time. Reality faded, leaving only calm. After his back, she massaged his arms, then his glutes. She finished by giving him a foot rub.

"A present for you," she whispered. "Do you want a happy ending?"

He rolled onto his back. "I would love one, but you—"

"You've been very generous with your time," she said. "And you have none to spare. This is my way of saying thank you."

Stryker couldn't take his eyes off her as she stroked his shaft and ran her soft fingers around the wet head. With his balls in one hand, she took her time massaging him. With a sultry smile, she leaned over him and kissed him while he fondled her breasts. Her pace never changed, nor did the pressure. The build was luxurious, the release explosive. As he floated in bliss, she kissed him, then cleaned him up.

"I'm going to make us breakfast," she whispered. She gave him one more tender kiss before she pulled on her tank top and shorty shorts. "C'mon, Pima."

He opened his eyes. "Emerson."

In the doorway, she turned back.

"You are a witch and I've fallen under your spell."

She waggled her eyebrows and was gone. On a very satisfied, groan, he rolled out of bed and padded into the bathroom. He had no memory of the last time he'd felt *that* relaxed.

After throwing on his clothes, he found her sipping coffee at the table, staring out the bay window. He poured himself a mug and sat. "Thank you."

"If only life was always that carefree." Her smile was sad. "Being a cop keeps things real, you know?"

He wrapped his hand around the back of her neck and kissed her cheek. "You want me to relax you like that?"

"Another time," she said. "That was for you."

"I loved it."

She rose. "I'm making omelets. You hungry?"

"I'll help."

Together, they made breakfast, then sat at the table. After a few bites, he asked, "Why wasn't your brother one of the officers honored?"

"Because he died of a drug overdose."

He ran a hand over her back for comfort. "That's tough. I'm sorry."

She forked egg into her mouth, swallowed it down with orange juice. "The police found his body behind a dumpster. He was jacked with so much heroin and fentanyl, he didn't stand a chance. Someone wanted to make damn sure he didn't survive." Tears filled her eyes and his heart broke.

"Drug abusers can be good at hiding their addiction," he said.

"Here's the thing about Doug. He didn't smoke weed in college. He never did drugs of any kind. Never smoked or vaped. He broke up with someone because he found out she was a total coke head, but not before he tried to get her help. When she wouldn't stop using, he moved on. He participated in the Ironman, more than once. He was into eating healthy and taking care of his body. He was super muscular and fit like you. I am convinced someone killed him and made it look like he'd OD'd."

"What kind of work was he doing?"

"Undercover with ACPD. One night, about a month before he died, he confided that he was close to making several arrests. I think he wanted me to know in case something went wrong."

"Did the department investigate his death?" Stryker asked.

"They did, but it went nowhere because there were no witnesses and no one saw or heard anything. I asked to see his police reports and was denied access. I was told that sometimes cops do drugs in order to fit in. That's bullshit."

"I'll help you," he said.

Her eyes grew large. "What?"

"I'll help you."

"No, you don't have to."

"Try to stop me. Your super powers aren't that strong."

She smiled through the tears in her eyes and grabbed the coffee pot. As she topped them off, she said, "Maybe another time. You've got so much going on."

"What do you need?"

She returned the carafe and sat down. After pausing to drink, she studied him for a minute. "To read his police reports."

"What am I looking for exactly?"

"He never told me what group or organization he'd infiltrated."

"Coulda been organized crime, drugs, government corruption. Lots of options. I'll see what damage I can do."

She placed both hands on his face and kissed him. "Thank you. I have to follow my gut on this one."

"We can do it together."

"I like the sound of that," she said.

So do I.

His phone buzzed with an incoming call. "It's my Veep," he said to Emerson before answering. "What's goin' on?"

"Cooper just got here," Brooks said. "I think we've got a chance of convincing him to suspend the government accounts only. Can you join me?"

"Be there in thirty." Stryker hung up.

She started clearing the table.

"Let me help you," he said.

She snaked her arms around him and kissed him. "Go. Now." She walked him to the front door and unalarmed. "Good luck."

He flashed a smile. "I stole one of your hair ties." He hopped on his bike, pulled on his helmet, and took off.

As Emerson dressed, she felt sexually satisfied and…hopeful. Happy was too much of a stretch. She hadn't been happy in months.

Despite it being the weekend, she had a lot of work to do, so she stopped by the precinct to check out the key to April's apartment, then drove to the apartment complex. Once inside, she spoke with April's next-door neighbor. The chatty woman knew very little.

As she made her way to April's apartment, her phone rang with an incoming call. "Detective, Easton."

"Hey, Detective, it's Lyle Barnham, *DMV* Magazine. How ya doin'?"

She was hoping Lyle had forgotten about her. "Hi, Lyle."

"If you're working today, any chance I could join you?"

Refusing him wasn't gonna fly. She'd already gotten her hand slapped for that. "I'm at a crime scene."

He gasped. "There was another murder?"

"No, I'm returning to a crime scene of one of my victims. Do you want to meet me?"

"Sure."

She gave him the address and hung up. Before entering April's apartment, she covered her hands and shoes in disposable gloves and footies. While the tech team had already collected their evidence, she didn't want to contaminate the scene, especially if she found a reason to call them back. She went straight into April's bedroom. Her gaze fell on the now empty bed, the vision of April's body still fresh in her memory. A chill ran through her.

After searching through the bureau drawers, she found nothing besides clothing, all folded neatly. There was nothing in April's night table drawer that caught her eye, either.

Her phone rang. "Hey, Lyle. Are you here?"

"I'm outside," he replied. "Can you come down?"

Emerson wanted to leave him out there.

"Never mind," Lyle said. "A resident let me in. Where you at?"

She was waiting in the hallway when he sauntered in her direction. "Hey, Detective."

"Put these on." She handed him gloves and shoe coverings.

"I'm not gonna touch anything," he said as he pulled on the protective gear.

"Good idea."

"Why are you here?" he asked.

She was relieved he'd brought along a pen and a notebook. She couldn't deal with his phone shoved in her face while he pummeled her with questions.

Once inside, she closed the door behind him. "I'm looking for any evidence the crime techs might've overlooked."

She returned to April's bedroom and continued searching. To her surprise, Lyle didn't bombard her with questions. He stood quietly in the doorway. Emerson searched every pocket of April's clothes, but came up empty. She had no luck in the second bedroom, either.

"What crime was committed here?" Lyle asked when Emerson entered the living area.

"Remember the photos you saw of the woman who'd been murdered?"

"Yeah."

"She lived here."

"So tragic," he said. "Her family must be devastated."

"They are."

"Mind if I ask you a few questions about that?"

"Based on the complaint you filed against me, I don't think I can refuse you."

His shoulders dropped. "Sorry about that. My boss is pushing for stories that draw readers in."

"Don't you mean stories that sell magazines?"

"Did you locate her family?"

"Yes."

"What did you tell them?"

"That she died."

"What, exactly, did you say? Did you mention the crime scene?"

"What about the crime scene?"

"These photos you showed me were pretty creepy. I mean, a wedding dress. Who kills a bride on her wedding night?"

Rather than explain to Lyle that she was dealing with a possible serial killer, she said nothing.

"How was she murdered, again?"

"Autopsy report isn't back yet."

"Who did you speak to?"

"Her brother."

"Was he devastated?"

"Of course." She regarded him. "Why wouldn't he be?"

"I doubt *my* parents —" He shook his head. "I'm trying to get an understanding of how things go down during a murder investigation."

What the hell is going on with him?

"Does he have to visit the morgue to ID her?"

"Someone local did that."

"How do you go about finding this woman's husband?"

"So, you think both victims were killed by their husbands?"

"They were murdered in their wedding dresses. Who else would've done it?"

He's clueless. "I'm gonna get back to work," Emerson said. "We can talk more later."

Emerson checked under the sofa cushions. Crumbs. There was a small desk tucked in the corner. The antique reminded her of an old-style writing table. Emerson lowered the lid. A box of note cards with the words, "A world of thanks from April" lay unused in their plastic container. Emerson's heart ached. April would never get to use those cards.

She opened the bottom doors and pulled out a small wooden box filled with a couple dozen business cards. The top one was from a doctor's office. The next was from a hair salon. The third was a freelance photographer. She closed the lid.

Lyle knelt beside her. "What do you do with those?"

"I call them." Emerson slid the box into an evidence bag.

After checking the kitchen, and finding nothing, she told Lyle she was done. In the hallway, they removed their shoe covers and gloves.

"Where are you headed next?" he asked.

"I'm going to a wedding gown consignment boutique in Alexandria."

"Can I tag along?"

She gave him the address, but he ended up following her. After introducing herself to the shop owner, Emerson asked about the designer.

"That designer was very popular a few years back. I've got several different styles. The dresses are organized by price. Do you have a picture of the gown?"

The coroner had removed Gloria Stanton's dress and a crime tech had snapped a pic of it on a hanger. Emerson showed the saleswoman the picture.

"I have several of those."

While Emerson went through the dresses, Lyle spent a moment chatting with the owner. A few women entered the store, so Lyle moseyed over.

"Any luck?" he asked.

Emerson pulled a gown. "This one is similar to the dress found on one of the victims."

While Emerson waited for the owner to finish helping her customers, Lyle asked her if this type of crime happened a lot.

She was done answering questions. "Who else have you interviewed for your article?"

"Just you, so far. I'm talking with a crime tech, a Media Relations officer, two detectives, and a few more people."

"Have you interviewed Detective Cardoso?"

"Not yet," Lyle replied.

The boutique owner ambled over. "Sorry to keep you waiting."

Emerson held out the dress. "Do you remember speaking with anyone about a dress like this?"

A bridal party entered the shop.

"I'm sorry. Can you come back during the week?" the woman asked. "Saturdays are my busiest and I'm short staffed. Mondays and Tuesdays are slow."

"Thanks for your help. I'll be back." Emerson snapped a picture of the wedding dress.

As she and Lyle headed out, he asked if she wanted to grab a sandwich. "We can continue discussing your case. I love my job, but yours sounds way more exciting. Plus, you've got a badge and you get to carry a gun."

"It's not like crime shows on TV. I spend a lot of time chasing leads that go nowhere. Plus, I work some crazy hours."

"I think I'd like to be a cop. Maybe one day. It would be so cool to hunt down a killer, but probably way more frustrating."

"Why is that?"

"They're almost impossible to catch."

Lyle followed her to a nearby eatery. After ordering and paying, they found an empty table outside.

"How long have you worked for *DMV* Magazine?" Emerson asked.

"A while."

"Do you write multiple stories at a time?"

"They're in depth, so I focus on one at a time." He bit into his sandwich. After swallowing it down, he said, "I did a story on Internet scams. It took me months, but it was the magazine's top selling issue all year."

"Good for you. You mentioned grad school. Where are you going?"

"George Mason."

"You must be busy. What do you do for fun?"

"Hang out with cool cops like you." He smiled. "How 'bout you, Detective? What do you do for fun?"

Stryker Truman. I do Stryker Truman. "I work a lot." She didn't want Lyle writing anything about her, so she asked him another question. "Are you from the area?"

"I'm a transplant from Florida."

"The cold weather must've been a shock. Had you seen snow before?"

"Oh, sure. My grandfather lives up here. We visit him every Christmas."

"We?"

"Me, and my mom and dad."

"Are you close to your parents?"

Lyle stiffened. "Not really, but they let me live in their guest house for free." That made him smile. "I like not having to pay rent."

"I hear you on that," Emerson said. "It's expensive around here. When you're not working on a story or studying, do you hang with grad school friends?"

"I'm too busy to party."

For some reason, Lyle didn't strike her as a loner, but it appeared he was. "Do you have someone special in your life?"

"I used to," he replied. "But things didn't work out." He finished his soda. "Hey, I thought I was the one asking the questions."

"You've asked plenty for one day."

"One more," he said. "What do you like most about being a homicide detective?"

"Catching the bad guys," she replied.

13

THE DINNER DATE

Stryker felt damn good, and he had the fiery detective to thank for the uptick in his normally dark mood.

After parking at his office, he turned his attention to his latest challenge—ensuring the FBI didn't suspend all operations during their investigation. As he made his way toward the building, his phone rang. Another blocked caller.

"What?" he growled.

"You having yourself a good morning, my friend?" Spinetti's gruff voice dripped in sarcasm. "I sure as hell am."

His blood turned to ice in his veins. "Stop calling me."

"I heard you had a break-in," Spinetti continued. "That must've been a bitch for ya. I gotta say, I hate when I'm having a good day and then, *bam!* some asshole comes along and fucks it up."

Every muscle in Stryker's neck went stiff and a growl shot out of him. "Admitting to a crime, Spinetti?"

"Listen up, motherfucker, I'm sitting here with nothing to play with but my dick. People talk. I listen. That ain't a crime."

"You come near me or my businesses again, I'll rip your no-good heart out and shove it down your—"

"You could get arrested for threatening a helpless old man in prison."

Stryker hung up and marched inside. Brooks was talking with an employee in the atrium.

"Where's Cooper?" Stryker bit out.

Brooks pointed across the lobby. Cooper was on the phone. Seething with anger, he waited for Cooper to finish. The familiar feeling pulsed through him, sending fury through every fucking cell in his body. His blood pressure shot up, he clenched his fists. Spinetti had orchestrated the whole thing from his damn prison cell.

After Cooper hung up, he made his way over to Stryker. "I've got good news."

"Spinetti called me again." A growl ripped from Stryker's throat. "That son of a bitch pulled this off from his fucking prison cell."

"He admitted to it?"

"He said, 'I heard you had a break-in.'"

"Relax, he's goading you. This is way out of his league."

"You think?" Stryker pushed back. "You told me you thought he had a contract out on me."

"You, not your company."

"Bro, his crew breaks in to the FBI pod, but no other pod is breached. C'mon, Cooper. Help me out here."

"Fine, I'll have an agent look into it."

"That's not gonna cut it."

"I said I'll have an agent look into it. Let it go, Stryker."

The two men glared at each other until Cooper pinned on a triumphant smile. "I've got good news."

At this point, Stryker was too pissed to care.

"We're only suspending your government accounts and I'll oversee the investigation to make sure it stays on track," Cooper said.

Stryker scraped his fingers through his whiskers. "What about Spinetti?"

"For fuck's sake, I had to sell this to every single person I talked to. I did this because we're friends—close friends—but you're pissing me the hell off right now."

Stryker had definitely struck a nerve. Cooper was one of his most laid-back friends. "You're right. I'm sorry, dog. You did go to bat for me and you hit a home run."

"Fuck the baseball analogy. You hate baseball."

Stryker chuffed out a laugh. "Look, I *am* grateful for what you did. Suspending the government accounts is bad, but shutting us down would have been a total cluster. Thank you."

"There, was that so difficult?" Cooper held up his hand. "Don't answer that."

"What's next?" Stryker asked.

"I've got to talk to Brooks." Both men approached Stryker's VP as he finished up with an IT employee. When she went back upstairs, Cooper told Brooks the good news.

Brooks broke into a grin and shook Cooper's hand. "Man, you are the best. This is a huge relief. I can live with this."

Cooper arched his eyebrow at Stryker. "See? Now, that's gratitude."

"What'd I say?" Brooks asked.

"I wasn't grateful enough," Stryker replied, "and Cooper was driving his point home because you were grateful enough for both of us."

With a chuckle, Brooks slapped Cooper on the back. "You've known Stryker longer than I have. He's the bad cop so, you and I have to be the good ones."

"You got that right," Cooper replied. "I'll be in touch with you early next week. If you find out that any of the other pods were breached —"

"I just got confirmation no other pods were broken into," Brooks explained. "So, you think the investigation'll run a few months?"

"I'm hoping a few weeks," Cooper answered.

"I'm taking off," Stryker said. "Brooks, you good?"

"I got this," Brooks replied.

"Thank you," Stryker said.

"Oh, sure, with Brooks you've got good manners," Cooper ground out.

Stryker laughed as he and Cooper walked outside. The bright sun had them fishing out their shades.

"What's the word on your promotion?" Stryker asked.

"I'm hearing rumors I'm moving west."

"Got other options?"

"No."

"You want another option?"

Cooper regarded him for an extra beat. "What are you thinking?"

"Something you might love."

"I'd love a beautiful blonde, a sunny day, and a yacht," Cooper said.

"You've got a boat."

"I want a bigger one."

"Emerson's friend, Danielle, you met her at Raphael's—"

"I remember her. She was hot."

"She asked about you."

"Nice." Cooper's smile fell away. "Won't matter if I move across the country."

"You might not have to," Stryker replied.

"Seriously? What's going on?"

"Give me a coupla days. I've gotta talk to someone. By the way, where's he serving?" Stryker asked.

"Who?"

"Spinetti."

"Oh, no, don't even think about it."

"Tell me, don't tell me. I'll find out."

"He's in a minimum-security camp in Cumberland." Cooper stared at him. "Let us do our job, Stryker. Do *not* poke the bear."

Stryker grinned. "Poking the bear is what I do best."

Two hours later, Stryker was signing in at the minimum-security prison in western Maryland. After leaving his weapon at the front desk, a guard escorted him to a visitation room. His blood ran cold as he made his way toward Spinetti. The fit, silver-haired man showed no emotion as Stryker took a seat across the table. Slight in stature with a weathered face, Spinetti crossed his arms over his chest.

Time to play this cool. Stryker remained silent and stone faced.

The prison garb was the only indication Spinetti was in prison. No shackles, no handcuffs. White collar prison was no picnic, but it was called "camp" for a reason.

"I musta gotten your attention if you drove all the way to fucking nowheresville." Spinetti smirked.

"The B&E at my company was impressive. I wanted to congratulate you in person."

Leaning forward, Spinetti steepled his fingers, as if in prayer. "I'm an eighty-year-old, retired businessman. At the end of my career, I get convicted of Internet fraud. I come to find out, you, Mr. Truman, are a fancy-pants hacker. The best in the biz, they tell me. You planted things in my computer, the FBI arrested me and voila, I'm in *camp* for the rest of my life. These assholes can call it whatever they want…it's still a damn prison."

"You dug your own grave, Spinetti."

"You interrupted a class I'm takin'. History one-oh-one. It's enchantin'." His smoker's laugh was thick with mucous.

"I want my laptops back before things get real ugly."

"Now you know how it feels when someone fucks with your business, but I got nothin' to do with your problem. I'm stuck here. What do I know about life on the outside?"

"Last chance."

Spinetti tapped his fingers on the table, his eyes cold. "What laptops?"

"If I don't get my computers back, you'll regret it."

"Again, with the threats." Spinetti's lips split open in a menacing grin. "Didn't your sweet lil' mama teach you manners?"

Stryker pounded his fist on the table. "Don't you fucking mention my mother," he growled. "She put scumbags like you away."

"Like mama, like son. You two deserve each other." Spinetti left and Stryker shoved out of the chair, sending it toppling over.

On his way out, Stryker picked up his Glock. Then, he drove for miles in a fuming silence. Spinetti was going to pay for what he'd done. Stryker didn't know how or when, but he sure as hell knew why.

Back at the precinct, Emerson plopped down in her chair. After lunch, she'd finally been able to ditch Lyle without hurting his feelings. The last thing she needed was him complaining about her again.

She pulled the business cards from the evidence bag and began making calls. The doctor's office would re-open on Monday. She called the hair salon and spoke with the stylist. The young woman told Emerson she'd cut April's hair a couple of times, but didn't remember anything about her. The third business card—Casey Quinn Photography—didn't have a phone number, email address, or website. She did an Internet search, but found nothing, so she Googled his name. There were dozens of men and women named Casey Quinn.

Nikki strolled up to her desk. "Hey, what's happening?"

"Zero," Emerson replied. "I got nothing. You?"

"Since we don't have April's phone, I filed records requests with all the wireless carriers. We'll hear back soon." Nikki peered into the small wooden box. "Whatcha got?"

"I found this at April's."

Nikki sat. "We can split them up." She glanced over her shoulder before leaning close. "I overheard someone in UC mention that Toby's working the case Doug had."

"What did he say?"

"He's made inroads with a drug gang."

"Anything else?"

"They're tight-lipped, so it's gonna be a while before he gets any legit names."

Emerson's hopes fizzled. *That's not news.* "Thanks for letting me know."

Nikki took a handful of business cards and returned to her desk. Turning back to her task, Emerson called the realtor.

"Hi, this is Cathy."

"Hi, Cathy, this is Detective Easton, Arlington County Police."

"I already donated."

"I'm calling about the homicide investigation of April Peters. I found your business card in her things."

"Hmm. I remember her. She contacted me a number of months ago. She wanted to rent, but everything I showed her was out of her price range. I suggested she use a roommate finder and share a place."

"Did she ever bring anyone with her when you took her apartment hunting?"

"No, she was alone."

"Did she mention a boyfriend, significant other, or a special friend?"

"I don't remember. Was she a short gal with purple hair?"

"No, she was average height with long, dark brown hair."

"Oh, I've confused her with someone else I had worked with. I'm sorry, I don't remember her."

After thanking her, Emerson hung up. "So frustrating."

Bing!

She glanced at the incoming email, then clicked on it.

"Are you reading?" Nikki called over.

"Sure am."

The results of the tox report were in. April Peters had died from asphyxiation due to strangulation. Like their first victim, the drug, ketamine, had been found in her blood stream.

Nikki rushed over. "How did we get this back so quickly?"

"The Captain must've called in a favor," Emerson said. "I've never gotten a tox report back this fast."

"You mentioned reviewing surveillance at the club. Any progress?"

"It's slow going. Everyone talks to the bartender, but a lot of the members are masked."

"Do you think the perp met April at The Dungeon?"

"Possible, but the first vic wasn't a member."

"I'm thinking we stake out the place," Nikki said. "It's easier to catch a killer if we put ourselves in his path."

"Good idea. I'll mention it to the owner."

Around three thirty, Nikki dropped the cards in the wooden box. "No luck."

Emerson flipped through the cards Nikki had taken. "With any of these?"

Nikki held up the librarian's card. "She had no clue who April was." Nikki flashed the pharmacy business card. "The clerk needs a warrant to disclose whether April had any prescriptions on file."

Nikki held up the nail salon card. "Another dead end."

Emerson flashed a card. "This is the second freelance photographer's card. I'm hoping she remembers April."

"What about the first one?"

Emerson showed her Casey Quinn's card. "No phone number and I couldn't find a website. There are dozens of men and women with this name. Another dead end."

"Not dead, just stalled," Nikki said. "I've gotta leave. We're taking the kids to a family birthday celebration. Tell me you're not working tomorrow. It's Sunday. You've been working these cases 'round the clock."

"I'm spending the day with my folks."

"How are they doing?"

"One day at a time," Emerson replied.

"Try to relax tomorrow. I'll see you Monday." Nikki grabbed her bag and left.

Emerson's cell phone buzzed with a call from Stryker and her heart skipped a beat. "Hey, what's the word?" she answered.

"Pissed off," he replied.

"That's two words. Does that mean the man I massaged to nirvana is gone?"

"Long gone. What are you doing?"

"I'm at the office, chasing my tail."

"You learn that from Pima?"

She smiled. "How'd things go with the FBI?"

"They're only suspending government accounts during their investigation."

"That's great. You gotta count that as a win."

"Have dinner with me tonight."

"You mean, at the club, while we work?"

"No, at my place."

Her pulse quickened. *Wow.* "I'd love to. What can I pick up?"

"Nothing. After, we can head to the club." He gave her his address. "What won't you eat?"

"Octopus, squid…anything with more than four legs."

That made him chuckle. "You eat steak?"

"Sure." She hesitated. "You up for this?"

"Yeah. How's seven?"

"See you then." Knowing he was her reward, she kicked up the effort and rolled through the business cards. Unfortunately, none panned out. Though frustrated, she didn't expect the evidence would fall in her lap. She'd just been hoping for a little break, that's all.

She shut down and went home to get ready. After playing with Pima, she showered, slipped into a sundress and sandals, and put on a little makeup. For Stryker, she threw her hair into a casual updo. *No, this is more like a drunk did my hair.* She pulled out the clips and pulled it into pigtails that she braided, starting at chin level.

At ten past seven, she turned down Stryker's street in an upscale neighborhood of Great Falls and stopped in front of his estate. *Whoa, that's impressive.* The magnificent stone-front, two-story home boasted impeccable gardens and a freshly-mowed, landscaped lawn. She'd envisioned him in something less...regal.

With a bottle of wine in hand, she made her way up the driveway.

For a woman who rarely got rattled, her heart was hammering away when she rang the doorbell. Part nerves, part excitement. *Is this a date? No, it's a working dinner and it's no big deal.* In truth, it was a big deal. She liked him, a lot.

He swung open the front door, and her heart ka-thumped in her chest. He'd worn a pair of baggy shorts, a tight gray T-shirt that accentuated his bulging biceps, and had pulled his hair up into a bun. She loved that he was barefoot. Chill Stryker was scorching hot.

"You look amazing," he said as she crossed the threshold.

He shut the door, wrapped those strapping arms around her, and kissed her breathless.

"Wow, that was intense," she murmured.

"We need to get in bed and stay there. I'm done with fucking reality."

"That bad?"

As he walked toward his kitchen, she admired the open floor plan. Modern décor filled the living and family rooms, the modern furniture perfectly suited to each space. His kitchen was downright spectacular. Masculine, yet filled with warmth. Dark-grain cabinets paired with a white marble backsplash, white marble counters and an oversized island with four elegant bar stools. Over the center island, dangling lights twinkled like stars. The stainless-steel appliances shone like new.

"Wow, your home is...it's beautiful. I love this kitchen."

"I bought the house as an investment. All I do is crash here and eat breakfast. I'm too busy to enjoy it."

"Did you furnish it?"

"My sister picked everything out. She did a great job."

Two New York Strip steaks waited on the counter beside several washed vegetables. Two large russet potatoes baked in the oven.

For the first time in years, Emerson wanted this to be a date. A regular date with a regular guy, but as she eyed the god of a man before her, she knew that Stryker was anything but regular.

"Steaks, potatoes, salad." His smile melted her. "You good with that?"

"Sounds perfect." She held out the Chianti. "For you."

"One of my favorite wineries." He set the bottle on the counter, lifted her onto the island, wrapped his arms around her waist and kissed her. "I can't stop thinking about you."

She kissed him back. "I know the feeling."

"Everything agitates the hell out of me, except you."

That made her smile. "I was once at the top of that list."

"And now, you're my sanctuary."

Oh, my God. Her heart soared. "So romantic." She tugged him close and kissed him. "You're mine, too," she whispered.

After holding her close, he kissed her temple. Without another word, he broke away to uncork the wine bottle. That's when she glimpsed the anguish in his eyes. The divot between his brows was there, too. Whatever demons haunted this man, they were always present.

He poured two glasses and offered her one. "To chasing justice," she said.

For some reason, that made him smile. "Chasing justice." He tapped her glass and they both drank down a mouthful.

"Good stuff," he said. "Thanks for bringing this."

"What's got you so angry?"

He pulled out a wooden cutting board and started slicing the hell out of a celery stalk. She put her hand on his shoulder. "Talk to me."

He tossed the diced celery into a salad bowl. "Heard of Carlo Spinetti?"

"No." She hopped down and held up the head of romaine lettuce. "Washed?"

"No. Spinetti's at a minimum-security camp in Western Maryland for Internet fraud. I helped the Bureau put him there."

"Nice," she replied, while rinsing the lettuce.

"I'm convinced he's responsible for the breach at my company." She studied him for a beat. "Oh, boy. What did you do?"

He shot her a smile. "What makes you think—"

"Oh, no, did you visit him?" She tore lettuce leaves and began dropping them into the bowl.

"I drove west and ended up in Cumberland."

Though she shook her head at him, she couldn't wipe the smirk. "How'd it go?"

"He's claiming to be a legit businessman and accused me of planting evidence on his computer that got him arrested." Stryker grew silent while sipping the wine, then he offered her his glass.

After sipping, she said, "Getting me drunk won't stop me from lecturing you."

"Sounds like something a girlfriend or wife would do."

"Being that I'm neither, I'm putting on my LEO hat."

"Here we go with the zodiac signs again."

"I'm serious. You're making this worse for yourself."

"The hit on my company was orchestrated by Spinetti."

"I get your need for control, but you gotta let the feds do their job."

He stopped slicing cucumber and shifted his gaze to her. The coldness in his eyes sent a shudder through her.

"But you aren't going to leave this alone, are you?" she asked.

"People get away with things every day," he replied. "Might be a lie. Or it could be something like killing April Peters or Doug Easton."

That got her full attention.

"You told me about your brother, but not because you trust me. You knew I'd do more than offer you sympathy. You wanted help."

She stilled. She was chastising him for protecting his business, even though she was willing to circumvent the rules in order to get justice for Doug.

"I'm sorry," she said. "You're right."

"I get that you're doing your job, but sometimes it takes more than following the letter of the law to make things right," he said before moving on to slice up a red bell pepper. "As I see it, the bad guys are winning."

"My hands are tied." She dropped a handful of cherry tomatoes into the salad. "I've got to follow the law."

"Well, I don't." He lifted the tray of steaks. "Time to grill these bad boys." With a wink, he walked onto his screened porch while his words echoed in her head.

He was right. His desire for justice was no different from hers. *Would I exact revenge if I found the person who killed Doug?* She stood there mired in thought. Would she trust the system to bring that person to justice, or right the scales herself? A shiver ran up her spine, the hairs at the back of her neck stood on end. For the first time in her life, the answer wasn't clear to her.

She walked through the spacious porch and onto his deck, where she found him grilling. Their eyes met. He placed his hand on her back over her tat and caressed her skin. His touch affected her like no other. She inhaled a deep, calming breath and let it go.

"Thank you for keeping this real," she said. "You trust me and I'm grateful for that."

He leaned down, dropped a light kiss on her lips. "One step at a time, right? For now, all I need to know is how do you like your steak."

She chuffed out a laugh. "Medium."

After he flipped the meat, she said, "You're right. I've always followed the law, respected the rules that were put in place. The ones that the lawbreakers disregard. If we found the people who killed my brother, I want to believe I'd turn them in. But I don't know. I'm ashamed to think that I might want to take their lives because they took Doug's. I took an oath to serve and protect, not break the law myself. This should be cut and dry for me, but it's not and that worries me."

He clasped her hand, kissed her palm. "I never said I was going to do anything once I got answers. I only said I wanted to find them. I've been searching for the truth for twenty years. Some days, I doubt I'll ever find it."

I'm lost. What's he saying?

He lifted the grill lid, checked the steaks.

"What are you talking about?" she asked.

"Nothing. Wanna eat outside?"

"Are you talking about your mom's killer?"

A brief sadness flitted across his face. This man fascinated her, yet she knew so little about him. He'd been generous with his time and understanding about her phobia. He'd forgiven her for charging him with a crime he hadn't committed, and he was mired in his own problems at work.

Step it up and be there for him, like he's been there for you.

He set the cooked steaks on the spare plate. Ignoring her question, he said, "You okay eating on the porch?"

"Absolutely."

They returned to the kitchen, plated their meals, and sat side-by-side at the round patio table on his screened porch. "This room is beautiful. I would live out here in the warm months."

The oversized room was first class all the way. A six-chaired table and fully-stocked bar filled one half of the room, and a gathering space filled the other half. Large, wrought iron chairs with deep cushions flanked a cream sofa that faced the stone fireplace. A large flat-screen TV was mounted on the wall.

"Life is complicated," he said. "Don't overthink our conversation. I'm glad you're here with me." He tipped the wine glass to his lips and drank.

She dragged her gaze away to slice into her meat. "My steak is perfect." As she chewed, she mulled if she should press him for information. He was so closed off.

Do it.

"Tell me what happened to your mom."

He said nothing while he chewed, and swallowed his food down with another mouthful of Chianti. "I invited you over because I wanted to chill with you. We've been thrown together to chase a killer. Don't you want to talk about something else besides—"

"Not really." She stroked his arm. "I want to talk about something—*someone*—who matters to you. You've been doing nothing but help me. First, with my case, then, my phobia, and then, I threw Doug in because, well, three's a charm."

He stayed quiet.

"And let's not forget all the mayhem happening with your company." She forked salad into her mouth and paused to eat it. "Like I said, you're fearless. I admire that about you."

"You're pretty damn fearless yourself, Easton."

Stryker liked making Emerson smile, especially when he complimented her. Her cheeks flushed and the strong-willed detective softened. He liked both sides of this intriguing woman.

In truth, he didn't want to talk about his mom. That would only further frustrate him. Spinetti had pissed him off plenty for one day.

"Tell me about your day," he said.

She regarded him for a few seconds, her gaze floating over his face while she furrowed her brow. "Is this your way of telling me you don't want to talk about your mom?"

"Not now."

"I found a box of business cards at April's apartment. My partner, Nikki, and I spent the afternoon calling most of the people."

"Any luck?"

"No. But Nikki had a great suggestion. Can you get us a fake membership or put us on your VIP list at your club?"

"What's she thinking?"

"We'd hang out at the club and see if we could lure the killer, assuming he's there."

"You'll attract every hetero man in that place. Most'll want to bed you. The rest'll want to set up some kinky scene with you. A few will want to talk to you before they do the first two."

"Not interested in any of that."

"You'll have to weed through them if you want to find the killer, if he's even there."

"So, you think it's a dumb idea?"

"I think it's a brilliant idea, but not if you're together—"

"Right, we're more vulnerable alone."

He sliced off a piece of steak and slid it into his mouth. She paused to watch him. "Mmm, you're so damn hot." Her voice had taken on a husky edge.

"Because I'm eating steak?"

"I find everything about you sexy. You want to make a federal case of it?"

"Only if it gets me into your bed."

"What about *your* bed? Is that off limits?"

"Bringing a woman home feels like a relationship."

"Got it. No problem."

Ah, hell. I've insulted her. "Emerson."

She looked over at him. The pain in her eyes about killed him.

"I didn't mean that. It's just...I'm not an easy man to get to know."

"No worries. This is a forced work thing that's turned into a convenient sex thing. I'm not reading anything—"

He stopped her with a kiss. One long searing kiss that turned him hard as fucking steel.

"All we do when we're not having sex is stare at fucking screens on a wall. I invited you here because I want to be with you. I want to stare into your beautiful eyes and not talk about work, for once."

Her gaze softened.

"I like you so fucking much. I want you all the damn time. I wake up thinking about you. I fall asleep thinking about you. I can't get enough of you."

"Ohmygod," she whispered.

"If we didn't have so much on our plates, you'd be my dessert. I would love you all night long. I would restrain you and fuck you. I would tease you and worship you. I would fall asleep with you in my arms, in my bed. And I would want to do it all over again tomorrow." He pushed out of the chair, walked to the end of the porch, and stared into his backyard.

The ticking wall clock thundered in his ears. *She needs to know.*

Slowly, he turned to her. "I stopped feeling the day my mother died in my arms. You've got me in a tail spin. I don't want to let you in, but I can't stand being so damn walled off whenever we're together. Being with you is torture, but being without you is worse."

She went to him and placed soft palms on his face, then stood on her toes, and kissed him. "The more I learn about you, the more I admire you. You're a complicated man and that's what interests me most about you."

Her kiss was filled with so much tenderness, the armor around his heart cracked a little.

"I'm not afraid of where this will lead, even if it never leads anywhere," she whispered. "Stay walled up if that makes you happy. I can hang on to my claustrophobia if it serves me. I think our issues are holding us back from being better versions of ourselves."

He held her in his arms and gazed into her eyes. *She's so damn smart.* "You're right. As hard as it is for me, I'll stop pushing you away."

14

THEIR NAUGHTY LITTLE SECRET

On the way to the club, Stryker anchored his hand around her thigh. He stroked her silky skin with his thumb. Back and forth, again and again. At a red light, their eyes met.

"What do you think about Nikki and me hunting for the killer at your club?" she asked. "Besides wearing masks, we'd be disguised. Wigs, for sure."

"Good plan, but I'm more concerned with what happens after you two leave."

"How so?"

"If the killer is using the club to troll for his next victim, he could follow you home."

"True."

"Let's isolate a few suspects on the surveillance, first, so you can target them when you work the floor."

"Smart," she said as he parked in his spot. "Thank you for dinner."

As they made their way toward the entrance, he snaked his arm around her waist, pulled her close, and kissed her. Bypassing the people waiting to get in, they walked to the front door.

"Hey, dude," someone called. "You gotta wait in line like the rest of us."

"Handle him," Stryker said to Tank.

Tank jogged over to the guy. "Hey, dude, that's the owner."

"This is why I use the back door," Stryker said to Emerson as they slipped inside.

The pulsing music pounded through him. He breathed in the familiar smell of booze and warm bodies moving to the seductive rhythm, their sensuous dances already heating up the dance floor. *Tonight, we're gonna play.*

"Is Parker working?" she asked.

Stryker checked the club's schedule on his phone. "He's on Tuesday's schedule." Clasping her hand, he made his way to the bar. "Whatcha drinking?"

"Water."

"Two waters and a scotch, neat," Stryker said to his mixologist. "Make that a double."

A masked man sidled close. "Love your tat," he said to Emerson.

"Thanks," she replied.

"You two in a scene tonight?" asked the member.

"No," Emerson replied.

"If you guys are gonna play, would you like an audience?"

"You into watching?" Stryker regarded the member.

"Big time."

A masked woman walked over and dropped her arm around the man. "Hey, there. Me and my guy are into whatever. You two up for that, too?"

This was one of the reasons Stryker didn't hang on the floor anymore. The scene had grown old. He wasn't interested in strangers, didn't want an audience, had zero interest in a group fuck.

"We're not," Stryker replied. "Been members long?"

"Years," said the woman. "We love having an open relationship."

"You ever leave with anyone or hook up outside the club?" Emerson asked.

"Nah," said the man. "We play here."

Stryker collected the drinks. "Have fun."

Emerson made her way toward the stairs. Instead of passing the elevator marked "Private", she stopped and tapped the down button.

"Nice." He stood in front of the scanner and the light turned green.

An unmasked gal moseyed over. "Where you headed?"

"Private party," Stryker replied.

"How can I get on that list?"

Emerson pulled Stryker close. "Sorry, it's closed."

"Dang, you two are hot. I'd love to be a third wheel." She chuckled.

"I don't share," Stryker said as the elevator doors slid open and they stepped inside. He stood in front of the retina scanner, tapped the down button, and the doors closed.

Emerson sucked in a lungful of air, and then another. "Ohgod," she whispered.

The doors opened. Squeezing Stryker's arm, she stepped into his private office. "Take a minute and center yourself." He set their drinks on the console and returned to her. Clasping her hands, he stared into her eyes. "You're doing great."

"I'm freaking out a little." She eyed the stairs over her shoulder. "I'm safe and I'm seconds away from the main floor." She repeated it like a mantra, then leaned up and kissed him. "Let's work."

Stryker logged in and pulled up the surveillance for L1. "This footage goes back a month. I'm going to work on getting past ACPD's firewall so I can find Doug's reports."

"Thank you for doing that." Emerson swigged down a mouthful of water.

"Music?" he asked.

"Of course." She shot him a sweet smile. This woman was doing it for him in every single way. Her determination spurred him on.

He admired her grit and how she was forcing herself to confront her phobia.

Stryker pulled up his playlist that included classic rock, R&B, soul, pop, country and classical. An eclectic list of favorites that soothed the monsters in his head and calmed his troubled soul.

Stryker hadn't hacked into the ACPD's files in years. Ten long ones, to be exact. Now, technology had become more sophisticated and hacker resistant. Even so, he was confident he could breach the firewall. He pulled up a software program and logged in. Then, using a different computer, he started writing code. The back and forth between computers continued.

When he finished, he set the program to run.

Shifting his attention to the sultry detective alongside him, he watched her work. She'd furrow her brows, her eyes sweeping left to right. She'd pause, rewind, study someone, then continue watching. She'd pulled out her police notepad and jotted several notes. Her laser focus reminded him of how intense she'd been when he'd first met her. She was hell-bent on finding the person running a prostitution ring out of his club. Her questions had been razor sharp, her gaze searing. As far as she'd been concerned, he was guilty. Case closed. His resentment had run deep and he'd been vocal about how much he had despised her.

Now, as he drank in her delicate features, he admired her tenacity. Never one to forgive, he'd given her a pass. Absolved her of her wrongdoing and moved past it. Now, he couldn't get enough of her. And his interest went beyond the physical. He wouldn't be helping her with her brother if he didn't have feelings for her.

Stryker's loyalty ran blood deep. He would do anything for his family and close friends. But the rage and revenge that carried him from day to day still ruled his thoughts and actions. *What would she think if she learned the truth about me?* He imagined telling her, "I'm a cold-blooded killer." *Would she dump me on the spot or arrest me?* His money was on both.

"Hello, Parker," she said, crashing into his thoughts.

She zoomed in, then glanced over at him. "Check this out." Parker was tending bar on L1 when a masked woman showed up. After serving her, she stayed at the bar. Emerson fast-forwarded. Parker spoke with the other bartender, then joined the woman. They moved to a quiet corner and talked. Fifteen minutes later, Parker returned to the bar and the woman left the club.

Emerson switched to an external camera, but the positioning of the cameras, paired with where the woman had parked, made it impossible to read her license plate.

"That doesn't look like a Virginia tag," Stryker said.

He ran the woman's masked face through IDware, but she wasn't a member. "Employees are comped two guest passes a month."

Emerson jotted something in her notepad. "Be right back." Pushing out of the chair, she headed toward the bathroom.

In the middle of the room, she pulled to an abrupt stop. As she hugged herself, she lowered her head. Rather than go to her, he waited. If she needed his help, she'd ask.

As if she knew he was watching, she said, "I'm good," then continued on to the bathroom. When she returned, the triumph showed in her eyes.

"Nice job, Easton."

She sat on his lap and kissed him. "I wouldn't be able to push past it if it weren't for you. Thank you." As she gazed into his eyes, she ran her fingers over his beard. "I want to tell you something."

"Okay."

"It's part of my prisoner fantasy."

He raised his eyebrows. "Okay."

"When I'm captive, my abductor does things to me."

"Like what?"

"Sometimes I'm tied up, sometimes not. He forces me to blow him, he goes down on me, has sex with me. I even imagine he's, um...he—" She stopped.

"It's okay," he said. "Not judging."

"He comes on me."

He nodded. "CNC. Consensual non-consent."

Relief had her inhaling a calming breath. "It's called something?"

He nodded. "You're not alone."

"I want to act those out with you," she flicked her gaze to his bed, "naked and restrained on your bed. In my fantasy, I fight it, but in reality, I'm aroused as hell."

Pausing, he considered her request.

"I'll do it," he said. How could he not? Making Emerson happy had become a priority for him.

Her searing kiss sent his blood rushing south. Emerson was a strong aphrodisiac. Her alluring scent, coupled with their intense embrace, had him stroking her tongue hard. But they had to stay focused, so he slowed the kiss down.

Her eyes were alight with energy. "I can't wait." Then, she eyed the laptops in front of him. "What are you doing?"

"I wrote code to get past the department's firewall. While that runs, I'll pull April's cell phone records."

"How? Nikki hasn't determined which wireless provider April used."

He shoots her a smile. "I got this."

"Thank you." She kissed him before returning to her seat.

"Anything for the detective."

Ten minutes passed while she reviewed the surveillance video.

"Look at this," Emerson said. "It's that blond again. And he's doing the same thing."

Together, they watched as she fast-forwarded through the evening. Blondie cozied up to the bar, ordered a glass of white wine and nursed it. As people came and went, he'd strike up a brief conversation, but he was more interested in observing than talking.

"It's like he's doing a psych study," she said. "Everyone else is totally into talking, flirting, being seen, dancing. This guy is the total opposite."

"He wants to blend in and not be seen. I might be able to finesse the program to find him, which'll speed up the process."

Stryker's report finished running and he clicked on a different screen. "I've got April's phone records."

"You're really good with computers," she said. "Were you, like, a computer genius as a kid?"

"No. I played competitive sports year 'round."

"Did you study comp sci in college?"

He could brush over her questions and stay high level, or he could tell her the damn truth. As he stared into her eyes, he opted for the latter. "I got into computers in high school because I wanted to find the person who killed my mom."

"How old were you?"

"Fifteen. I became obsessed, but I didn't know what I was doing and was terrible at it. It wasn't 'til college that I started getting good."

She swiveled toward him. "But you haven't found that person, have you?"

"Not yet." *Tell her.* "In my twenties, the FBI arrested me."

"For what?"

"Hacking them."

"Did you go to prison?"

"I got lucky. My lawyer proposed a deal, and they accepted. I worked off my crime by hacking into their files, then helping them with the fixes, for free. That's when I started TCS."

"How long did this deal last?"

"Seven years. I still help them with some off-the-books jobs, but most of the time they pay me for hacking in and doing the fixes, or passing the problems along to their teams."

She smiled. "Thank you for telling me that."

April's call and text logs populated onto the screen.

"Are any of these numbers Parker?" she asked.

After pulling up his employee files, he matched a number on April's phone with Parker's number. "That one."

"They talked about getting together for lunch, but she ghosted on him."

"That's not a reason to kill someone," Stryker replied.

"No, but she was dead two days later," Emerson said. "Check these texts from a different number."

Emerson read the texts out loud: "'Let's meet up Saturday. Park still good?' April replied with, 'Yes, 10am.'"

"A few days later, she got another text from the same number," Emerson said. "It says, 'Pics came out great! See you tonight.' April replied with, 'Looking forward to it.'"

"That's the last text she sent," Stryker said. "I'll run that number and see who owns it." Stryker plugged the number into a different software program. "This'll take some time." He pushed out of the chair and stretched. "We need a break."

Raising his arms forced his shirt to ride up, exposing his toned abs. Emerson eyed his muscular torso. "Tie me up," she murmured.

That got his attention. "And?"

When she pushed out of her chair, lust filled her eyes. "I want to feel trapped, then surrender to that fear. I trust you."

The tension he carried in his shoulders turned to steel. "I don't deserve your trust."

"Well, you have it."

She was turning herself over to him. Submitting to him. If she knew the truth about him, she would never trust him so freely. Guilt mixed with desire was a dangerous combination. He wanted her. He also wanted to be truthful with her.

Stepping close, she dropped the sundress straps off her shoulders. Lust and the need to burrow inside her had him hardening. He admired her full breasts and swollen nipples, her hourglass curves, and the black thong covering her pussy. She kicked off her sandals and wiggled out of her thong. "I need this. So badly."

Tying someone up and taking them against their will wasn't a fetish Stryker had any interest exploring. But as he stared into Emerson's soulful eyes, he felt compelled to please her.

Do it, for her.

"Time to play," he said.

Her throaty moan rumbled through him. "Yessssss."

Being around Emerson was exhilarating. But, experience had made him a master at control, at understanding his partner's desires, then executing on them.

"Colors work for safe words," he said. "Green means you're okay. You feel safe and you want to continue. Yellow is a warning. Red is a hard stop."

Desire flashed in her eyes. She ran her tongue over her lower lip. "Understood."

He collected her pigtails in his hand and pulled them back, forcing her face upward. "What do you need?"

"It's dirty," she whispered.

"Tell me." Stryker released her hair.

"In my fantasy, some guy owed you millions, but he didn't have it," she began. "I was his virgin girlfriend." Pausing, she shot him an adorable smile. "Just go with it."

The feeling hit him like a bolt of lightning. *I'm falling in love with her.*

"But," she continued, "you wanted *me* in exchange for that debt. I'm forced to live with you for a year and I'm at your mercy. Tonight, you're introducing me to your dark world."

"How, exactly?"

She sucked down a deep breath. "I want your face between my legs, pleasuring me until I climax."

This time, he offered her an assuring smile. "You sure about this?"

She nodded. "I'm nervous and excited. It's a heady combination. You're great at helping me explain what I want."

"Do you want pleasure, pain or both?"

"Mostly pleasure. But I am your prisoner, so light pain."

"Are you resigned to being my prisoner or fighting me on it?"

"Fighting, then surrendering."

"Got it." He pulled the rumpled bed linens away. "Lie down on your back in the center of the bed. "Raise your arms over your head, spread your legs, then bend them at the knees."

He secured her wrists and ankles with the Velcro wraps, then stood back and admired her. She was a living piece of priceless art. Beautiful and supple, brave and strong willed.

"I'm going to blindfold you. When I remove the blindfold, the fantasy starts."

"Okay."

"Any questions or concerns?"

"No." She shuddered in a shaky breath. "I can't believe this is happening. My heart is pounding so hard."

He would never have pegged her for someone who wanted to be held against her will. But she hadn't asked him to scrutinize her. She had simply trusted him.

"I'm going to be checking in with you," he said.

"Uh-huh."

He didn't have a blindfold, so he used a tie he kept there for days when he'd spent the night and needed a change of clothes. After covering her eyes, he dropped a light kiss on her mouth.

She lay still. As he began taking off his clothing, her breathing increased, her chest rising and falling faster. She tugged on the arm restraints and groaned.

He stood at the foot of the bed naked. "Hello, prisoner. Today, we meet." He removed her blindfold, kissed her hard. "You want some bread, you do as I say."

"I'd rather starve, first." Emerson's cheeks were flushed, her eyes alight with energy.

"You okay?" he murmured.

"Green."

"My cock is big and thick. You're a virgin, no?"

She fought against a smile. "None of your business."

He loved how she was enjoying this.

"You watch me touch myself. Learn what I like." Standing beside the bed, he wrapped his hand around his shaft and stroked it. Her gravelly moans tore through him. His wetness oozed out and he coated the head. Up and down and around the head. His gaze never left hers. She was fixated on his shaft.

"You're an evil, vile man," she croaked out. "I hate you."

"Hate is a powerful emotion, prisoner. Will you still hate me when I bring you pleasure?"

Her glare was so convincing, he hitched a brow before climbing on the bed. Now, on his knees, he raked his gaze over her sublime body. His stroking continued, but the real pleasure came from Emerson.

She felt safe enough to confide her dark fantasies. He would do right by her. He stopped touching himself, leaned down and kissed her.

She jerked her face away. "You don't get to kiss me."

With a firm touch, he forced her to look at him. "I get to do whatever the hell I want to you."

"Fuck you," she murmured.

"You're mine. I *own* you," he ground out.

Her breathing was jagged, her cheeks pink with color.

"Tantric breath," he murmured, and placed his palm on her diaphragm. Two relaxing breaths and she nodded. "Green."

"Prisoner, I'm going to suck your fantastic tits."

"Ohgod, yes," she exclaimed. "I mean, no, no, don't do that."

He kissed her again, this time pushing his tongue into her mouth. Greed and desire had him kissing her harder. She raked her teeth over his tongue and stroked his with wild abandon. Desire sent a constant throbbing to his aching dick.

Her eyelids were heavy with lust. "You gotta stop."

"To break you in, I'm going to eat you. Next time, I come inside your hot little snatch."

"You will never break me," she said, panting hard.

He kissed her again and she fought against him.

"Stop," he bit out. "And take your fucking punishment."

"You're a demon," she rasped.

"How are you doing?" he asked.

"I'm so aroused," she murmured. "I can barely hang on."

He took her engorged nipple into his mouth and sucked. He fondled her other, pinching lightly. "Stop, you shouldn't be doing this to me. I'm a virgin."

While he sucked her nipple, she murmured, "Eat me."

"You do not get to tell me what to do."

"Please, Stryker," she whispered. "I'm dying for you."

Love was the last thing on his mind, but as he kissed her breasts and her abdomen, then the sides of her body, he knew exactly what he was feeling. He was falling in love with this woman and he hated himself for not stopping things now, before he got in too deep. Before he broke her heart and ruined his own life by ending things between them.

Forcing himself to re-focus, he placed his mouth between her legs and licked the length of her opening. She was drenched in arousal.

"I'm gonna come pretty fast."

When he slid two fingers inside her, she bucked and groaned. "No, no, you have to stop. Free me."

He stroked her with his tongue while her moans turned feral and she started writhing beneath him.

"Yes, yes, ohhhh, yesssss." She convulsed hard and shook while he pleasured her through her orgasm. When she relaxed back down and let out a long, relaxed sigh, he stopped.

Leaning over her, he kissed her gently, but when she slid her tongue into his mouth, he gave her back what she needed. Hard, fast strokes until she slowed the kiss. Peering down at her confirmed his feelings. Emerson was his person.

"You did good, prisoner," he said. "Tonight, you get extra grub. Tomorrow, I fuck you."

"What about now?" she asked, her eyes blazing with desire.

"That was your first CNC role play. No more tonight."

"I loved being your prisoner," she murmured. "Thank you for taking such good care of me."

"I love taking care of you, Emerson." He removed the restraints, then pulled her into his arms. He rubbed her back and kissed the top of her head while she ran soft fingers over his chest.

They stayed together for several minutes. No words, just tender caresses and soft touches. Then, he broke the silence. "Are you okay?"

She lifted her face and offered a relaxed smile. "That was super intense. I've been stressed about this case, plus, I've been so angry about my brother. This is the most chill I've been in a while. I've had that fantasy for so long, it doesn't seem real that I actually experienced it."

He was concerned that the intense sex high might leave her feeling blue tomorrow. But he didn't want to take away from her joy by warning her, so he stayed silent.

"If I got a membership, would you play with me in a suite?"

"You don't need to buy a membership. I'll set one up for you."

Pushing onto her elbows, she regarded him. "I can pay for a membership."

"To play in a suite, you'd need to purchase an L3 membership. That entitles you to everything on all floors. It's seventy-five grand a year."

Her mouth dropped open, then she laughed. "How much are they, for real?"

He hitched a brow.

"Oh, wow."

"I'm not saying you can't afford a membership," he said. "But why pay when I own the club? Let me do this for you."

"That's too much," she said.

"Emerson, I like you…a lot. I like working with you. I love our intimacy and how you tell me what you want, what you need. If you want to play in a suite, I can make that happen."

"Thank you. I just didn't want you to feel like you had to—"

He kissed her. "You're fine."

On the way home, he wrapped his hand around her thigh and she threaded her fingers over his. This constant need to connect with her, to touch her, to be near her, struck him as odd. Despite being around people all the damn time, he considered himself a loner. He valued his independence and the feeling of being unfettered, but there was something compelling and necessary about being with Emerson. It didn't feel like he was losing his freedom, it felt like he had found something he didn't realize had been missing.

Her.

"I'll set up your club account tomorrow before I head to Heather and Gordon's. You wanna join me?"

"I'm spending the day with my mom and dad. It's hard without Doug, but we're finding our way."

As he pulled into his garage, he said, "Stay with me, tonight."

"As much as I want to, I've gotta get home. I've got a ton of things to do in the morning before I head to my parents'. Thank you for tonight. I had a great time."

He walked her to her car, drew her into his arms, and kissed her goodnight. She tightened her hold around him, then broke away.

"Should I follow you home again?" he asked.

"I'll text you when I get there." She slipped into her car and drove away.

Maybe I should slow things down—way the hell down—before this relationship gets away from me and we both end up wrecked over it.

15

SUNDAY FUNDAY

As much as Emerson wanted to stay with Stryker, she needed time alone. She'd never acted out a fantasy with anyone and she needed to process what had happened. She entered her house, turned off the security system, and waited until the garage door closed before locking up and reactivating the alarm. Pima was waiting.

Meow, meeeeeooooow.

"Hi, sweet boy." She rubbed his soft coat before heading upstairs to shower. She didn't feel depressed, per se, but she was struggling with how she felt. *Maybe I should have talked to him about this.*

After a quick shower, she crawled into bed and texted Stryker. "You awake?"

"You okay?" he texted back.

"I'm not sure how I feel about tonight."

Her phone rang. "Hey," she answered.

"I had a feeling this might happen," Stryker said.

"I don't regret that I acted out a dark fantasy," she said. "And I'm glad it was with you."

"What are you feeling?"

"Elated, but kinda sad—which makes no sense—and a little…I

don't know...ashamed or guilty. The guilt comes from liking what we did, because it's dark."

"You've had these fantasies for a long time," he said. "Tonight, you made it happen. Big difference."

"I'm not one to get caught up in my emotions," she said. "It's not like I don't have them, but I don't dwell on them. This feels different."

"So, there's this thing that can happen after a high like you had tonight."

"A low?" she asked.

"Exactly," he explained. "And it's something to know for the future. You have a right to enjoy your fantasies. If you can sleep it off, do that. If you feel bad in the morning, I'll come over."

She smiled. He was going out of his way to make sure she was okay. "Thank you for being there for me."

"You want me to come over now?"

"I'm okay."

They ended the call. She turned out the light and fell asleep.

In the morning, she felt better. She liked what they'd done and accepted it at face value.

After going for a run, she typed out a text to Stryker. "I'm okay today. Thanks for a great evening and for walking me off the ledge after. Have fun with your fam." She added a thumbs up and a heart emoji, removed the heart, then added it back. Before she changed her mind again, she sent it.

Dots appeared.

"Good morning, beautiful. I set up your club account." He sent her the link and a temporary username and password. "Once you log in, you can change everything. I'll miss you today."

"I'll miss you, too," she texted back.

After breakfast, Emerson created an account at The Dungeon, named herself "Prisoner Girl" then went looking for Stryker's online account. When she found his photo, her heart skipped a beat.

He'd left his hair down, and had worn his black leather jacket and a simple black mask.

I've got it so bad for him.

She read his profile. He identified as a male who liked women. He was into role play and edging. Penetration was optional and he didn't do oral. *But he does with me.*

When she skimmed his club name, she stilled. He called himself Justice. "No way. There's no way he's *my* Justice."

As she went upstairs, she couldn't shake the thought that they were the same man. *Both men lost their moms. Stryker is Heather's nephew and she started the survivor group.*

In the bathroom, she applied smoky eyeshadow, black eyeliner and lots of mascara. She covered her cheekbones in dark rouge, then coated her lips in black lipstick. She found the long, brown wig she'd used for Halloween and pulled that on. With her black mask in place, she snapped a selfie. With her account set up, she changed it to "private", removed the wig and washed her face.

As she headed to her parents', she wondered if Stryker was her late-night friend from the survivor group.

Only one way to find out. *It's time for coffee with Justice.*

Stryker walked into his aunt and uncle's home and was barraged with children. Screaming, happy children all running in his direction. Sundays were insane and he loved the mayhem. His close friend, Dakota, had married his cousin, Providence. They had two children, Sammy and Graham. His sister Trudy and her husband, Mark, had three kids of their own.

He hugged the oldest three, then grabbed the two youngest, tucking one under each arm like packages. The squealing and giggling was just shy of deafening.

"Uncle Syker Tooman!" Aaron yelled. "Tickle monster."

Dakota and Providence's eighteen-month-old son, Graham, started giggling.

After entering the kitchen, he set both kids on the floor. "Can you pay with us, Unca?" Graham asked. "We run."

The first ten minutes was always controlled chaos. Hugs, back slaps, and bro-hugs. He'd take his crazy family and their outpouring of love over the misery he and Trudy had endured after his mom died and his dad left. Despite Dakota and Providence's children being his second cousins, they called him uncle, too.

After greeting Dakota and Providence, and Trudy and Mark, he asked his Aunt Heather and Uncle Gordon about their other daughter, Megan.

"She and Leigh are in New York, picking up a puppy to foster," Heather replied.

"Show him the picture, Nana," Sammy Luck said. "He's the cutest puppy in the world."

The conversations flowed, as did the laughter. This sacred time was Stryker's refuge. He didn't think about work, or the vigilante missions he'd completed, or the ones coming up. He simply chilled with his family.

As he headed out back to play with the kids, he thought of Emerson. How was she doing? Was she having a good day? More importantly, would she fit in with his family?

She would.

He chased the kids around the backyard playing tickle monster until he tired them out. Once the kids had cooled off, it was time to chow down. Everyone sat around an extra-long table, Gordon led a prayer of gratitude, and they dug in. While the conversations were fluid, Heather always made sure to ask each child what made their week special.

One by one, the children touted their gratitude for something. A good grade on a test, or a new friend, or something kind they did for someone else.

"Stryker," said Heather, "why don't you tell everyone about the honor you received?"

Stryker blanked. "I got nothing."

"You were honored at the law enforcement fundraiser."

"What's that?" one of the kids asked.

"I gave money to some people who didn't have enough money to buy food," Stryker explained.

"Yay, Uncle Syker Tooman," Aaron said.

"That was generous of you," Sammy echoed.

"He did the same for us," Stryker's brother-in-law Mark said. "Thanks for the credit card. We decided to split the groceries every week. You pay half. We pay half."

"Wow, that was kind," Gordon said.

"No splitting," Stryker said. "Use the card." Stryker didn't like all this attention, so he redirected the conversation to Dakota. "How's the exciting world of real estate?"

"I talked to Sammy's class at career day," Dakota said with a smile. "Now all the kids want to sell houses when they grow up."

"Is that what you want, Sammy?" Stryker asked.

"I want to have my own marketing company, like my mom," Sammy replied. "She carries a gun to work and I think that's cool."

Silence.

Dead silence.

"How do you know about Mom's gun, Samantha Lynn?" Dakota asked.

"I saw her get it out of the secret room one day before she went to work."

No one said anything for almost a minute.

"I'm glad you told us, Sammy," Providence said. "Do you know how to get into that room?"

She shook her head as Dakota and Providence exchanged glances. Stryker knew that they stored their Glocks in a locked room. And within that room, their weapons were stored in a locked gun case.

"We've talked a lot about gun safety," Dakota said to his daughter.

"I know and I understand," Sammy replied. "I don't know how to get into that room."

Again, Dakota and Providence exchanged glances. Stryker was confident that conversation with their daughter was far from over.

"I have news," Trudy said, after everyone had finished eating. "I invited Dad over today. He'll be by for coffee."

Another bomb had been dropped in the middle of what should have been a chill family get together.

Stryker's blood pressure kicked up. "Not good."

"Trudy, that was very inclusive of you, dear," Aunt Heather began. "Since not everyone wants to see him, getting buy-in beforehand might have been a good idea, don't you think?"

"I didn't think it was a big deal," Trudy replied.

"It is to me, sis." Stryker stacked the dishes and carried them into the kitchen. A few seconds later, his aunt moseyed in.

"You okay?" Heather asked.

"Hell, no," Stryker replied. "He's not part of this family, and I will not welcome him back."

"Please don't leave."

"I'm not leaving." He put his arm around her. "I don't scare that easily."

"You don't scare at all," she said with a smile. "You have nerves of steel."

They cleaned up in silence while conversations floated in from the porch. With the dishwasher loaded, Stryker started scrubbing the pans. At some point, Dakota wandered in. "Stryker, you wanna go for a walk?"

"Yeah."

This was always the best part of Sunday Funday. He and Dakota would grab Graham and take off for the neighborhood playground.

"Let me change Graham's diaper, first." Dakota went looking for his son.

"So, how are you and Emerson getting along?" Heather asked while drying a pan.

"Where's that coming from?" Stryker asked.

"Well, for one, I saw how you two interacted at the fundraiser. Please don't take me for an idiot, Stryker." With a smile, she patted his back.

"I made her dinner last night."

"Very nice. She's lovely and very smart. She mentioned working with someone who was helping her overcome her phobia. I'm guessing that was you."

"How do you know so much?"

"You couldn't keep your eyes off her. She left the room upset and you went after her. But, no worries, your secret is safe with me."

Dakota walked in with Graham.

"Nana, I had poopie diaper," Graham said. "Can you play with us?"

Heather lifted the small child and kissed his cheek. "This is your special boys-only time. You three have fun." She set her grandson down. "We'll play when you get back."

They walked outside to find Stryker's dad making his way up the driveway with a bouquet in one hand and a bottle of wine in the other. Stryker's chest tightened. Seeing his father sickened him.

"Hey, Stryker," Tyler said. "Good to see you again. You're not leaving, are you?"

"Taking a walk."

"Thanks again for the tour of your company. It was very impressive." Tyler set down the bottle of wine to shake Dakota's hand. "I'm Tyler, Stryker's dad."

"Dakota Luck. This is my son, Graham."

After a moment of bullshit small talk, Stryker suggested they take off.

"I look forward to catching up with you," Tyler said before ringing the doorbell. Gordon opened the front door and welcomed him inside.

Agitation clouded Stryker's thoughts. "What a piece o' work. He turns my stomach."

Dakota strapped his son in the stroller and the three ambled toward the playground. "You handled that well."

"He ghosts on his children after his wife dies, then rolls back into town twenty years later like nothing's happened. He's got some nerve."

"He's not worth your time," Dakota said.

"No, he's not," Stryker replied. "Let's change the subject. Are you hiring any ALPHA operatives?"

Dakota and Providence ran the top-secret government organization.

Dakota slapped him on the back. "Finally! You're coming on board."

Stryker chuckled. "I'm asking for Cooper."

"I thought he liked working at the Bureau."

"He misses fieldwork. Sitting on his ass in meetings isn't his thing. Plus, he's up for promotion out west and he doesn't want to go."

"You think he'd make a good operative?"

"Damn good."

"I'll call him."

They arrived at the playground and Dakota unstrapped Graham, then took him out of the stroller. "You want to go on the swing, buddy?"

"Yes!"

Dakota lifted him into the toddler swing and pushed him.

"You're a good dad, Dakota," Stryker said.

"Thanks, man. I love my kids. They keep me young and remind me what's important."

"How are things with you and Providence?"

Dakota smiled. "Keeps getting better."

"I started seeing someone, kinda," Stryker said. "It's complicated."

"Women always are. Who is it?"

"Daddy, done," said Graham.

Dakota slowed the swing to a stop, then unstrapped Graham. "What's next, Graham?"

"Slide with Unca."

Every Sunday, weather permitting, this was their ritual. The tot slipped his small hand into Stryker's and the three of them made their way over to the slide. Stryker helped the tyke climb up. It was tight, but Stryker managed to maneuver through the small jungle gym. Graham plopped down, Stryker sat behind him and they slid down.

"Yay! Again!" Graham exclaimed.

After doing it five more times, Stryker turned the sliding gig over to Dakota and watched as father and son played together.

"Is this what love does to people?" Stryker asked.

Dakota chuffed out a laugh. "Looks that way. So, who's the woman?"

"Emerson Easton," Stryker replied.

"How do I know that name? Wait, isn't she the cop who arrested you?"

"That's the one."

"You must like her a lot if you're willing to look past that."

I'm crazy about her. Stryker bit back a smile. "I must."

"Bring her by some Sunday. We'll be nice."

"Or scare her away."

They stayed until Graham had had enough. As Dakota was strapping his son into the stroller, four linebacker-sized teenage boys wandered onto the playground. Two were smoking weed and one was vaping.

"Look, a coupla dads with their baby," said one of the teens. "What's your kid call you? Dad One and Dad Two?"

"You carryin'?" Stryker murmured to Dakota.

"Yup. You?"

"Same."

"Take it down a few, guys," Dakota said. "This is my wife's cousin."

"Sorry, dude," said one of the teens. "We's thought yous guys was faggots."

Stryker strode over and glared down at them. "Mind your own damn business and stop judging. Who the fuck do you think you are? God?"

The biggest kid stepped into Stryker's space. "Yeah, man, I am God. Whatcha gonna do about it, pussy?"

Stryker wanted to punch the kid's lights out. Instead, he pulled out his phone, tapped his IDware app, then snapped a pic of the teens. Seconds later, he had what he needed. "Three of you have a juvi record. Shoplifting, mugging, vandalism. Hmm, one of you killed a dog." He narrowed his gaze and stared from one to the other. "Get your shit together, boys, or you'll end up in prison."

Stryker made his way back to Dakota and Graham. As the three of them headed toward home, Dakota said, "You hear him coming?"

"Yeah, I think he's gonna jump me. Keep going. I got this."

The kid was coming in fast. Stryker turned to face his assailant and the blade pierced his shoulder, sending pain shooting down his arm. He grabbed the kid's wrist, yanked it backward, and twisted hard.

"AAAAIIIEEEEE!" screamed the teen as he dropped the knife.

He held on to the kid while Dakota called 911. The other three kids took off.

"Hey, don't leave me!" shouted the teen.

But his friends were long gone, having already vanished into the nearby neighborhood.

"Police are on their way," Dakota said, then made another call.

Before Stryker could stop him, Dakota was on the phone to Providence.

The patrolwoman arrived and called out Stryker's blood-stained arm. "You need an ambulance?"

"I'm fine," Stryker replied.

The Sunday-Funday crew showed up at the playground, concerned etched on his family's faces as they took in the scene.

After the cop took Stryker's statement, she asked, "You pressing charges?"

Stryker slid his gaze to the now scared-looking kid. "No, I'm not."

"Oh, man, thank you so much. I'm sorry. I'm really sorry I stabbed you."

"Make smarter choices," Stryker said.

"I'll take you back to your parents or guardians," the cop said to the kid. "Since you attacked this man, I'm cuffing you."

The teen didn't resist when the cop slapped cuffs on him, then led him away.

"I'll drive you to the hospital," Uncle Gordon said, examining the stab wound. "You need stitches."

"Let's go home," Stryker said. "I got a better idea."

As the family walked back to the house, Stryker was grateful Tyler didn't hover or act like a concerned father. He knew his place. He was the Omega.

Once back at the house, Stryker found fast-sealing super adhesive glue. He handed it to Dakota. "We'll use this to patch me up."

"You've got to be kidding," Gordon said. "You need stitches."

"Back in a minute," Stryker said.

He shut the bathroom door and yanked off his shirt, ignoring the pain in his shoulder. After washing the wound, he found Dakota on the screened-in porch.

"Close 'er up," Stryker said.

Dakota worked quickly to seal the wound.

"I've never seen that done before," Tyler said. "Pretty cool." His phone rang. Instead of answering, he excused himself and vanished inside.

"I really wish you'd gone to the hospital," Gordon said.

"This isn't the first time I've been glued back together," Stryker said to his uncle.

With the wound sealed, Stryker pulled on his shirt and poured himself a scotch. While he'd downplayed the incident because he wasn't going to the hospital, his arm was throbbing pretty good.

He and Dakota headed into the backyard, where Providence was watching the kids.

"You should have walked away," Providence said.

"I did walk away," Stryker replied.

"How's your shoulder?" she asked.

"Nothing a little liquid medicine won't cure." Stryker raised the glass and downed the booze. "I've reached my limit for fun. I'm taking off."

"Stay out of trouble," Providence said.

"It follows me," Stryker said, before pulling Dakota in for a bro-hug and kissing Providence on the forehead.

"Love you," she said to him.

Stryker climbed the steps to the porch. Heather and Trudy were sitting at the table talking. "I have a psych question for my genius aunt."

Trudy rose. "That's my cue." She glanced out back. "Where's Dad?"

Stryker pointed to his uncle, relaxing nearby in a chaise lounge. "Gordon's right there."

His uncle shot him a proud smile. "Thank you, son."

Trudy glared at him. "I wish you'd talk to Tyler. He's a nice guy."

"Not interested," Stryker replied.

On an eyeroll, Trudy headed down the stairs.

"How do you desensitize a person?" Stryker asked, sitting beside Heather.

"Depends on what it is."

"Closed spaces."

Her gaze lingered on his while the corners of her mouth lifted. "If I were treating a patient for claustrophobia, I would try replacing their negative reaction with a positive one. Everyone is different, so every reaction is, as well. It's tricky because you don't want the positive replacement to be associated with the negative feelings."

"Like?"

"Laughter is positive. Love is positive. If the person has a favorite type of music, that can be used. So, in an elevator, for example, you could play a favorite song. Over time, the goal is that the negative feeling of being in the elevator is replaced with the happy feeling brought on by the song."

"Got it."

"Food can be a good stimulus, but it can also be a crutch, so I'm wary of using food as a tool. Words are powerful and mantras can also work. Phobias are complicated. Take a spider. I would show my patient a picture of a cute, baby spider. We might spend time learning about spiders and how they're helpful to the environment." Heather folded her hands on the table. "Did that help?"

"I'll let you know." He kissed her cheek. "Did I ever thank you for stepping in for Trudy and me?"

"I'm sure you must have."

"Thank you both for taking us in and raising us. You and Gordon went from two kids to four. And I was pretty messed up, so I know it wasn't easy."

"You were a fifteen-year-old boy who'd just lost his mother. Teenagers are unusual creatures." She smiled. "You and your mom were close. She died and your dad couldn't handle the loss, so he escaped. It's not that uncommon. Maybe you could give him a chance."

"Not happening." He pushed out of the chair. "Thanks for your help. I love you."

"I love you, too. Good luck with the claustrophobia," she said with a smile.

Stryker headed out.

Tyler was talking on the phone in the driveway, a cigarette

dangling from his mouth. He didn't remember his dad being a smoker, but he didn't remember much about him at all.

Tyler ended the call, stomped out the butt and ambled over. "You taking off, son?"

"Yup." He wanted to tell him to stop calling him 'son', but it was less effort to say nothing. "Where you been all these years?"

"Florida."

"What were you doing there?"

"Sales, like I did up here."

"Why'd you leave?"

"I was broken over Mom's death and having trouble functioning."

"Cry me a fuckin' river."

"I thought it would be best for you and your sister if you stayed with Heather and Gordon while I got myself together."

"Does that mean you got yourself together now? All pretty and ready to step in and be an amazing dad? That job is filled. Gordon stepped in. He and Heather went to every game I played. Football, basketball, lacrosse. I don't remember you doing that when you were around. They helped me apply to colleges and paid for me to go. They made sure Trudy and I felt loved. They included us, like we'd been their kids for-fucking-ever. You were a mediocre dad, at best. I'm not interested in seeing you again. Sunday Funday is for family. You aren't."

Stryker got in his car and drove away, but his agitation stayed with him all the way home. Though he wanted to see Emerson, he needed to learn about Carlo Spinetti. If Spinetti was guilty of something beyond the Internet scam, he would find it. If there was anything Stryker was good at, it was rooting out evil.

"Takes one to know one," he ground out as his fingers flew over the keyboard.

16

CHASING BLONDIE

Tuesday, late morning, Emerson called Parker and asked him to swing by and answer a few more questions.

"I already told you everything I know," Parker pushed back.

"You and April were friends. What would you do if she asked you for help?"

"I'd help her."

"Well, Parker, I'm asking for her, because she can't."

"What time?"

"I'm here now."

"Be there in twenty."

When he arrived, Emerson asked an officer to escort him into an interrogation room. Nikki joined her to watch Parker through the one-way mirror. While waiting, Parker nibbled a fingernail and stared at the floor.

"You think he's our guy?" Nikki asked.

Emerson continued watching him. "He didn't tell me about his prior, which makes me suspicious."

"Makes me wonder what else he's hiding," Nikki replied.

"He doesn't have an alibi for the first night April Peters went missing." Emerson glanced over at her partner. "Can you ask about the dates in April when he took vacation? Those coincide with the dates Gloria Stanton was killed."

"Got it."

The women left the observation room and walked next door. Emerson introduced Detective Cardoso.

"Let me get you a water," Nikki said.

She left and Emerson eased down in the chair across from him. "Thanks for coming in, Parker. I'm struggling with this case and could use your help filling in the gaps."

"I didn't kill her."

"No one accused you of that."

He stopped fidgeting.

Nikki returned with a bottle of water. With a trembling hand, Parker drank down half the bottle as Nikki leaned against the wall.

"You talk to a lot of people at the club," Emerson began. "Have you heard anyone say anything about April's death?"

"I talk to everyone, but I got no time to chat," he replied. "Every night is crazy busy, but Fridays and Saturdays are insane. These members fork out big bucks to get first-class service, so we smile and we serve 'em."

"Did you ever see anyone single April out, you know, try to get to know her or ask her out?"

"April was pretty, so sometimes I'd overhear a guy say something, you know, like hitting on her. She never responded." A sad smile touched his eyes. "She was a good person. She didn't deserve to die."

"No, she didn't," Emerson said.

"You took a few days off in April," Nikki said. "The fifteenth and sixteenth."

"Yeah, so?" Parker furrowed his brows. "Do I need a lawyer or something?"

Dammit. "Totally up to you. Whatever makes you comfortable." Emerson leaned back in the chair and grew silent.

"Why those dates?" Parker asked.

"There was another murder around that time," Nikki answered.

His eyes darted from one detective to the other. "I was with my sister."

"Great. Can she confirm that?" Nikki pressed.

"Uh, yeah...um...sure."

"Can I get her name and number?"

As Parker rattled it off, Nikki jotted it down.

"I'm curious," Emerson said. "You never mentioned your prior conviction."

Parker swallowed hard. "Oh, boy."

"Can you tell us what that's all about?" Nikki asked.

"I broke a restraining order and got arrested. I served my time and learned my lesson."

Emerson pushed for why he didn't honor his former girlfriend's request when she told him no.

As Parker explained, Emerson studied him. He was jittery, but she expected that. She was searching for nonverbal clues that would tell her the real story. He appeared to be telling the truth, but she'd get Nikki's input.

"I was stupid," he concluded. "I thought I could change her mind, make her see we were good together. I won't do that again."

"How do you know you wouldn't do that again?" Nikki asked. "I mean, you did say you knew you guys were good together."

"Prison sobers a guy up, fast. I never wanna go back there."

"One last question," Nikki said. "Are you into taking pictures?"

Parker paused, his gaze darting between the women. "Sure." He held up his phone. "Isn't everyone?"

"What kind of pics do you take?" Emerson asked.

"Nothing special. A sunset or something funny."

"What about people?" Nikki asked. "Do you take pictures of people?"

Parker flicked his gaze from one woman to the other. "I think I'm done answering your questions. If you want to question me again, I want a lawyer."

Emerson walked him out and found Nikki back at her desk. "What do you think?" Emerson asked.

"We don't have any evidence," Nikki said. "I called Parker's sister. She didn't answer and the phone wasn't set up to leave messages."

Emerson nibbled on her lip. "She's his alibi for the first murder. Without her, he's got no alibis for either case."

"I'll let you know if I talk to his sister."

"I'm heading back to a second-hand bridal boutique." As Emerson made her way downstairs, she checked her phone. She hadn't heard from Stryker since Saturday and wondered if her prisoner fantasy had been too much. Rather than overthink it, she typed a text. "Is your company back online today?" She didn't like that, and retyped. "Thinking of you. Is your company up and running?" She sent it, jumped in her car, and drove to the bridal shop in Alexandria.

The store was quiet and the owner had more time to assist Emerson. After Emerson reminded her what she was looking for, the woman pulled out a stack of notebooks from behind the counter. "I keep notes to help me remember. My memory isn't what it used to be." A few minutes later, she said, "Here's an entry from March. A young man did swing by. You'd think I'd remember a man shopping alone for a wedding dress. His name is KC." Emerson tried making out the owner's notes, but the abbreviations and poor penmanship made it impossible.

"Did you get his last name?"

"No, but he did purchase four dresses."

"Didn't that strike you as odd?" Emerson asked.

The woman continued reading. "Here it is. He's a photographer and he needed a few dresses for a photo shoot."

Have I found the killer? "Did he tell you anything about the shoot?"

"Nothing I remember."

"Did he say if the pictures would be posted anywhere, you know, to promote his business?"

The woman checked her notebook again. "I wish I'd written that down."

"That would have been great publicity for your boutique."

The owner shook her head. "How did I miss that opportunity?" She reviewed her notes again. "I didn't get a phone number for him. Hmm, here's something. All four dresses were size eight."

"Did he pay with a credit card?"

While the woman checked, her phone buzzed with an incoming text from Stryker.

"TCS is up and running except for gov't accts. Meet tonight, 9?"

"Congrats! Nine works," she replied.

"He paid cash for the dresses," said the shop owner, plucking her from her thoughts of Stryker.

Cash is another dead end. "Do you remember what he looked like?"

The woman paused. "I remember he was such a nice young man. So friendly and polite."

"So, he was young?"

The woman smiled. "Everyone is young to me. I've had this shop for over forty years."

"Was he tall with dark hair?"

The owner shook her head. "That's not ringing any bells with me."

"Shorter with blond hair and a beard and mustache?"

"Sorry, no."

Emerson glanced around. "No surveillance cameras?"

"I don't have a problem with shoplifting. It's hard to sneak out with a wedding gown."

"If the gentleman who bought the gowns returns, please don't tell him I was asking about him."

"No problem."

"And call me right away." Emerson left her card.

"Did he do something wrong?"

"He's a person of interest in two homicides."

The woman gasped. "Am I safe alone here at night?"

While the shop owner didn't fit the killer's profile, she wanted to encourage her to be safe. "You can lock the door when you're alone or change your policy to appointments-only in the evening. If a man comes into your store and you're not comfortable, call 911." Emerson thanked her for her time and left.

As she drove away, her hope fizzled. Emerson believed she'd found her guy, but she had nothing beyond that. No contact info, no description. Then, the realization hit her. The killer had purchased four dresses.

He's hunting his third victim.

Stryker smiled like a proud papa as his computer systems came online. His entire staff had gathered in the atrium and cheered while the monitors on the far wall lit up. It had taken an extra day, but they were back in business.

"Team, we're up and running," he announced. "Government accounts are suspended until the investigation is completed. Check with your manager for your short-term assignment."

Stryker had spent the past two days meeting with his executive team to ensure his employees were reassigned during the Bureau's investigation. Company rumors had been flying that his government hackers would be laid off. No one was losing their job.

As the teams made their way back upstairs, Cooper strode into the building.

"Hey, great timing," Stryker said. "We're back in business."

"We need to talk," Cooper said. *"Now."*

"My office."

The two men jumped into an elevator with several chatty employees. Normally friendly, a silent Cooper stared straight ahead. Floor by floor, employees hopped off, leaving the two men alone on their way to the top floor. "You look pissed," Stryker said.

"I am pissed," Cooper said as the doors slid open and the men walked to Stryker's office.

Once there, Stryker closed the door. "I musta done something."

"You sure as hell did." Cooper pulled up a video on his phone. It was of Stryker visiting Spinetti in prison.

"What's the problem?" Stryker asked. "I paid an old man a visit. Kinda nice of me, don'tcha think?"

"Are you fucking kidding me? I told you to stay away from him. I get that you do not like being told what to do. I've known that forever. But this? This is unacceptable. How the fuck am I supposed to go to bat for you when you pull this kind of crap?" Cooper glared at him.

"Relax," Stryker said, but his words were futile. Cooper looked like he was gonna breathe fire out his nostrils.

"He told his lawyer you threatened him," Cooper continued. "I walked in to a shit storm this morning. You do this again and I won't bail you out. The Bureau will suspend TCS indefinitely and take their time investigating your company. You will have to fire your employees. You will lose business. Your attorney fees will be insane. This will drag on for months." Cooper stared at him. "Am I clear?"

"Spinetti is guilty of orchestrating the B&E. He's not coming after the Bureau. He's coming after me. For some reason, this is personal. And I sure as fuck will stand up to him."

Stryker's phone buzzed with an incoming text. He read it and a growl shot out of him. It was Spinetti. "Perfect timing," he said, and showed Cooper.

The text read: "You won't beat me."

"Hmm," Cooper said.

"I helped the Bureau put Spinetti away," Stryker said. "That *favor* meant nothing to me. It's one of dozens I've done over the years. I didn't think twice about Spinetti until he called and threatened me. Have I ever backed down before?"

"No." A second passed. Cooper's anger broke and he cracked a brief smile. "Remember that bully when we were—"

"In third grade," Stryker said.

"Yeah. Wasn't that kid in fifth grade?"

Stryker nodded.

"He was picking on the special needs boy at recess."

"Larry was a good kid," Stryker said. "We used to play with him sometimes so he wasn't alone."

"You beat that bully pretty good."

Stryker smiled at the memory. "It worked, didn't it? He stopped picking on Larry."

Cooper nodded. "I have no idea how we've stayed friends this long. You drive me insane, man."

Stryker held up his phone so Cooper could see Spinetti's text again. "What would you do?"

"I'd want to respond, but I'd let it go," Cooper replied.

"That's where we differ. I won't."

"You built this company from nothing. Don't lose everything because you can't control your anger."

"If your mom was murdered and died in your arms, but her killer was never found, you'd be pretty fucking angry, too."

Cooper sighed. "I'm sorry, bro. I get that—"

"I love you, Coop, but you *don't* get it. You don't get the rage I carry around because someone got away with murder. She didn't deserve to die. She was doing her damn job. That's not a reason to kill someone."

"All right," Cooper said. "For the record, let us do our job. But I know warning you is pointless."

Stryker pulled him in for a bro-hug. "Get outta here and go save the world from bad guys."

"I'd love to, but I sit in meetings all day."

"About that... expect a call," Stryker said.

"What does that mean?"

"Your life is about to change, for the better."

"Will I be thanking you?"

"Damn straight, brother."

Cooper left, closing the door behind him.

Alone in his office, Stryker re-read the text from Spinetti. "You won't beat me."

"Watch me," he texted back.

That evening, Stryker stood near The Dungeon entrance talking to Tank. As Emerson made her way over to him, their eyes met across the parking lot. His gaze stayed locked on her and a rush of excitement sent butterflies fluttering in her stomach. His energy drew her to him like a magnet. She hadn't seen him in days and she'd missed him...a lot.

He was wearing black leather pants that hugged his massive thighs, a tight black T-shirt that stretched against his sinewy muscles, and black boots. He wasn't just a handsome man with a killer body. He was determined and fearless, loyal and so damn smart.

She wanted to jump into his arms and kiss him for days. But that's not how Emerson rolled. She'd play things chill and keep the vibe lowkey.

He flashed her a chill smile, sending a hit of adrenaline through her. "Hey."

"Hi."

They stood too close, closer than two working professionals would stand. As he stared into her eyes, his expression turned primal and his pupils blackened. She glanced at his mouth, desperate to kiss him. But she was there on official police business and she needed to keep her hands—and her mouth—off him.

He gripped her shoulder and sparks whizzed through her. "Detective Easton, good to see you again."

She loved the deep register of his voice, his relaxed cadence that set the mood. But she wasn't fooled by his laid-back persona. That anger he carried in his soul poured out of him and she wanted to gobble it all up and get lost in him.

"How's it going, Detective?" Tank asked.

"Going all right. You?"

"Ready for another rowdy evening," Tank replied.

"I'll be around if you need me," Stryker said to Tank.

"I'm sure I will," Tank said.

Stryker led her inside the club and toward the stairs.

"I can take the elevator," she said. "And I need to question Mavis."

After the scanner cleared him to enter and the doors closed behind them, he was on her. His mouth on hers, his arms enveloping her. He was all man, all testosterone, and all encompassing. She buried her fingers into his hair and tugged fistfuls of soft strands. Their kiss turned wild, his lusty groans making her weak in the knees.

The doors opened, their kiss ended. She tugged down her summer sweater, and stepped into the quiet, dimly-lit hallway on L3.

So much had changed in such a short amount of time. In less than a month, she'd felt things with him that she'd never felt with anyone else. She loved being in his life and sharing hers with him.

They stopped in front of Mavis's closed office door. "She's not expecting you." Stryker knocked.

"C'mon in," Mavis said.

Stryker pushed open the door and Emerson entered the smoky room.

A lit cigarette dangled from Mavis's lips. She flicked her gaze from one to the other, then crushed the cigarette in the ashtray. "What's up?"

"Detective Easton has more questions."

Emerson sat in the guest chair. Stryker shut the door, leaned against the wall. She glanced over at him before addressing Mavis. "I heard you had a few days off," she began. "Go anywhere fun?"

"Visited my son and his family at Virginia Beach."

"Nice," Emerson said. "I wanted to talk to you about Parker Sandler."

"What about him?"

"Did you know he and April were friends?"

Mavis shook her head. "I've got over fifty employees. People rotate in and out monthly. Some nights I'm interviewing, other nights I'm letting someone go. I'm serving drinks or breaking up a fight. I have no idea who's banging who."

"What's your impression of Parker?"

"He shows up on time, does his job. He calls out sick a coupla times a month with a migraine, which is a pain in my ass. I gotta find someone to work for him or do it myself."

"Have any staff or members complained about him?"

"I keep a record of complaints." Mavis typed a few keystrokes. "Nope, nothing."

"Did you know Parker was convicted of stalking his ex-girlfriend?"

"I'm sure I did." Mavis tapped on the keyboard again. "Yup, it's here on his application."

"You weren't concerned about hiring a stalker or someone who doesn't understand the word no?"

"I wouldn't have hired him if I thought he'd be trouble. Newbies are on a sixty-day probation period. He got through that no problem. He needed a job. I needed a mixologist."

Another dead end.

"Thanks for your help." Emerson rose.

"I'll be around for a few if you need me," Stryker said to Mavis.

They left Mavis's office and headed down the hallway. "Elevator or stairs?" he asked.

"Elevator."

Once in his office, she glanced over at him. The knot between his brows was deeper than normal.

"What's going on with you?" she asked.

Exasperation rolled off him in angry waves. "More shit, different day."

"Talk to me."

He did not. Instead, he fired up the computers.

"I'm not working until you tell me what's wrong."

"We're short on time and the list is long." He turned toward the console, typed in his password.

She knew *exactly* what he needed to help ease his frustration.

He pulled up what they'd been working on last week. "We got hits on Blondie. He was here a couple of weeks ago, Tuesday night."

They watched the video of Blondie entering the club. Instead of holding up his phone so the hostess could scan his QR code, he whispered in her ear, then slipped her something.

"Did you see that?" Stryker asked.

"I sure did."

"He paid her to get in."

"Are you going to speak with her?"

"Not yet," Stryker replied. "If she tells him, we lose him."

Blondie sat at the bar, ordered a glass of wine, and camped out there. Over the course of the evening, he talked to several women, danced with three, and walked one gal out at the end of the night.

"She fits his profile," Emerson said. "She's got long, dark hair."

The two chatted at her car. Before she left, he handed her a business card. Stryker zeroed in on the woman's face and pulled up IDware. While the program searched for a match, Emerson asked him to print out screen shots of Blondie talking to her.

Bing!

Match found

The member went by KW. He tapped her profile, found her credit card, along with her contact info.

Karen Watters had an L1 membership and lived in DC.

Emerson jotted down the woman's contact info. "This is great."

Stryker's phone rang with a call from Mavis. He hit speaker. "What's up?"

"I've got two guys on L2 about to beat the living hell out of each other."

"On my way." Stryker hung up. "Come with me," he said to Emerson.

"I'm okay."

That elicited a brief smile. "Nice. I'll set the monitors to 'live' so you can see what's happening real-time." Once he'd done that, he vanished up the stairs.

A shudder ran through her. *I can do this.*

After a calming breath, Emerson pulled the pictures of Blondie from the printer and slid them into her oversized handbag. Then, she turned her attention to the monitors on the wall.

She glanced from one to the next, then spotted a blond man talking to a woman with long, dark hair. *That's Blondie. He's here!*

On her way upstairs, she texted Stryker, "Blondie is on L1. Going to talk to him."

The first floor was wall-to-wall members. When she got to the bar, Blondie wasn't there. She squeezed around the clubbers on her way to the dance floor.

There he is! Blondie and the brunette were standing near the dance floor talking. He had his hand on her shoulder and was whispering in her ear. As Emerson got closer, Blondie slid his gaze to hers. They locked eyes.

A couple stopped in front of Emerson, blocking her way and cutting her off. *C'mon.* When she scooted around them, Blondie was gone.

No, no, no. On her tiptoes, she swept the room, back and forth. Then, she caught him heading for the exit. *Go!* She hurried outside.

Where'd you go? Emerson rushed over to Tank, talking to a member in line. "Tank, did you see a blond man walk by?"

"Nope, sorry."

She scanned the area and spotted him, hurrying down the

sidewalk. He turned the corner and she followed. Once she cleared the corner, she saw him across the street, cutting through the shopping center parking lot toward the grocery store, the lights illuminating the area outside the store. Emerson pursued him.

Rather than head inside, he made his way toward a car waiting at the curb near the closed dry cleaners.

He spoke to the driver, then hopped in the back seat. The car took off. Emerson strained to see the tags, but the car sped away too fast. She stopped in the middle of the parking lot.

I lost him.

Either Blondie had an accomplice, or he'd called an Uber.

Stryker pushed through the swarms of bodies, but Emerson wasn't on L1. He strode outside. She wasn't in the parking lot, either.

"Hey, boss, looking for the detective?" Tank asked.

"Yeah, where is she?"

"She went after some guy." Tank pointed. "Took off down the street."

Fire burned through Stryker as he jogged down the sidewalk. *What was she thinking going after him alone?*

He rounded the corner. No Emerson. When he glanced across the street, he saw her walking back through the mostly empty parking lot. What she didn't see was the car creeping behind her. He broke into a full-on run, his long stride eating up the pavement.

The car pulled diagonally in front of her, blocking her way. Both the passenger and driver got out. Two large men on the prowl. Emerson pulled her Glock.

"Whoa, baby," said one of the guys. "Why the heavy artillery? We just wanna say 'Hey.'"

"Back off," Emerson shouted.

Breathing hard, Stryker pulled to a stop by her side. "Get the fuck away from her."

"Get lost, dude. Baby, get in the car."

"I'm a cop," Emerson said. "You two need to get in your car and drive away now."

Anger seethed from his every pore. Stryker wanted to take both these guys down. "You heard the detective. She's cutting you a break you don't deserve. Get the hell outta here."

Both men retreated into the car. The passenger spit out the window. "Rot in hell, motherfuckers." The car sped off.

Emerson re-holstered her weapon, but she wouldn't look at him.

Tamping down on his fury, Stryker said, "You scared the hell out of me."

"I'm so pissed at myself," she bit out. "So fucking pissed."

"Are you okay?"

"No, I'm not okay. I'm so obsessed with finding the killer that I ran after Blondie without thinking it through. I should have let him go." Fear flashed in her eyes. "If I didn't have my weapon, they could've taken me."

"I would've killed them, and died myself, before I let them take you."

She wrapped her arms around him and hugged him. With her in his arms, he could breathe. She was safe.

"Thank you," she whispered.

When she pulled away, he said, "Let's get outta here."

"I need to question the woman who was talking to Blondie."

They returned to the club. After walking through the sea of people, twice, Emerson wanted to scream. Not only had she lost Blondie, she couldn't find the woman he'd been hanging with. Despair had her blood running hot.

Turning to Stryker, she said, "I'm calling it. Where are we going?"

"My place," he replied.

17

CLAIRE-MARIE

Stryker, on a Harley, was the hottest thing Emerson had ever seen. As she followed him home, she imagined her arms wrapped around his hard torso while they flew down an open road.

Inside his house, he set his helmet and leather jacket on the kitchen table, then pulled her into his arms. Gazing into his fiery eyes brought the heat, every damn time.

"I've missed the hell out of you." His embrace was strong, but his kiss was soft. "I have a surprise for you."

"You do?"

"I got past the department's firewall. You wanna see if we can access Doug's police reports?"

"You are so good to me." She kissed him with so much energy, he cracked a smile.

"That's because I like you so damn much."

"I feel the same way." She kissed him again, this time, deepening their embrace.

"We're knocking this out, then I'm taking you to bed."

They sat side-by-side at his kitchen table and Stryker logged in to his laptop. Once he'd accessed the department's website, he was able to get into Doug's online file. Together, they read several of Doug's reports to get an overview of his UC work.

Doug Easton had infiltrated a tight-knit drug gang in Northern Virginia. According to his notes, they were the region's premiere seller of heroin and opioids. Small, but powerful, they called themselves The Trinity. Doug had risen through the ranks, earning himself a position that gave him access to the gang's leader, known only as The Father.

"None of these guys use their real names," Emerson said.

After skimming a report, Stryker would open another one. It was almost one in the morning when Emerson said, "Last one for now. I've got an eight AM meeting with the chief toxicologist."

Stryker clicked on a report and they started reading.

"Here we go," he said. "He got a name."

"Donny Farraday," Emerson read.

According to Doug's notes, Farraday had been pushing heroine and opioids for decades, and staked a large area of Northern Virginia as his turf. It didn't take Stryker long to find Farraday on social media. The guy loved posting pics of himself with strippers.

After a quick search for Farraday on the dark web, Stryker found X-rated photos of him and a woman. Ten minutes later, Stryker learned the woman wasn't a woman at all. She was a sixteen-year-old teenager.

"This guy is dumb as fuck," Stryker said.

"Thank you for doing this for me." Emerson caressed his face with the back of her fingers before dropping a soft kiss on his lips.

He stood and held out his hand. "Let's go to bed, baby."

As she entered his bedroom, she squeezed his hand. He'd left a box with a bow on his bed.

"You bought me an electric toothbrush. Or you bought yourself one and put a bow on it."

On a chuckle, he handed her the box. "For you."

"Thank you," she said, before kissing him. "This sleepover was premeditated."

"Guilty as charged."

With her new toothbrush in hand, she said, "I cannot believe how much you spoil me."

"Neither can I, but I love it."

They brushed their teeth, stripped down, and got into bed. Then, she eyed his shoulder. "What happened to you?"

"I got stabbed."

"*What?*"

After he told her about the teens at the playground, she gently kissed his healing wound.

"Mmm, that helped."

She dotted his shoulders and chest with kisses before returning to his mouth. When he drew her into his arms, she felt home. This was where she was supposed to be and this was her person. She felt it in her bones and in her soul.

"I'm falling in love with you," he murmured.

I've already fallen, so, so hard.

"Me, too." While she didn't like withholding her truth from him, she viewed him as a free spirit when it came to women and commitment. Because of that, she'd tread lightly.

She opened his night table drawer and extracted a condom. Having made her intentions known, she kissed him again. She loved the intensity of his embrace, the passion in his lovemaking. His touch electrified her and her body surrendered to his. His powerful thrusts took her over the edge, but it was the tenderness in his eyes that brought a tear to hers. This man had captured her heart in every way possible.

They lay together, sharing a pillow and facing each other. The tension he carried between his brows and the tightness in his jawline were gone. Serenity replaced angst, leaving his true beauty to shine through.

He kissed her palm. "You deserve to be with a good man, Emerson." He fell silent. "That's not me."

Emerson had been soaring high in the sky, floating amongst the clouds. His words sent her plummeting to the cold, hard earth. Hurt and confused, she said, "I thought you were falling in love with me."

"I am." More silence while he searched her eyes. "I'm not the good guy you think I am."

"What kind of man are you?"

"I'm ruthless and vengeful." He sighed. "You deserve better."

Pain shot through her chest. "That's not your choice to make. Not even you have that kind of power over me." It was late and she didn't want to get into it with him, so she rolled away, hoping to shut out the pain.

Stryker spooned her, his warm body blanketing hers. She wanted to ask him why he was pushing her away, but his harsh words stopped her. *I'm ruthless and vengeful.*

As he drifted to asleep, she wondered who Stryker Truman really was.

Emerson woke early and left Stryker's before the sun crested the horizon. Beyond thanking him for his help, she said nothing more. If he was pushing her away, that was on him.

Once at home, she called Karen Watters, the woman who'd been last seen on video surveillance talking to Blondie. When she didn't answer, Emerson left a message, then sent a follow-up text. Hoping to hear back, she left for her meeting.

Emerson sat across the desk from Arlington County's Chief Toxicologist, Dr. Rebecca Jardin. The doctor handed her a report. "These are the ME's results, along with my tox report for April Peters. I just emailed this to you and Detective Cardoso."

"Thank you. That was fast."

"Chief Watson is pushing for results."

"Did you find anything?" Emerson asked.

"Yes," replied Dr. Jardin. "Like Ms. Stanton, Ms. Peters also had a high level of ketamine in her bloodstream. The drug can be snorted, injected, or drunk. Both victims ingested it with wine. Since it's tasteless and odorless, the victim is at a terrible disadvantage."

"Isn't it a tranquilizer?" Emerson asked.

"Its primary use is to sedate animals, but it's become a popular street drug. When used in small doses, it induces calmness and hallucinations. It also evokes dizziness, slurred speech, and diminished reflexes."

Emerson jotted down a few notes.

"It's been used as a date rape drug," the doctor explained. "In both these cases, the killer used the drug to incapacitate his victims, before strangling them."

Emerson finished up the meeting and checked her phone on the way out. Karen Watters had texted her back.

After a few back-and-forths, the women agreed to meet in thirty minutes at a coffeeshop on the Hill. Emerson jumped in her car and drove over the Potomac towards the Capitol.

Emerson entered the busy eatery and found Karen Watters sitting alone. "Thanks for meeting with me," Emerson began.

"I hope I can help," Karen replied.

Emerson showed her a photo of her speaking with Blondie in the parking lot of The Dungeon. "Do you remember meeting this man?"

"Oh, sure," Karen said. "We started talking at the bar."

"What did you two talk about?"

Karen paused to sip her iced coffee. "Some of the outfits and tats that caught our eye. He loved my hair. I'd worn it down. It was nothing, really, but he made a big deal over it." She pointed to her hair. "I usually just pull it back for work."

At a glance, Karen Watters fit the killer's type.

Emerson redirected her attention to the photo. "What's he handing you?"

"His business card. He wanted to take some test shots of me, then possibly hire me for a photo shoot."

"What kind of photo shoot? Did he mention any details?" Emerson asked.

"Like what?"

"The location or the type of clothing you'd be wearing for the shoot."

"I didn't give him a chance. I took the card and left."

"Did you meet with him?"

Karen furrowed her brow. "No."

"Why not?"

"Something was off about him. He was fine all night, but when he asked for my number and I wouldn't give it to him, he got… kinda pushy. Like, annoyed because I told him no."

"Did he give you his number?"

"No. He said he was between phones, whatever that means."

"Have you been back to the club since then?"

"Once."

"Did you see him?"

"No, but I wasn't looking for him and I wouldn't have spent any time with him if I had."

"Why not?"

Karen shrugged. "Not interested in him or his photo shoot."

"Do you have his card?"

"I think so." Karen started digging through her bag. She pulled out the card and set it on the table.

CASEY QUINN
FREELANCE PHOTOGRAPHER

Using a tissue, Emerson folded a napkin around the card and tucked it into her bag.

"You've got my number. If you see him at the club, text me. Do not leave with him or meet him anywhere."

"I wasn't planning on it. Why are you interested in talking to him?"

"He's a person of interest in two homicide cases I'm working."

Karen's eyes grew large. "Yikes, well, I'll definitely stay away from him."

Back at the office, she and Nikki read through the ME's report on April Peters.

The killer's most recent victim had died from asphyxiation as a result of strangulation. The ME estimated April's time of death between nine on Wednesday evening and three in the morning on Thursday. A single fingerprint found on April matched a partial on Gloria. A single blond hair was found on the wedding gown, but there was no root, so DNA was inconclusive. April had no skin under her nails. She had not been sexually assaulted.

Emerson was relieved April had not been raped, but since her body offered no clues, they had hit another dead end.

"I'll talk to my informants," Nikki said. "Someone might know who's selling ketamine on the street."

Right around noon, a uniformed officer escorted Danielle over to Emerson's desk.

"Hey, what are you doing here?" Emerson asked.

Danielle folded into the chair. "I'm trying to be chill about this, but a coworker at Claire-Marie's office called me this morning. She hasn't shown up for work all week."

Not wanting to panic her friend, Emerson asked, "Have you talked to her this week?"

"No. I called and texted her a bunch of times after I talked to her coworker, but she hasn't called me back."

Oh, boy. This isn't good.

"Let's swing by and check on her," Emerson said, while shouldering her bag. "Do you have a key to her condo?"

"Yeah."

On the way out, Emerson asked, "When was the last time you guys talked?"

"We texted over the weekend." Danielle checked her phone. "Saturday."

"Was she okay?"

"As far as I could tell."

Emerson read the text exchange between the sisters. Nothing looked unusual about the messages. "Was she seeing anyone? Could she have gone out of town, maybe camping, and doesn't have cell signal?"

Danielle paused. "She didn't say. The last time I saw her was when we went to dinner at Raphael's."

"Do you guys use a location app like Find a Friend?"

"No."

They left the building. Danielle hugged herself and Emerson stroked her back. "We'll find her." Emerson's gut roiled as Danielle unlocked her car.

"I know she's a free spirit and all, but it's not like her to ghost on her job." Danielle's brows were pinched together.

"Have you talked to your mom or dad to see if they've heard from her?"

"No. I didn't want to worry them. Knowing them, they'd jump in the car and be here this afternoon."

While Danielle drove, Emerson called Claire-Marie, then put the call on speaker. It rang several times, then went to voicemail. Emerson hung up.

"I'm trying not to let my imagination get away from me," Danielle said. "She could be sick and not able to call for help."

Though Emerson tried to calm her friend, she didn't want to tell her Claire-Marie was okay, because she didn't know. Fifteen minutes later, the two women hurried inside the condo building.

Danielle inserted the key and opened the door. The dreaded odor smacked Emerson in the face. *God, no.* Adrenaline pumped through her and she pulled the door closed.

"What are you doing?" Danielle said.

Emerson stood in front of the door, blocking her friend from going inside. "You can't go in there."

"Why not? That's ridiculous."

Dread curled around Emerson's heart. "She's not okay. Stay here."

The color drained from Danielle's cheeks. Emerson went in, but before she could shut the door, Danielle flew into the apartment.

"Claire-Marie? Are you here?" Danielle screamed as she rushed past Emerson.

Emerson grabbed her arm. "Stop!"

Danielle yanked her arm away, then covered her nose and mouth with her hand. "What smells so bad?"

"Look at me." Emerson spoke calmly, though she was shaking. Danielle did.

"I think Claire-Marie is dead."

"Claire-Marie!" Danielle yelled, while bolting through the condo. "AAAIIIIIIIEEEE!!!!!"

Emerson ran after her. Claire-Marie's lifeless body sat stiffly in the oversized chair in the corner of her bedroom, her dead eyes staring straight at Danielle.

Danielle started shrieking, then fell to the ground, sobbing. Emerson pulled out her phone and called for backup. "This is Detective Emerson Easton. I've got another wedding gown victim." She gave the location and hung up, then dropped beside Danielle.

Emerson put her arms around her friend, and Danielle's sobs turned into wails. As she held her, her heart broke in so many ways. The killer had outsmarted her again.

"Danny, we need to go into the living room," Emerson said. "Let me help you."

Danielle stared into Emerson's eyes. "Oh, my God. Who would do this to her? How did this happen?"

Emerson helped Danielle to her feet. Instead of leaving, Danielle stared at her sister.

"She's posed," Danielle uttered. "Like a doll or a mannequin. What is this?"

"It's the serial killer," Emerson said, pushing away the defeat that hounded her. He was winning and Claire-Marie had become another victim in his sinister game. "I will find him and he will pay for what he's done."

When Emerson escorted Danielle into the living room, she broke down again in Emerson's arms. Danielle's gut-wrenching sobs tore at her, but Emerson pushed down her own sorrow and stayed strong for her friend.

"Do you want me to drive you to North Carolina?" Emerson asked.

"Oh, no, my mom and dad." Danielle wiped her cheeks. "This is going to kill them."

Two officers arrived, along with the paramedics. Emerson spoke with them before turning her attention back to Danielle.

"I can drive you to your parents'," Emerson said.

Shaking uncontrollably, Danielle hugged herself. "No, you need to stay and find the bastard. I'm going home to pack, then I'm taking off."

"I'll let Stryker know," Emerson said, wiping away her friend's tears. "I'll ask an officer to drive you home in your car."

"Find him, Em. If you don't, I will." Danielle's eyes grew cold. "And I'll kill him myself."

Emerson spoke with a patrolwoman, who escorted Danielle out.

Emerson stood in the living room feeling responsible for Claire-Marie's death. *I knew about Claire-Marie's photo shoot, but I didn't make her cancel or go with her.* Even though she'd warned the women, it hadn't been enough to save Claire-Marie.

She had failed her friends. Her throat tightened, the emotion on the verge of exploding out of her. She couldn't lose it here. She had a damn job to do.

The crime tech team arrived. One of them handed her shoe covers and disposable gloves. As they dispersed through Claire-Marie's home, Emerson went into the kitchen.

The sink was empty, the kitchen was spotless. *He's cleaning up after himself.* When she found no dishtowel, Emerson opened all the drawers. She opened the hall closet and found a matching set of three. *He cleaned up and took the towel with him.* Emerson asked the crime scene photographer to take a picture of the three matching towels.

Back in the bedroom, she studied her latest victim. Thirty-five-year-old Claire-Marie Fox stared back with lifeless eyes. Dressed in a white wedding gown, the train had been draped over her legs. If it wasn't for her ashen skin and purpling of her neck, it would seem like she was sitting there relaxing.

Only she wasn't. She was dead. A fury erupted inside Emerson and she released a muffled cry. Someone was killing innocent women and had turned it into a game of cat and mouse. She had to change things up, let him think he was winning.

One of the crime techs walked over with a bagged phone. "Detective, we found this under the vic's bed."

A lucky break? Emerson was not feeling lucky, but this was the first time they'd found a phone.

"Thanks for telling me."

Her head pounded and the ache in her heart wouldn't stop.

Her partner, Nikki, entered the bedroom. "I got here as soon as I heard." Her gaze fell on Claire-Marie. "He staged this one differently. What's he trying to tell us?"

"I know her," Emerson whispered.

"Ohmygod, no," Nikki replied.

"This is my best friend's sister."

Nikki stepped forward and Emerson held up her hand. "I'm okay," she lied. "I've gotta push through this." Emerson squelched down the tidal waves of emotions threatening to burst forth.

"I'm sorry," Nikki whispered. "I'm so sorry."

After a few seconds, Emerson nodded as she swallowed down the mounting grief. "I think he's going for shock factor. The chair is opposite the door. Claire-Marie is the first thing we saw when we walked in. He's letting us know he can command the room. He's in control."

"I have news," Nikki said, "and you're not gonna like it."

How much worse could the day get? Her best friend's sister was dead.

"I never heard back from Parker's sister, so I called him. His phone went right to voicemail, which means he turned it off, or it's out of juice. I swung by his apartment. No answer. I've requested a search warrant."

"You think he's running?" Emerson asked.

Nikki shrugged a shoulder. "Something isn't right. Do you know if he's been at work?"

Emerson hadn't seen him at the club last night, but he could have been working on L2. Rather than assume his whereabouts, she called Stryker. His phone rang, then rolled to voicemail. She sent him a text. "Can you tell me if Parker's been at work the past few days?"

No dots appeared. "I might not get an answer until later."

"Hey, Detectives." Lyle stood in the bedroom doorway, a uniformed officer by his side. "Can I come in?"

"Terrible timing," Emerson mumbled. "What are you doing here, Lyle?"

"I heard on the police scanner, so I came right over." He shifted his attention to the victim and laid his hand over his heart. "I can't believe this happened again. It's so sad."

"This is an active crime scene and you can't be here," Emerson said.

"Wait, Detective," Lyle blurted. "I'm wondering if the captain would want you to go public with the story. I can help with that. You know, change up the focus of my piece. Isn't it time the public was warned?"

Emerson addressed the officer. "Please escort Mr. Barnham out and don't let anyone else in."

"Let's go," said the policeman.

"I can help you solve this," Lyle said over his shoulder as he was led out.

"I'm done answering his questions," Emerson said. "I don't care how many complaints he files against me."

"I think he's got a point," Nikki said. "We need to talk to Captain Perry. I know they don't want to fuel the killer by giving this a lot of media attention, but if we don't do something different, nothing's gonna change."

Stryker spent the entire morning and half the damn afternoon stuck in meetings. When the last one ended, he high-tailed it to his office, stopping at his assistant's desk. "No interruptions for the next fifteen."

He went into his office and shut the door. At his desk, he logged in to a secure portal and entered his sixteen-digit security code. A screen opened and his cousin, Providence, appeared in the window.

"Hey, cuz," she said. "What's the word?"

"I need your help with a drug gang in the DMV. The Trinity."

"Never heard of them. Give me a few." While Providence searched for information, Stryker checked his phone. He had missed calls from Cooper, Danielle, and Emerson. His pulse kicked up when he saw that Emerson had called…until he read her text. "Can you tell me if Parker's been at work this week?"

Dammit. He'd hoped she'd moved past his fuck up, but her text was work related. That morning, she'd bolted with barely more than a peck goodbye. He regretted saying anything to her, but he had to tell her the truth about himself.

He clicked the phone app that tracked employee hours and found Parker. "Hmm."

"Sorry this is taking so long," Providence said.

"It's all good," Stryker replied. "I'm working."

Parker had requested time off Tuesday and Wednesday. Mavis had scheduled another mixologist to work his shifts.

Stryker texted Emerson. "Sorry I missed your call. Parker requested off on Tues & Wed."

"I'm back," Providence said. "I don't have much on this group. I see that a UC named Doug Easton had been working the case. File shows he's deceased. Who are they and why are you interested in them?"

"I'm helping a friend out," he replied.

"I'm sorry I don't have more info."

"Did Dakota talk to you about Cooper Grant?" Stryker asked.

"I reached out to him, but haven't heard back. You might want to give him a heads up. I doubt an ASAC with the Bureau would accept an invitation to tour a meat packing company."

That made Stryker laugh. ALPHA Meat Packing Company was the agency's cover.

"I'll talk to him." Stryker ended the video call and left his office in search of a caffeine hit.

His assistant flagged him down. "A Detective Easton is waiting for you in the atrium. Do you want her sent up?"

"I'll go down." As he passed the executive conference room, Brooks waved him in.

After sticking his head inside, he asked, "You guys still meeting?"

"We could use your help with something," said one of his execs.

"No can do," Stryker said. "I've got another meeting."

He took the stairs, entered the lobby of his building, and found her. A rush of heat blanketed his chest. She did it for him every damn time. When she turned, her expression caught him by surprise.

"Hey, I'm glad you came by." He never showed affection at work, but something was wrong, so he pulled her into his arms. "What's going on?"

She glanced around the spacious lobby. "Where can we talk in private?"

"My office, top floor. Elevator or stairs?"

"Elevator."

She hesitated a brief second before stepping inside. Once the doors closed, he rubbed her back.

"Thanks," she murmured, but said nothing more.

She's here to end things. Dammit to hell. I royally fucked this up.

As he passed his assistant, he said, "No interruptions."

"Can I get the detective a coffee?"

Emerson shook her head and they went into his office.

Behind his closed office door, he leaned his backside against his conference table. Sad eyes stared up at him, then clouded with tears. "Danielle's sister, Claire-Marie, you met her at Raphael's." A tear streamed down her face. "She was murdered by the Wedding Gown Killer."

He held her while her sobs ripped through her. She was shaking hard and trying to get a handle on herself, but the emotion poured out of her. He cradled her and kissed the top of her head. His heart broke for Danielle and their family, but the rage that lived at the surface burst forth like a volcano spewing white-hot lava.

Emerson dug out a tissue and wiped her eyes, then took a moment to compose herself. "This is personal. I failed. I failed my best friend and her sister. I failed their entire family."

"Emerson."

She steeled her spine. "But this isn't about me. This is about finding the madman and stopping his killing spree. I don't care if you don't want to be with me. I don't care that I'm falling in love with you and you can't reciprocate. None of that matters because it's not about us. I need your help. You in?"

He loved her spirit. He loved that she put it out there and wasn't holding back. He loved her commitment and her humanity. She allowed herself to be vulnerable with him, was strong enough to admit her feelings, but stayed focused on the task.

"I handled last night poorly. Love is complicated for me and I'm sorry I hurt you. I won't make that mistake again."

"Thank you. But you don't have to—"

He dropped one gentle kiss on her lips. "I love you, Emerson. I love you with my entire being. Getting this close to you scares the fuck out of me. I think you deserve better—"

This time, she kissed him like she was unleashing her anger, her sadness, and her fear onto him. And he took it without hesitation. He would walk through fire for this woman. He would protect her and fight for her. And when he told her the truth about himself, she would make up her own mind about how she wanted to proceed. For now, he would enjoy every minute with her, knowing one of them would be his last.

"I love you, too, but I can't think about us," she said. "Not until I find this killer."

Those three little words seeped into his bitter soul and chipped away at the armor surrounding it. "I'm in. Whatever you need."

They sat side-by-side on his sofa.

"Tell me what happened." He held her hand and stroked her soft skin while she filled him in.

When she finished, Stryker said, "I'll let Danielle know she can take as much time as she needs," he said. "When are you meeting with the club member, Karen Watters?"

"I met with her. She confirmed Casey Quinn is a freelance photographer who asked her to do a photo shoot."

"We find that photographer, we find the killer," Stryker said.

"While you're probably right, Parker's gone missing."

"He was scheduled to work this week, but asked for Tuesday and Wednesday off."

"I've gotta let Nikki know."

After speaking with Nikki, Emerson stood. "Nikki's putting out a BOLO for Parker. I've gotta get back to work. Thank you for...." She trailed off. "Thank you for being my rock."

He rose. "I will help you find this psychopath." Clasping her shoulders, he stared into her eyes. "Whatever it takes."

On the way back to the station, Emerson forced herself to think about the clues, pushing down the grief over Claire-Marie. Parker Sandler had no alibis and was missing. Casey Quinn was stalking women at the club and inviting them on photo shoots.

Are these two men the same guy? Is the killer hiding in plain sight?

18

THE HIT

Back at the station, Emerson found Nikki at her desk. "I feel like I'm going in circles," Nikki said. "Parker's MIA and this Casey Quinn doesn't exist."

"Don't you find it strange that Lyle showed up today?" Emerson asked.

"Not really. The media listen to police scanners all the time," Nikki replied.

"Where were all the other reporters?"

"I saw a few in the parking lot when I left. Didn't you see them?"

"No. Who verified Lyle's creds?"

"Media Relations. What are you thinking?"

"I'm following my gut." Emerson returned to her desk and called downstairs to Media Relations. "This is Detective Easton in Homicide. I'm calling about Lyle Barnham, the reporter from *DMV Magazine*. Can you tell me who verified he works for the magazine?"

"I did." Her tone turned crisp. "What's the problem, Detective?"

"I need the name of the person you spoke with when you cleared Lyle."

"Just a minute."

Emerson waited. And waited. And waited. Finally, the MR officer came back. "Sorry about that. I spoke with the publisher's assistant." She rattled off a phone number and hung up.

Emerson dialed.

"Mr. Lisson's office," answered a woman.

"This is Detective Easton with Arlington County Police. I want to verify employment for one of your journalists."

"I'll transfer you to HR." The line went silent. Emerson waited and waited, but the call didn't connect. She called the main number and asked for HR.

"This is Becky."

Again, Emerson explained she was looking for information on one of their journalists.

"What's his name?"

"Lyle Barnham."

"Hold on." Becky came back on the line. "What did you say his name is?" Emerson repeated herself. "He's not on staff, but we have over twenty freelance journalists who pitch ideas and write stories for us. Some already have the finished product, others don't. Let me transfer you to freelance."

"Freelance," answered a man.

After identifying herself, Emerson inquired if a Lyle Barnham was a freelancer.

"I'll check." The man hummed a tune while Emerson waited. "Yup, I've got a Lyle."

"Lyle Barnham?" she confirmed.

"No last name. Just Lyle."

"Is there a phone number or email address for him?"

"Nope. We get a lot of interested writers who want to contribute a story, but never surface with the finished product. We used to chase the leads, but we don't have time. Our staff churns out the stories fast enough."

"So, if you don't have his contact info, does that mean he's never published with the magazine before?"

"Not necessarily. The writer includes their contact info with their submission. Makes it easy if we have questions."

"Thanks for your help." As Emerson hung up, Captain Perry entered the bullpen, then headed in her direction.

"Easton, can I have a word?" asked the captain.

"Of course."

Captain Perry sat in her guest chair. "I just found out that Claire-Marie Fox is a friend of yours. I'm very sorry for your loss."

"Thank you."

"Detective, our jobs are difficult enough, but when a case becomes personal, it can be…" She paused. "It can be hard to detach. Why don't you take a few days to—"

"With all due respect, Captain, I don't need time off. I need to find the person who's killing these women before he does it again."

Captain Perry nodded. "We're drafting a press release and the chief is holding a press conference later today. We're going public with the Wedding Gown Killer and alerting women to his M.O."

"Good. Something has to change because he's definitely got the upper hand."

On a nod, Captain Perry left.

That evening, on her way home from work, her cell phone rang. "Detective Easton."

"Hi…um. This is Parker Sandler's sister, Debbie. You've been trying to reach me. I'm sorry I haven't been available. Could you meet us at The Dungeon tonight?"

"Us?"

"Me and Parker."

"There's a BOLO out for him."

"A what?"

"He'll get arrested if a cop spots him. Give me your address and I'll meet you now."

"We're driving back from Philly. Here's Parker." Emerson pulled into her driveway. "Detective, I promise you I'll be there tonight."

"What time?"

"We can meet you on L2 at nine thirty."

"I'll be there." The line went dead and she called Nikki. "I heard from Parker Sandler and his sister. I'm meeting them at The Dungeon tonight."

"I can't join you," Nikki said. "I'll be on a stakeout for another case."

"No worries," Emerson replied. "I've got this."

That evening, Stryker and his crew pulled into the abandoned strip mall. The shops had shuttered years ago and the structure sat untouched. The place was like a ghost town in the middle of a bustling section of Alexandria.

The guys were alone. Brooks cut the headlights, drove around back, and stopped in front of the rear entrance to an athletic apparel store.

"I'll be your eyes across the street in the fast-food parking lot," Brooks said.

Stryker, Sin, and Rhys pulled on their night goggles. "If Farraday doesn't show, we follow Plan B," Stryker said before pulling on his leather gloves.

"I'll be behind the dumpster," Rhys said. "It's not as close as I'd like, but I can make it inside the building in—" He glanced over his shoulder. "Less than ten seconds."

"Good luck," Brooks said. "I got your six."

The three men exited Stryker's SUV and Brooks drove away. Sin pulled out his lock pick and went to work while Stryker and Rhys kept watch.

Too many seconds passed.

"What's the problem?" Stryker asked.

"The lock is rusted. I can't get under the bar to release. I'm gonna have to shoot—I got it." He opened the door.

"See you in a few," Rhys said, before jogging toward the

dumpster, fifty feet away.

Stryker and Sin walked inside. The back room was littered with boxes and plastic bags. Several rats scattered toward the front of the store.

"I'm in place," Rhys said through the comm. "There are some monster rats out here."

"Here, too," Stryker murmured.

The door leading into the retail area lay propped against the wall. They entered the body of the shop. Used syringes and trash were strewn everywhere.

"I'm in place," Brooks said.

After Stryker and Sin cleared the manager's office and employee break room, they took positions in the manager's closet, where they'd stay hidden until buyer and seller arrived.

"A white convertible pulled in," Brooks said. "Wait. Not our guys. It's getting back on the road."

"Eyes on another vehicle," Brooks said. "Heading toward the back. Two occupants. Rhys, you're up."

"Copy that," Rhys replied. "Eyes on vehicle. Pulling up to the building. Killed the engine. Two men exited, one's got a duffel bag. Neither is Farraday."

POP!

"He shot the lock out," Rhys whispered.

"Idiot," Stryker mumbled.

The two men entered the back room. Stryker made out the words "shit hole" and "a shit-ton of opium".

"Show time, ladies." Brooks's baritone voice rolled through the earpiece. "Another vehicle is heading your way. I can't see inside. Tinted windows."

A moment later, Rhys said, "Eyes on Farraday. Confirm, eyes on Farraday. He's got two men with him." A pause. "Farraday plus one moving into building. His guard is carrying two duffel bags. One guard, outside. He's mine. On my way."

"Here we go," Stryker said.

"Let's do this," Sin said.

"Now!" Rhys huffed out.

POP! POP!

"One down," Rhys said.

Stryker and Sin flipped up their night goggles and charged into the room, now illuminated by the dealers' phone flashlights.

POP! POP! POP! POP! POP! POP!

Stryker took out the buyer and his guard. Sin shot Farraday's guard and he dropped.

"What the fuuuuuuck!" screeched Farraday.

Sin blocked the doorway leading into the store. Rhys stood at the back exit. Both men turned on their phone lights.

Stryker pointed his gun at Farraday. "On your knees. Hands behind your head."

Sin walked over and pointed his gun at Farraday while Stryker opened the bags. One bag was filled with cash, neatly stacked. The other two contained bags of heroin.

"You cops?" Farraday asked.

"Businessmen," Stryker replied.

"What the hell! If you wanna make a deal, all you gotta do is ask, man. You didn't need to pop my guys."

"Thanks for the tip," Stryker said. "I got a coupla questions."

"You're crazy," Farraday said. "I don't have to tell ya nothin'."

"He is crazy," Sin said. "So, answer his questions."

With his gun still pointed at Farraday, Stryker asked, "Who killed undercover cop, Doug Easton?"

"You wanna talk to me about a cop? What the fuck do I know about some cop?"

"Wrong Answer." *POP!* Stryker shot him in the shoulder.

"Fuuuuuck you! You motherfucking lunatic!"

"I'm only gonna ask one more time. Who killed Doug Easton?"

"My boss."

"What's his name?" Stryker growled.

"Barca, Jimmy Barca."

"Show me on your phone."

With trembling hands, Farraday pulled up Barca's number and showed it to him. Stryker took the phone.

"Hey, man, you gotta gimme that back."

"No problem. You answer my questions, you get your phone." Stryker glared down at Farraday. "How'd he do it?"

"I set up the meeting. Barca pumped him full of heroin and fentanyl, just like his boss told 'em to."

"Repeat what you told me about Easton."

Stryker tapped the video app on Farraday's phone and Farraday repeated what he told Stryker. When Farraday finished, Stryker stopped the video, turned off the phone, and shoved it in his pocket.

"Hey, that's my phone," Farraday complained.

"Who's Barca's boss?"

"I don't know his name, I swear." Beads of sweat trickled down Farraday's forehead. "I only know him as The Father."

"Get him up," Stryker said.

Sin and Rhys pulled him to his feet.

"You've been very helpful," Stryker said. "You been running your business for long, Mr. Farraday?"

Farraday pressed his hand against his bleeding shoulder. "A while."

"What do you sell?"

"I'm the number one distributor of opioids and heroin in the DMV," Farraday said, puffing out his chest.

"Not anymore."

POP! POP! POP!

Farraday hit the floor, blood oozing from his chest. Stryker picked up the buyer's phone and called 911.

"What's your emergency?"

"Drug deal went bad," Stryker said, altering his voice. He gave her the address and hung up, then he wiped the phone and dropped it next to Farraday.

"Brooks," Stryker said. "We need a pick up."

"On my way," Brooks replied.

At nine thirty, Emerson arrived at the club, ready to hear the truth from Parker. Like every night, the place was packed, the line of eager members was twenty people deep. There were no parking spots out front, so she drove around back and parked. Instead of walking around to the front door, she stood in front of the back-door scanner. To her surprise, the light turned green and she opened the door. *Stryker gave me complete access.*

She made her way to L2 via the back stairs. That scanner turned green and she entered the second floor.

The vibe on L2 was so different from the mayhem downstairs. Sultry jazz filtered down from ceiling-mounted speakers. Seductive lighting bathed everyone in a soft glow. Here, club members were decked to the nines. Emerson was downplaying it in black jeans, a tightknit shirt, and lightweight leather jacket, but she was on official police business. She scanned the room and found Parker behind the bar. As she made her way over, she caught his eye. After acknowledging her, he spoke to the other bartender, then walked over.

"Thanks for meeting us," he said. "My sister's waiting in a booth."

The woman was sitting alone, her back to the room. Masked and wearing what looked like a wig, she offered a timid smile. "Hi, I'm Debbie, Parker's sister."

Emerson slid across from her and Parker sat beside his sister. "I'm Detective Easton." She showed Debbie her badge. "Thanks for meeting me."

After a tight nod, Debbie sipped her coffee.

"I understand Parker was with you on April fifteenth and sixteenth. Can you tell me about that?"

The young woman leaned forward. "I left my husband in April—April fifteenth, to be exact—and moved from Dayton to

Philadelphia. He was abusive and controlling. I tried leaving him a year ago, but he promised he'd be nice, so I went back. He's a liar." She shuddered. "I couldn't trust anybody but Parker. He met me in Philly and helped me find an apartment."

"Can I see your driver's license?" Emerson asked.

With shaking fingers, Debbie set it on the table. Emerson snapped a picture. "What can either of you show me that puts Parker there that weekend?"

"He took a bunch of pictures while," Debbie said.

Parker handed his phone to Emerson. "There's at least twelve. When you're done, I'll show you when they were taken."

A waiter topped Debbie's mug and Emerson ordered an iced tea.

Emerson scrolled through photo after photo. Brother and sister in front of the Liberty Bell, another selfie of them eating Philly cheesesteaks, one in front of an apartment building, one of Debbie signing a lease.

"We had the best weekend," Debbie said. "I felt free." She smiled at her brother. "He told me I could do it and I did it. I left my husband."

Emerson returned the phone to Parker. He tapped on the photo app and showed Emerson the dates and locations of the pictures. They were all taken in Philly on the fifteenth and sixteenth.

"Why didn't you just tell me this when I asked you about it?" Emerson asked him.

"That's on me," Debbie interjected. "I swore Parker to secrecy. I was terrified my husband would somehow find me. He told me if I ever left him again, he'd hunt me down and kill me. When Parker left me in Philly, he had no way to contact me because I left my phone in Dayton. I had squirreled away a little money, so I lay low the first month. Didn't even buy a burner. When I got a phone and called him, he told me he'd been accused of killing someone. I'd gotten a job waiting tables, but I came down as soon as I could. There's no way he killed anyone."

"Thank you for contacting me," Emerson said. The server

returned with her beverage and she drank down half the glass. "Parker, I have one more question. You requested time off this week. Where were you?"

"I've decided to move to Philly to be near my sister. I used to work construction, so I lined up some interviews and drove up on Sunday. The club is closed on Mondays and I took Tuesday and Wednesday off."

"Is your sister your alibi again?" Emerson asked.

"Yeah." He clicked on his phone. "I also have emails confirming my interviews and the thank you emails I sent after. Would those work as an alibi?"

"I'll need to speak with someone who can verify you were there," Emerson replied.

"If they think I'm in trouble, they won't hire me."

"I'll be discreet," Emerson explained. "Text me their contact info when you get home. I'll cancel the BOLO, so you won't get arrested, but do not leave town without telling me. If you hear back from a prospective employer, let me know."

"No problem," Parker replied.

"How long are you in town?" Emerson asked Debbie.

"I'm driving home tomorrow morning."

She smiled at Debbie. "Congratulations on your new life. It takes a lot of courage to start over. I wish you the best."

"Thank you," Debbie replied. "I'm happy to be free."

Emerson dropped cash on the table before sliding out of the booth.

Parker had alibis for Gloria Stanton and Claire-Marie. All three vics were the mark of the same killer. Emerson would call to verify his alibi, but her gut told her he wasn't the killer.

One step forward, ten back.

Rather than leave, she took the stairs to L1. As she made her way through the crowd, she scanned for Casey Quinn. Even though it wasn't his regular night, she was hoping for a break. With Parker no longer on her watch list, the photographer had become her primary suspect.

He wasn't at the bar, or on the dance floor, so she decided to leave. She made her way to the back door, stepped outside, and stopped short. Stryker and three other men were exiting a black SUV. All four were dressed in tactical gear, night vision goggles in their hands.

What the hell?

In silence, they made their way toward the fire escape stairs. She followed. For large men, they were stealth. One by one, they started climbing. Stryker must have sensed someone watching. As he put his foot on the first metal step, he turned in her direction. He paused for a split-second, while surprise flashed in his eyes. Rather than come over to her, he climbed.

She watched in silent shock as they made their way to the third floor. At the top, Stryker must have said something because all four men looked in her direction. She didn't wave, didn't smile. She couldn't make her legs move. Then, they disappeared inside. A few seconds later, her phone buzzed. She read his text.

"We need to talk."

No shit.

Fire burned in her belly as she strode to her car. She did not know him, at all. Who was he, really? What was he doing? That sure as fuck didn't look like he'd come from a game of laser tag or paint ball. Those men looked like they'd been on a SWAT mission.

His words, "I'm ruthless and vengeful", crept back into her consciousness.

Her drive home was filled with questions, but no answers. Once at home, she opened a bottle of wine and poured herself a healthy glass. Sitting on her living room couch, she sipped while Pima batted around his silver tinfoil ball. When he dropped it on the sofa, she threw it. He flew off, ran after it, and pawed it around before capturing it in his mouth like prey, and returning it to her.

She had no idea how long she sat there, sipping her wine and throwing that tinfoil toy. Had Doug been around, she could have confided in him. He had kept all her secrets. But he was gone. She thought of Danielle and wondered how much she knew about her boss.

She trusted her best friend enough to tell her what she'd seen, but Danielle was consumed by grief and Emerson would never burden her.

Her phone rang. It was Stryker. Her heart did its normal flippy thing, but she was too angry to care. "Yes," she answered.

"I'm out front. Can you let me in?"

Needing answers, she opened the front door. His hair was damp. She glared at him for a long second, turned on her heel, and walked into the kitchen. He shut the door and followed. As she refilled her wine glass, she asked, "Do you want a glass or something stronger?"

"Wine is fine."

Pima came tearing into the room and over to Stryker. "He wouldn't be that thrilled to see you if he'd seen what I saw."

"What *did* you see?"

She hitched an eyebrow. She had been duped, lied to. He had warned her but she hadn't listened. He had told her he wasn't a good guy, but she had been too gaga to listen. Too stupid to walk away. And now, she loved him. How was she supposed to walk away from that?

"Enough," she replied, and returned to the living room.

They sat on opposite sides of the sofa, sipping their wine in a frosty silence. She missed him, yet he sat three feet away. She wanted to curl up on his lap and kiss him senseless. She wanted to pull him into her bed and love him all night long. Her world was complete when he was in it and she was happiest when he was by her side.

Except for now. Now, she was too furious to utter a damn word.

19

THE TRUTH

Stryker had a situation. This wasn't something he could anger away. He couldn't ignore it, couldn't pretend it didn't exist. He loved Emerson, had fallen hard for her. And he wasn't going to walk from this challenge. But this was new territory for him. First and foremost, she was a woman. His woman, but did she see herself that way? Second, she was the damn law. She hadn't seen him commit murder, but he had. If he kept that from her, he was a vigilante *and* a liar. That wasn't the kind of relationship he wanted with her.

He shifted in her direction. She looked over. He saw her anguish, felt her anger. But beneath that, he glimpsed her sadness. Was she sad that she had seen him or sad that he had kept something from her?

"You want to talk now or in the morning?" he asked.

"Who said anything about you staying?"

"I'm not leaving until we've had this conversation. I need to know if now or later works better for you."

"Now."

"I talked to Donny Farraday, the man your brother—"

"I know who Farraday is," she bit out. "What did he tell you?"

"He set up a meeting with your brother, and some guy named Barca killed him."

"Did he give you any trouble?"

"Nothing I couldn't handle."

"Who made the arrest?"

"No one."

She set her wine glass on the end table. "You let him go?"

"No."

She tucked her feet under her, turned toward him, and tapped her fingers on the back of the sofa. He sipped the wine, wanting something stronger, but letting that urge drift away like seaweed that washes in with the tide, then back out to sea.

"He's a drug dealer in The Trinity gang," Stryker said. "Familiar with them?"

"No."

"Barca takes his orders directly from the leader. He calls himself The Father."

"How ironic. Did you get his name?"

"No, but that's who I'm going after."

She raised her eyebrows and waited. While he wanted to believe that was the end of the conversation, he knew she had more questions.

Pima jumped on the sofa cushion between them. Big, yellow eyes stared up at Emerson, who rubbed his head. Loud purring filled the tense silence. Then, Pima padded over, sat on Stryker's lap, and stared up at him. When he rubbed the cat's head, his purring intensified. Then, he peppered in an occasional meow, like he was talking.

In that second, Stryker wasn't just in love with Emerson. He'd fallen in love with that insane cat. Pima had gotten her to smile.

Stryker moved to the center cushion.

"You can't use my cat to get in good with me," she said.

He stroked her hand. And breathed easier when she didn't pull it away. Stryker felt like the walls were closing in. He wanted to go outside where the night breeze would wick away the heat.

Never rattled, he was going to put it all out there and risk everything for the woman he loved. He kissed her finger, then her hand, then leaned back. He ran his fingers through her long blonde hair, letting the wisps tickle his digits. Then, took her hand in his again. When he looked into her eyes, she was waiting.

"You want the truth, don't you?" he asked.

She nodded.

"I love you and I'm taking a risk. Isn't that what love is? Risking everything for that special person. Putting that person first—"

"Did you kill Farraday?"

"Yes."

She snatched her hand away. Her gaze turned cold. He was going to lose her. Instead of pushing off the sofa or screaming, she just stared into his eyes. "I've been under the illusion you're a hacker, but you're a cold-blooded killer."

"Yes, to both."

She picked up her wine glass, sipped. "How can justice be served, how can my brother's memory be honored, if you take out the evidence?"

"I'm going after the leader," he explained.

"So, you're gonna kill this Barca, too?"

"Yes."

"I need more, Stryker. Loving me isn't enough. I don't know what to think. I don't know what to say. You're admitting to murder. I'm assuming the men who were with you are also guilty."

He refused to comment on his crew, so he stayed silent.

Pushing off the sofa, she stood in the middle of the room. Hands on hips, she glared at him. "Who are you, really?"

"For the past ten years, I've been searching for my mother's killer."

"And you haven't found him?"

"No."

"Who else are you killing?"

"Drug gangs."

Her mouth dropped open, her eyebrows jutted into her forehead. "I'm a police officer. I took an oath to uphold the law. How could you let this"—she pointed to him and to her—"happen?"

He rose, but he didn't go to her. They stood five feet apart, but it felt like five miles.

"I couldn't stop it," he said. "What's happening between us is bigger than two people working on a case or getting kinky together. I'm yours. You own me. And you're mine. You. Are. My. Woman. I feel your love, your rage. It's—"

She plowed into him with so much intensity, he staggered back. But he stopped their momentum and folded her into his arms. Their ferocious kiss had him growling through the building euphoria. Her groans were filled with anger. She was attacking him with her mouth and he drowned in their passion.

"Fuck you, Stryker," she gasped. "You should never have come into my life. I fucking hate you. So, so much."

Their kisses were intense one minute, soft and nurturing the next. She was grinding against him while clawing his back or fisting his hair. Her breathing was jagged, her eyelids heavy with lust.

She ripped off her shirt and he eyed her bare breasts. He loved her angry, wanted all of that fury.

Seconds later, they were naked. But it was the intensity in her eyes that turned him into a feral animal. She pulled him on her as she lay on the carpeting. Their mouths found each other, their kisses a fiery combination of bites and agitated strokes. He broke away to take her nipples into his mouth. Within seconds, he had her mewling and writhing.

"I'm on the pill," she rasped out. "Fuck me."

He speared her, the euphoria stealing his thoughts and calming his rage. More pleasure than he deserved. He wanted her to have it all, and him none. He didn't deserve her. But he couldn't live without her.

"I fucking love you so much," he murmured as he moved inside her.

"You can't love me," she uttered. "No love. Just hard fucking that doesn't mean a thing."

He stopped moving inside her. "This isn't a fling or a thing that lasts for a few years. This is our forever."

Though she dug her fingernails into his back, the harshness around her eyes vanished. "Don't say that," she whispered. "This isn't supposed to mean anything. This is my goodbye fuck."

He bit back a smile. He got that she was furious, but behind her anger, he could see the love in her eyes. "Then, we better make it damn good."

He started moving inside her again and she kissed him. But her kiss was filled with so much love, his heart melded to hers and his soul bound with hers.

She reached between their legs and cradled his balls, sending streams of pleasure through him. He broke the kiss and fondled her breast, teased her nipple with his finger, then with his tongue. Making her happy was all that mattered to him.

"I still hate you," she whispered.

He smiled. She tried not to, but failed. Her smile filled him with hope. "Loving you is going to kill me," she said.

"No, it's not."

"So cocky."

He teased the orgasm out of her. And when she shattered beneath him, he let go, allowing the ecstasy to chase away his demons.

They lay together and stared into each other's eyes for a long time. She was his entire world. When she kissed the tip of his nose, he had been forgiven. And he could breathe again.

"Is there more you need to tell me?" she whispered.

"Only that I adore you. I killed to avenge Doug and I'll do it again."

"I'm not looking for revenge," she replied. "I'm chasing justice."

20

COULDA BEEN DEAD

Emerson was mired in turmoil. Her heart and soul were telling her one thing, her mind the exact opposite. She'd fallen in love with a vigilante. She couldn't un-fall in love with him. She couldn't erase him from her memory. She couldn't bring herself to arrest him, either.

In silence, she set the house alarm, then continued to glower at him. "Yes, you're staying," she said as they climbed the stairs. "But I'm not happy about it."

"Angry Emerson is better than no Emerson," he said.

They went into her bathroom and she turned on the shower. They stepped in, the hot water washing away any remaining evidence of their torrid lovemaking. She loved the intimacy of bathing with him. They'd each pulled their hair up and she appreciated how she could see his face free of his long, wild hair. She traced his thick eyebrows and ran her wet fingers over his whiskered face. When she leaned up and kissed him, he held her tightly in his arms.

She lathered the soap and ran her hands down his deltoids. Hard muscles that didn't give way to soft fingers. She loved how his gaze never left hers, how his hands were in constant motion whether he was stroking her back or kissing her. She sudsed his chest, his steel abs, his relaxed cock. Then, she knelt and washed his thick, strong thighs and calves. There was no part of him that was off limits to her, no part she didn't explore. She would enjoy this man for however long she allowed him to stay in her life. And for now, this moment was all she had.

When she finished, he rinsed off, took the bar of soap and created his own lather. Large, sexy hands stroked her body. Back and forth, up and down. There was no part of her that he didn't touch. They were without limits or borders. Never before had she been so willing to allow someone to know her this intimately.

After she rinsed away the soap, he drew her close. Then, he peered into her eyes and smiled. "You are my forever."

She wanted to believe that, but she was still too shocked by his admission.

They got into bed, like everything was okay. But nothing was okay, not really.

"Pima," Stryker called. "Come here, demon kitty."

The cat came whizzing into the bedroom, jumped up, and walked over his legs and up to his chest. He stared down at Stryker.

"This is my secret weapon," Stryker said, patting the animal. "I need crazy kitty on my side."

"You're gonna need a lot more than that cat to save you. You've put me in a terrible situation. I know I confided that I want to leave the department, but now you've forced my hand."

"Babe, you gotta trust me on this."

She turned out the light and he spooned behind her. She lay there thinking about the man in her bed. By hunting for his mom's killer, he'd become one himself. And she had envisioned spending the rest of her life with him. *What am I gonna do?*

His phone rang in the middle of the night, waking her from a deep sleep.

"Truman," he answered. "I'm not at home. Hold on while I check my security cameras."

Emerson turned on the table lamp.

"I slept through the alerts," Stryker said. "No police. Did you turn off the alarm? I'll handle it from here. Thanks for the call." He hung up, bolted out of bed, and pulled on his clothes.

"Someone broke into your house?" she asked while dressing.

"Looks that way." He grabbed his Glock. "Is your vest here?"

"Yeah."

"Put it on?"

"We don't have—"

"Do it."

She took the extra minute to put on her Kevlar vest before holstering her Glock. "Where's your vest?"

"Club."

"We'll stop there and grab it." He opened his mouth to speak and she put up her hand to silence him. "Don't argue with me."

He said nothing.

As he drove, she re-played his security videos. Two people dressed in black and wearing black ski masks sliced through the screen door on his back porch, then cut the glass on his French doors. Once inside, the kitchen camera videoed them hurrying up the stairs. The camera in his bedroom activated when they walked into the room and sprayed his bed with gunfire.

Emerson gasped. "Oh, my God."

He glanced over. "What are they doing?"

"They just unloaded on your bed," she murmured. "If I had kicked you out…" She couldn't finish that sentence.

Someone tried to take me out.

Seething with anger, Stryker pulled into The Dungeon parking lot and parked at the back door. Then, he set his gaze on Emerson. "You saved my life."

Once in Travesty, he unlocked the gear room and put on his vest.

She stood in the doorway, staring at the cubbies where his crew's gear hung.

"I never would have suspected this was back here," she said.

"That's the idea."

They left the club and drove into his quiet neighborhood. From the front, his house looked undisturbed, but Stryker new the destruction that waited inside. He pulled into his garage, cut the engine.

"Ready to clear?" he asked.

"Absolutely."

With weapons in hand, they walked through the first floor. Other than the hole in the French door, nothing had been disturbed. Next stop, his basement. All good down there.

Despite seeing the video, nothing could have prepared him for the destruction in his bedroom. His bed and his headboard were riddled with bullet holes.

Spinetti's putting the screws to me.

"I'm bagging the slugs and shell casings," Emerson said. "Do you have any plastic baggies?"

She snapped a few photos of his bed before bagging what she needed. Then, she turned her full attention on him. "We are not a team if one of us is lying or withholding information. Are we clear on that?"

"Got it."

"Who do you think did this?" she asked.

"Spinetti's crew."

"Going forward, you're wearing a vest."

"Then, so are you."

"Me? I'm not a target," she replied.

"If you're with me, you are. We both wear vests."

"Fine. Whatever it takes to keep you alive." She glanced around the room. "Let's pack you up. You're staying with me."

He could crash at the club, but this was a no brainer. "You know, Easton, if you wanted me to move in with you, all you had to do was ask."

"Not funny." She threw him some shade. "I'm still angry with you, but there is no way you're dying on me."

He threw clothing into a couple of leather overnight bags, snapped a few pictures of the bed. As he turned out the light and shut the door, a chill traveled down his spine. Was their intent to kill him or terrorize him? He didn't fucking know.

He texted the pictures to Cooper. Within seconds, his phone rang. "Are you okay?" Cooper asked, his voice groggy. "When did that happen?"

"A couple of hours ago, but I wasn't here."

"Spinetti?" Cooper asked.

"It's gotta be. Before you lecture me, I'm not going to visit him in prison."

"Good choice," Cooper said. "Need a place to crash?"

"I'm staying with Emerson, but thanks." Stryker ended the call, then called a twenty-four-hour glass repair company.

"They'll be here by two this morning," he told Emerson.

Emerson brewed a pot of coffee before sitting at his kitchen island. "How did you end up living with your aunt and uncle?" She sipped the hot drink.

He couldn't have the kind of relationship he wanted if he wasn't open with her. Easing onto the chair beside her, he paused to sip the joe.

"A few months after my mom died, my dad started traveling for work again. He asked Heather, my mom's sister, if Trudy and I could stay with her and Gordon for a couple of weeks until he sorted things out. He showed back up last month." Every muscle in his body tensed.

"He wasn't there for you guys, at all."

"My past shaped me into the person I am." *A cold-blooded killer.*

"Tell me about your mom."

"She was the best. She always put my sister and me first. I played a lot of sports and she never missed any of my games. Not one."

"Did she work?"

"She was a prosecutor."

"How did she die?"

"She was gunned down outside our house one night." He hated talking about this. "I couldn't save her. She died in my arms."

"Oh, God." She reached out and held his hand. "I'm so sorry. When did this happen?"

"Twenty years ago."

"Where?"

"Arlington," he replied.

She studied him for a few seconds. "You think her death is gang related."

"I do. She put away several drug kingpins."

"I've fallen in love with a vigilante," she murmured.

The repairman arrived and installed a new glass door. When he finished, Stryker and Emerson left.

On the way to her place, she said, "I admire that you're going after your mom's killer. I didn't do that when my brother died."

"Not everyone can do what I do. My cross and dagger tat is there for a reason."

"What does it mean?"

"A reminder of God's wrath when I die."

"That hasn't stopped you, though."

"No, it hasn't."

Back at Emerson's, she gave Stryker a spare house key and told him the codes to her garage door and home security system.

"I think the people who burglarized your company also broke into your home. You're being hunted." She pulled her secondary weapon out of her safe. "I'll drop the bullets and shell casings off this morning so forensics can analyze them. Going forward, we watch each other's backs."

Despite her anger, she loved him. He would spend the rest of his life cherishing every moment with her for as long as she would have him.

They stripped down and crawled into bed. She snuggled close. He inhaled her beautiful scent and held her in his arms, running his fingers over her bare back.

"I love you, Emerson."

Even in the semi-dark room, her smile made his heart pound faster. "I can't walk away from you. I hate you too much." She kissed him. "Still raging mad at you."

He smiled. "How 'bout I get the name of The Father from Barca and you go after him and arrest the son of a bitch."

She laid her head back down on his chest. After a long minute, she said, "Bring me with you. I need to meet the man who murdered my brother."

Emerson entered the precinct at eight thirty, feeling like a zombie. She hadn't been able to shake the thought that if she had sent Stryker home, he'd be dead, his body slammed with bullets. His life over.

Her heart clenched as she entered the crime lab. After completing the paperwork, she dropped off the slugs and shell casings before continuing on to Homicide. As promised, she'd worn her vest, but only to make Stryker wear his. Which he had.

She grabbed a cuppa joe and started reading emails. One from Parker caught her eye.

> Detective, here's an email from my future employer. She mentions the date of my interview, along with my start date. I'm going to give my notice at the club tonight. Good luck catching April's killer.

Emerson replied. "Thanks for the email. Good luck with your new job."

Nikki dropped into the guest chair. "How are you holding up?"

"Going through the motions, but my heart is broken."

"I'm so sorry, and I'm here for you, whatever you need."

"Thanks," Emerson replied. "We're gonna find him."

"The tip line has been slammed with leads about the Wedding Gown Killer," Nikki said. "I think every bride-to-be is terrified out of her mind."

"Real brides aren't his target," Emerson said. "Our plan has gotta work, but he's so cunning."

"He left Claire-Marie Fox's cell phone," Nikki said. "He'll slip up again or get cocky from all the press. What happened with Parker?"

"His sister verified his story, plus, he took a bunch of photos in Philly that put him there at the time of Gloria Stanton's murder." Emerson showed her the email from Parker and brought her up to speed on their conversation. "I'll verify he interviewed with these companies, but I'm confident he's not our guy."

"That leaves us Casey Quinn." Nikki sipped her coffee.

"And any leads from the tip line." Emerson's phone rang. It was Danielle. "I'm gonna take this," she said to Nikki. "It's Claire-Marie's sister."

"Back to chasing leads." Nikki returned to her desk.

"Hey," Emerson answered. "How are you?"

"Hanging in there," Danielle replied. "Made any progress in the case?"

"I can't discuss details, you know that."

"It's me, Em."

"No breaks, not yet."

"My dad was asking about funeral arrangements. What should I tell him?"

"We can't release the—Claire-Marie has to stay with us until the medical examiner has …" She trailed off. She had to handle this differently. "Tell your parents it's going to be a few more weeks. Can you suggest a memorial, for now?"

"I'll mention it."

"How's your mom doing?" Emerson asked.

"She's at home. My brother's here and he's been great. Can I ask you something?"

"Of course."

"How do you process all this death? I mean, we've never really gotten into the details of your work, but this is what you do. I can't get past my hate. I'm angry all the time now. I fantasize about finding him and killing him. I don't know who I am anymore."

Emerson's heart clenched. She wished her best friend was sitting in front of her, so she could comfort her. She wished she could turn time back. She wished she could have saved Claire-Marie. She wished for things she had no control over.

"In the beginning, it was hard," Emerson said. "Over time, I learned to put some distance between the cases and me. Death sucks, which is why I don't stress over the little things. But with Claire-Marie, it's different. This is personal and I can't make the pain or the guilt go away. I'm angry, too, and I'm going to find him."

"Don't feel guilty, Em. You warned us. You even gave Claire-Marie your mace. It's not your fault. I'm gonna spend a few more days here, then I'm coming home." Danielle hung up and Emerson shifted her gaze out the window.

She wasn't making the progress she'd hoped for and the man she loved had a giant target on his back. *Oh, yeah, and he's also an assassin. And I'm going to meet my brother's killer. I'm no better than my vigilante boyfriend.*

Some days, the department was busier than others. Today, there was a full house. The walls were closing in on her. She couldn't think. She couldn't stay there and focus. She shut down, collected her laptop, and checked in with Nikki. "I'll be working from home for the rest of the day. Call or text if you need me."

On her way out, Emerson went into the Property and Evidence room, found the boxes from Claire-Marie's condo, and took the bagged cell phone, along with two pairs of disposable gloves.

Twenty minutes later, Emerson was staring at her corkboard wall of case photos in her home office. She had pinned pictures from each of the crime scenes, along with pictures of Parker and Casey. She removed the pictures of Parker and tossed them on her desk.

Her phone rang with a call from Nikki. "Tell me you have good news."

"I just spoke to a woman who said she met Casey at The Dungeon. She said he didn't hit on her, but he did give her a business card. She wasn't interested and didn't give him her number, but—get this—she ran into him at her neighborhood breakfast shop where she was picking up bagels with her boyfriend. She said he approached her like all 'hey, what a coincidence', but when her boyfriend walked over, he left."

"Did she describe him?"

"Blond with a beard and mustache. It's definitely him. That's his M.O."

"That's great news."

"Did you add me to the list at The Dungeon tonight?" Nikki asked.

"I completely forgot. I'll do that as soon as we hang up."

"What time tonight?" Nikki asked.

"Nine."

"If he shows, we bring him in for questioning," Nikki said before hanging up.

Emerson texted Stryker. "Can you put Detective Nikki Cardoso on the list for the club tonight? First name only. Thanks."

Seconds later, her phone rang, and she answered without looking at her screen. "That was fast."

"Detective, it's Lyle Barnham."

"Oh, hey, what's up?"

"My story is done and my editor wants me to get your final approval. I'm at the police station. Are you here?"

"I'm working from home."

"Can I swing by?"

Eager to ask him some pointed questions, she gave him her

address and hung up, then refocused her efforts on the wall of pictures. *C'mon, there's a clue here that I'm overlooking.* The longer she stared, the more frustrated she became. Casey always wore a mask and dressed in long-sleeved shirts and pants, so if he had any tats, they were well hidden. She studied each of the victims, searching for a clue she hadn't seen before.

"Hey, baby."

Stryker's deep voice startled her and she whizzed around.

"Whoa, what's got you so jumpy?"

"I didn't hear you come home. What are you doing here?"

"I forgot my wallet, or I left it at my place after I paid the repairman."

"You had it when we left."

"Then, it's upstairs."

"Did you add Detective Cardoso to the list?"

"She's all set." He dipped down and kissed her. "Be right back." He left her office and she turned back to her wall of photos.

Ding-dong.

She looked through the peephole and stared at Lyle. *Are you the killer?* She swung open the door. "Hi, Lyle. C'mon in."

"Hey, Detective, how's it going?" He stepped into her small foyer.

"It's nice outside. Let's sit on my back deck."

As she headed toward the kitchen, he said, "That's impressive."

Lyle stood in her foyer, staring at the wall of crime scene photographs in her office. She walked back over. "Go on in."

He set his backpack down, walked over, and began eyeing the pictures, one at a time. "You've got the newest ones, from the third victim."

She thought she heard his breathing shift.

While adjusting his glasses, he eyed the pictures of Parker on her desk. "Who's this?"

"A POI—person of interest—whose alibis cleared."

Lyle pointed to a photo of Casey. "Looks like you're tracking someone. Who's that?"

"Another POI. That photo was taken at The Dungeon. Ever heard of it?"

"No, I don't go clubbing. Do you think he killed these women?"

I do think he killed those women. She studied his eyes, framed behind those oversized glasses. *Are you Casey Quinn?*

"You've never mentioned any hobbies," she said. "Besides school and writing, what else do you do?"

"I don't have time for much else. I've been thinking about getting a dog, so I've done some research on that."

"What about taking pictures? Are you an amateur photographer?"

He laughed. "No, but if I had a dog, I'm sure I—"

Stryker appeared in the doorway. "Hey, babe, I found them." His gaze slid to Lyle. "How ya doin'?"

"Lyle Barnham, Stryker Truman," Emerson said, then added, "Lyle's been interviewing me for *DMV* Magazine."

"Nice." Stryker tossed her a nod. "I'm taking off."

"I'll talk to you later," she said.

After Stryker left, Lyle asked, "Is he your boyfriend?"

Emerson wasn't answering his questions, especially the personal ones. "Do you need me to fact check your story or sign off on anything?"

Kneeling, Lyle ruffled through his backpack. "That's weird. I must've left it with Detective Cardoso."

"The entire piece?"

"I only brought the first two articles with me." Lyle stood. "Sorry I wasted your time."

She glanced at the laptop in his backpack. "I've got a printer."

"That's a friend's laptop from school. I lent her mine so she could copy my notes and I took hers so she wouldn't have to lug both around."

He's got an answer for everything.

"All right, then, I'm good with the story if Nikki okayed it."

He glanced at his watch. "Yikes, I've gotta get to class."

She walked him out and stood on her front porch as he took off on foot, disappearing around the corner. She closed the door behind her and followed. Lyle hurried toward the convenience store at the corner. There were several cars in the lot and she couldn't see which car was Lyle's. *Dammit.*

The heat of the midday sun burned down on her as she made her way back home. *He's got the same slim build and appears to be the same height, but he looks nothing like Casey. And they've got different walks. We've gotta pull Casey in for questioning tonight.*

Once inside, she called Nikki. "Did Lyle stop by and show you his story?"

"If he did, I missed him."

"He said he left it with you."

"It could be on my desk. I've been running around."

"If you put a blond wig, and a beard and mustache on him, do you think he could be Casey Quinn?"

"Seriously?"

"I don't trust him."

"You don't trust anyone."

She has a point.

"Casey is cunning and manipulative, smooth, too," Nikki said. "Lyle seems—I don't know—like a sweet guy, maybe even a little naïve. I don't see it. Okay, I'm back in Homicide. There's no story on my desk. Hold on, let me see if someone saw him." A few seconds later, she said, "No one did. Did you get me on the list for tonight?"

"Yeah. I'll meet you on the first floor. Casey usually ponies up to the bar."

"Got it," Nikki said. "What time?"

"Around nine and I'll be wearing a brown wig," Emerson said. "Do you need a mask?"

"I've got one from a party I can use. See you tonight."

Emerson set her phone down and stared at the pictures of Casey Quinn.

Casey didn't wear jewelry, but Lyle wore a watch on his left wrist. Lyle wore glasses, Casey didn't. *Casey could wear contacts or Lyle's glasses could be fake.*

Lyle was right handed, but Casey was handing the woman a business card with his left. She studied the pictures of him at the bar. He held the wine glass in his left hand. Despite their obvious differences, Emerson couldn't shake the thought.

Have I been working with the killer this entire time?

"You better show up tonight, Casey Quinn," Emerson said. "I've run out of time."

Stryker walked into the pet store and down the cat toy aisle. Too many options. He picked out a catnip mouse, a fishing pole toy, a tower of tracks, and a mountain house with scratching posts.

Stryker had no idea what he was getting himself into with demon kitty, but he loved Emerson, and Pima was part of the package. With the items in his cart, he wheeled his way over to the dry food.

What the—

There must have been a dozen different brands. A customer stopped nearby.

"Whatcha lookin' for?" she asked.

Even though the woman didn't work there, he wasn't about to reject help. Maybe she was a well-informed cat lady.

"Quality dry cat food."

"This is the best. It's made from real food, like tuna." She pointed to a different bag. "This is good, too, and much easier on the wallet. I love your hair, by the way."

"Thanks." He held up a bag of food. "What about this one?"

"My cat got the runs from that one."

He re-shelved the bag.

"That one is a middle-of-the-road and it's been around for decades."

Stryker placed a bag of her top recommendation into his cart. "Thanks for your help."

She grabbed a bag of the same food and followed. "I don't make it a point of picking up guys in a pet store, but...are you attached? I mean, you wanna have coffee sometime or get to know each other on social media?"

Stryker stood in line. "Thanks, I'm with someone. This is for her cat."

"That's so sweet. She's a lucky gal."

He set her bag of food on the conveyer. "Lemme buy this for you."

"That's okay," she said.

"That last bag is for the woman behind me," he told the clerk.

"Nice," said the employee. "Paying it forward." After Stryker paid, he turned back to the woman. "Thanks for your help."

His next stop would be more of a challenge. As he drove out of the shopping center, his phone rang and he tapped the speaker on his nav system.

"Go," Stryker said.

"Stryker, it's Dad, er, Tyler. How are you doing?"

He shook his head. *Why won't this man leave me the hell alone?* "What's up?"

"Your sister's birthday is coming up and I wanted to throw her a surprise party." Stryker rolled his eyes. "She mentioned that you own a restaurant with a private dining room. Any chance I can rent that or hold her party there?"

Not happening. "It's booked solid months in advance."

"Well, dang. You ready to get together for coffee sometime? It would be great to catch up."

"I went to college, got a job, started a company." *And I hunt for Mom's killer.* "You've been gone for twenty years. What have you been up to?"

"Let's meet for coffee and I'll fill you in."

Stryker pulled into the boutique jewelry store parking lot and cut the engine. "I'll give that some thought. Gotta run."

"I look forward to hearing from you," Tyler said.

Don't hold your breath. Stryker killed the call and got out of his car.

After a saleswoman buzzed him inside, she said, "Welcome, do you have an appointment?"

"No."

"Did you have something in particular in mind you wanted to purchase today?"

"No."

She offered a warm smile. "First time jewelry buyer?"

He smiled. "That obvious?"

"Let me find someone to help you." The woman disappeared into the back.

Stryker perused the glass counters. He had no idea what he wanted to give Emerson, only that he wanted her to know how serious he was about her.

A different woman greeted him. "Hello, how can I help you?"

"I'm looking for something special for my girlfriend." He had no idea where to start.

"Okay, let's see if we can narrow that down. Does she wear jewelry?"

"She wore a diamond necklace to a formal event and she wears a ring. And earrings sometimes."

"Is this for a special occasion?"

"No."

"What does she do?"

"Police detective."

"Hmm, that's helpful."

After looking at more jewelry than he'd seen in his lifetime, he settled on a diamond ring. Set in platinum, two brilliant round diamonds were separated by a gold X. The pattern repeated all the way around the ring. "This sixteen-stone ring is our most popular. What size is she?"

Stryker had no idea. "Medium. Mmm, could be small."

The saleswoman laughed. "I'm going with a size six. If it doesn't fit, bring it back and we'll find the right size. Make sure you bring her along."

As he drove to Emerson's, his thoughts drifted back to his dad, and the hatred he'd long buried rose up to the surface. *Why now, old man? What do you want from me?*

He parked in Emerson's driveway, entered through the garage, and dropped the cat bags in the kitchen. Not wanting to startle her again, he called out, "Baby, I'm home."

"In my office."

After hiding her gift in the bedroom, he walked into her office. "There's my woman."

Her brief smile was laced with angst. "I've convinced myself that Lyle is Casey Quinn."

"That reporter I met?"

She pushed out of her chair, raked her hands through her hair, and harrumphed. "I've gotta take a break."

As she walked past him, he slid his arm around her waist and pulled her close. "Take it down a few notches." He touched the area between her furrowed brows.

She inhaled a calming breath, rose on her tiptoes, and kissed him. "You're right. What time is it?"

"After six."

With his arm still around her, they sauntered into the kitchen. "You went shopping?"

"I got a few things."

Her beautiful smile replaced the worry lines. "I love housing vigilantes. Turns out, that's my favorite thing to do. Who knew?"

Pima walked into the kitchen and stretched, then went over to the bags and rubbed against them. Stryker carried them into the living room and sat on the floor. Emerson joined him.

As he pulled the toys from the bag, Pima started purring.

"You bought him a three-story track chaser and a house with a scratching post. He doesn't need any more reasons to love you, but these are gonna seal the deal."

After biting into the catnip, Pima went berserk. He started rolling around, then jumped up and went on a tear with the toy in his mouth.

"I'm encouraging his lunatic behavior." Next, Stryker pulled out the bag of dry cat food.

"Good luck," Emerson said.

"He'll eat it."

She straddled him and sandwiched his face in her hands, dipped down, and kissed him. "Thank you for doing this." She pushed off him.

"That was fast," he said. "Get your ass back down here."

"I can't stop obsessing over Lyle."

Though Emerson's mood lifted while they made dinner, she couldn't stop thinking about work. "Can you take a picture of Lyle and use IDware to see if he and Casey are a match?"

"I can, but those two don't look anything alike," he replied while flipping the chicken on the stovetop. "You need a grill, woman."

"I don't need a grill. I need to catch two killers." He rubbed her taut shoulders. "A psychopath on a killing spree and the lunatic trying to take you out."

Emerson pulled the corn on the cob from the boiling water. "Have you talked to Danielle?" She stirred the vegetables sautéing in the skillet.

"This morning," he said. "I told her to take as much time as she needs. She told me that if you don't find the killer, she will. I get what she's going through. It's like a switch gets flipped. Instead of drowning in grief, fury takes hold."

Stryker poured dry cat food into Pima's bowl. "Why do you think that reporter is Casey Quinn?"

"He's been obsessed over my case, and I've caught him in a couple of lies."

Stryker set the cat bowl on the floor. "Welcome to the human race. Everyone lies." He left the room.

She plated their food, filled their wine glasses, and waited at the kitchen island. Stryker returned with Pima under his arm, the animal's loud purrs competing with the music playing in the background.

He knelt, set the cat down, and placed a few pieces of dry food in his hand. Pima smelled the food, rubbed the side of his face against Stryker's fingers, then smelled the food again. With his tail in the air, he moseyed out.

As Stryker sat beside her, she hitched an eyebrow. "Cat, one. Man, zero."

He raised his glass. "Watch me win this food war." She tapped her glass against his. They sipped the wine and started eating.

After slicing off a piece of chicken, he said, "I need to tell you my plan for Barca."

21

PARTNERS

At almost nine o'clock, Emerson slid onto the bar seat on L1 and ordered a sparkling water. Hoping to blend into the crowd, she'd worn a short black skirt and a snug top that revealed cleavage, and stilettos. Her eyes were framed in a black mask, and she'd hidden her blonde hair under a long, brown wig.

Ten minutes later, Nikki arrived and sat across the bar from Emerson. She'd worn a purple mask and pulled her dark hair into a ponytail.

Stryker sat alone in the owner's booth. But he wasn't alone for long. Women paraded by, most stopped to say hello. Some even slipped into the booth with him. As Stryker nursed his drink, he seemed to know exactly what to say to ensure they didn't overstay their welcome.

As Emerson waited for Casey, she wondered what life would be like with him. She wasn't intimidated by, or jealous of, all the attention he was receiving. He was strikingly handsome, with a killer body, and an attitude that screamed "fuck off". That, along with his sexy man-bun and permanent scowl, was an absolute chick magnet. Who wouldn't want to get to know a man who wore his anger like a second skin? He commanded power and attention wherever he went.

There was no question he loved her, but was he a forever kind of man? Her heart wanted to believe he was, but was he the type of man she could be with for the rest of her life?

He's a killer and I'm still a cop.

As if he could hear her thoughts, he pushed out of the booth, leaving the starry-eyed women to fend for themselves. With every step, her heart pounded faster. Despite some members' attempts to chat him up, Stryker didn't stop for anyone.

One testosterone-laden step at a time, he made his way toward her. When he squeezed in beside her and brushed against her shoulder, she had to fight the smile.

"Excuse me." She loved the deep timbre of his voice, his slow, sexy cadence that turned her inside out.

But the pull was too strong to ignore and she found herself staring into his eyes, wanting desperately to kiss him.

"You are fucking gorgeous," he murmured.

The bartender appeared. "Hey, Stryker, what can I get you?"

"Macallan, neat."

"Coming right up."

Stryker dropped his arm around the back of Emerson's barstool and her pulse quickened. His penetrating gaze made her heart pound hard and fast.

As the bartender served him, Stryker dropped a hundred on the bar, and collected the drink. "Keep the cash," he said to his employee. Then, he shifted toward Emerson. "You're coming home with me."

"That's not happening," she murmured, "because *you're* coming home with *me*."

He flashed her a wicked smile before heading back to the booth.

The time ticked by quickly because the crowd was in constant flux. But at almost midnight, her hope fizzled. If Casey was coming, he would have shown hours ago.

Emerson handed the mixologist fifty dollars.

"This is way too much."

"I didn't order any alcohol. This should help offset some of the tips you didn't make."

Emerson made her way over to Nikki and squeezed in beside her. "When Lyle stopped by today, he saw the pics of Casey in my home office," she whispered to Nikki.

"I'm having a hard time making the connection that those two are the same person," Nikki said. "Are we calling it?"

"Yeah, let me get Stryker and we'll walk you out."

When Nikki drove away, Emerson slunk close. "I need your help."

"With all that pent-up frustration?"

Leaning up, she kissed him. "I have Claire-Marie's phone from evidence. Any chance we can download the data?"

That wasn't what Stryker had in mind, but he could see the tension on her face, and knew the higher ups were looking for answers.

Once in the dungeon, he got to work. Using his IDware, the system found several hits. They saw the moment when Casey made his move. Claire-Marie had been talking to friends, then went to the bar for a drink. Within seconds, a masked Casey appeared beside her. The two started talking. Then, two people at the bar left and Claire-Marie and Casey sat.

"This is heart breaking," Emerson murmured.

He caressed her back, hoping to comfort her. "You can do it."

Over the course of that evening, Claire-Marie and Casey sat at the bar, then moved to the dance floor. After two dances, Casey walked her back to her friends and left.

"He's smooth," Emerson said. "He didn't touch her, didn't slow dance with her, didn't hug her goodbye."

The second time they met, Claire-Marie was at the club with a different masked man.

"Who's that?" Emerson asked.

Stryker used IDware to identify the member. "He goes by Zeus. Real name is Rob Consuelo. He's been a member for four years."

That evening, Claire-Marie spoke briefly to Casey in passing. The third time, Casey was waiting at the bar when she arrived. He went right over when he saw her and stayed by her side all evening. This time, he walked her to her car.

Before she got in, he handed her a business card. "Claire-Marie told us she met a photographer at the club, then ran into him at the grocery store."

"He's stalking them, finding out where they live, then staging a run-in."

"He's creating a false sense of security," she said. "I need one more thing."

"What, babe?"

"A background check on Lyle Barnham."

While the background check ran, Stryker checked the program pulling the data from Claire-Marie's phone. "We've got the cell phone data."

There were thousands of texts, phone calls, and photos. He downloaded the data into a report they could filter. When he searched for Casey Quinn in her address book, he got a hit.

"This might be him," Stryker said. "She's got a 'Casey' in her contact list, no last name." He aggregated the data and threw the text thread onto a wall monitor.

She covered his hand with hers. "I love working with you."

Stryker leaned over, kissed her. "Me, too, baby."

Emerson squeezed his hand, then read the text thread out loud. "See you Sat," Casey had texted. "Perfect weather for test shots."

A few days later, Claire-Marie texted back. "Saturday was great! I have to cancel our photo shoot. Sorry! Work deadline."

"Casey never replied," Stryker said. "A few days later, she sent another text to him."

"So glad we ran into each other," Emerson read out loud. "Thx for coffee. See you later with the gowns!"

Emerson shook her head. "He's a master at gaining their trust."

Stryker pulled up a computer program. "I'm gonna call him, but block him from tracing it." He typed in the number. After a few seconds, the line connected, but the call went to a computerized message.

"This number is not set up to receive voice mail."

Stryker disconnected. "He knows what he's doing. I can't triangulate a phone that's off, but I can create a program so when he turns it on, the system will capture his location and notify me. And just to piss him off, I'll download his phone data."

Her smile brightened her eyes. "I love how smart you are."

"We make a good team."

She nodded before checking the time. "It's late. Let's take off."

After Stryker wrote the program, he saw that Lyle's background check was completed. They read the report.

Lyle Barnham was twenty-five years old and a resident of Palm Beach, Florida. Three years ago, he graduated from a small Florida college. Since then, he'd had a string of jobs. Pizza joint, grocery store, and courier. He was the only child of Tee and Carla Barnham.

"There's nothing of relevance here," Stryker said. "Where does he live now?"

"Somewhere up here with his parents." She pushed out of the chair. "Thank you for doing all of this."

When he rose, she pulled him into her arms and held him tightly. Then, she whispered, "I love you, Stryker Truman. Why did you have to be a vigilante?"

He kissed her. "Why did you have to be a cop?"

Back at home, she poured herself a half glass of wine, and a finger's worth of scotch for him. She took his hand and led him into the family room. He set down his glass. "Back in a second."

He retreated upstairs and returned with the small gift bag. Her gaze went from him, to the bag, and back to him.

After collecting his glass, he eased down beside her and set the bag on the sofa cushion. "For you."

"Oh, wow," she said. "What's this for?"

"Love."

Eyeing the bag, Pima hopped up, shoved his face inside, then tried climbing in. Stryker pulled him out and tossed the cat nip across the floor. He tore after it.

Emerson extracted the gift box, then opened the hinged ring box and stared at the jewelry for several seconds. "Wow, Stryker, this is *stunning*."

He pulled out the ring and she offered her right hand. After slipping it on, he said, "It fits."

"Perfectly." She kissed him. "Thank you. I've never received anything this…gorgeous."

"That's how I feel about you."

She captured his face in her hands, and stared into his eyes. "I love you, too." Her kiss was fierce and powerful and the look in her eyes was full-blown love.

The following evening, Emerson and Stryker sat at the poker table in the Travesty room discussing possible scenarios for dealing with Barca, including the one where they both ended up dead.

"Not an option." Emerson pulled up a photo on the laptop. "Barca's a career criminal with priors," she read from his rap sheet. "Possession and distribution of heroin, armed robbery, grand theft, rape, and attempted murder. He did time a few years back, but got out when the verdict was overturned on a technicality."

Stryker studied a recent picture of Barca.

"He goes from shaving his head to letting his hair grow long," Emerson said, swiping through more pictures of their target. "And he loses the beard and mustache when he wants to change up his look."

Stryker pulled on his leather gloves before opening Donny Farraday's burner phone. "I sent Barca a few texts from Farraday's phone last night."

They read through the texts together.

"We got a prob," Stryker had texted as Farraday.
"Meet me at the bar," Barca replied.
"Not safe. I got eyes on me. Abandoned shopping center, route 236, Alexandria. Tomorrow night 930."
"You gonna be alone?" Barca texted.
"Fuck yeah," Stryker replied. *"Make sure you aren't followed."*

"You set the trap, now we execute it," Emerson said.
"You sure about this?" he asked.
"Yes."
Stryker rose. "Let's get you armed."

Emerson followed him into the back room. Instead of letting the drug enforcement unit handle Barca, she was doing it herself. Was this the right choice? *It's my only choice.*

Dressed in black, she'd pulled her hair into a snug bun. She dropped her handbag in an empty cubby while Stryker set his wallet and cell phone in his.

Stryker slid his burner phone into his black jeans. "Burner's in my right pocket."

"Got it," she said.

Since she couldn't use her service weapon, he handed her a sidearm and a secondary weapon, which she tucked inside her ankle holder, before securing the primary in a holster, alongside her taser.

Stryker secured his weapons, which included two Glocks and a switchblade. He handed her a comm device, which she fitted inside her ear. After testing them, they picked up their night goggles and left out the fire escape.

Emerson said nothing as Stryker drove his SUV to the abandoned shopping center in Alexandria. She wasn't nervous, wasn't scared, either. She was simply determined to learn the truth. When he wrapped his hand around her thigh, she gazed over at him. The man she adored stared back, but the lines around his eyes were etched deep. Stryker Truman was going into killer mode.

Twenty minutes later, they parked in the back of an abandoned strip mall. They were alone. With their night goggles in place, they exited the vehicle. Emerson's heart rate kicked up and her palms grew moist inside the leather gloves. Wrapping her fingers around the Glock calmed her down.

The fire door was closed, but the lock was broken. Per their plan, Emerson left the door partially open. Rats scurried out of the filthy room. A few chairs were tossed in a corner and Stryker moved one to the middle of the floor. Emerson eyed the blood-stained floor as they made their way through the space.

As planned, they stood in the dark hallway on either side of the door that led to the back room. Weapons at the ready. They'd arrived early, so she closed her eyes and centered herself. Focused, deep inhale. Relaxed, silent exhale. When her heart rate slowed back down, she holstered the Glock and pulled out the taser.

She thought of the brother she had admired and loved her entire life. She remembered the moment when she had identified his lifeless body, so her parents wouldn't have to, and the pain that had shattered her soul. Her life hadn't been the same since.

Her thoughts floated to her mom and dad. Their gut-wrenching sobs had been heart breaking to witness. She had shoved aside her own grief to help her parents through theirs. Her dad had fallen into a deep depression. Her mom had confided that she wasn't sure she could find her way back and was terrified her only remaining child would also die young. Images of her broken family flashed through her mind. Then, she thought about the countless times she'd asked for help investigating Doug's death. And the countless times she was told the tox report was conclusive. Her brother was a user who had overdosed on the very drugs he was trying to get off the streets.

Enough was enough. Emerson was taking action and getting justice for her brother.

A car pulled up. She stood tall.

This was it. And she was ready.

Stryker felt no remorse or guilt over what he was about to do. He would never apologize for righting a wrong, especially a deadly one. Anger whirled around him as he counted car doors being closed. One. Two. Three.

As he expected.

"This is a shit hole," said one of the guys.

Phone lights shone into the dark room. Stryker and Emerson quietly lifted their night goggles.

"Yo, Farraday, where the fuck are ya?"

"Maybe he ain't here," said another.

"Then, whose SUV is that?"

"Now," Stryker whispered and stormed into the room. Emerson rushed in behind him.

Stryker zeroed in on his targets. *POP! POP! POP! POP!*

Barca's bodyguards dropped.

Emerson fired the taser, hitting Barca. He began convulsing and hit the floor. Moving fast, Stryker pulled Barca to his feet and shoved him into the chair. Emerson snatched off the taser barbs, and shone her burner phone's light directly at Barca.

"How ya doin, Barca?" Stryker asked.

"Who the fuck are you?"

"I've got a few easy questions. You answer 'em, we're good. You don't, you get punished. I could take a finger. I might sink my switchblade into your stomach." Stryker knew he had the advantage. Barca had just pissed himself from the taser.

"An undercover named Easton worked you for information. Who was he looking for?"

"My boss. Douche thought he could take him down. What a fuckin' idiot." Barca snickered.

"Now, see how easy this is," Stryker said, his voice low and relaxed. "Who killed him?"

"Farraday," Barca replied.

Stryker pressed his knife against Barca's throat. "He told me that you offed him."

"Whatever. Farraday set up the meeting and I took care of business."

"How?"

"Shot him full of heroin and fentanyl. He didn't see it comin'. I kinda felt sorry for the guy. He was doin' his job, like the rest of us. Tryin' to make a livin'."

"Who told you to kill him?"

"My boss, The Father."

"Why?"

"Like I just told ya, Easton got too close to the source."

"I need The Father's name."

Barca shook his head. "No can do."

Stryker pressed the tip of the blade into Barca's skin and blood trickled down his neck. "You don't know it, do you?"

"Sure, I do. I been to his mansion. Even driven with him in his fancy limo."

"Last chance to tell me."

"You'll have to kill me. I'm no snitch."

Stryker drove the knife into Barca's shoulder and he cried out. "Fuuuuck. You son of a bitch."

Though Stryker wanted to beat the living hell out of him, he lowered his voice. "C'mon, Jimmy, tell me his name."

"I can't," Barca said. "He'll kill me."

"So will I, my friend. You got a better chance with me. What's his name?"

"Go to hell, you motherfucker."

Stryker drove the knife into Barca's guts and he lunged for Stryker. Stryker shoved him back and he stumbled over the chair and crumpled to the floor.

Emerson shone the light on Barca's face. "Answer his question or he'll rip your heart out and shove it down your throat. Who ordered Easton's death?"

Barca spit blood. "I don't answer to no bitch."

Emerson walked around him, then kicked him in the kidney. "You and I are gonna see each other again, in hell." Then, she kicked him in the head. "You have no idea who you're dealing with. Tell him the name of The Father or I will beat it out of you." She kicked him again.

"Stop!" Barca groaned out. "My God, bitch, you're insane. The Father is Spinetti. Carlo Spinetti."

22

STRYKER'S LOVING FAMILY

Stryker's brain absorbed the words, despite everything happening in slow motion. When he slid his gaze to Emerson, she was staring at him.

"Carlo Spinetti," Stryker uttered. "He's The Father?"

"That's what I said. Now, call me a fuckin' ambulance."

"Gimme your phone, Barca," Stryker bit out.

With trembling fingers, Barca handed it to him.

"Repeat what you told us about Easton and Spinetti."

"C'mon, man, I'm bleeding pretty bad, here."

"Repeat it."

Using Barca's phone, Stryker videoed Barca's confession. When he finished, Stryker turned off the phone and pocketed it.

"One more thing," Emerson said. "Easton was a good cop, a good son, and a good brother. He spent his career trying to put thugs like you in prison. What's your big contribution to society? You're pumping everyone full of drugs. You're the fucking problem."

POP!

She pierced Barca between the eyes.

A lifeless Barca stared up at them, but Stryker wasn't taking any chances. He fired his weapon twice into Barca's chest. Emerson picked up the shell casings without stepping in the blood pooling around them.

"Ready to get outta here?" he asked.

"Spinetti," Emerson uttered. "He's in prison for Internet fraud. So, who's running his empire?"

"Babe, we gotta go."

They eyed the three dead men one more time before stepping into the night. Once outside, they climbed in the SUV, removed their goggles, and took off. The miles ticked by in silence. He glanced over at her. No surprise, she was deep in thought.

"Talk to me," he said.

"I can't. Not yet. Are you calling it in?"

"No," Stryker replied. "I don't want Spinetti to get word of Barca's death."

They returned to the club via the fire escape, and slipped unnoticed into Travesty. There, Emerson fished the shell casings from her pocket. "I've never committed a crime," she murmured. "I don't know how to dispose of evidence."

He took them from her. After opening his wall safe, hidden behind the back wall of his cubby, he dropped Barca's cell phone next to Farraday's, along with the shell casings.

She gave him back his handguns and put the night goggles on the shelf. "Is this my cubby?"

"No. You took out Doug's killer, that's it. You're a cop, Emerson, and a damn good one."

"I'm damaged goods, now."

He stroked her cheek, kissed her. "Not to me."

"Once I solve my case and help you with Spinetti, I'm out."

They drove home with the windows down. The evening breeze felt good against his skin, but Stryker didn't deserve to feel good. He deserved no reward for what he'd done. For what he'd allowed Emerson to do. "Another nail in my coffin," he mumbled.

"What?"

"Nothing."

"Thank you for tonight," she said. "No matter what happens between us, I will take this to my grave."

He pulled into Emerson's driveway and cut the engine. They went in through the garage and were greeted by an excited Pima.

Meow-meow-meoooow.

Up the stairs he flew. In the kitchen, he paraded back and forth in front of his dish.

"Check it out," Stryker said, "He ate the dry food."

"No, he didn't. I dumped it and gave him moist food." Emerson sat at the island. "How do you make peace with what just happened?"

"You don't," he replied, matter-of-factly.

Stryker shook the container of cat treats and Pima started doing his possessed two-legged dance. Rather than give him the treats, he pulled out a handful of dry kibble and dropped them into his dish.

Pima ate one, then another.

"Only you," Emerson said.

Stryker patted the cat, which elicited his bizarre purr-meow combo. "Good boy, Pima." He stroked the cat, poured himself a scotch, and sat beside Emerson.

She said nothing while he sipped his liquor. After he'd finished, he dragged over his laptop. "If Barca was telling the truth, Spinetti has people on the outside running his drug ring."

"Isn't he in a minimum-security camp?" she asked.

"Yeah."

"Hack in and see if he's had any visitors."

Stryker got busy trying to access the prison's surveillance systems. He lost track of time, but when Emerson set a plate of chicken and pasta with red sauce in front of him, along with a side salad, he stopped working.

"We didn't eat dinner," she said.

He'd been so laser focused, he didn't realize she'd been cooking for the past forty minutes. "Thanks, baby." He dug in. "Delicious."

She peered at his screen. "How are you doing?"

He continued typing, then shot her a smile. "I'm in."

Using a mugshot of Spinetti, Stryker ran his IDware going back six months. While the search ran, he ate.

"Why aren't you eating?" he asked.

"I can't stomach anything. I'm still processing what happened."

"Babe—"

"I'll eat tomorrow, when my guts aren't tied in knots."

He turned back to the computer. "When the Bureau asked me to help with the Internet scams, I found nothing connecting Spinetti to a drug ring."

"He's got wide-reaching tentacles." She poured herself a glass of water and stood beside him.

He put his arm around her and rubbed her back.

Ping!

Stryker glanced at the screen. "We got hits."

Together, they watched a video from four months ago. A flashy blonde wearing oversized sunglasses entered the visitation room. After a hug and a kiss on each cheek, she sat across from Spinetti. Her light blonde hair was styled in a fashionable updo and her pant suit screamed big bucks.

"Check out that wedding band," Emerson said. "Those diamonds are gigantic."

"Could be his wife, girlfriend, mistress."

Spinetti and the woman talked for twelve minutes, but they spoke in hushed tones, so the audio couldn't capture their conversation. Even though the woman kept her sunglasses on, Stryker paused the video, captured her image, then transferred it to IDware. While that search ran, the video jumped ahead two months, when Spinetti had a second visitor.

A young man walked in and Emerson gasped. "No way. That's Casey Quinn."

"It sure as hell is," Stryker replied.

The blond man with the beard and mustache hugged the old

man before sitting across from him. The two spoke, also in quiet murmurs, for twenty-three minutes.

"Did you see how much Casey smiled?" Emerson asked.

"Yeah." Stryker toggled to the check-in camera and zoomed in. "I can't make out his name."

Emerson leaned close. "It looks like scribble. I'm not piecing this together at all. Casey knows Spinetti. Casey's been sneaking into The Dungeon. Have I gotten this all wrong? Is he stalking you?"

Stryker started up the video again. "Is there another camera in that room?" she asked. "I want to catch Spinetti's face when Casey walks in."

While Stryker went hunting for access to a different camera, Emerson started pacing, back and forth, her hands buried in her hair. "Think," she whispered. "What is their connection?"

After several minutes, Stryker was able to hack into a different camera in the visitation room. "Got it."

When Casey entered the room, the old man lit up, his smile uncontainable. During his conversation with Casey, he stayed engaged. Never once, did he appear disinterested.

"It's either someone important to him or they're discussing Spinetti's business," Stryker said before jumping back to the video of the woman signing in at check-in.

He zoomed in. "Back it up and stop just when she finishes signing in," Emerson said.

After Stryker did, she stared at it for a long minute. "That looks like first initial C, last name Barm...Barrhum...Barram."

"Oh, Jesus, it's Barnham," Stryker said. "Is she related to Lyle Barnham?"

Emerson gaped at him. "So, my hunch that Lyle and Casey are the same person might not be so insane. But, why are they visiting Spinetti in prison? What's their connection to him?"

Stryker opened a new browser window and pulled up a website. "I'm going to run a basic background check on Spinetti. If they're close relatives, they'll show up on the report."

While waiting, he swiveled toward her and pulled her close. "How's my baby doing?"

She squeezed in between his legs and kissed him. "Your baby is losing her mind." She rested her forehead against his. "What are we missing?"

"Answers," Stryker replied. "But we'll get them. And then, you know what we're gonna do?"

"Sleep for a week."

He smiled. "Vacation. Sun, sand, you and me."

"That sounds perfect."

Bing!

Together, they read the report. "Spinetti had four wives," Stryker read out loud. "Two he divorced, two died. He has one daughter, Carla Spinetti Barnham."

"Lyle is Spinetti's grandson," Emerson said. "This is blowing my mind."

"And a possible serial killer," Stryker added.

"It's time to bring Lyle Barnham in for questioning."

Emerson woke at five in the morning. *So much for sleep-in Sunday.* Stryker was sleeping on his stomach, facing her. The knot between his brows was gone, and she paused to appreciate his peaceful expression. His hair had fallen across his cheek and she wanted to sweep it away, then kiss his beautiful face. *Is this it? Are you the one?* Her gut told her yes.

She slinked out of bed, threw on her bathrobe, and headed downstairs. She made coffee and sat in her bay window while it brewed. The quiet neighborhood was cloaked in early-morning serenity. She wanted to tell her parents the truth about how Doug had died, but it was too soon. The blood on her hands hadn't even dried.

When the coffee finished brewing, she padded into her office, mug in hand. She wrote the word "Spinetti" on a piece of paper, moved several photos on her corkboard, then, tacked that paper in the center. Stepping back, she stared at the web, trying to make sense of everything.

"This has gotta be a family business."

She rubbed her pounding forehead. *None of this makes sense.*

Just after seven, Stryker padded into her office. "Morning, baby, what's going on?"

"I've got a drug lord who murdered my brother and is trying to take you down, and his grandson might be a serial killer. Are these somehow connected or am I dealing with two completely different cases?"

"You'll figure it out." He placed his hands on her head, kissed her forehead, then kissed her lips. "Come with me to Heather and Gordon's. They're having a Memorial Day party this afternoon. Take a break and clear your head."

She smiled. "Okay. I'll bake brownies to bring with us."

"Babe, seriously, you don't have to do that."

She moseyed out of her office. "I'll probably stress-eat half the batch before we even get there."

That afternoon, Emerson texted Lyle. "It's Detective Easton. I've got new information regarding my case you'll want to include in your story. Meet me at the station tomorrow, 11am and I'll update you." She hit send.

Dots appeared. "Sounds good," Lyle replied. "See you then."

Stryker strolled into the kitchen wearing leathers. "I'm riding my bike to Heather and Gordon's. You wanna ride with me?"

"Sure."

He eyed her slowly, up and down. "Better go upstairs and change."

She stared at her shorts and T-shirt. "What should I wear?"

He held out his hand. "Let's find something that protects you."

As soon as they walked into her bedroom, she threw her arms around him and kissed him. "You bought me more presents."

Laid out on the bed were leather pants, a leather jacket, leather gloves, and a helmet.

"You gotta ride safe," he said, and kissed her. "I checked your sizes before I bought all this."

"You are spoiling me so good."

"Busted." As she changed, he asked about Lyle.

"He's meeting me at the station tomorrow morning."

She finished dressing, pulled her hair into a ponytail, and took her helmet. She packaged up the brownies and they left. Once in the driveway, he stored the dessert, pulled on his helmet and his gloves, then mounted his Harley. "Hold on to me and lean into the turns. I'm taking the back roads so you can get used to riding."

"How do you know I didn't have a biker boyfriend and rode all the time?" With a smirk, she tightened her chinstrap and climbed on behind him.

She loved holding on to her man, loved the feeling of freedom as he rode out of her neighborhood. With everything raining down on them, she needed this moment to let her thoughts trail out behind her and vanish in the wind. As they made their way to his aunt and uncle's, she was looking forward to a relaxing evening.

Stryker pulled into a tree-lined neighborhood with neatly kept two-story houses, and parked in the driveway of a brick-front home. He cut the engine and she hopped off, then removed her helmet. He disembarked, pushed off his helmet, and handed her the brownies. Together, they made their way toward the house.

As soon as they entered, a pack of happy children ran in their direction. A toddler yelled, "Uncle Syker Tooman is here!"

Stryker's smile stole her breath. His face lit up, his laugh contagious. After hugging the three older children, he lifted the two smallest tykes into his arms. "Graham and Aaron, this is my *special* friend, Emerson. This is Graham and this is Aaron."

"Do you play tickle monster?" Aaron asked.

"Absolutely," Emerson replied with a smile.

"Ready for mayhem?" Stryker asked.

She nodded. In truth, she couldn't wait. The kitchen was packed with so many people, the overflow spilled into the family room. Stryker set the little ones down as Heather made her way over. "I'm delighted to see you." She gave Emerson a warm hug.

"I baked some brownies. If you've got a plate…"

"That was so nice of you. Let's put them out and watch them vanish in seconds." After hugging Stryker, Heather smiled. "I'm happy to see you two together."

A tall, sturdy man with dark hair and bright blue eyes wandered over. "You must be Emerson. I'm Dakota Luck."

One by one, Emerson met Stryker's family. Emerson couldn't remember the last time she smiled for that long. Everyone took their proverbial punches with Stryker and he loved it.

She met Dakota's wife, Providence, and their daughter Sammy. She met Stryker's sister, Trudy, her husband and their children. And she said hello to Stryker's uncle, Gordon.

"We'll be back," Stryker said, pulling Emerson out of the room. "If we don't get outta these leathers, we're gonna melt."

He brought her into the living room, where they removed their leather riding wear to reveal their summer shirts and shorts beneath.

"My vest is driving me crazy," Emerson said. "Plus, it's so obvious we're wearing them."

"We keep 'em on," Stryker said.

When they returned to the kitchen, Heather and Emerson plated the brownies, which were devoured as predicted. Everyone made their way onto the screened porch, while some ventured into the fenced backyard. But what intrigued Emerson the most was Stryker. She couldn't get over how much he smiled, and how attentive he was with the kids, especially the little ones. The tension and anger he carried around with him like dead weight vanished. And she did not expect that he would be such a hugger. He hugged everyone hello. She'd been talking to Heather when she heard his belly laugh.

Dakota had said something to him and he could not stop laughing. The joy on his face was breathtaking.

"See something you like?" Heather whispered.

"I do," Emerson said with a smile. "He's so different here. Relaxed and happy. We've been working together and he's very intense and driven. It's nice to see he has a lighter side."

"Did you and Justice ever get together?"

Emerson laughed. "Not yet, but I'm pretty sure I know who he is."

Stryker moseyed over. "What's the word, ladies?"

"We're talking about our favorite subject," Emerson replied.

"Must be me," he said with a grin. "I'm going to help Gordon with the grilling." He kissed Emerson and took off.

"I'm so happy for you both," Heather said. "I'm glad he took his time finding his person. And I'm thrilled that person is you, Emerson."

"Thank you, Heather. I'm pretty crazy about him."

Providence ambled over, her daughter by her side. Providence was tall with short, dark hair and pretty gray eyes. Sammy was a mini Dakota with dark hair and bright blue eyes. Mother and daughter had worn matching sundresses with a pretty floral design.

"We're excited to see Stryker brought someone with him today," Providence said.

Heather excused herself to check the grilling status.

"Did you get to ride on Uncle Stryker's motorcycle?" Sammy asked.

"I did."

"My dad says I can do that when I'm one hundred." Sammy scrunched up her face. "That's too old. I'm getting my own motorcycle when I'm twenty."

"Is that so?" Providence asked.

"Uh-huh, definitely," Sammy replied.

One of Sammy's cousins ran over. "Sammy, come play with me."

"Okay." Sammy hugged her mom. "I love you, Mom."

"I love you, sweetheart."

Emerson put her hand over her heart. "She's absolutely adorable and so affectionate with you."

"Sammy is Dakota's biological daughter. I adopted her after Dakota and I got married. We're very close." Providence paused to watch her child play. "Stryker said you're a police detective. Do you like your work?"

"I love it, but I'm leaving after I solve a high-profile case I'm working on."

"Is that why you're wearing a vest?" Providence asked.

"Yeah," she said and nodded.

"Are you staying in law enforcement?"

"I'd like to. I'll know better once I start interviewing. How 'bout you? Do you work?"

"I'm a marketing consultant. Not much to say about that." Providence tossed a nod toward Stryker. "He's fallen pretty hard."

Emerson smiled. "Me, too."

Talking with Providence came easily. Spending the evening with Stryker's family helped put him in perspective. He was a complicated man who loved his family and was haunted by his past.

After dinner, the adults sat around the table on the screened porch while the children played nearby. Stryker's phone buzzed with an incoming call and the adults began booing.

"Don't answer it," Dakota said.

"Voicemail," Providence echoed.

Laughing, Stryker pulled out his phone and pushed away from the table. "It's Cooper, I gotta take it." He answered. "My family is so pissed at you right now." As he went into the house, Emerson heard him say, "What about Spinetti?"

Conversations resumed. When Stryker returned, a shadow had fallen over his face, his brow knitted in frustration. "I've gotta take off." He swept his gaze over the adults, pausing on Emerson.

"That's my cue." Emerson rose, plate in hand.

"Stay," Providence said. "We'll take you home later."

"Thanks, but I've got a ton of work to do," Emerson said, before regarding Stryker. "Can you drop me off?"

"Yeah," he replied, curtly. Whatever Cooper had told him had gotten under his skin.

They pulled on their leathers and returned to the porch to say goodbye.

"Emerson, make sure Stryker brings you next Sunday," Heather said.

"We're having our first sleepover with all five grandbabies," Gordon said. "There will only be a *next* if we survive tonight." Everyone laughed. "Heather, honey, *what* were we thinking?"

"It's going to be a blast, right, kids?"

All five children shouted their excitement in unison.

"Help us," Gordon said, and everyone cracked up.

Emerson hugged Heather goodbye. "Thank you for having me. I had a lot of fun."

Outside, Emerson asked Stryker about his call.

"Spinetti's attorneys might have found a loophole. He could be getting out of prison."

"Oh, no."

"I'm swinging by Cooper's to talk to him. He lives ten minutes from your place. Come with me."

"I'm gonna work," she said. "You can tell me all about it when you get home."

With a nod, Stryker pulled on his helmet.

After strapping hers, she hopped on the back. When she wrapped her arms around him, the tension gripping his back was palpable. Once they reached Emerson's, he pulled into the driveway and cut the engine. "Let's clear the house."

She dismounted and pulled off her helmet. "I'm fine."

"It'll take five minutes." They went in through the garage and into the house. She turned off the alarm and they checked every room. They were alone. "I love you," he said.

She smiled. "I love you."

One brief kiss and he was gone.

As he rode away, she closed the garage door and waited until it hit the floor before retreating inside. She found Pima scratching on the post of his new house and stopped to rub him before she went upstairs to shower.

She stripped out of her clothes, happy to remove her vest.

As the hot water pounded her back, she thought about Spinetti getting released and the danger Stryker would be in. She finished showering, dried off, and walked into her bedroom. After dressing in a tank top and shorty shorts, she padded downstairs.

Movement caught her eye and she turned. Everything went into slow motion. Strong arms wrapped around her and a wet towel was pressed over her nose and mouth, stifling her scream. She flailed and kicked, but things turned hazy…and slow…and dark.

23

SAVING EMERSON

Stryker leaned his backside against Cooper's kitchen counter. "You sure about this?"

"That's what I'm hearing." Cooper tossed his empty beer bottle into recycling. "You sure you don't want something to drink?"

Stryker shook his head. "What if I told you Spinetti was using the Internet fraud business as a cover for something else?"

Cooper chuckled. "I love the way you think, but we were thorough in our search."

"We missed something."

"Like what?"

"He's the head of one of the DMV's biggest drug rings."

Cooper stared at him for several seconds. "Seriously?"

"The Trinity. He's The Father."

"I need evidence to re-open the case."

"You'll have it. Until then, not a word, to anyone."

"Of course not. So, I had an interesting conversation with Providence," Cooper said. "I'm meeting with her next week."

"Don't fuck this up."

Cooper laughed. "Thanks for...I'm not sure what. You wanna clue me in?"

"It's an opportunity few get."

"That's it?"

"I gotta go."

"How are things going with Emerson?"

"I'm thinkin' of making things official."

"Assuming she'll have you."

Stryker laughed. "I gotta go. I need a coupla days to get you what you need on Spinetti." Stryker pulled him in for a bro-hug.

"You're wearing your vest. Smart move."

"Not my time to die." Stryker showed himself out.

As he mounted his bike, his phone binged. He almost ignored it, but, thinking twice, pulled out his phone and glanced at the screen. The killer had turned on his phone and the program Stryker had written was alerting him. Stryker tapped the app. Up popped the phone's geolocation.

Adrenaline slammed through him.

He throttled up, popped the clutch, and, burning rubber, he rocketed into the night.

As Emerson came to and the fog cleared, her heart started pounding hard and fast. Lyle was staring down at her, her own gun pointed at her face. She was a prisoner. Secured to her office chair at her wrists and ankles.

"Hey, sleepyhead." Lyle's dead-eyed smile sent a shiver through her.

Lyle had shoved a washcloth in her mouth. She sat there, helpless and fuzzy-headed, trying to come up with a plan.

"I'm going to remove the gag. If you scream, I'll shoot you. Do you understand?"

She nodded. He pulled out the cloth, and she sucked down a lungful of air, and then another. "How did you get in? My house alarm was set."

"One day, when you went on a run, I was parked nearby and saw you punch the code on your garage door opener. Then, I stalked you. It's amazing how easy that is to do. People never pay attention to who's behind them."

He'd found the scotch and tipped back the bottle. After swallowing, he grimaced. "After you and your boyfriend left on his bike this afternoon, I got into the garage and hid. You guys came home, went inside, and unalarmed. When he left, I came in and waited for you. It was so easy." His eerie smile made her want to throw up. "And here you are, hard at work, trying to catch the Wedding Gown Killer."

"Why are you doing this to me?" She needed to play this cool, stupid, almost. She forced a smile. "Is this a joke or something?"

He set down the handgun and moseyed over to her wall of photos. "Tsk, tsk. I'm not happy with you. You know too much, and you wanted me to come to the police station tomorrow so you could charge me with murder."

"Why would you say that?"

"I didn't know you were looking for me until I stopped by here and saw all these photos." He paused to stare at them. "I love admiring my handiwork."

On a sigh, he turned back to her. "Not even the great Detective Easton can stop me from having my fun. In fact…I want us to have a little fun *together*." He patted her head before breezing out of the room.

She yanked on the knots, but the zip ties only dug into her flesh. *I'm trapped.*

A few moments later, he returned. He'd removed his reading glasses and put on the blond wig and fake beard and moustache. In his arms, he held a white wedding gown. Her stomach dropped. *Oh, God, no.*

"This is for you." He laid it across her desk. "It's too big, but we'll make it work."

Despite her bone-dry mouth and frenzied heartbeat, she was

going to continue playing this cool. Ignoring his disguise, she pushed on. "Lyle, I didn't ask you to the police station to arrest you. I was going to offer you an apprenticeship, working in the homicide department."

He stared at her, blinking. Had she hooked him?

"Lyle? I'm Casey. Casey Quinn, freelance photographer." His soulless smile made her shiver.

"You told me you wanted to be a police officer and I can help you. Tying me up isn't gonna get you the job."

"You can't fool me. I'm a suspect in the Wedding Gown Killer case." Lyle pointed to the photos on her wall. "You were looking for me. I saw you at the club a week or two ago."

"Why didn't you say hello? I thought we were friends."

"Friends? Ha! What a joke. I know what you're trying to do. You're no different from everyone else in my life. My parents hate me. *Hate me*! Do you know how furious that makes me?"

Emerson wanted to scream. She wanted to cry out for help. Instead, she encouraged him to keep talking. She needed to buy herself some time. "Why do they hate you?"

He swigged more scotch. "My mother has belittled me my whole life. I was never good enough, never smart enough. I never lived up to her expectations and became a big, fat loser. This'll show her I can accomplish something."

"I'm sorry. That sucks." She meant it.

"My dad's no better. He pretty much ignores me. Always has."

Spinetti had been genuinely happy to see him. "What about a grandparent? Do you have a special relationship with your grandma or grandpa?"

He smiled. "My grandpa pities me, but someone framed him for a crime he didn't commit. Now, he's stuck in prison."

She needed to keep him talking about everything, anything. Could she diffuse him? Could she appease him and get him to untie her?

"I'm sorry to hear that," she said. "That must be tough for both of you. Can you visit him?"

"Yeah, but he's...I can't talk to him about my parents because he always sides with them. I just make stuff up so he'll be proud of me."

"Like what?"

"Last time I visited him, I dressed like this and told him I'd gotten the lead in a play. He was so proud of me." His eyes grew cold and a chill slithered down her spine. "My life is one big fucking lie."

Keep stalling him.

"You're a journalist and in grad school. That's something to be proud of."

He snickered. "I lied. I'm not in college. I don't even have a job. I called the magazine and told them I wanted to write the piece, but I never did. Not a single fucking word."

His life is so tragic.

"It's not too late," she pressed on. "You know so much about the case. Write that story. I'm sure they'd print it."

He hopped on the desk, facing her. "I'm always amazed at how easy it is to fool people. They're so malleable. They see what you want them to see. They believe what you want them to believe. I spent a lot of time in that wedding gown store, but when I returned as mild-mannered, dopey Lyle, the store owner had no clue I was the same person who bought those dresses." He threw his head back and laughed.

Like most psychopaths, he was a master at conning and manipulating people.

Lyle picked up the dress and cradled it in his arms. "None of that matters, now. I need you to put this dress on, Detective."

If he untied her, she might be able to overpower him.

He held up the dress. While he stared at it, a coldness settled into his eyes. "My fiancée had a dress like this."

Did she die? Leave him at the alter? Emerson didn't want to ignite his anger by asking the wrong question. So, she stayed silent, hoping he'd continue talking.

"She dumped me two days before our wedding. All she said was, 'I met someone else'. She gave me the ring and left." He glared at Emerson. "I killed eight women in Florida and I was on a roll, here, too. You're trying to stop me. You're ruining my fun, Detective. You're ruining my life!" He threw down the dress and stomped on it. "First, my bitch mother hates me! Who does that to her own child?" He started flailing his arms. "My dad never wanted me. And then, my fiancée rejects me!"

He picked up the gun and stared at it, his finger on the trigger.

Emerson's heart sank. He was going to kill her.

Stryker cut the engine, threw his bike down, and ripped off his helmet. As he ran toward Emerson's end-unit, he surveyed the townhouse. Garage door was closed. The front room was lit up, but the blinds were closed. *Emerson's office.*

He slowed outside the window to listen, and pulled out his Glock.

"Lyle, you need help," Emerson said. "Killing these women isn't going to bring your fiancée back to you."

"Back?!" Lyle yelled. "I don't want her. She married some loser. She's used goods. But the women I kill, they're so trusting, so nice. They're so eager to be in front of the camera, they'll do anything. Now, it's your turn, Detective. I'm going to untie you and you're going to put on this wedding gown!"

Stryker bolted up the front steps, shot out the lock, and threw open the front door. He raised his weapon.

BANG! BANG!

Hit in the chest, Stryker staggered backward. Lyle turned to Emerson and raised the gun.

POP! POP! POP! POP!

Lyle dropped to the floor.

Stryker and Emerson locked eyes, the frantic energy whirring around them. He rushed to her and knelt down. "Are you hit? Are you okay?"

"Not hit." She was trembling so hard. "Are you?"

"He got me in the vest. Mighta fucked up a rib, but I'm wearing my vest." He cut the restraints with his blade, pulled her into his arms, and hugged her so hard. Despite her shaking, she broke away, pulled off his leather jacket and yanked up his T-shirt.

"Emerson, is now really the time?"

"Shut up." She helped him remove the shirt, then the vest. "One bullet pierced the vest in the upper chest and the second in the stomach."

Then, she lifted his undershirt. His skin hadn't been punctured. "Thank God. Thank you for getting here in time." She hugged him again. When he held her in his arms, he realized how close he'd come to losing her.

She broke away and checked Lyle. "No pulse." Then, she ran out of the room, returning with her phone. "This is Detective Easton, ACPD. The Wedding Gown Killer is in my house. He tried to kill me. I need police and an ambulance."

"Are you hurt?" asked the operator.

"No. My boyfriend got here in time and shot him in self-defense."

"Is he breathing?"

"No."

"First responders are on their way," said the operator.

Emerson hung up and bolted out of the room.

A dark, red pool was expanding beneath Lyle's body, which lay face up on the white wedding gown, now turning crimson. Emerson came flying into the room and laid towels around his body to absorb the blood. "I didn't see Pima."

"I got this, babe." Stryker took off in search of the cat. "Pima!" He checked inside the cat house, then took the stairs, feeling the pain of the shots with each step. He strode into Emerson's bedroom and smiled. Pima's head was sticking out from between their pillows.

He sat and the cat started purring, then squeezed his way out. "How's my little buddy? You gotta know, I still think you're nutso." After giving him a quick rub behind his ears, he closed the bedroom door and went back downstairs.

The police had arrived and Emerson was giving her statement.

"This is Stryker Truman," Emerson said.

"I understand you've been shot," said the policewoman. "Let's get you checked by a paramedic."

"I'm good. My vest took the bullets." He regarded Emerson. "You saved my life *again*."

"And you saved mine," she replied before turning back to the responding officer. "It's been a stressful evening."

"I can imagine."

"There's a lot of evidence that needs to get bagged," Emerson said. "Lyle Barnham's cell phone, the wig, the wedding gown."

"Crime techs are on their way." The officer left them to speak with the paramedics, who were heading out without Lyle's body.

"Pima was hiding between the pillows on our bed," Stryker said. "I closed the door so he can't get out."

She wrapped her arms around his waist. "Thank you for taking care of us."

He kissed the top of her head. "No one's taking my woman, or her crazy cat, away from me."

Her sweet smile was the most beautiful thing he'd ever seen.

"How'd you know I was in danger?" she asked.

"When Lyle turned on his burner, the program pinged me." Stryker pulled out his phone. "All his data downloaded."

Emerson peered over while Stryker flipped through Lyle's photos.

"Oh, God," she murmured. "He posed with the bodies. Look, he even took his wig off. Poor man. He was such a mess."

"How can you feel sorry for him?"

"He told me his mom hated him and his dad didn't want anything to do with him. Sounded like Spinetti felt bad for him, but his relationship with his grandfather was built on lies. I don't think he was born a monster. I think his parents created one. When his fiancée dumped him, he snapped."

"Yeah, like a psychopath." He pulled her into the living room, away from the fray. "I'm sorry I didn't make the connection that Lyle and Casey were the same person."

"Your job was to hack into the systems. It was *my* job to find the killer." She exhaled a long sigh. "I am so relieved his killing spree has ended."

"Me, too, baby," Stryker said, pulling her into his arms. "Me, too."

Nikki came flying into the house. "Are you okay? I heard two people were shot."

"I got hit in the vest," Stryker said. "And I took Lyle out."

"I'd be dead if it weren't for Stryker," Emerson replied.

"Thank you for saving my girl," Nikki said.

"No other option," Stryker said, peering into Emerson's eyes.

"I'll get a search warrant for the Barnham residence," Nikki said.

"And the guest house," Emerson added.

"Right." As Nikki stepped away to handle that, Captain Perry entered Emerson's foyer.

"I'm sorry I put you in harm's way, Easton. Clearly, Lyle Barnham wasn't properly vetted. How are you doing?"

"I'm good, thanks to Stryker," Emerson replied.

"Your heroic act will be acknowledged by the department," Tiana said to Stryker.

"I'm no hero," Stryker replied. "But I know two people who are."

24

LYLE'S FAMILY

At four in the morning, Emerson rang the doorbell of the Barnham estate. With search warrants in hand, Nikki stood beside her, while the uniformed officers waited in their cars. Telling someone they'd lost a loved one was one of the hardest parts of Emerson's job.

If that wasn't bad enough, she had to tell Carla and Tee that their only child had been a serial murderer.

After a few minutes, Nikki banged on the front door. "Arlington County Police!"

A sleepy-looking woman in a bathrobe answered the door. "What's going on?"

"Are you Carla Barnham?" Nikki asked.

"Yes."

"I'm Detective Cardoso. This is Detective Easton. We'd like to come in and speak with you about your son, Lyle."

"Ah, hell, what's he done?" Carla swung open the door and escorted them into the living room, but she didn't sit.

"Do you live alone, ma'am?" Nikki asked.

"I live here with my husband. He's on business in Florida, flying home this afternoon. Do I need to bail our kid out of jail or something?"

"I'm sorry to have to tell you this, but your son is dead," Nikki said.

"Lyle?" Carla asked. "No, he's in the guest house, where he spends most of his time. Lazy bum."

"I'm sorry, Mrs. Barnham, but he's not there," Emerson said. "We can check with you, if you'd like?"

Carla fished a pack of cigarettes out of the bathrobe pocket, along with a lighter. "How'd he die?"

Emerson and Nikki exchanged glances. Carla's lack of emotion astounded her.

"I had identified Lyle as a person of interest in a string of murders in the DMV," Emerson began. "You might have seen something about them on the news or social media."

"You mean the Wedding Gown Killer?" Carla asked.

"Yes," Nikki replied.

"Are you telling me *my* kid killed those women?" She lit the cigarette and inhaled a long drag.

"We believe he did," Emerson replied. "When I asked him to meet me at the station, he broke into my home and tried to kill me. He was stopped just before he did."

Carla stared at her while the smoke swirled in her face. "Do I need to ID his body, now?"

What a cold-hearted bitch. "No," Emerson replied.

Carla took a few steps toward the front door. "I'll let my husband know when he gets home. Where's his body?"

"With the medical examiner. We can release him after the investigation has been completed." Nikki held up the warrants. "We need to search your homes for evidence."

"I'll let you into the guest house," Carla said. "That's where he lived."

"We also need to search your home," Emerson said.

"No, you don't," Carla objected. "Lyle didn't live with us."

"Based on the severity of the crimes, the warrant applies to the entire property." Emerson called one of the officers waiting outside. "We're starting the search."

Carla crushed the cigarette in an ashtray. "You don't have the right—"

"The warrant gives us the right," Nikki explained.

"I'll be back in a few." Carla moseyed toward the stairs.

Emerson stood at the base of the winding staircase leading to the second floor. "Mrs. Barnham, you can't go upstairs."

Carla strode over and glared at Emerson. "You can't boss me around in my own home. You two need to leave, *now*."

"Step away from Detective Easton," Nikki said.

Carla shoved Emerson out of the way, then took off for the stairs. Nikki grabbed Carla by the wrist. "You're under arrest for impeding our investigation and for assaulting an officer."

Two uniformed officers entered the home. "What's going on?" one of them asked.

"I didn't agree to this search and I have my rights. This is my house and you need to get the hell out of it!"

"Mrs. Barnham isn't cooperating," Emerson said. "Can one of you take her in and put her in holding until we complete the search?"

While the officer cuffed Carla, she yelled, "I'm calling my lawyer and suing you for breaking and entering."

As the officer led her down the driveway, Carla's rants could be heard in the house.

"We'll have to search for keys to the guest house," Emerson said.

They found no keys in the kitchen, so while several officers began searching the home for evidence, Nikki and Emerson headed to the guest house.

"The main residence is massive," Nikki said.

At the quaint entrance to the guest house, they pulled on disposable gloves. Emerson tried the door. It was locked.

"That would be too easy," Nikki said.

The women split up, looking for an unlocked window. Emerson found one on the south side. "Nikki," she called. "I've got one."

It took some work, but they opened the window. Emerson pulled on shoe coverings, climbed in, and opened the front door.

When Nikki turned on the light, they stared at the photos covering two walls in the living room. "Wow, that's a lot of pictures."

Lyle had photographed his victims and taken selfies posing with them, both in and out of his disguise. Emerson's stomach roiled. Lyle Barnham was the worst kind of evil.

A shoebox filled with jewelry sat on the kitchen table. Emerson recognized a ring worn by Claire-Marie and a cell phone she presumed was April Peters's. Beside the keepsake box lay the missing dishtowels from his victims' kitchens, folded neatly.

On the counter, they found three vials of ketamine from a veterinary clinic.

"He could've broken into the animal hospital," Nikki said. "Or he paid someone for the drugs."

In addition to the photos and keepsakes from the victims, their search turned up two laptops. The only rooms used were one of the bedrooms and the kitchen, but there was hardly any food in the fridge. "He was all alone," Emerson said. "And his parents lived a hundred feet away from him."

As the sun cleared the horizon, one of the officers popped her head inside the guest house. "Detectives, you're gonna want to see to what we found."

"I'll finish up here," Nikki said.

Instead of leading Emerson into the main house, the officer brought her into the four-car garage. "I found a bunch of laptops behind some boxes and turned one of them on."

Stryker rode up to the sprawling estate, pulled off his helmet, and dismounted. Four police cars and Emerson's vehicle were parked out front.

Twenty minutes earlier, he'd gotten a notification that one of his stolen computers had been activated, which included a photo of a police officer taken by the laptop's camera and the GPS coordinates of its location. Then, Emerson had called and asked him to swing by.

A police officer greeted him. "Mr. Truman?"

"Yup."

"Detective Easton is expecting you. Hang here for me while I get her."

Stryker leaned against his bike. The sand-colored stucco home reminded him of the southwest. The elaborate gardens were perfectly manicured and the lush aroma of flowers filled the air. *Bought with Spinetti drug money.*

Emerson emerged from inside, her beautiful smile halting his breath. Seeing her was always the best part of his day. "Hey," she said.

"Hey, babe."

She peered up at him. "You were right about Spinetti orchestrating the break-in at your company."

"How many laptops did you find?"

"Ten."

Though agitated that Spinetti's daughter had stolen them, he was relieved they weren't in the hands of a terror cell. "Have you arrested the Barnhams?"

"Mrs. Barnham wouldn't let us search the home and she assaulted me, so she's being held at the station. Her husband is out of town."

"Whoa, back up. She assaulted you? You okay?"

"I'm fine." He hitched a brow. "Really," she replied.

"How'd she handle the news about Lyle?"

"She was more concerned about our searching the property."

"Charming family, the whole lot of 'em."

"Can you log in to one of the laptops for us, to prove they're yours?" She handed him a pair of disposable gloves and led him into the garage.

He entered the admin password and, as he expected, the computer booted up. "How's it going here, otherwise?"

"The guest house is filled with evidence. Dozens of photos of the victims and a box of keepsakes."

"How you holding up?"

"Adrenaline."

One of the officers walked into the garage. "Detective, check this out." He set the evidence bags on the workbench. Two bags with a handgun in each. Inside the other were photos and papers.

After introducing Stryker to Officer DeCampo, she extracted the snapshots. "Looks like your company," she said to Stryker.

He flipped through the pictures while Emerson unfolded several pieces of paper. "These are their plans for the break-in," she said. "Officer DeCampo, can you run these in for me?"

"Now?" DeCampo asked. "Don't you want us to take everything at the same time?"

"Give me one second." She re-bagged the evidence, handed it to DeCampo, and walked Stryker out of the garage. "Don't say a word about this to *anyone*, especially your FBI friend. You gotta trust me."

"I do." He dropped a quick kiss on her lips, then took off down the driveway.

Emerson pulled out her phone and called her captain. "How's it going, Easton?"

"Very well, Captain. Earlier, you told me you'd help me any way you could."

"What do you need?"

"We found two guns in the main house. I need them matched against slugs I left with forensics for another case."

"What do I have to do with that?"

"I need your help getting it pushed through ASAP."

"You want to tell me why?"

"Someone tried to kill Stryker. Based on the photos and other evidence we've found, I think the weapons used are the same ones we found here."

"Why wasn't I told about this?"

"At the time, it wasn't linked to any of my cases, and I didn't want you to pull Stryker from helping me if you thought his life was in danger."

"Understood. When can I expect the weapons?"

"Within the hour." Emerson hung up and told DeCampo to run the evidence in.

"Sure thing," he replied. "I found a small storage room in the finished basement with several sealed boxes. Can you tackle that while I'm gone?"

As soon as DeCampo left, Emerson made her way downstairs. The expansive lower level housed a billiard table, a ping pong table, and a home entertainment center. There were pinball machines and a small dance floor, along with a sauna and a lap pool.

She found the unfinished storage room. The officer had already sifted through three boxes. Emerson opened a box. It was filled with photo albums. She opened a second box. It was filled with holiday cards from decades ago. *This is a waste of time.*

Another box was filled with record albums. She opened one filled with brown packing paper. Beneath that lay a smaller, leather box. Taped to the box was a hand-printed note.

DO NOT DESTROY

Inside was a gun and a mini tape cassette player with a tape inside. Emerson pressed "play". After listening once, she listened to it again. Only, this time, she recorded the conversation into her phone so there would be no chance of anyone erasing it.

Emerson Easton had hit the motherlode.

25

EXECUTING THEIR PLAN

After speaking with Nikki, Emerson hightailed it back to the precinct. Once there, she found Captain Perry in her office. "C'mon in. Have you heard from the lab yet?"

"Not yet." Emerson sat across from her captain and pulled on a pair of disposable gloves. "While in the Barnham basement, I found this." Emerson played the tape for the captain.

When it ended, she ran her idea by her superior officer.

"You have my full support," said Captain Perry, before picking up her phone. "It's Captain Perry. I've got Detective Easton with me. Can you check on the status of the ballistics report for me? It's the Truman case."

Adrenaline was pumping through Emerson. There were a lot of moving parts to her plan.

"Yes, I'm here." Captain Perry slid her gaze to Emerson. "Thank you." She hung up and nodded. "The slugs you extracted from Stryker's headboard are a match with the guns pulled from the Barnhams. Now, we've got reason to detain Carla Barnham."

"Please don't share the findings with anyone. I don't want her tipping anyone off."

"She's in a holding cell without her phone."

"Carlo Spinetti is in prison, but that didn't stop him from getting himself a burner and using it to call Stryker." Emerson stood. "Thank you for your support, Captain."

"Keep me posted."

After jumping in her car, she called Nikki. "How are things going?"

"We're finishing up."

Emerson glanced at the time, then did a double take. "Is it really quarter to six?"

"Yes, did this day fly by or what?"

"Did anyone find a house key?"

"Yeah, we found one. Are you coming back here?"

"Yeah, but traffic is heavy. Let me know where you hide the key." Emerson ended the call, then called Stryker.

"Hey, baby," he answered. "What's the word?"

"We need to talk. Where can we meet?"

"I'm at the office."

Her phone rang. "Lemme call you right back." She answered, "Detective Easton."

"It's DeCampo. I've got the information you need."

"Great, and you're going to tail him?"

"As soon as we get eyes on him."

Emerson ended the call with DeCampo and called Stryker back. "Can you leave now and meet me at your house? You'll need your vest and your weapon."

"Got em both," Stryker replied. "What's goin' on?"

"I'll explain when I see you. I love you."

"I know you do." She heard the smile in his voice.

In twenty minutes, she was going to wipe that smile right off his face.

DAMAGED

Later that evening, Stryker found the key, hidden under the rock in the front garden of the Barnham estate, and let himself in. The police had spent hours conducting their search of the main residence, and it showed. The place looked like a tornado had whipped through.

Stryker didn't care if the home had surveillance cameras tracking his every move. Though he could have turned on the lights as he meandered from room to room, his night goggles provided him with optimal viewing. The tick-tock of clocks sounded the seconds as he waited in the living room.

Twenty minutes later, Emerson texted him. "Go time."

The garage door opened, a car drove in, and the door closed. Tee Barnham entered the kitchen and flipped on the lights. Stryker slipped into the shadows of the dark living room.

"What the hell?" Tee Barnham's dress shoes clicked against the tile floor as he walked through the kitchen. "Carla! Carla! Are you home?" Stryker caught a glimpse of him as he rounded the corner and hurried up the stairs.

"Holy fuck!" Tee yelled. "What the hell happened here?"

As he came flying back down, the doorbell rang. He flung it open. "What?" he bellowed.

"Hello, Mr. Barnham," Emerson said.

Stryker loved how cool she was in pressure situations. Just another day in the life of Detective Easton. *My Detective Easton.*

"Now's not a good time," he blurted, then, added, "oh, you've got the police with you. Perfect. Are you a neighbor? We've been robbed. The house is a complete disaster. Was your house hit, too?"

"I'm Detective Easton with Arlington County Police. Can I come in?"

"Yes, yes. I'm concerned my wife might have been taken."

From where Stryker stood, he had a clear line to Emerson. He loved her confidence and calm demeanor.

"C'mon in, officers," Barnham said to the two uniformed cops.

"They'll wait outside while we talk," Emerson said, closing the front door. "Mrs. Barnham isn't here."

"Where is she?"

"We'll get to that in a minute. Can we sit?"

"My home has been burglarized and my wife is missing. No, we cannot sit."

"Mr. Barnham, your son, Lyle, is dead."

Silence.

"I'm sorry, what? Was he killed during the home invasion?"

"There was no home invasion. He was killed when he broke into my home and tried to kill me."

"What are you talking about?" Stryker couldn't miss the annoyance in his tone.

"I'd been trying to capture the Wedding Gown Killer. From the evidence we'd collected, your son was that person. He figured out I was close to making an arrest and he tried to kill me."

The silence hung heavy.

"*He* was the monster terrorizing those women?" Barnham choked out.

"Looks that way."

"Did you do this to my home?"

"The police conducted a search of the compound for evidence."

"Where the hell is my wife!" Barnham hollered.

Stryker shook his head in disgust. *Still yelling.*

"She refused to let us conduct the search and she assaulted me, so she's being held at the Detention Center."

"I've got to get her out of there," Barnham said. "You'll be hearing from my attorney."

"You're not going anywhere." Emerson's brusque tone caught his ear. "I have something you need to hear."

Walking with purpose, Emerson headed for the kitchen. Barnham followed. A chair was dragged over the tile. "Sit," she bit out.

In stealth mode, Stryker moved closer, so he could see Barnham.

Emerson sat across from him at the kitchen table. After pulling on latex gloves, Emerson pressed "play" on the cassette tape.

"How'd it go?" asked the first man.
"Just like we planned," said the second.
"And?"
"I killed her."
"You sure she's dead?"
"I shot her twice in the head and she fell to the ground. I don't see how she could've survived that. My son, Stryker, came home—"
"I thought you said he'd be out."
"He was supposed to be at his high school, getting ready for their football game. I have no fucking idea why he came home."
"What happened next?"
"He pulled her into the foyer and performed CPR. Then, he held her."
"Did you stay until the police showed up?"
"No, I came here after the kid stopped doing CPR."
"Give me the gun." Pause. "Get your ass back to your office and stay there. I'll get rid of the weapon. You act like the grieving husband. No contact with Carla, at all. No texts, no phone calls, no sneaking around. Do you understand me?"
"Yes, sir."
"The police will investigate you, but you've got an alibi. They won't find the weapon. You've got no motive."
"I asked her for a divorce and she told me she wanted us to go to counseling."
"Dammit. Did you meet with a therapist?"
"No."
"Did she set up an appointment?"
"I don't know."
"That might be a problem. Don't mention the marital issues when you're questioned by the police."
"I won't."

"You also need to play the part of a doting dad."

He laughed. "Jesus, you're asking a lot."

"You can fake it for a little while, can't you?"

"Yes, sir."

"Once the police clear you—and they will—you'll move to Florida."

"With Carla."

"And Lyle."

"Right, of course, sir."

"You'll marry my daughter and be a good father to your son. Hell, I spend more time with your kid than you do."

"I'll do my best."

"If I find out you even look at another woman, I'll slit your fucking throat."

"I'll be faithful to Carla. You have my word."

"That's good, Tyler. Welcome to The Trinity, son."

"Thank you, Mr. Spinetti."

Stryker emerged from the shadows. Tee Barnham startled and the color drained from his cheeks. "Oh, heyyyy, Stryker."

Stryker loomed over him, forcing him to tilt his face up. Seething, he said nothing.

Barnham shot Emerson a furtive glance.

Stryker wrapped his hand around his father's throat and pulled him to his feet.

"Do something," Barnham croaked to Emerson.

Emerson didn't move.

Stryker tightened his grip. Barnham's face reddened. He wanted to choke the life out of him. Several seconds later, he released him. Barnham wheezed in a few mucus-filled breaths.

"What the hell is going on here?" Barnham rasped out.

"Vindication, Tyler Truman." Despite the hatred raging through him, Stryker kept his voice low and calm. "This is where I'm supposed to feel satisfaction that I've found my mother's killer. But I don't. I want to take your life in exchange for hers. But you need to rot in solitary confinement. You, alone with your demons, for decades."

"I think there's been a huge misunderstanding," Barnham said.

"That's you on the recording," Stryker ground out. "And that's Carlo Spinetti, also known as The Father. You must be The Son. The one who killed his first wife and married his mistress. You were gone all the time…on business. But it wasn't business. You had two families." Stryker's stomach turned. "You sicken me."

"I…um, er—well, it's just that—"

"You were a non-existent father the first time around. You'd think you'd get it right for round two, but Lyle turned into a psychopath, a serial killer. Bravo, Tyler. It doesn't get any worse than that."

"I never wanted to be a dad. I wanted to be wealthy. Mission accomplished." Barnham's demonic smile made him look insane. "I was living my best life when you helped the FBI take down my father-in-law. I was highly motivated to eliminate you, but not before we ruined you, first."

"You didn't ruin me." Stryker smiled. "I ruined you."

"We'll see."

"Your life was filled with bad choices that included trusting Spinetti."

Barnham jumped up and raised his arm to strike Stryker. Moving fast, Stryker shoved him back. Barnham crashed into the chair and fell backward. Stryker glowered down at him. "Get this scumbag outta here."

Stryker pulled him to his feet so Emerson could slap handcuffs on him. "You're under the arrest for grand theft, the attempted murder of Stryker Truman, and the murder of Amanda Truman." After she mirandized him, the officers placed Barnham inside the patrol car.

Relief washed over Stryker. He had found his mother's killer, and by doing that, he had freed himself. At long last, Stryker's twenty-year search had come to an end.

"I'm headed to the station to add the recorder into evidence," Emerson said, as the cop car pulled away.

Stryker removed the wire he'd been wearing. "I'll keep this, just in case."

"Good call," Emerson said, removing her wire. "We'll use mine."

"Where can I find you later?"

"In bed, right next to you," she said, then she furrowed her brow. "How are you doing?"

"I wanted to choke him dead and leave him to rot."

"I know you did."

He pulled her into his arms. "You found my mom's killer."

"*We* found her. And we found my brother's killers, too."

"This is it. It's you and me, baby. No other option."

Rising up, she kissed him. "No other option."

Stryker waited until Emerson pulled onto the street before he slipped into his Mercedes and headed into the night.

First stop, the club.

A woman stopped him in The Dungeon parking lot. "Aren't you Stryker?"

"Whatcha need?"

"You, for starters."

"I'm off the market." Before going inside, he made a call.

"Yo, Stryker, my man, how you been?"

"Are you still interested in buying The Dungeon?" Stryker asked.

"Hell, yeah."

"It's yours."

"You kiddin' me?"

"I'll call my broker and he'll take care of everything."

"The Dungeon is gonna be mine. Time to celebrate." The call ended.

Time to move on.

Stryker found Mavis in her office. "The Wedding Gown Killer is dead."

Mavis smiled. "Whew, what a relief."

He showed Mavis a picture of the hostess who let Lyle into the club. "Who's this?"

"That's Becky. She's working tonight."

"The killer bribed her to get in. He was using the club to stalk women."

"Oh, no, that's awful."

"Becky needs to go. Can you get her up here?"

"Give me thirty. I gotta find someone to cover for her."

"Be back in an hour." On his way downstairs, Stryker made another call.

"Yo," Cooper answered.

"You at home?"

"Yeah."

"I'm swinging by. Be there in ten." Stryker walked outside and dialed again.

"Hello, Stryker," answered Tiana Perry. "How'd it go?"

"Emerson arrested Barnham."

"Excellent."

"We need to talk. Can you meet me in forty?"

"Where?"

"That park near your house," Stryker said. "I'll text you ten minutes before I get there." He ended the call and drove to Cooper's.

Once there, the two friends sat at the kitchen table. "Beer?" Cooper asked.

"I'm good." Stryker pulled out a bag with two burner phones. "I'm telling you this in confidence."

"Got it."

"Doug Easton was undercover with ACPD. Six months ago, his body was found behind a dumpster and his death ruled accidental OD. He'd made inroads with The Trinity."

Cooper's eyes widened. "From what little I know about that crime family, no one in law enforcement had made inroads."

"Doug was Emerson's brother and she was convinced he was murdered. Together, we got to the truth. His POC was a drug runner named Donny Farraday. He worked for Jimmy Barca who reported to The Father."

Cooper nodded.

"The Father is Carlo Spinetti."

Cooper's eyes widened and he pushed out of his chair. "Seriously? How the hell did we miss that?"

"His daughter, Carla Barnham, and son-in-law, Tee Barnham, were running the drug operation in Florida. When Spinetti went to prison, they had to move up here."

"You're blowing my mind."

"There's more," Stryker said. "Emerson and I took out the serial killer."

"The Wedding Gown Killer?"

"It was Spinetti's grandson, but he wasn't in the business. You ready for the kicker?"

"There's *more?*"

"Barnham killed my mother."

Cooper's mouth dropped open. "What?"

"Barnham is my father—ex-father—Tyler Truman."

"Holy hell. That is one fucked-up family."

"Circling back to The Trinity and Spinetti. Barca and Farraday are dead and they confessed before they died. Their full confessions were videoed on their phones."

"How'd you get the phones?"

"I know a guy who knows a guy."

"Bullshit," Cooper said. "You're not being straight with me."

Stryker bit back a smile. "I'm giving these phones to ACPD Captain, Tiana Perry. The Bureau can have them after she hears the truth about how Doug Easton died."

"Now I know why I haven't seen you in weeks. You've been busy."

Stryker pulled on disposable gloves and played both Farraday and Barca's confessions for his friend.

"Thanks for the heads up," Cooper said.

"Anytime, my brother."

On his way out, Stryker texted Tiana. "On my way."

Ten minutes later, he arrived at the park, located in her upscale neighborhood. He was alone. Tiana pulled up and he slipped into her sedan.

"These are for you." He set the phones on the center console. "Donny Farraday and Jimmy Barca worked for The Trinity crime family, run by Carlo Spinetti. Someone got their videoed confessions. Doug Easton was murdered because he was close to arresting Spinetti."

"How did you get these?" Tiana asked.

"Friends in low places. ASAC Cooper Grant, with the Bureau, will take these off your hands when you're done with them."

"I'll touch base with him," she said.

"One more thing. This conversation never happened." He exited the vehicle.

"Stryker," Tiana said. "Thank you."

He returned to the club and found Becky in Mavis's office. After showing her a video of her speaking to Lyle, she admitted to taking money.

"Do you let non-members in a lot?" he asked.

Becky shrugged. "I've done it before."

"You like workin' here?" Stryker asked.

"It's a job." she said, blowing a bubble.

Stryker slid his gaze to Mavis, then back to Becky. "You can't do that."

"Fine, whatever."

"Unfortunately, we have to let you go," Mavis said.

"No problem." Becky stood.

"I'll walk you out," Mavis said.

Stryker rode down the elevator with them.

In the parking lot, Mavis lit a cigarette. "You know, Stryker," she exhaled the smoke, "you're a real softie, you know that? You couldn't even fire that gal."

Stryker chuffed out a laugh. "You think I should become more of a tough guy?"

"Wouldn't hurt, you know."

"Thanks for the advice," he replied. "I'll keep that in mind."

26

JUSTICE & BOOMSLANG

After parking in Emerson's driveway, Stryker opened his Survivor app and typed a message to Boomslang. "Hey, Boomslang, wanna get together for dinner? My treat. Just friends."

A few seconds later, dots appeared, then her reply. "How's Thursday?"

"That'll work. I'll make res and text you the deets."

She replied with a thumb's up emoji.

With a smile, Stryker let himself in and found her crashed in bed. He patted Pima, stripped down, and crawled in beside her. She rolled toward him and kissed him. "Hello, my love."

"Hi, baby. How's my detective doing?"

She tucked his hair behind his ear and kissed him again. "I'm good. You?"

"Better, now that we're together."

Her sweet smile warmed his heart.

"I will always miss my brother. You'll always miss your mom," she said. "We'll never be whole, but we're going to heal, together. I adore you in a way I didn't know was possible. I miss you when we're not together and I'm excited when I see you." She paused. "Tell me I haven't become co-dependent."

He laughed. "You're fine. You've got a case of the Cupids. Me, too. Pretty damn bad."

Their kisses were soft and tender. He moved over her body, taking his time to appreciate her. He loved how responsive she was to his touch, to his kiss. Her coos grew into moans, but when she started gyrating beneath him, he rose over her.

"Do you want me, Emerson?"

Her heavy-lidded gaze was the best medicine for his soul. "Always."

Once nestled inside, he murmured her name and her eyes fluttered open. "You saved me, you know that, don't you?"

"Saved you from what?" she asked.

"Not living my best life." He stopped her smile with a loving kiss. As she wrapped her limbs around him in a protective cocoon for two, he smiled back.

"Does that mean I'm stuck with you?" she whispered.

"No other option."

"I can live with that."

He made love to her with everything in him that was good and she responded with a ferocity that left him breathless. Emerson's love had freed him from a life of revenge and fury, and he would cherish her for the rest of his days.

In the aftermath, when they were snuggling close, Pima jumped on the bed and stared at Stryker.

"Hey, crazy cat. You're stuck me with, buddy." Stryker rubbed the cat's head and Pima started purring. When demon kitty had had enough, he plunked down at the foot of the bed.

"I know you're gonna attack my toes in the morning," Stryker murmured.

Emerson peered into his eyes. "I need to tell you something."

"Okay."

"I'm not adverse to children."

"Did we just make one?"

She smiled. "I meant, down the road. What are your thoughts on children?"

"I have one condition about kids—that I only have them with you."

She kissed his cheek. "I'm in no hurry. Plus, you haven't even met my mom and dad."

"That's easy to fix. Invite them to dinner at my place, so I can grill."

"I love that idea. I'll do it in the morning."

"If we stay up much longer, it will be the morning." He turned out the night table light. "There is one thing I've missed since you came into my life."

"Other women?"

"Hell no," he replied. "Sleep."

Laughing, she snuggled close.

As he drifted off to dreamland, he thought about his mom. *I love you, Mom. Now, you can rest in peace.*

Emerson walked into the kitchen with her stomach tied in knots. "The cinnamon rolls smell so good." She eyed the spread on the island. "This is a lot of food."

They sat and ate, only Emerson spent more time pushing the food around on her plate than actually eating it. She sipped some coffee, then set down her mug. "We haven't talked about what to do with Farraday and Barca's videoed confessions."

"I gave their phones to Tiana Perry."

She stared at him. "You're gonna have to give me more than that. Does she know I know about this? What did you tell her? Am I going to get arrested?"

"Relax, babe." He put his hand on hers to calm her. "You are *not* getting arrested. I told her I got them from friends in low places."

"So, I don't know?"

"No."

"Well, I'm resigning anyway. Not today, because I've got too many loose ends to wrap up, but I'm going to quit the force. I killed someone. I'm a dirty cop."

"What will you do?"

"I don't know. All I've ever wanted to do is save the world from bad guys."

"You know, I've got other friends in *high* places you might want to talk to about a career opportunity."

"Doing what?"

"Saving the world from bad guys."

"And?"

"I'll let them discuss the specs with you."

She kissed his cheek. "Thanks."

"I'll make a call." He tossed a nod at her plate. "But you've got to eat something, first."

"You are not my mother."

Ding-dong.

"Danielle's here." Emerson rose. "I want her to hear about Lyle from me."

Emerson answered her front door. After a long hug, Emerson brought Danielle into the kitchen. She didn't want to stare at her bestie, but Danielle looked different. Besides having dropped a few pounds, there was a hardness in her eyes that hadn't been there before Claire-Marie had been murdered.

She wished she could change the past, bring Claire-Marie back. Bring all three victims back. But she couldn't, and her heart felt heavy.

Stryker pushed out of his chair and hugged Danielle. "I know I said this on the phone, but I'm sorry for your loss."

"Thank you."

"How are you doing?" Stryker asked.

"Still fighting mad," Danielle replied.

"I'll give you two some time," he said.

"You don't have to leave," Danielle said.

He smiled. "It's fine." Then, he slid his gaze to Emerson. "Babe, can I use your office?"

"Of course."

After Stryker left the room, Danielle put her hand over her heart. "I love that he called you babe."

"Me, too." Emerson poured two small glasses of orange juice. "You look like you've lost weight, Danny. Have breakfast with me."

"I haven't felt like eating lately." After Danielle filled her plate with two pancakes and some scrambled eggs, the two friends sat at the table.

After a few bites, Emerson said, "I've missed you."

"I've missed you, too."

"Are you doing any better?"

"Not really."

"I wanted to let you know...the Wedding Gown Killer is dead."

"Good." Danielle didn't smile.

"I thought you'd be happy to hear that."

"Happy? No. Relieved? Yes. What happened?"

Emerson explained about Lyle and Casey and how he ambushed her.

When Emerson finished, Danielle shook her head. "It's bad enough that I lost my sister, but I would have completely fallen apart without you. I know that sounds—"

"I get it. I would feel the same way if something happened to you."

Danielle drank down the orange juice. "I've been a rule follower my entire life. Since Claire-Marie died, I've been going on the dark web to find bad guys. All I want to do is stop them before they hurt someone else."

"You want to talk to someone about how you're feeling?"

"I am talking to someone. My mouth is moving. You appear to be listening to me."

Emerson smiled. "I mean, like, a therapist."

"No. I'm good."

Her best friend wasn't okay, but Emerson was in no position to lecture her. She'd been consumed by Doug's death and had exacted vengeance, herself.

"Thank you for telling me," Danielle said. "Can I tell my parents and Noah?"

"Absolutely."

"I'm happy something good came out of all of this tragedy," Danielle said.

"What?"

"You and Stryker fell in love. You two are perfect for each other. You deserve your happily ever after, Em."

"You deserve yours, too," Emerson replied.

"I'm not looking for love," Danielle said. "I'm looking for revenge."

THE FOLLOWING MORNING, Emerson was summoned to Captain Perry's office. Her palms were clammy as she eased into the guest chair.

Here we go.

"A CI provided me with evidence that your brother's death was a homicide. He was killed by two members of the drug ring he'd infiltrated," the captain explained. "The order came from its leader, Carlo Spinetti."

Emerson paused, as if hearing this news for the first time. With the truth, came a mix of emotions. Relief and anxiety coursed through her, but her heart broke for her brother. A good man who had died trying to make the world a better place. The truth had come out because she had taken the law into her own hands. And now, she had to live with that scar on her soul.

"I know, it's a lot to take in," Captain Perry said.

Emerson found her voice. "I never believed he was using, and

I'm grateful the truth came out so Doug's good name can be restored. He was a good cop."

"One of the best," the captain replied.

"Is this something I'm able to share with my mom and dad?"

"Yes, of course," Captain Perry replied. "On behalf of the department, our condolences, again, for your loss."

"Thank you."

The captain offered a warm smile "Congratulations on your excellent work regarding the Wedding Gown Killer."

"Thank you. It was a total team effort." Her phone buzzed, but she ignored it.

"It always is," Captain Perry said. "I hope you take a few days off. You deserve it."

"Once I get my paperwork in order, I will." Emerson stood.

On the way back to her desk, Emerson read the text from Stryker. "Can you interview this afternoon, 4pm? Company is in Tysons."

"Wow, that was fast!" she replied. "Yes, that's awesome. Thank you and love you."

"Love you." He included the address in the text.

"What's the company name?"

"ALPHA Meat Packing," he replied.

"LOL!" she texted. "Seriously, what is it?"

"That's it."

Emerson did an Internet search for ALPHA Meat Packing, but got no hits.

She texted Stryker. "How can you send me to a company that doesn't exist?"

"Stop Googling and TRUST ME."

Back at her desk, she continued working.

An hour later, her phone buzzed with a text from Justice. "Hey, Boomslang, confirming dinner tonight. I made res at Raphael's. How's 7?"

Even with everything going on, she loved that he hadn't forgotten. "Looking forward to it," she replied.

At three forty-five, she drove to the end of a quiet street in Tysons and pulled into the parking lot of ALPHA Meat Packing Company. The four-story building had reflective glass covering the windows. With a few resumes in her tote, she headed to the front door. It was locked, so she pressed the button on the security pad. *It has a retina scanner. This must be a secure site.*

"Can I help you?" asked a woman.

"This is Emerson Easton. I have a four o'clock."

The buzzer sounded and she entered the building. "Hello, Detective," said the receptionist. "Welcome to ALPHA Meat Packing. Ms. Luck will be with you shortly."

"As in, Providence Luck?" Emerson asked.

"Yes."

Why does Stryker think I want to be a marketing consultant at a meat packing company?

There was nothing in reception that provided her with any information about the organization. No brochure, no business cards. Nada.

A moment later, Providence appeared. With a warm smile, she shook Emerson's hand. "Good to see you again, Emerson. C'mon back."

Providence's windowless office wasn't what Emerson had expected. Two desks were pushed together, facing each other. A lone laptop sat closed on one of the desks. The other was void of anything. There were no pictures, no artwork by Sammy or Graham, no awards, no business books or marketing magazines.

On the other side of the room was a shiny conference table surrounded by six mesh office chairs. A lone office plant took up space in a corner, but Emerson couldn't tell if it was real or plastic. She'd expected a room filled with personality. This had none.

Moreover, she didn't want to be rude, but she had no interest in marketing.

Providence gestured to the conference table and Emerson sat in one of the chairs near the head. "Congratulations on catching the Wedding Gown Killer." Providence folded into the seat at the head of the table. "That's a big deal."

"Thank you."

Providence slid a piece of paper over to Emerson. "This is a non-disclosure. If you'd like to learn more about ALPHA, you'll have to sign this."

Emerson read the document and signed.

"I understand you're thinking of leaving ACPD."

"I am. Do you know why?"

"Stryker told me that you love being a LEO, but weren't sure ACPD was going to work for you, long-term."

"That's right." Emerson had no idea where this conversation was going.

"ALPHA is a top-secret organization buried in the bureaucracy of DOJ. We report directly to the President. We all have covers. Our primary job is to take out the worst offenders that get off on a technicality or break out of prison. Repeat offenders that have eluded law enforcement from the local to the federal levels."

"Take out? As in, kill them?"

"Not always, but yes, that's a necessary option, in some cases."

"So, you're not really a marketing consultant."

"No," Providence replied with a smile. "I co-run ALPHA with Dakota. His cover is his real estate company and he splits his time between the two."

"Is Stryker in ALPHA?"

"No. But not for lack of trying."

"What would my cover be?" Emerson asked.

"That's a detail we'd figure out if this turns out to be the right fit for both of us."

The interview continued for another forty minutes. When it ended, Providence gave her an abbreviated tour.

"The organization used to be an hour away, but I needed to be closer to my children. We can hop on the beltway and be at either Reagan National or Dulles in minutes. We're in DC in twenty."

"What would I be hired to do?" Emerson asked.

"You'd be an operative."

When they returned to Providence's office, Emerson's mind was made up. "I would love working here." She fished out a resume and handed it to Providence.

"Thanks, but I'm familiar with your career. Plus, Stryker recommended you and I trust him completely." She extended her hand. "The position is yours. Let's discuss starting salary and benefits."

Forty minutes later, Emerson walked out with a verbal job offer and a tentative start date. Just like that, she was going to be an ALPHA operative.

I've gotta be dreaming.

When Emerson got home, Pima greeted her and they went upstairs. A beautiful bouquet of peach and pink roses was perfectly arranged in a vase. She inhaled their beautiful robust scent before reading the card.

All my love, always.
Stryker

How romantic.

Then, she read the sticky note taped to the table. "Meeting a friend for dinner. Be home around nine."

"Yeah, me, too," she said with a smile.

Stryker couldn't wait to find out if Emerson had accepted the job. But he wasn't sure how she'd feel, learning he was Justice.

He sat in the private dining room of Raphael's, a bottle of champagne chilling in the bucket. In order to create a more intimate experience, the staff had pulled the curtains closed on both sides, leaving only the glass front exposed.

He spotted her the second she entered the restaurant. She spoke with the host and was escorted toward the private dining room. His heart pounded harder. When their eyes met, her smile was filled with love.

"It's good to finally meet you, Justice. I'm Boomslang." She extended her hand. When he captured hers in his, he knew. This was his forever woman. His soul mate. His life partner.

He kissed her cheek, letting his lips linger an extra second. "Hello, baby."

"Hello, my love," she said.

"Did you know?"

"I suspected it when I learned your club name is also Justice. You?"

"Your boomslang tat, plus, you texted me a picture of Pima."

"You've known for a while." Leaning up, she kissed him. "I'm glad it was you."

"Me, too." Stepping back, he checked her out. "You look amazing."

She'd worn a halter maxi dress with black stilettos.

That elicited a smile. "You clean up pretty good yourself, Justice."

He'd worn a dress shirt and black pants, and pulled his hair into a half-up top knot.

"Your half-up man-bun is so sexy," she murmured.

He shot her a smile. "I did it for you."

After seating her, he sat at the head of the table and clasped her hand. "Tell me about your day."

With a grin, she said, "You sound so domestic."

The waiter knocked on the glass door, then entered. "Hello, ma'am. I'm Henry, and I'll be serving you and Mr. Truman this evening." He filled Emerson's water goblet and topped off Stryker's. "May I open the champagne?"

"Go for it," Stryker said, before turning to Emerson. "The chef is preparing a sampler dinner. Four appetizers and four main courses to choose from."

"That's a lot of food."

Henry popped the cork, poured their bubbly, and left.

"It's samples, but enough to share if we both like the same thing," he said.

She draped her small hand over his large one. "We do like the same things and I love sharing with you."

She told him about her meeting with Captain Perry and he couldn't contain his smile when she told him she'd accepted the position at ALPHA. "There is one thing that disappoints me about the job, though."

"What's that, babe?"

"I won't be able to work with you."

Stryker grinned. "I could be convinced."

"I would *love* that."

"I'd have to work out the details. I'd be splitting my time—"

"Like Dakota does."

"My woman is in the know."

"Will you consider it?"

He nodded, then raised his champagne flute. "Here's to a lifetime of kickin' butt and—as you put it—saving the world from bad guys."

She tapped his glass and sipped. "Delicious. Thank you for the roses. They're beautiful and I loved the note." She leaned over to kiss him, but he didn't meet her halfway. "Hello? Kissing."

It was now or never. He kissed her, pulled out the ring box, and got down on one knee. Her surprised expression was both priceless and adorable. "This—us—is forever. No other option. Marry me, Emerson."

He opened the box. She glanced at it, then back into his eyes. She placed her soft hands on his face and kissed him. "Yes, I will marry you." With a smile she added, "No other option."

After sliding the engagement ring onto her finger, he kissed her before pulling her out of the chair and wrapping her in his arms. They shared a loving smile.

"I'm happy you forgave me or this little love affair would never have happened," she said.

"You are the best part of my life and I want to spend the rest of my life showing you that." He kissed her forehead.

Several restaurant patrons started applauding. Stryker acknowledged them with a smile, then added, "She said yes!"

The entire restaurant broke out in applause and Emerson turned around and waved. "I'm gonna marry this man!" Then, she turned back and kissed him again.

Once seated, she studied the ring. The brilliant radiant-cut diamond was flanked with two halos of small round stones. "This is unbelievable. It's so incredibly beautiful and big. Wow. How did you know I liked the radiant-cut diamond?"

"Danielle."

"I'm worried about her. She's not okay."

"No, she's not. I talked to her about losing her sister. She didn't say much, but that's nothing new with her. I told her to take off as much time as she needs, but she said working full-time is keeping her mind off things."

"She's so angry," Emerson said.

"I get that."

"I know. I do, too."

Stryker leaned over and kissed her cheek. "All you can do is be there for her."

As their server returned with their appetizers, Emerson admired her ring. When he left, they tried each appetizer, one at a time.

"Can we hire the chef for our wedding?" Emerson asked. "This is delicious."

"Ready to get married?"

She shot him a smirk. "Not today. What I do need is a cover for my new job. Thoughts?"

"That's easy," Stryker replied. "I'll hire you as my security advisor at TCS."

"Great idea. That's perfect. I have one more question to ask you."

"Okay."

"What are you doing after dinner, Justice?"

He laughed. "No plans, why?"

"I reserved a room at a spicy nightclub called The Dungeon." She leaned close. "I bought this latex outfit and I've been *dying* to crack the whip."

"I'm all yours, Boomslang," he replied. "All yours."

EPILOGUE

December, Six Months Later

Emerson walked down the stairs and spotted Stryker in the family room. Her heart flipped at the sight of him. He'd pulled his hair into a man bun and was rocking it out in his black tux.

Then, she saw what he was doing, and laughed. He was shining a laser light on the floor and Pima was chasing it like a maniac. He slid his gaze in her direction and let out a long, slow whistle.

She wore a deep violet gown with a slit up the side.

"My God, woman, you are gorgeous. Wow." He flicked off the laser light and met her at the foot of the staircase.

Standing on the last step, she stared into his eyes. "You look damn hot yourself. You were born to wear a tux and my job will be unwrapping you at the end of the evening."

He shrugged. "We'll see."

"I love when you play hard to get," she said, before dropping a soft kiss on his lips.

Emerson loved living in Stryker's home, which they'd turned into *their* home.

"Did you see him chasing the laser?" Stryker asked. "Crazy cat was leaping off the furniture."

Emerson laughed. "You ready to head out?" She clicked off the lights on their nine-foot Christmas tree.

After helping her into her winter coat, he shrugged into his. He set the house alarm and they climbed into his SUV, parked in the garage.

"I got word that Spinetti's trial starts in January," Emerson said. "And I've been called by the prosecution to testify."

"That'll be a circus." Stryker pulled out of the driveway.

"I also heard Carla Barnham's trying to get her sentence reduced, so she turned on her husband."

"As long as he stays in prison, I don't care what happens to him," Stryker said.

She laid her hand on his thigh and he blanketed her hand with his. "I need your help with a case," she said.

"Which one, babe?"

"A Maryland gang that's been trafficking women. Providence and I agree it would be smart for me to partner with someone. Well, you, actually. We need someone ruthless."

"I'm flattered," he said, his voice thick with sarcasm.

She laughed. "I'll check your TCS schedule and set up a strategy meeting next week."

Fifteen minutes later, Stryker pulled into the driveway and cut the engine. As Emerson emerged from the vehicle, he strode around and offered his hand. Holding hands, they headed up the walkway. He rang the doorbell, then opened the door.

"Mom, Dad, we're here," Emerson called.

Rick Easton was sitting alone in the living room. "Hey, guys," Rick said, rising to his feet. "You both look great."

"Dad, I can't remember the last time I saw you in a tux," Emerson said. "You look so handsome."

"Thank you, dear. Mom is just finishing up."

"How are you doing?" Stryker asked her dad.

"I'm good. Tia's been a little emotional. This is a big day for us," Rick said gesturing to the sofa.

Stryker eased down and Rick returned to his chair as Emerson started up the stairs. "Be right back."

She found her mom slipping into her heels. "Mom, you look beautiful."

Tia Easton wore a conservative black dress and a simple strand of pearls. "Thank you, dear. I wore waterproof mascara in case I cry."

"It's totally fine if you do. Hopefully, tonight, will help us heal."

Once everyone had piled into Stryker's vehicle, they headed over the bridge and into DC. Stryker valet-parked in front of the upscale hotel.

The grand ballroom was filled with guests. As they made their way toward their table, Stryker slid his arm around Emerson's waist.

"Doing okay, babe?" he asked.

She shot him a little smile. "I am."

Gratitude filled Emerson's heart. Tonight, her beloved brother would be honored as a hero who died in the line of duty.

They ran into Captain Perry and her husband. After hugs and hellos, Tiana said, "We're still pretty mad at this guy"—she gestured at Stryker—"for stealing you away from us."

"I couldn't resist," Stryker said while caressing Emerson's back. "Emerson brings a lot of value to TCS."

"I'm sure she does," Tiana said.

Stryker and Emerson escorted her mom and dad to their table. To Emerson's surprise, Heather and Gordon were there, as well.

"There they are," Heather said, and hugged all of them.

"I didn't know you guys were coming," Emerson said.

"We're family," Gordon said. "We show up."

"Did you know they were coming?" Emerson asked Stryker as everyone took their seats.

"Of course." He lifted her hand and kissed her finger. "They want to pay tribute to your family."

"I am marrying into the best family."

"Me, too, baby," he replied.

The event began when Chief Watson stepped up to the podium. "Good evening, and welcome to the twelfth annual Acts of Heroism Ceremony. Tonight, we share a stage with first responders from all over the DMV as we pay tribute to our own. Firefighters who ran into burning buildings, paramedics and EMTs who breathed life into someone who would otherwise have died, and police officers who ran toward danger, not away from it. Some of these brave men and women lost their lives because they placed others first. We will carry their spirit forward by remembering them in our hearts, forever. Our ceremony of honor will begin immediately following dinner."

Detective Nikki Cardoso and her husband joined them at their table and the two women talked shop for a few minutes.

"I'm pretty excited to be in your wedding party," Nikki said. "Have you guys set a date yet?"

"No," Stryker replied, taking his fiancée's hand in his. "Emerson is a hard woman to pin down."

"My new job was pretty intense for the first three months," Emerson said. "Somewhere in all of that, we moved into Stryker's home, then got busy readying my townhouse—Doug's townhouse—to sell. We haven't had a minute to plan a wedding."

"After we moved, our crazy cat had a nervous breakdown," Stryker added, and they all laughed.

"When we moved, our cat was a wreck, too," Nikki said. "Poor thing stopped eating, but she's okay now."

"That's not a problem for Pima," Emerson said. "Stryker has him eating out of his hand."

"We're talking about a spring wedding," Stryker said.

"Or a Christmas wedding," Emerson added. "Next year."

"Tell me all about your job," Nikki said. "What do you do at TCS?"

Stryker gave her hand a little squeeze and she squeezed back in return.

"I'm in charge of security for the facility and for the systems. It keeps me super busy." She paused to sip her water. "Did you hear that Carla Barnham threw her husband under the bus?"

And just like that, Emerson had redirected the conversation away from her work. She loved being an ALPHA operative and loved when Stryker joined her on a mission, too. She had found her dream job. When she slid her gaze to Stryker, he was waiting.

The love in his eyes told her everything she needed to know. Her dream man was also her forever man.

Their entrées were delivered and the conversations continued. Stryker glanced around the table. When Heather and Gordon had learned the truth about his mom's death, they were furious with Tee Barnham. As the months passed, they were able to process what had happened and move beyond the anger. They couldn't change the past, but they found comfort knowing the truth, and that justice would be served.

Stryker's sister, Trudy, had taken the news about Barnham the hardest. Learning that their father had murdered their mother, and that their dad had a secret family, had shaken her to her core. She'd apologized to Stryker, and her aunt and uncle numerous times, promising she'd never be that gullible, ever again.

Emerson's mom and dad had been warmly welcomed into Stryker's extended family, not only participating in Sunday Fundays, but hosting several of them.

"You good?" Emerson whispered.

"Yeah, baby. I am. You doing all right?"

Her sweet smile made him happy...as happy as someone with a chip on his shoulder could be.

Stryker teased Emerson that ever since she'd come into his life, he wasn't getting enough sleep, but the truth was, he never stopped pushing. Running TCS and jumping in on a few ALPHA missions was the perfect work balance. His club had sold, so he and Emerson used one of the spare bedrooms in their home as their own private dungeon.

He had a feeling, however, that one of these years, it would become the nursery. And he was ready for it all. Marriage, kids, but no more damn cats. Crazy Pima was plenty.

When the plates were cleared away and the dessert bar had been opened, Stryker retrieved two coffees and a piece of chocolate fudge cake.

"Is this leaded?" she asked when he set the coffee down in front of her.

"Yeah. No good?"

As she pressed the mug against her mouth, her lips curved in a sexy smile. After sipping, she murmured, "You know this'll keep me awake for hours."

He winked. "I sure do."

They shared a laugh.

The fire chief kicked off the ceremony. Though it was a somber event, lighthearted stories were shared as a way to remember the fallen in happier times. When Captain Perry took the stage, Emerson took Stryker's hand.

"Losing our own is hard. We form tight-knit groups and close bonds, so when someone dies in the line of duty, it's an unbearable loss that never leaves us. I'd like to honor a man who served his community, first as a beat cop, working his way up to undercover. His exemplary career spanned twelve years. He loved his job and never shied away from the challenges. Undercover detective, Doug Easton, was determined to make inroads with The Trinity, the

DMV's longest-standing drug gang and the area's biggest supplier of heroin and opioids. Twelve months ago, Doug Easton died of an apparent accidental drug overdose. When the gang's leader was exposed, the truth came out. Detective Easton was murdered by the criminals he was trying to take down."

A picture of Emerson's brother in uniform appeared on the large screen behind Captain Perry.

"Doug Easton is a recipient of the Acts of Heroism Award for his valor while serving. Tonight, we're excited to announce that the Easton family has started a foundation in his honor, dedicated to helping those struggling with drug addiction."

Applause filled the ballroom. When the room grew quiet, Captain Perry continued. "Accepting the award on behalf of the Easton family, is his sister, former detective, Emerson Easton."

Emerson made her way to the podium. After accepting the plaque from the captain, she addressed the crowd.

"On behalf of the entire Easton family, we are thankful that Doug's honor has been restored. He loved being a police officer, and his undercover work brought him a great sense of pride. We were devastated to learn that he had died, and refused to believe it was from the drugs he was trying to get off the streets. While we will never be able to thank the person or persons who uncovered the truth about Doug's murder, we are forever indebted to them." She slid her gaze to Stryker. "The truth has helped our family heal." She held up the plaque. "Thank you."

As Emerson made her way back to the table, her loving smile filled him with a deep sense of gratitude.

She sat beside him, kissed his cheek, and whispered, "Thank you."

Together, they had found peace. As Stryker stared into her eyes, he knew they would always have each other's back and love each other unconditionally.

"No other option," he murmured before kissing her forehead.

"No other option," she replied with a smile.

A NOTE FROM STONI

Thank you so much for reading DAMAGED! I love crafting romantic suspense stories that draw you in and keep you engaged. If you were, then I did my job.

My fave trope is enemies-to-lovers and I had the best time giving Stryker a real chip on his shoulder because of what Emerson had done to him. But true love can't be stopped, can it?

Creating Stryker and Emerson's world was a thrill, especially since I included a few of the characters from The Touch Series, my wildly popular romantic suspense novels that follow six sexy, wealthy, and very powerful men and six independent, strong-willed women as they weave their way to their own happily ever afters. If I'm a new-to-you author, check them out while waiting for book two in The Vigilantes Series.

It's always fun to hear from readers. You can drop me a note at Contact@StoniAlexander.com.

To learn about my upcoming releases, be the first to see a cover reveal, or participate in a giveaway, sign up for my Inner Circle newsletter at StoniAlexander.com. When you do, I'll send you my steamy short story, MetroMan.

All of my books are available exclusively on Amazon and you can read them FREE with Kindle Unlimited.

Cheers to Romance!
Stoni

ROMANTIC SUSPENSE
The Touch Series

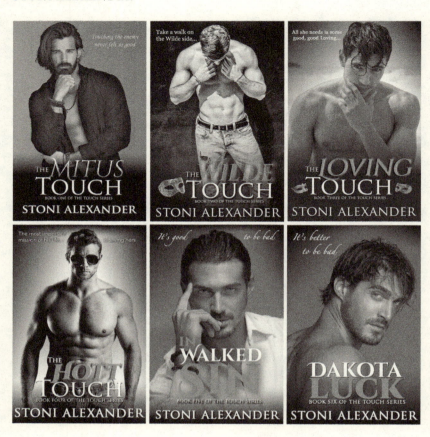

ROMANTIC SUSPENSE
THE VIGILANTES SERIES

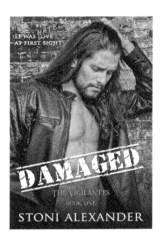

Looking for a sexy standalone?

CONTEMPORARY ROMANCE
Beautiful Men Collection

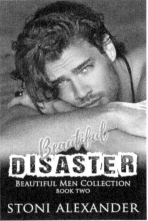

Grab them or Read FREE with Kindle Unlimited!

ACKNOWLEDGMENTS

Anyone who knows me, is well aware that I love crafting stories, and how grateful I am to be doing it every day. I'm perfectly happy tap-tapping away on my keyboard, while my imagination comes up with a zillion different situations and scenarios. It's definitely the best job I've ever had. I'm having so much fun, it doesn't even feel like work!

The following people support me, cheer me on, and remind me that there's no way—*no freakin' way*—I could do this on my own.

Johnny, after all these years, you still do it for me in all the ways. Thank you for being the best part of my life. People grow apart or they grow together. Life with you is my favorite adventure.

Son, just thinking about you makes me smile. Thank you for always throwing your support my way. You have turned into such an amazing young man. Never, ever, stop chasing your best self.

Friends and Fam, thank you for keeping me sane…or, at least, trying.

Nicole, you rock it every time. Every. Single. Time.

Author friends, I am in awe of your talents and love our special connection. We're alone in our heads every day. We create worlds out of nothing and the people in them are real to us. We get that, and each other, and for that, I'm immensely grateful.

ARC Team, thank you thank you! You lovely ladies make me smile so big.

Readers, I appreciate your loyalty. I am especially thankful when I hear from you. Your support is like receiving a beautiful and unexpected gift for absolutely no reason.

Muse, why do we steer toward the dark side? Why are we so fascinated by the push and pull between light and dark, good and evil? The next two books in this series are filling my head with some crazy ideas. It's time to get back to work…

ABOUT THE AUTHOR

Stoni Alexander writes sexy romantic suspense and contemporary romance about tortured alpha males and independent, strong-willed females. Her passion is creating love stories where the hero and heroine help each other through a crisis so that, in the end, they're equal partners in more ways than love alone. The heat level is high, the romance is forever, and the suspense keeps readers guessing until the very end.

Visit Stoni's website:
StoniAlexander.com

Sign up for Stoni's newsletter on her website and she'll gift you a free steamy short story, only available to her Inner Circle.

Here's where you can follow Stoni online. She looks forward to connecting with you!

- amazon.com/author/stonialexander
- bookbub.com/authors/stoni-alexander
- facebook.com/StoniBooks
- goodreads.com/stonialexander
- instagram.com/stonialexander

Made in the USA
Monee, IL
12 February 2022